Robert Ryan was born in Liverpool. He has written for many national newspapers and magazines. He lives in north London with his wife and three children. He is author of the bestselling novels *Early One Morning*, *The Blue Noon*, *Night Crossing*, *After Midnight*, *The Last Sunrise* and *Dying Day*. For more information on Robert Ryan you can visit his website: www.robert-ryan.net.

Also by Robert Ryan and available from Headline

Underdogs
Nine Mil
Trans Am
Early One Morning
The Blue Noon
Night Crossing
After Midnight
The Last Sunrise
Dying Day

EMPIRE OF SAND

Robert Ryan

headline
review

First published in 2008 by HEADLINE REVIEW
An imprint of HEADLINE PUBLISHING GROUP

First published in paperback in 2008 by HEADLINE REVIEW
An imprint of HEADLINE PUBLISHING GROUP

2

Cataloguing in Publication Data is available from the British Library

ISBN 978 0 7553 2926 7 (B Format)
ISBN 978 0 7553 4425 3 (A Format)

Typeset in Janson Text by Palimpsest Book Production Limited,
Grangemouth, Stirlingshire

Printed and bound in Great Britain by
Clays Ltd, St Ives plc

Headline's policy is to use papers that are natural, renewable and
recyclable products and made from wood grown in sustainable forests.
The logging and manufacturing processes are expected to conform
to the environmental regulations of the country of origin.

HEADLINE PUBLISHING GROUP
An Hachette Livre UK Company
338 Euston Road
London NW1 3BH

www.headline.co.uk
www.hachettelivre.co.uk

For Deborah

Use your enemy's hand to catch a snake
                 – Persian proverb

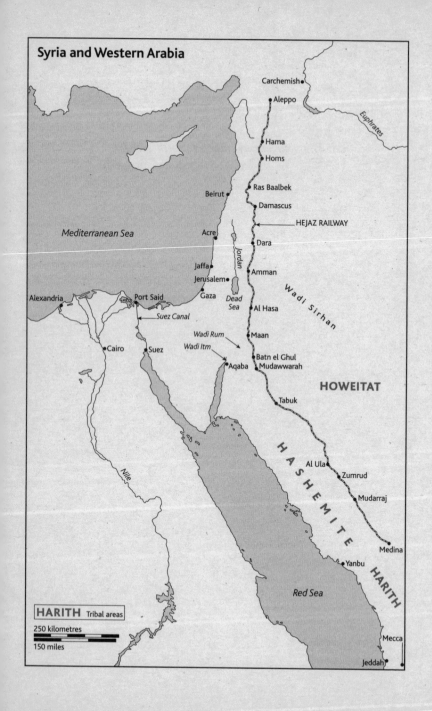

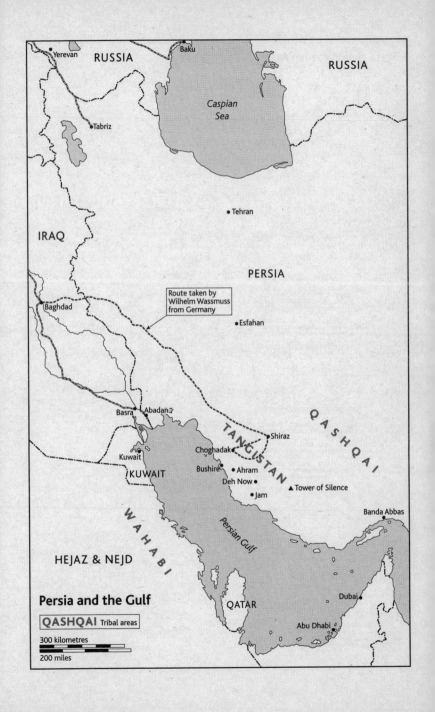

Prologue

Palestine, August 1917

I

The riders appeared at the far end of the gorge just as the last echoes of the gelignite explosion died away. It was Hassan, the Egyptian foreman, who spotted them first, pointing with his rhinoceros-hide whip to the distant bend in the desert canyon, where a stream of mounted men had emerged, travelling at a fast trot. Sergeant Sam Rollins wiped some of the grit from his eyes and squinted through the curtain of dust that still filled the air. 'For cryin' out loud. What now?'

Ten miles to the south of the road crew was the port of Aqaba, British held; ahead of them, once they had blasted a clear path through the Itm Pass and on to the plateau, lay the Turkish army, the Hejaz railway and, ultimately, Damascus. The camel riders were approaching from the direction of the enemy positions.

It could, thought Rollins, be a forward patrol of the

3

Imperial Camel Corps. If so, they would be on sleek, white Sudanese camels. Hassan, though, shaded his eyes, studied the group intently, noted the hue and decoration of their mounts, and pronounced: 'Arab!'

Rollins was aware that, although the Arabs were in revolt against their Turkish masters across the whole of the Levant and Arabia, not all loved the British. Some northern tribes, sceptical of the colonial powers' promises of Arab self-rule, had remained loyal to Constantinople.

The sergeant walked back along the wide sandy floor of the valley to where Bloodhound, his latest Rolls-Royce armoured car, was parked. Rollins clicked his fingers at Humphries, Bloodhound's gunner, who was lurking in the rest area they had created in one of the fissures that split the canyon walls. The corporal leaned forward and spotted the new arrivals. Humphries quickly dropped the butt of his cigarette, crossed to Bloodhound, and slid inside the revolving turret on the rear of the armoured car. He spun the Vickers-Maxim to face the oncoming riders.

Rollins indicated that the six Indian riflemen he had been assigned should also take up a defensive position, as well as his Egyptian machine-gun unit. The modern firepower of the work party ensured that they could hold their own in a fight with any marauding Arab bandits.

The two dozen locals, scraggy half-naked workmen, charged with clearing the stones and rocks that might rip the tyres or bend the steering rods of the armoured cars, had stopped to watch the Arabs, but Hassan shouted at them to carry on working. They bent once more, shovelling, brushing and lifting the rubble, but at half the usual pace, their eyes drawn by the fast-approaching camels. Rollins could smell their apprehension.

The Rolls was in shadow now, but some of the armoured panels were still as hot as skillets from a day-long roasting in the sun. Rollins was careful where and how he leaned against the machine as he rolled a cigarette from the tobacco dust which the native traders sold to them at outrageous prices. It was such poor fare, it was a feat just to keep a fag alight for more than a few seconds. The same tinkers normally came back the next day with overpriced boxes of matches, knowing the soldiers would quickly have exhausted their own supply. It was possible the new arrivals were also traders, looking for nothing more than a vast profit.

'Arab no good,' said Hassan, who was city-bred and had little time for the men of the desert, even back in Egypt. 'Thief. No good.' And just in case Rollins had missed the point, he spat loudly.

As they came closer, Rollins could see that the loping camels were richly brocaded, with elaborate saddles and harnesses. Some of the decorative tassels reached almost to the ground. The riders, however, were a ragged-looking bunch. It occurred to Rollins they might be camel thieves who had raided a more prosperous group. He counted twenty-one of them, most with modern rifles slung over their shoulders. Something told him these were no cigarette vendors.

When they were fifty yards away, one of the Arabs raised an arm and the party slowed and stopped. The lead camel knelt and its rider dismounted. The man was dressed in grubby, heavily stained clothes, thick with yellowy dust. He wore a red and white *keffiyeh* pulled over the lower half of his face. Rollins heard Hassan hissing through clenched teeth in disgust at this beggar.

'Sarge!' It was Humphries, his voice muffled by the metal of the turret, asking for guidance. 'You want me to fire a cautionary burst?'

'Just take it easy, son.' Rollins had been in the desert for more than two years, first in Persia, then the Western Desert and now Palestine. He knew you had to treat these nomads firmly or they'd rob you blind. Or worse. He took a pull on his cigarette, left it dangling in the corner of his mouth, and stepped forward with his arms by his side, palms forward. He began to swing his hands at the approaching Arab, as if shooing away a pigeon. 'Go, go on. Nothing for you here. *Talla! Ishmi!* Clear off!'

The man, barefoot he noticed, carried on coming and behind him, another Arab barked an order that Rollins understood was an instruction to dismount. The remaining camels flopped down, allowing their riders to slide out of the saddle. The air thickened with the odour of the pack. Rollins sensed he was losing control of the situation.

'*Ishmi!*' he repeated forcefully.

'Sergeant Rollins, you took my advice, I see.'

The cultivated voice was soft on the ears, a balm after days of barked Arabic and harsh cockney and brum. The cigarette fell from his lips, but Rollins didn't notice. He was looking at the eyes, as steely-grey as the polished metal of the Rolls-Royces had been when they were unloaded at Aqaba. Rollins leaned forward for a closer inspection and was startled by what he saw. 'Lieutenant Lawrence?'

The man pulled down his scarf, revealing a face that was far more gaunt than Rollins remembered. The boyish grin, however, was unmistakable. 'Actually, it's Captain now.'

'Yes, sir,' he gulped. 'Good to see you, sir.' Rollins threw him a salute.

'Oh for God's sake,' Lawrence said with obvious irritation. He held out his hand and nodded over his shoulder at his escort. 'Do you think we bother with all that nonsense in the desert?'

Awkwardly, the sergeant took the offered hand and his was quickly wrapped in a double-grip of sinew and calluses. The desert had roughened him up, Rollins thought.

'I do believe you have Captain Noel with you,' said Lawrence.

'He's Major Noel now. Promotion came through with new orders.'

Lawrence's eyes sparkled with amusement. 'A major? Is he indeed? Well, it seems we are all going up in the world, Sergeant. No regrets?'

'None, sir. You gave me good advice.' It was Captain Lawrence's doing that Rollins had ended up in the elite Armoured Car Brigade.

Lawrence strode over to the Rolls and began to circle it, remembering another, similar, machine. 'Better than ours, eh? Fighting De Luxe?'

'Quite a chariot this one,' Rollins agreed. 'Stronger back axle, double springs, armoured plating on the radiator, fully swivelling gun mounting.' That reminded him. He banged on the door panel. 'It's OK, Humphries, you can get out of there. Captain Lawrence is one of ours.' He signalled his other units to stand down, too.

Lawrence stooped to inspect the metal-studded tyres. 'Dunlops.'

'Much better than the Bryants, sir. We still have to clear the bigger rocks out of the way, though. They haven't quite got the hang of strengthening the steering arms.'

'We heard the explosions. Dynamite?'

'Gelignite.'

'Electrically fired?'

'Fuse and electrical, depending.'

'Do you have any spare cable? We've been rather busy on the railway.' He meant the Hejaz line from Damascus to Medina, ostensibly designed to deposit pilgrims within easy reach of Mecca, but primarily a way of cementing Ottoman control over the region. 'They've sent only short lengths of cable. It means we are uncomfortably close when we take out a locomotive.'

'I'll see what I can do, sir.'

'Good man.' As he stood, Lawrence grimaced and touched his back. 'Bet you wouldn't mind trading that' – Rollins indicated Lawrence's camel and then tapped the Rolls – 'for this.'

'Ghazala?' The sergeant realised this was the camel's name. 'She's a grandmother. Her latest foal died and she mourns now and then. We have the hide, which we let her sniff, and that stops her for a while. But it might be time to turn her out.' There was clear regret at the thought. 'So I might well join you in the cars once you have cleared your roadway. How would that be?'

'Marvellous!' said Rollins.

'Now, Major Noel was headed where?'

'He didn't say. But he left a parcel for you.'

'For me?'

'Well, he said a British officer would be along to pick it up. It's from Eastman in Cairo, he said.'

Lawrence laughed. 'Yes, that's mine. Wonderful.'

Rollins indicated the cleft in the cliff face. 'If you'll follow me, sir. And would you like to freshen up? There's water for washing.'

Lawrence shook his head. 'I can't wash till my bodyguard wash. It would be impolite.'

The twenty men were a bodyguard? Rollins didn't know much about Arabs, but he was well aware that such a personal force conveyed considerable status. 'I'm not sure there's enough for them.' He suddenly realised how that sounded. 'I mean, there's not much spare—'

'I know what you meant, Sergeant. Let's get my parcel and cable. Ablutions can wait.'

As they walked over the rough ground, Rollins looked down at Lawrence's naked feet and his own army boots. 'How do you manage?'

Lawrence also lowered his gaze, as if surprised to see he was sandal-less. One of the toes rose at an unnatural angle. It looked to Rollins as if it had been broken and had healed badly. 'Practice, I suppose.'

Rollins noticed the work of clearing rocks had slowed almost to a halt. 'Hassan! Get them back to work.'

The Egyptian cracked his whip and the natives began to

pick the valley floor clear of debris once again, this time under the disdainful eyes of Lawrence's escort.

Lawrence broke away from Rollins, strode over and put a hand on the foreman's shoulder, letting it rest lightly. 'Hassan, my friend. There are two boys in my group. See them? The pair throwing stones at each other?'

The two lads were at the far side of the bodyguard, running around in circles, occasionally tossing a rock in the other's direction. 'Farraj and Daud, of the Ageyl tribe. Servants, supposedly, but really the bane of my life.' It was said with both frustration and affection. Now Lawrence raised and firmed his voice, so that it carried down the canyon to his subjects' ears. He used the version of his name that the Arabs often affected, as they found the real thing a tongue-twister. 'If they cause you any trouble, tell them you have Orrans's permission to use the whip on them.'

The two boys froze, and then fell to the ground, their hands covering their heads, as if blows were already raining down on them.

Lawrence smiled and leaned in close to Hassan, so that Rollins couldn't hear. 'But the others, the Harith, but especially the Howeitat, are not to be alarmed in any way. They are the men who crossed the Desolate, took Aba el Lissan and sacked Aqaba. Many have prices on their heads.' The Egyptian's eyes widened. When he had passed through the ruined port with the armoured cars, he had heard all kinds of stories about the men who had traversed the bleakest of deserts and taken the city by surprise and of the fate of any Turk unfortunate enough to be in their way.

'Yes, sir.'

'Call me Lawrence. Where are you from, Hassan?'

'Cairo.'

'Which part?'

There was a moment's hesitation, before the foreman decided the Englishman would not be able to distinguish one district in Cairo from another. 'Darb al-Ahmar.'

'I know it well.'

'You do?'

A flicker of regret played across Lawrence's features. 'I had a good friend there, once. You must miss it.' He slapped Hassan on the back. 'I hope you get back home soon.'

'You too, sir.'

It was Lawrence's turn to wait before replying softly, with a smile. 'Me? I'm already home.'

The crevice that served as a storage depot had a rough curtain across the entrance to keep out the worst of the heat and the flies. Rollins unhooked this and unfurled it back to reveal the road gang's supplies. Lawrence's eyes widened when he saw the amount of explosives and detonators.

'Drink?' offered Rollins. 'We have some decent water.'

'Thank you.'

Rollins noticed that Lawrence had slumped slightly once he was out of sight of his men, and the light dimmed from his eyes. He was, thought the sergeant, like a stage actor, come to take a breather in the wings, unclip his collar and smoke a cigarette. Lawrence took the mug of warm water from Rollins and drank. He smacked his lips. 'The

11

well at Mahrg?' It was a small oasis, back towards Aqaba.

'Yes. How did you know?'

'The salt. Very distinctive.'

It had never seemed particularly brackish to Rollins.

'The Bedu know their wells like the French their wines,' Lawrence explained. 'It takes a while to learn the trick, but I am getting there.' He held out the cup. 'Can you spare another?'

While he waited for a refill, Lawrence shrugged off his *bisht* – the camel wool outer-coat – and examined the stores. As Lawrence picked up a pair of binoculars and held them to his eyes, Rollins saw that the man's *thaub* tunic was covered in a fine spray of black dots down the front. In the centre, over the breastbone, was what looked like an inky handprint. 'Is that blood, sir?'

Lawrence put down the field glasses and accepted the mug once more. He lowered his head and looked at the blot, pulling the shirt away from his skin. 'Yes.'

'Yours? Are you hurt?'

Lawrence continued to examine the stain. When he looked up, his gaze was somewhere else far distant, and Rollins realised he was remembering just how the blood came to be on his clothing.

II

It often took two hours to lay the mines properly. To make sure he had adequate time before the trains started running, Lawrence had crawled on his belly across the cold sand towards the Maryland steel rails of the Hejaz railway well before the sun had done much more than threaten an appearance. His passage had left a series of swirls and troughs in the fine soil, as if a giant serpent had passed that way. Next to it were lighter marks left by Ali when he helped bring out the sacks of explosives. Lawrence would have to take his time erasing all these, lest a hawk-eyed driver or engineer spotted the telltale tracks of a saboteur.

It was worth the risk, though. On this section of the railway the single track ran through a wide, sandy valley. The line was straight for the most part, deviating only when confronted with one of the huge rocky outcrops that had been created by some geological upheaval eons ago and then shaped and honed by the desert winds into grotesque shapes. These massive striated islands were barriers that resisted the blasting of engineers, so the rails had to be curved around them. Destroying such a section of track was a dividend, because they were much more difficult to replace than the standard linear pieces, each one having been custom-made. The Turks could have a normal stretch of steel rail replaced in hours; damage to bends took days to put right. And if you took out a loco as well, that was more than a bonus. Rails were comparatively simple to find or fabricate; for the Turks to source a replacement engine in wartime was nearly impossible.

Directly opposite Lawrence, on the far side of the track, was one of the rocky outcrops, an unusually symmetrical flat-topped protuberance, some fifty feet high, layered like a French confection. It was due to this miniature plateau that the German engineers had been forced to create the sweeping

13

diversion that curved towards Lawrence. It was because of this outcrop that Lawrence had chosen this exact spot to painstakingly lay his mines.

Stretched out flat on the ground at right angles to the steel track, Lawrence began excavating the hole for the first mine – actually a sandbag, filled with gelatine explosive, stripped of its paper wrapping – with his bare hands. He carefully scooped a hollow, ignoring the sharp ballast stones that cut his skin. Although he had a steel entrenching tool next to him, he could not risk even the slightest brush of the blade with a rail. Such a noise carried for miles in the still air. As he had made his stealthy way to the track on his stomach, he had heard sounds – the slamming of a door, the stamp of a horse – from the station he knew to be almost four miles away. So, the first six inches of the hollow were dug manually, before he switched to the tool.

It was slow work. There were four mines to place, linked to each other by an electrical wire, so they could be detonated in series. His shadow grew long over the sands, then began to shrink again as the sun climbed, but Lawrence didn't begrudge the time. The mines had to be concealed well enough for one of the Turkish patrols to walk straight over them, and they had to be placed for maximum effect. Two of the mines he would secrete under the centre of the metal sleepers. That would then distort both rails with a single explosion as the stretcher was thrown into the air. The second pair he positioned against the bottom flange at the expansion joints where two rails met, in contact with the fishplate.

Lawrence had learned all this by continuous trial and error

in the past months. He had seen both mines and bricks of guncotton make a tremendous din, throwing up tons of sand and grit, besmirching the blue sky, but hardly bending the rails. Others had been discovered minutes before a train was due to pass over them because of their careless disguise.

Even while he scratched at the soil, he kept one ear cocked for any unnecessary sound from other members of his raiding party. Behind him was a ragged ridge of sand dunes, where Auda, the Howeitat outlaw, and his small group of eleven were concealed, rifles, he hoped, at the ready. But not too ready. It had taken a long time to teach the tribes that firing lots of bullets was not the same as those rounds doing some good. No, he wanted them to engage only if a Turkish patrol appeared and looked like stumbling upon him.

Between the ridge and the railway was a sandy hillock anchored by a sparse covering of thorny plants. Behind that lay Ali, a vigorous young man of nineteen or perhaps twenty, who was, strictly speaking, Lawrence's servant, the eldest of three given to him by Emir Feisal, the son of the Sherif of Mecca. Lawrence treated Ali, though, not as dogsbody but as apprentice. He was strong, keen and a quick learner.

His job was to ferry the explosives out to Lawrence, but that day, Ali was also in charge of the plunger that would detonate the sequence of four mines. In an ideal world, he, too, would be on the ridge with Auda, but they were desperately short of electrical cable. They would have to risk detonating as close as they dare. Normally, Lawrence would ensure he was the one on the handle, the man most exposed, but Ali took such great delight in the explosions, almost as much as Lawrence did, that he felt cruel denying him the opportunity. They would blow the line together.

The risen sun was burning his back by the time the four holes were deep enough for Lawrence to place the mines inside them. He carefully attached the wires to the primer charge before he slid each into place, and tugged on the connections. Another hard lesson learned, from a trestle bridge that failed to blow because the terminals had come loose. Going back to reconnect them at night, under the nose of enemy soldiers, had been a tense and exhilarating time. Lawrence had rarely felt so alive as when he blew the structure to matchwood the next morning.

Satisfied with the positioning of the mines and the quality of his connections, Lawrence scraped back the earth over the top of the devices, making sure the darker subsoil went in first, holding back a whitish layer of stones to blend in with the lighter shades of the surface. He stroked and prodded and scraped at the ballast as if he were icing a cake, until he was happy that the craters containing the explosive charge were as invisible as possible.

Now he reversed his early morning crawl out to the railway, working backwards, burying the detonation wire as he went and sweeping the sand with the hem of his cloak in an attempt to conceal both his passage and the position of the cables. By the time he reached the scant coverage of the hillock, he was panting and his mouth felt parched from the sand dust. Ali uncorked the water bag and passed it to him. Lawrence sipped gratefully and settled, his back to the mound, facing the ridge where he could just make out the dark oval of a head.

He signalled for the man to drop down, but the Arab raised an arm, as if in greeting.

'Auda,' said Ali and Lawrence laughed softly. As if it would be anyone else. The hook-nosed, toothless Howeitat was a fearsome fighter who had killed two Turkish tax inspectors, thus ending his temporary alliance with the Ottoman Empire. He had therefore not hesitated to join Lawrence when he heard of his plans to drive the Turks out of Arabia, Palestine and Syria and to take Damascus. The gold, and the promise of pillage, had helped, of course. Auda had shown his commitment to the cause by smashing his false teeth, declaring they were made in Constantinople and he would have nothing Turkish in his mouth while the Ottomans occupied his lands. It was a powerful gesture, even if it was sometimes impossible to take the gummy rogue seriously. But Lawrence knew dozens had died because they hadn't paid Auda enough heed. Tall and erect, the man not only looked like a bird of prey, he sometimes acted like one.

'Oh for God's sake,' Lawrence moaned as loud as he dared when Auda virtually stood up. The man thought he was invulnerable.

'Orrans.' Like many desert Arabs, Ali had trouble with the name 'Lawrence' and had found his own strangled version. He followed the young man's pointing finger. 'A train.'

So there was. That was what had caused Auda to break cover. A thin pillar of white woodsmoke was just visible against the glare of the morning sky, indicating a locomotive. A troop train, he hoped, running down to Medina, to reinforce the beleaguered garrison. Lawrence allowed himself a small whoop of joy.

17

That's when he heard the aeroplane.

It was still far in the distance, not much closer than the loco, but the buzzing of the biplane was suddenly clearly audible. Lawrence had known for a long time, since his escapade in Persia two years earlier, that air power was going to be a decisive factor in this war. Nevertheless, he found himself cursing the machine as it swooped back and forward over the tracks, like a nervous gadfly. Sometimes it was galling to be proved right. Lawrence examined the ground he had spent so long grooming. To his eyes, the line of cable to the railway was no longer carefully blended into the landscape, it looked as if elephants had been dancing in the sand. If the observer were half decent, he would spot it immediately. And, of course, the Arab raiding party.

Auda appeared on the dune, his camel behind him, followed by Ghazala, Lawrence's mount. For a second Lawrence wondered what Auda was doing, and then realised his motives. A group of men hiding in dunes was highly suspicious. A camel train wasn't, not in this country, and the nomads often followed the railway, because the stations always had water to trade. Unless Lawrence had blown the storage tanks to bits, which he had taken to doing. Locomotives were surprisingly thirsty vehicles and it was a simple way to disable them.

Lawrence gave a sharp whistle and Ghazala's head turned towards him. She hesitated, just to establish that this was not blind obedience but a willing partnership of equals, and trotted down the slope towards him.

By the time the spotter plane reached them, the actors were in place and the play was in motion. Auda, on foot, was leading a tethered camel, at the head of a string of mounted men, none of whom appeared to have modern weapons. The procession had slowed because one camel had fallen out of the line. Around that errant creature a timeless scene was being enacted: an angry Arab merchant was beating his servant, laying into him with fists and feet.

As the German-built plane came in, the Arabs all looked up, shading their eyes to get a better glimpse of the strange machine. Some of the men waved. Others shook their heads, as if scared.

And all the time the train chuffed nearer. It was pulling two passenger carriages and, at the rear, a windowless baggage car, Lawrence noted. He had been hoping for boxcars, a dozen or more, crammed with Turkish troops or a carriage flying a general's flag. But even so, taking out the loco would be worth the explosive. The thought that he might have to let it pass unharmed caused him a twinge of anxiety.

The pilot brought the plane around for another look at the group, and Lawrence stopped attacking Ali. He could clearly see the machine gun mounted next to the observer. Lawrence too, waved, but there was no response from the crew. He felt the gritty wash of the propeller as the plane roared overhead and he briefly closed his eyes. The engine note became angrier and the biplane banked away.

'Shall we still blow it?' asked Ali, brushing the dust from the mock beating off his clothes. The noise of the loco filled their ears, and they could smell its smoke. The train was on the bend, apparently heading straight for them. They could see the armour plating on the front. That won't save you, Lawrence thought.

'Wait,' he said. *Not while there is a machine-gunner in the air.*

Lawrence calculated the time before the engine was over the mine. It wasn't long. The aeroplane had flown up the line and had come back, heading directly for the billowing plume issuing from the engine's smokestack. Lawrence knew the aeroplanes had limited fuel supply; they could not shadow the train for ever. Furthermore, as the day heated up and the air thinned, they lost lift. It was a brave pilot who would linger far into the morning.

Sure enough, this one dipped down, wagged its wings above the loco, and sped off north.

Lawrence held his breath, willing the aircraft not to turn back. It shrunk to a point where it was hard to tell the plane from the spots on his retina caused by sand glare.

The train was almost level now, just entering the apex of the wide curve that took it around the long, low rock.

Auda was hastily leading his men up to the ridge again, seeking the protection of the slope.

The driver had spotted the activity; he hauled on his whistle twice, alerting the station ahead, and begun to slow. The engine crews were getting jittery, it seemed. He should be flattered.

Lawrence flung himself down beside the plunger on the detonator and waited for Ali to join him. Now the engine was loud in his ears, he could hear the thump of pistons, the hiss of steam and the protest of brakes.

Lawrence risked a look over the hillock and a bullet whizzed by. The engineers carried rifles and often took pot shots at any lingering Arabs, just in case. The driver, clearly suspicious at the behaviour of Auda, applied full braking, sending sparks flying. The front wheels of the loco slid past the mine. The boy wound the charging handle and moved to the plunger, but Lawrence held his hand. Although it was slowing, the train's momentum still took it around the bend. Lawrence caught his breath, waiting till the boiler was above the spot where he had lain for those two hours. 'Now, Ali. Now.'

The earth rippled and the surface sand danced like fine rain as the first mine detonated and the engine lifted clear of the tracks. There was an anguished squeal as the whole train bucked and shuddered. The other three mines blew in rapid succession, a rolling thunder that sent vicious whiplashes down the length of the cars. The wounded loco left the track and began to head straight into the desert, sending up a huge spume of earth around it.

A series of shockwaves hit the saboteurs and Lawrence felt the superheated air scorch his cheek. He didn't duck; he couldn't take his eyes off the death throes of the machine, which had a terrible majesty, like the final moments of a prehistoric beast.

The carriages, too, had jumped the distorted rails, the bogeys digging into the soft sand, some shearing off. The front car bent in the centre with a loud creak and toppled on to its side, still hauled through the earth by the weight of the disintegrating locomotive. Doors and windows began to flip off the carcass, spinning away over the desert floor.

Ghazala gave an alarmed honk and sprinted uphill towards Auda.

An internal explosion burst the body of the engine open

and a column of steam seared high into the air. A wheel flew over Lawrence's head, humming as it went. Had he been a few inches taller, he would have been cleanly decapitated. It was the signal to get clear.

Lawrence grabbed Ali and pulled him away from the hillock as shards of metal pitter-pattered around them like hot rain, soon joined by showers of coal and wood. As they ran an impact shook the ground beside them. Lawrence barely had time to recognise it as a man, the top of him scalded raw by steam, the bottom a tangle of bloody stumps. He pushed Ali before him and they stumbled up through the loose soil.

They had almost made the ridge when a fist-sized piece of debris caught Lawrence between the shoulders and sent him sprawling. His face buried in the earth, he began to slide downhill. For a moment he thought he must suffocate as sand was forced up his nostrils. A hand grabbed his hair and pulled his head back, halting his progress.

'Ow.'

He looked up at Auda, the Arab's gums showing as he smiled. 'Are we to take Damascus lying down, Lawrence?' Auda never had any trouble with his name.

A bullet cracked close to Auda's ear, but he didn't flinch, and simply looked with irritation at the train. It had slithered to a halt, shrouded in smoke, vapour and dust. Through the haze, soldiers could be seen emerging from the shattered windows of the passenger carriages, some of them already firing at the raiders. The baggage car, however, had remained upright, and, from the terrified whinnying they could hear, it contained horses.

22

'Are you hurt?' asked Auda.

'No.'

Lawrence raised a hand and Auda yanked him to his feet. Auda's men were returning fire at the Turks, and Lawrence saw at least two hit. They were improving.

Lawrence crouched down. There was activity on the far side of the luggage car, protected from his view.

'Auda—' he began.

From behind the train a dozen horsemen came galloping, their heads down to present a smaller target, their rifles aligned along their steeds' heads, eating up the ground separating them from the ridge. The air came alive with gunfire as the Ottoman soldiers in and around the train set up a fusillade to protect the riders.

'Cavalry,' Auda announced with annoyance. Few of the Turk's fighting units impressed the Arabs; the Hejaz was not where crack infantry was deployed. The mounted soldiers, however, were different. They were the cream of Enver Pasha's forces. Auda was tempted to stand and fight. Lawrence could sense the Howeitat leader was torn between taking spoils from the train and taking casualties.

A muzzle flashed from between the ruined carriages and there came the sharp tapping of a Spandau machine gun. A line of sand below the ridge sprayed into the air as the gunner struggled to find the range.

'Time to go,' said Lawrence quietly. 'There will be other trains.'

Auda nodded, barked an order and his men immediately stopped firing and mounted their camels. Lawrence crested the ridge, pulled Ghazala down and slid into the saddle. In less than a minute, the Arab raiding party had taken their animals down on to the hard-packed earth at the base of the slope and urged them on. The camels moved swiftly into their top, racing speed.

Far too soon for comfort, they felt the snap of bullets at their backs. Mimicking their pursuers, the Bedu made themselves small in the saddle and Lawrence did the same. None looked to see if the Turks were gaining. Lawrence knew that the Turks' courage diminished the further away they were from the security of the railway and the foot soldiers. Also the camels had more stamina than horses, and had not been traumatised by being in a train wreck.

The Turks would also see that ahead were the canyons of the Ka'ma Hills, a belt of fissured limestone that would offer the raiding party shelter and defensive positions. For all the Turks knew, the main Arab army was camped in there and they were being led into a trap.

The firing became sporadic and then stopped and Lawrence risked a backward glance. The line of Turkish horses had halted. Behind them was the sand ridge and above that, a twist of grey smoke, staining the sky.

He allowed himself a smile.

After almost an hour, when they had emerged from the Ka'ma's twisting Atam gorge on to the beginning of the hard salt flats, Auda called a halt. Lawrence, his buttocks aching from the gallop, was only too pleased to get off the wheezing Ghazala.

Auda also dismounted and came over to Lawrence, his face

24

grim. He would be angry at losing the loot, of course. Dead Turks were routinely stripped naked, everything of value stowed in saddlebags until, Lawrence knew, they felt they had enough booty to return home. The size of their welcome depended on the weight of those bags.

But it wasn't the money or spoils that concerned Auda this time. 'It is Ali,' he said. 'You must come.'

Two of Auda's men had lowered the youth from his camel and carried him to a small gully in the shade, where they had laid him down on his side and given him water. They stood and backed off as Lawrence approached.

The Englishman knelt down, took off his cloak and slid it under the boy's head. 'Ali. What happened?'

He pointed with a bloody hand. 'My back.'

'Can I take a look?'

'No.' He grimaced. 'It hurts.'

'Be brave. For me. For Orrans.'

He gently rocked the lad on to his front and tried not to exclaim at the sight that greeted him. He rolled him back on to his side, careful to keep a smile on his face. The boy's handsome brown face was creased in pain, covered in a film of sweat and he was biting the tip of his tongue. Lawrence could barely imagine the kind of agony he must be in, especially after the headlong dash on the camels. A Turkish bullet had hit the centre of his spine, ripping through clothes, skin and bone. He had seen fragments of white vertebrae in the wound, and shreds of wool. 'Can you move your toes? No? Move your leg for me. No? Well, that's fine. It's just shock.'

Lawrence was aware of someone behind him. Auda stepped past and knelt, looking into the boy's eyes. He kissed his forehead and said something Lawrence didn't catch.

When he stood, Lawrence could see Auda had left his revolver on the bed of the gully, just out of Ali's sight.

'He knows,' Auda said.

What the lad knew was that they couldn't leave him. The Turks had taken to roasting captured raiders over open fires, no matter how badly wounded they were. Nor could Ali ride on with such a terrible injury; he wouldn't survive with so much filthy fabric in the wound anyway. If the bleeding didn't kill him, the poison in his blood soon would. It would not be a nice death, not one to be proud of.

Auda walked away. Lawrence, Ali's master, would have to perform this mercy. The boy reached up and grabbed his tunic, pulling him close. He managed a brave smile. 'Orrans. Do not worry. I will see my father, and my brother. I will tell them about you. I will tell them what an Englishman can do. It has been good, hasn't it?'

'Yes, Ali,' he replied as he reached for the revolver, the words hardly managing to leave his lips. 'It's been good.'

III

Rollins remained quiet once Lawrence had finished his story.

'We buried him there, on the edge of the flats. A warrior can be interred where he falls, you know. He'll still be taken into paradise. I didn't always appreciate that. I shall dedicate the next train we blow, the one with your cable, to Ali. So, to answer your question, no it's not my blood.'

There were so many other questions Rollins wanted to ask, not least how an Englishman had come to lead a band of brigands – as the Turks saw them – across the deserts of Arabia and Palestine. And did he really believe the boy was in Paradise? Wasn't that heathen nonsense, all that stuff about virgins and gardens and endless streams of cool water? But he didn't feel he could quiz the man.

'My apologies, Sergeant, I have talked on for too long. I have been in the desert ten months now. It's why I am talking too much. With a friend. I hope you don't mind.'

Rollins was quietly pleased to be nominated a friend. 'Of course not, sir.'

Lawrence allowed himself a yawn and a stretch. It was like watching a feral cat, thought Rollins.

'Perhaps you need to rest.'

'Rest? Not till the Sherif's flag flies over Damascus, Sergeant. Help me on with all this.'

Once Lawrence's cloak was in place, he took a deep breath, holding it for a minute, then two, then three.

Lawrence's face began to redden.

'Sir.'

An upraised hand silenced Rollins.

At around the four-minute mark, Lawrence allowed the air to leak out of his lungs. He then made half a dozen fast inhalations and exhalations. With this he seemed restored, his eyes blazing once more, his chest puffed out. He wagged a finger at the driver. 'Not a word, Rollins, not a word.'

The sergeant wasn't entirely sure what he was meant to keep quiet about, but he nodded solemnly. 'Of course.'

Lawrence quickly selected sticks of gelignite, cable and detonators and placed them in various pockets. Like a wily poacher, the goods had simply disappeared from sight, lost in the folds of his native garb. 'Excellent. Now, that parcel?'

'Oh, right.' Rollins, who had quite forgotten about the item left for Lawrence by Major Noel during the story, fetched the box from a makeshift shelf. There was a note attached, which Lawrence unfolded and read. He frowned as he digested it.

'Bad news?'

'What? No. Yes. Allenby wants to see me.' General Edmund Allenby was the commander of the Egyptian Expeditionary Force, the conventional counterpart to Lawrence's less formal army. His brief was to smash the Turks by taking every major city in the region, with Jerusalem being the ultimate goal.

'The Bull? Ah, well. Best go and see him then.'

'Not until I have spoken to Noel.'

'The major didn't leave a forwarding address, sir. How will you find him?'

'Another Englishman in the wilderness?' Lawrence seemed amused by the idea that there would be any difficulty. 'There are ways, Sergeant, there are ways.'

They left the storage area and walked across towards the bodyguards who, sensing it was time to leave, quickly packed up their bread and dates and began urging their camels back on to their feet. Lawrence paused and watched them with pride as they took to their mounts. 'You know, Sergeant, there are terrible setbacks like poor Ali. Some days the mines don't blow. Other days the wind doesn't stop howling. And I have politics and lies, monstrous lies, snapping at my heels. But, right now, there is nowhere else on earth I'd rather be.'

Watching the band of desert-hardened ruffians assemble, and imagining the rigours of criss-crossing this country in their company, Rollins couldn't quite see why, but he could tell Lawrence was sincere. 'I am pleased to hear it, sir.'

'I'm a lucky man. And I will see you shortly, Sergeant Rollins, for another ride in a Rolls-Royce,' Lawrence said as he slipped the box into his saddlebags and stepped on to Ghazala. 'And thank you.' The old camel rose with a series of grunts and coughs, unfolding like a hinge.

'Good luck, sir.'

Lawrence leaned over towards him and kept his voice low, as if addressing a fellow conspirator. 'We've come a long way since Persia, haven't we, Sam?'

Now, as they both grinned at the memory of those few days, the sergeant could see Lawrence was still the same man who had blown into Banda Abbas like a sand devil, full of wild ideas, trailing a bewildered Captain Quinn and two Arabs with him and dragging an English airman and a young car mechanic called Sam Rollins into his schemes. 'No argument there, Captain.'

Lawrence replaced the cloth over the lower part of his face and uttered a short phrase: 'Hut-hut-hut.' Ghazala darted forward, and Lawrence settled into the saddle, rolling with the animal's gait.

Rollins stepped back several paces as the bodyguard pulled

their animals around to follow Lawrence back towards the bend in the gorge, urging them on with short sticks or sharp commands. The camel train left in a swirl of dust. At the rear came the two boys, Lawrence's servants, busy trying to tie something to the tail of the camel immediately in front.

With Lawrence and his retinue gone, the canyon of Wadi Umt suddenly seemed darker and emptier and Rollins felt the first chill of the evening to come. 'We should call it a day,' he yelled to Hassan. 'Pack it up.'

'Blimey, Sarge. Your mate. Captain Lawrence, was it?' Humphries, the gunner, had moved to Rollins's side. He was rolling a cigarette, puzzled by what he had just witnessed, a mixture of awe and disbelief in his voice. 'Where the bloody hell did he come from?'

Part One

Two Years Earlier

One

Pas de Calais, France, 1915

The ground was never still beneath their feet. It vibrated and heaved under the continuous barrage. Every pool of standing water shimmered in the early morning light, the surfaces rippling and dancing as the shells pounded the earth. The bombardment from the British and French artillery had started at two in the morning, ripping a mile-long gash in the night sky with its blurred muzzle flashes, filling the Allied soldiers' skulls with its constant rumble. It was now nearly five, and the sun was rising to witness a freshly ruined countryside surrounding the roofless village of Richebourg l'Avoué.

The line trenches that the 1st Gloucesters were moving through had been built by the French and then abandoned, before being called into action once more for the assault against the new German front. In the interim, the duckboards had rotted away, the parapet splintered and the sandbags had split and spilled their filling. The exposed sump at the bottom was a sludge of sewage, sand and mud, through which they had to march.

Second Lieutenant Frank Helier Lawrence, the second youngest of the five Lawrence brothers, stepped aside into one of the boltholes that dotted the length of the communication trench to allow his men to pass. His feet sunk into the mulched straw beneath his boots and he heard the splash of the rats he had disturbed. As the drawn and sometimes frightened faces flashed by, he began speaking to each in turn. 'Well done. Keep it moving. Watch your step. How's the leg, Corporal? That's the spirit.'

Platitudes, but he could think of no better strategy and the men seemed grateful that he made the effort. There were too many officers who stayed mute, taking counsel with their own fearfulness. Lawrence wasn't afraid, simply resigned to the likely outcome of his time in the trenches. But his throat was unnaturally dry, despite the thick, pre-sweetened tea he had consumed. Some of the mugs had been fortified with the nip of rum that his orderly had begun adding. He didn't drink alcohol, but the old farm worker insisted it was medicinal, tried and tested in the fields at home. 'Good for the chilblains.' Lawrence would certainly risk the wrath of his teetotal mother to quell the itching of his feet, which were quite immune to the MO's white powders. So he took his rum and swore he would pray for forgiveness later.

The sun had inched higher in the sky, but the smoke shells had created a haze. As the light became stronger, the faces passing became tinged with yellow, as if the company had all

34

come down with jaundice. Coupled with their bleary and bloodshot eyes, it made them look like an army en route to hospital, rather than war. But then every eye in the British Expeditionary Force was inflamed, from lack of sleep, the constant scratching of dust and dirt and the clouds of smoke that enveloped them day and night.

'Well done, there. Lift your feet, it's easier than dragging them, Private. Helmet, man, helmet.'

He snapped out the praise and gentle chiding with a confidence he no longer felt. He had been in France for just three months, which made him an old hand. Of the ten officers on the square when he joined, four were dead, four wounded and one missing. He felt he was carrying the torch for that group, keeping their spirit alive.

He touched the envelope in the inside pocket of the silk-lined oiled Burberry he was wearing. Not To Be Opened Until My Death, it said on it. He was the last of the ten still standing, as far as he knew. You had to be prepared. So, in the letter, he told his parents and his brothers, Bob, Ned – as they called Thomas Edward – Will and Arnold, not to grieve, but to accept God's will.

He thought of Ned in Cairo, tried to imagine what it must be like to feel warm and dry, to be free of lice, to let the sun warm a clean face. At least T.E. was out of harm's way there, with his maps and diaries. His over-active older brother might protest at the crushing boredom in Egypt, but right now Frank would give a lot to be bored.

He hoped Ned remained there, away from the war. Of all of them, he'd had the most rotten childhood, and had received more than his fair share of beatings from Mother, because he would always accept responsibility for any of his brothers' misdemeanours. When Frank had asked why, T.E. claimed he knew for a fact that the cane hurt the others more than him. Perhaps there was some truth in it; he broke his leg once and nobody discovered it for days, such was his stoicism.

Although Frank wished Ned safe in Cairo, something told him his brother was unlikely to settle for a quiet war.

'Lawrence.'

It was Captain Blunt, who was holding a piece of paper out to him. 'Slight change of plan,' he shouted over the grumbling of the guns. 'The major wants to move your men to this section here.' He jabbed the crude drawing. 'Designated Rapier. You wait—'

Both men started, as if they had received an electrical jolt. It was a second before they realised the cause of the shock. The barrage had stopped. All that was left was the residual ringing in the ears. A breathless hush fell over the column of men, who slowed, as if to catch the precious silence. The noise of the mud sucking at their feet was clearly audible with each step now.

'Good Lord.' Blunt checked his watch. 'Thought we had another thirty minutes.'

'Perhaps they've run out of shells,' said Lawrence. It wasn't an entirely facetious remark. It had happened before.

'Best get into place. Good luck.'

Lawrence pushed his way through the trudging men, slithering as he went, his hand often plunging into the sodden sides of the trench as he struggled for balance, until he reached his sergeant. He indicated the man should go to the head of the column. 'Tell them to wait at the holding point,' he said. 'Then we'll move right. Not lef—'

The earth shuddered and muck and stones rained down on them, sending up plumes of black water from the bottom of the trench.

There was a pause, perhaps two heartbeats long, in which they heard the distinctive growling cough of the German guns, before the air seemed to flutter and the concussion tossed them around like skittles. As they tried to regain their balance, a third wave of shells landed, these ones screaming and whistling as they came, so that the ground-shaking thud of the explosion signalling their detonation seemed like a welcome relief.

There was another pause and every man in the dugout counted, till thirty seconds had passed. Then, a full minute. It was a ranging exercise. The Germans would adjust the artillery's clinometers and start again, this time targeting the forward trenches. The very ones the 1st Gloucesters were heading to. Even the early morning light was gone now, the sun blotted out by a curtain of black particles that hung over the field, rising up to fifty or more feet.

A voice barked from the rear. 'F'God's sake. Get moving, come along. Ain't you lot ever been shelled before?'

There was a ripple of rueful laughter. The sergeant straightened and tried to wipe the dirt from his face, with no success. 'Sir, you were saying?' His officer was still bent double. He touched Lieutenant Lawrence's shoulder, but the man slumped into one of the timber supports and slid down, his face gathering splinters as he went, blood from the shrapnel wound in his head leaving a dark glistening trail on the filthy wood. The sergeant didn't need to check any further; he'd seen this more times than he could possibly calculate. Young Frank Lawrence was dead.

Two

Persia, 1915

Captain Edward Noel, the British Army's Political Officer at Bushire, led his mount up a stony slope, the hooves skittering and sparking on the loose, pebbly surface. His small scouting party had left the date palms behind and, away from any flood plain, the land had grown scrubby, dotted with tamarisk and blackened camel-thorn, all the way, it seemed, to the distant mountains. The desert here was a drab, dusty grey and monotonous. It reminded Captain Noel of a vast, baked spoil heap.

As the band of men, horses and camels crested the rise, they could see clearly the interruption in the overland lines of the Anglo-Persian Telegraphic Company that ran from the British Residency at the port of Bushire, north to Baghdad and Tehran. The wires had been pulled down but, confirming that this was no idle vandalism or vicious act of nature, a stretch of the telegraph poles had been yanked from their seatings and carted off. To a people who lived in a land without great forests, with many thousands of square miles devoid of even the smallest trees, the use of stout timber to hold flimsy spools of copper seemed wasteful and arrogant. Whoever had attacked the property of the Anglo-Persian Telegraphic Company had taken its wood as booty.

Not in its entirety, however. One column of timber was left standing, proud of a thin stand of acacia, although its function had altered, for it was a telegraph pole no longer. Where it had once cradled delicate filaments of metal, it now supported two bodies, hanging from its short, stubby arms. It has become a makeshift gibbet.

Apart from this gallows, the only other visible structure was a blockhouse, constructed of rough cement, unpainted to merge into the landscape. Even from a distance, Noel could see the scorch marks that had discoloured it. It had been put to the torch. He turned and looked over his shoulder, but Lieutenant Johnson and the three sepoys under his command had already drawn their weapons and he had no need to warn them of the need for vigilance. Behind them, the camel master, a turbaned Indian *drabi*, held back. If the raiders were still around, he had no desire to be caught in the service of the English, even if he was carrying nothing more threatening than baled hay and water.

There was a flapping around one of the hanged men's heads and oil-dark wings were briefly silhouetted against the sky. Noel felt a shudder of revulsion.

He walked his horse around the suspended men, trying to

ascertain how long they had been there. The pair were still in khaki shorts, the upper torsos were naked, and, even under the reddening of the skin inflicted by the sun, he could see the dark red criss-crosses of a flogging. The eyes had already been gobbled out and the tongues that lolled out of the mouths were pockmarked and torn by the carrion's pecking.

The shot from behind made his horse buck. Noel instinctively ducked, although the round went well above his head. The magpies and hooded crows that had come to feed on the rotting bodies took to the air with petulant cries. The sound of the discharge screeched across the desert.

He turned to see Johnson, his revolver raised, a curl of smoke clinging to the barrel.

'You fool,' Noel said.

'Sir? I just wanted to shift those bloody birds.'

The lad looked queasy, as well he might. He hoped the boy didn't have too much imagination. These men, one English soldier, one Scots telegraph engineer, had not had an easy death. But making such a racket was a foolhardy response, even if it was to save the men the indignity of any more deface-ment by the birds.

He suppressed the urge to bawl the lad out. 'Go softly, soldier. Put the gun away. Cut them down, bury them.'

Johnson hesitated before he replied. 'Sir.'

'Feed the animals while you are doing so. Quick as you like'.

Noel took off his topee and wiped his brow. Using field glasses he examined the stony waves of the desert, the ridge behind him, the gently rising foothills to the right. The sun hadn't reached its zenith yet; there were still shadows to give depth and perspective to the view. At midday, the land would become a flat and featureless glare. He concentrated on the soot-coloured foothills, blurred by the ripples of a heat haze, which gave way to mountains with fiery sandstone cliffs, hard, unyielding granite peaks and a series of treacherous passes, which led, eventually, to Shiraz, a deceptively beautiful city of sparkling, water-filled gardens, rich with the scent of roses. It was charming and graceful on the surface, but cruel at heart.

Nothing moved within his range of vision except the constantly shifting air. Yet he knew the sound of a gunshot could be heard many, many miles away and this wilderness was never as empty as it seemed.

Noel nudged his Arab mount over to the blockhouse to investigate further, for he was still one body short of a full tally. There had been three men sent out to examine the lines, one engineer and a pair of armed escorts with horse and mule. He had no doubt where the animals had gone, but had they also abducted the third man? If so, there would be a ransom demand.

He found the corpse at the far side of the cement structure and acknowledged that there would be no note arriving at Bushire, offering an exchange for a trunk of sovereigns. This third body was completely naked. Four wooden tent pegs, each a foot long, had been driven into the earth at an angle, and twine had been used to bind his limbs at wrist and ankle and he had been stretched out in a star-shape.

The captain tried to keep his mind detached while he examined the remains. Where the man's genitals should have been, there was nothing but a gaping red and black hole, the surface shimmering with the gorged, luminous bodies of thousands of flies as they shifted and jostled to find their feasting spot on the great wound. The man's face was savagely blistered and it looked as if he had puffed his cheeks out in exasperation. The lips had been stitched together with some kind of rough thread. Noel had no doubt what he would find inside the mouth if he snipped the sutures. Nothing had yet attacked the eyes of this one, apart from a smaller battalion of flies, but there appeared to be no pupils. They had rolled up inside themselves, no doubt an extreme reaction by the body to having the eyelids removed.

The captain slowly took some water from his canteen, making sure his actions were cool and measured. Inside the white heat of anger burned bright. Unlike the majority of his compatriots, Noel liked this country, admired its people, but sometimes even he found himself cursing it and them.

Noel swilled the water around his mouth and dragged his gaze away from the poor mutilated soul before him. He swallowed, then cleared his throat to make sure his voice, when it came, was strong and resilient.

'Johnson!' he yelled. 'We have a third—'

The spasm around his head told him he was under fire. The distinctive crack that followed suggested it was a Mauser, a German rifle, rather than a Martini or the homemade *jezeel* muskets more commonly used in these parts. A whorl of dust was thrown up from the blackened cement wall.

There came more pops and snaps, and he whirled his Arab, looking for the gunmen's position. There was no indication of where they were, just the same featureless scrub marching off into the distance. Smokeless powder, another signifier that they were wielding unusually modern weapons for south-west Persia. Then a flash of cloth, a figure sprinting between positions, a desert wraith that disappeared within seconds.

His Indian *drabi* had already turned and fled, racing for the rise over which they had come, whipping his camel with an urgency that suggested he wouldn't stop until Bushire. He had dropped the tethers of the other beasts, although two of them were padding after him, honking in dromedarian alarm as they went.

Noel saw Johnson abandon his shovel and try to mount his horse. He had one foot in the stirrup, when the bullet caught him. A lick of blood splashed up the animal's flanks and it began to prance, as if it were dancing on fiery coals.

Noel rode over there as quickly as he could manage, and scooped Johnson over the saddle, grabbed the reins and followed the *drabi*'s example by seeking cover. Johnson, one arm limp, managed to struggle upright.

His three sepoys were already back on their horses and firing, but blindly. 'Just ride, you idiots!' he cried at them.

Sprays of gravel kicked up around them as rounds hit the desert floor. This suggested to him they were at the edge of range for a Mauser, which was around five hundred yards. Unless the guns were fitted with a telescopic sight, and who in the desert would have those?

Johnson had just taken the reins for himself when the second round punched out a large section of his right shoulder. He screamed and slumped forward, but stayed in the saddle. They were ascending the rise now, only feet from safety. Noel heard a high whistle close to his ear, followed by a louder crack, a sure sign of a near miss. Telescopic sights.

The routed Englishmen crested the ridge and Noel could not believe the scene that greeted him.

At the bottom of the slope was the Indian camel master, kneeling next to the bulk of his bloodied animal, which was braying in agony and kicking at the earth, sending up clouds of grit. Hovering above the poor man, a curved blade was glinting in the sun, arrested at the apex of its arc, ready to sweep down and sever the head from the body. Behind the weeping guide and his trap-faced executioner, set off to one side, a cluster of Tangistani was jabbering excitedly, yelling at each other. Every man had a gleaming Mauser over his shoulder, but they made no effort to unsling them. What was on the ground in front of the group was far more exciting a prospect for them and each was pressing their case for a turn behind it. It was a sledge-mounted, water-cooled Maschinengewehr 08, the German Army's much-feared machine gun.

Noel had never seen one in action, but he knew the slaughter they had inflicted in France and he also knew that to hesitate before one was to die. He raised his Webley and fired into the body of the tribesmen, at the same time kicking his horse forward.

There came an order, shrieked at full volume and audible even over the noise of his pistol, the death throes of the camel and the scrabble of rocks and stones under hooves. As the sword started its swift journey through the bone and sinew of the Indian's neck, the MG08 began its mechanical chatter.

The air around him buzzed, as if a swarm of locusts had descended. He felt lines of white pain streak across his left arm and warm droplets spattered on to his chin. Noel fired one last shot at the executioner's head, gratified by the red mist that erupted from the rear of the skull, then felt a fist drive deep into his shoulder and his unfortunate mount buckled under him, pitching him to the ground, where he hoped death would at least come quickly.

It didn't. He lay there, listening to his lungs wheezing and whistling, his eyes closed. The pain built, burned fiercely, but held just the right side of unbearable. Some time had passed before he became aware of a shadow over his face. He raised his lids and squinted against the glare of the light. It was one of the warriors, but all he could see was the silhouette of the face and the shape of the hat. The sun behind him had blacked out his features.

The man kneeled down and leaned in close, so Noel could see his expression. He was wearing a satisfied smile, showing his yellow teeth, breathing the scent of almonds across the captain's face. He propped up the wounded man's head and held a goatskin water pouch to Noel's lips and he gulped some down. Like all the water of the area, it had a whiff of brimstone, but, for once, Noel didn't care as he swallowed greedily.

A fresh fire had started in his ribs and was spreading across his chest, as if someone had lit a fuse. The charge exploded somewhere beneath his sternum. He grimaced and gave an involuntary spasm, spitting out a jet of the water.

When he spoke, the man's voice was soft and caring, as if

he had taken no part in the massacre, that it was all circumstances beyond his control. 'With God's help and mercy, you might live long enough for someone to come looking and find you, Englishman. You understand?'

Noel nodded.

'Your wounds are not worse than they feel, I think.' The man took off his own hat and propped it on Noel's head, shielding his upper face from the sun. 'And I leave you the water.'

Noel tried to speak, to curse the man's capricious God, but his throat had closed with the pain.

The stranger unpopped the leather ammunition pouch from Noel's Sam Browne and it disappeared into the folds of his tunic. Noel's Webley and the other British weapons and their bullets were too precious to leave behind. 'My name is Zair Khidair. I am Khan of Ahram. You know Ahram?'

Another nod. It was a fortified village to the south of Bushire. He'd also heard of the Khan, had sent requests for meetings that had been ignored.

'They will ask you who did this.' He looked around at the field of the dead, the stones on which they lay flecked with darkening crimson. 'You can say it was me. Zair Khidair,' he repeated, banging his chest. 'Of the Tangistan. But listen.' He stood now, becoming a dark, featureless silhouette once more as the sun flared around him. 'Tell them we did it in the name of Woss Moss. You hear me? Woss Moss.'

Three

Cairo, 1915

When the news from France finally reached him, Second Lieutenant Thomas Edward Lawrence of the Intelligence Section's Geographical Services Department was working behind the *mashrabiyya* carved screen he had erected to delineate his corner of the map room. He was not, that particular morning, poring over cartographic renderings of the Levant or Arabia, but carefully stripping a Martini-Henry rifle to establish its provenance. The weapon had been recovered from a felucca, boarded on the Nile by Royal Marines, following a tip-off by Lawrence, which in turn came from one his spies in the Alexandria docks. There had been two cases of rifles hidden beneath the felucca's decking, along with a number of pistols, including British Webleys.

Ronald Storrs, the Oriental Secretary and Deputy Head of the Intelligence Section in Cairo, delivered the message in person. He grasped Lawrence on the shoulder as he handed it over, squeezing in a manner that told the young Lieutenant what it contained even before he opened the envelope. It was a War Office telegram, and addressed to him at INTRUSIVE, the Cairo office's telegraphic address. Lawrence placed it to one side on the table and carried on examining the rifle, giving Storrs a commentary as he did so.

Strictly speaking, the analysis of confiscated ordnance, let alone the running of spies, was outside the remit of a mere creator of maps, which was Lawrence's official status in Cairo. However, the lieutenant saw no reason to be constrained by the army's lack of vision when it came to its intelligence officers. His superiors would prefer him to stay focused on his duties within this stuffy room. He had other plans.

'Well used but very serviceable,' said Lawrence, as he turned the rifle over in his hands. 'First and second proofing in Birmingham,' he added, pointing to the stamps on the breech. 'With a London Proofhouse mark when the conversion to .303 was carried out. Which makes it a Martini-Enfield, not Henry. But there is also this.' He indicated a pair of arrows converging on a single, central point. 'A Sold Out of Service mark. It's ex-army. Ex-British army, I should say.'

'And the letters?' Storrs asked, pointing to an 'F' and an 'A' that bracketed the two arrows.

'Firozpur Arsenal. That's southwest Punjab. Someone is buying up ex-Indian Army weapons and shipping them to Cairo.'

With no good in mind, thought Storrs. He squeezed the shoulder once more. 'Well, we can worry about that later. You'd best read the telegram.'

The lieutenant nodded but made no move to do so. Eventually, after enduring a lecture on the .303 cartridge, Storrs left him to it, knowing the man would get round to it in his own good time.

Lawrence stripped the rifle down then reassembled it, the mindless rhythm distracting him from thoughts of the envelope and its contents. His hands barely shook, but he could feel the tremor within the muscles, the knotted tension. He took the Martini apart again and re-made it and then a third time, until he was satisfied his shakes were totally suppressed.

Then he opened the envelope. His throat dried as he read the terse statement:

Deeply regret to inform you that 2nd Lieutenant F.H. Lawrence Gloucester Regiment killed in action 9th May. Lord Kitchener expresses his sympathy.

That man's well of sympathy must be bottomless, he thought, his eyes stinging. He took a deep breath and held it, fighting for control. *Not here*, he thought. *Not now.*

At midday, a fresh batch of decoded signals was brought in by Captain Stewart Newcombe, the closest person to a friend Lawrence had in the building. They had met in Sinai before the war, when they were mapping the region for the military under the guise of archaeological work. After he had put down the paperwork, Newcombe stared at the folded telegram.

'Lawrence—' he began.

The thought of empty words, no matter how sincerely

meant, filled Lawrence with dread. 'I know. Best leave me to get on, eh?'

'Of course.'

Once he had gone, Lawrence read the new dispatches from Persia and Mesopotamia. There was a worrying report concerning a Captain Noel that took his attention. A telegraph repair party had been slaughtered, the rescue patrol attacked, their weapons taken. Including Webley revolvers. All done in the name of someone called Woss Moss.

Lawrence located Bushire on the map of Persia and traced his finger out into the scruffy hinterland. He pencilled a small 'x' at the spot where the atrocities had taken place. Next to it he wrote two letters, 'WM', and added a question mark. If it was significant, he'd be hearing that name again.

It was just coming up to one o'clock, the time when the British offices traditionally closed for four hours. Usually, Lawrence liked to work straight through, fuelled by syrup-sweetened coffee and biscuits. That day, however, he changed from the pumps he wore, initially the subject of much hilarity and derision, but now accepted as one of his many foibles, and slipped on his regulation boots.

He left the map room and stepped out into what passed for atmosphere in Cairo, a cloying mixture of jasmine, burning charcoal and excrement, carried on a fine breeze of desert dust, the last of the season's *khamseen* winds. The city was hot and stuffy, but enough of spring remained in the air to hold off the liverishness and lassitude that befell it in high summer. Lawrence walked through the courtyard of the hotel opposite the British embassy that housed the map room and

Military Intelligence offices, past the sentries, and through the iron gates to the street.

There, he slipped a coin to Munir, the boy he had hired to look after his newly acquired Clyno motorcycle. Lawrence had rescued the machine from the scrap heap at the Bab-el-Hadid barracks, a faux-Crusader castle opposite the railway station. The Clyno had originally been designed to carry a machine gunner in an open sidecar, and had been successful in France. However, trials in the desert had thrown up problems with sand penetration of the engine. Lawrence had rebuilt the carburation system and incorporated three extra-fine mesh filters that, although they needed washing and changing at least once a day, cured the problem of grit in the fuel needles.

'*Fein el cocktail Bokra?*' the boy Munir asked. Where is the party tonight? He was aware the lad was probably a spy, reporting his every movement to one of the many Syrians who held court at the coffee houses.

Lawrence hesitated and said softly: 'No cocktail *Bokra*.' The Egyptian was not to know that he never touched alcohol, no matter how it was dressed up. 'No cocktails tonight.'

Lawrence kicked the Clyno to life. Whereas Lawrence hated unnecessary noise created by human beings, and especially despised the mindless braying of so many of his colleagues, he loved the sound of a well-tuned and powerful engine, the sweetest racket on earth. As part of his improvements, he had unbolted the clumsy steel frame designed to hold the sidecar, thus increasing the machine's performance. He left Munir standing in his wake of petrol fumes.

Lawrence's first call was the Savoy Hotel, where he was

billeted. Here, for a consideration, the concierge could arrange for letters to by-pass the boorish censors, who thought even comments about the inflated price of tea subversive. He dropped off half-a-dozen newly written pages, to David Hogarth, his old Oxford mentor – now moved to Military Intelligence – one to each of his parents, and the longest and most detailed to the desert explorer and Arabian expert Miss Gertrude Bell. Postal delivery done, he headed south into the heart of the city.

The Sharia el Fasquiya was blocked – he could see mounted Cairo police and British MPs on foot, and a crowd of protestors, no doubt whipped up by the Egyptian Brotherhood – so he took to the side-streets, manhandling the bike along roads clogged with mules, carts and people, not a small proportion of the latter in uniform. There were newly detrained Australian and New Zealand units in the Greater Cairo area, many of which had caught the tram to the city for a taste of the usual pleasures soldiers seek when abroad.

They were pestered, as all fresh arrivals were, by the sellers of flyswats, swagger sticks, shoelaces, cigarettes, the scrawny bootblacks ('Kiwi polish, sir! Bigga clean, sir!') and the pockmarked pimps with their lurid promises of forbidden books and of women in the brothels and peepshows of the baffling maze of mud huts known as the Birka, a squalid quarter that was a hop, skip and a drunken stumble from the luxury of Shepheard's Hotel. It was said women of any colour, shape and size could be had in the Birka; Lawrence considered the same doubtless applied to the range of diseases.

The hustlers rarely bothered Lawrence. They were fully

conversant with the subtleties of Dominion uniforms – they could place a man by the crown of his slouch hat – and were aware of who was new in the city. Fresh, disorientated meat was always best for them. Plus Lawrence could snap back at them in their own language. To his own ears, his Arabic was no better than competent, but Dahoum, his young companion in Syria, had schooled him in an entire lexicon of spirited curses. Later, just before war broke out, a remarkable woman called Fareedeh el Akle had introduced him to the more refined aspects of the language. Put together, it meant the street rascals quickly appreciated that there were much softer touches than Lawrence.

He stopped at an orange seller's cart. The gaudily painted stall was manned by a sallow-faced boy with one sightless eye disfigured by the worm, and Lawrence bought four medium-sized fruits for a half-piaster, checking the skin for tell-tale signs that filthy water had been injected to make them feel plumper.

He picked up the avenue to Maadi, following the tramlines and the twin rows of pepper trees that marked the route to the city's desirable green suburb. But he did not take the boulevard all the way; he moved back through Old Cairo and across the bridge to the island of Roda and on to the west bank of the Nile.

Once on the relatively open highway, he lowered his goggles and opened up the machine, slipping into top gear and zipping by startled camels and their drivers. A few curses and shaken fists were directed his way because of the chalk-thick plume generated from the bike's studded tyres. He was on the acacia-lined Giza road, built to improve access to the pyramids, and its uneven surface sent judders up his arms and spine. He enjoyed the physicality of it and, such was his carefully maintained upper body strength – Lawrence liked to think of himself as a pocket Hercules – he had no trouble keeping the handlebars straight, even at considerable speed.

Ahead was the toothy outline of the city's famed triangular monuments, their edges feathered and the bases obscured by heat and the glare of the sky, so that they seemed to be floating above the desert on a carpet of smoke. Somewhere in their shadow lay the great encampments for the troops and the stables and corrals for the horses and pack animals of the British Army and its colonial allies. Instead of passing through this militarised area, he headed south, along an old route that led towards Memphis and the lesser-known pyramids at Saqqara.

With the knocked-about pyramid of Sahu Ra and its even less intact siblings in view, he took a right, on to a track that was little more than a trace in the soil. He rode for twenty-five minutes, watching the greenery grow patchy and fade as the irrigation ditches and their tall weeds petered out, passing one last sad date plantation, its brown-fronded trees stunted by continual thirst. He powered on, his dust-blackened teeth chattering as the Clyno bucked and bounced over the fringes of the Western Desert, until ahead was a series of low scrub-covered hillocks, with a single rocky outcrop that afforded enough shadow for him to park the bike. He had discovered that the loss of petrol in the cruel Cairene sun through evaporation was startling, and any shade helped cut down the waste.

55

In the lee of the rock, Lawrence heaved the bike on to its stand, hung his goggles over the handlebars, and unclipped the panniers, slinging them over his shoulder. He found what he was looking for after five minutes; a good solid boulder around three feet tall, its upper surface shaved billiard-table flat by the elements. On top of it he placed three of his oranges. He then paced out a hundred yards, set the bags down and lifted out his Colt automatic pistol. He unwrapped the protective oilcloth and examined the gun, working the action to ensure it was absolutely smooth. He selected one of the two magazines he had brought along, checked it was charged with the 200-grains ammunition and slid it home into the weapon's grip.

Then he placed the gun down at his feet and stripped off his tunic, tie, khaki shirt and undergarments, until he was naked from the waist up and could enjoy the aggressive feel of the early afternoon sun on his pale skin. He aimed the pistol with a two-handed grip, the palm of his left hand underneath and supporting the right, positioning the foresight level with the first of the small orange globes and bringing up the V of the rear sight.

There was no wind, and hardly any noise, just the scratching of a few grasshoppers in the hills. He pulled the trigger, felt the gun kick in his hand and saw the first orange snatched from its perch. The report rolled around him and there was the faintest of echoes, a fast receding whisper.

He paced out fifty more yards. Once again he fired and the second orange disintegrated into pulp as it was swept cleanly from the rock. He walked on, until he could barely make out the surviving fruit. It took him two rounds to unseat that one.

He held the warm gun in the palm of his hand and weighed it appreciatively and thought of Frank's letter about the weapon. Lawrence had used a Colt Peacemaker in Syria, but when a friend had purchased the later 1911 model and posted it to him, his brother had enthused:

The Colt is a lovely gun. The more I examine it the more I like it. There is a vast gulf between it and the ordinary revolver. If you want anything in connection with it which you don't want to write for, I could get it for you. They keep two weights of bullets, I think 200 and 230 grains. The lighter weight has considerably higher velocity and penetrating power, though I suppose less shock.

Frank loved his pistols, as did Lawrence. And now his brother was gone, killed in action on the Western Front, according to that telegram.

Lawrence walked back towards the rock. From the panniers, he took his water flask and drank, before splashing a handful on to his shoulders. Then he sat on the rock and let the ferocious heat of the afternoon attack his skin till he could feel the prickle of burning. It would hurt later, he knew, but he didn't care. He might not have the best physique in the world, but what he did have he had made strong and tough. With great care, he peeled the surviving orange and sucked the juice out of it.

Frank had always feared that Lawrence's love of the desert,

his quest for its solitude and silence, would kill him and had said so, his face etched with sadness at the thought of Ned gasping his last in some stony wasteland. Lawrence recalled flinging a quote from Marcus Aurelius at Frank when his brother had expressed concerns about his plans to travel across the Syrian wilderness looking at Crusader forts. 'It is not death man should fear, but he should fear beginning never to live.' Frank had agreed it was an admirable sentiment and had withdrawn any objection. But how much living could Frank have started at the age of twenty-two?

Not much. And how much living was Lawrence himself doing in Cairo? He was altering maps and writing his geographical essays and debriefing prisoners and filing his reports and he had his spies, both in the city and beyond, but did this amount to a life? Any right-minded jury would have to deliver the verdict: no. It was time wasted, potential squandered. Just as young Frank had been squandered.

Lawrence allowed himself to sink towards the grief he had denied himself at GHQ in front of the others. It was hard to imagine the lad he called his Little Worm was gone. He was consumed by a deep, ravening sadness at the thought and tears fell, staining the soil at his feet. He waited until the sobs had passed and blew his nose on his handkerchief. Poor Frank.

There was one glimmer of a blessing, a slender straw to grasp in all this. As far as he knew, Frank had died without discovering the truth about their parents, a truth that had haunted him since the age of ten. He half wished he had also remained ignorant of the facts.

Lawrence had known since he was young about the

hypocrisy at the heart of his parents' apparently conventional union, that they were not married, that they lived a lie. The disgraced master and his governess had uprooted themselves and their principles for something as vague as love, had condemned their offspring to a twilight place in society, denied them their birthright and their legitimate name. Is that why their mother sought solace in religion? And why she beat him when he fell below her intolerably high standards? To try and purge her own terrible sin, the falsehood they were living? In which case, it would have been better had they never borne children and sacrificed themselves completely on the altar of their selfish romance. But no, they produced five sons who would, often unwittingly, carry the burden through their lives.

Lawrence had had few friends at school – he could only think of one who deserved the term – which meant he relied on his brothers for socialising. They had their differences, of course. Arnold was still young, not yet a man, and Bob had inherited his mother's fervent brand of Christianity, which put him apart somewhat. There was no doubt he was closest intellectually and spiritually to Will, who was just a year younger than him, but with Frank he shared – had shared, he corrected himself – a love of machinery that vaulted the five-year age gap.

The pair had rejoiced in the thrill of toy yachts built from scrap wood, of watches taken apart and meticulously re-assembled and the mystery of why they never worked again; of improvised musical instruments and miniature hot-air balloons, sent soaring high over Christchurch meadow, or flimsy, delicate-winged gliders, launched on a stiff breeze, clawing a precious few minutes of flight before they went crashing into the Cherwell. Of cycles with engines, then motorcycles. Of guns.

He raised the Colt into the sky and emptied the magazine, a volley in memory of Frank Helier Lawrence, born 1893, died in the charnel house in France, 1915.

Wearily, he re-strapped the panniers to the Clyno and kick-started the engine and began the ride back to Cairo. He knew that his time working on maps must soon come to an end. Frank had participated in the war and the Germans had killed him before he had a chance to make a real difference. That gave Lawrence's craving for action a fresh, personal impetus. To strike a blow against the Kaiser and his allies the Turks would somehow help compensate for Frank's short-lived contribution to the conflict. Ned Lawrence would pick up his brother's fallen baton. It was time for him to make his mark on the war against the Ottoman Empire, Germany's sprawling ally. And he knew just where to begin.

Four

Persia

Captain Edward Noel survived the Tangistani bullet he took during the ambush and was discovered by British troopers before the desert sun broiled him. Recovering in the infirmary at Bushire, he had written a detailed report and sent it off to GHQ in Cairo, doubting that anyone would actually bother to read it, let alone wonder at the identity of this 'Woss Moss'.

He had put out feelers about the name and quickly unearthed the man's real identity. A German, it transpired, one of a group sent by Berlin to create trouble for the British in Persia and Afghanistan.

Spurred on by this discovery, Noel was quickly back at close to his best, the familiar handsome, blond Englishman who was not afraid to walk into any local village. Even with a stiff, bullet-scarred shoulder, Captain Edward Noel considered himself a match for any German agent provocateur in Persia.

So he had ridden out into the hinterland of Bushire in search of the man he now knew to be Wilhelm Wassmuss, primed by anger and armed with a small fortune in gold.

In massacring his scouting party, the German's followers had damaged Noel's reputation with both the British and the locals. So, wherever he went, he made sure the natives knew this was a personal matter, a question of honour, and that he was prepared to pay handsomely for information about his quarry.

Therefore, it was no surprise to him when a message arrived at his camp from the Khan of a small village, saying that they had an agent of the Kaiser called Wassmuss and two other Germans as 'guests', along with a great quantity of their baggage. Was he interested?

The messenger, tired and dirty from the lengthy ride, asked if he should return and demand Wassmuss be clapped in irons, as was the Persian way with brigands. However, despite the ambush that he had inspired, the Englishman thought of Wassmuss not as some petty criminal, but as an enemy combatant, who should be treated like a captured fellow officer.

'No,' said Noel after some deliberation. 'There is no need to be barbaric. Just ask the Khan to keep the utmost vigilance. But he can extend the usual hospitality to an enemy.'

Noel sent word to Bushire for sepoys and pack animals. He had plenty of faith in his abilities, but he was far from stupid. Trying to escort three Germans and their bags across hostile territory was impossible for one man. Even if he could keep a constant watch on his prisoners, there was every chance that the Germans' Tangistani allies would attempt to mount a rescue.

Bushire, for once, responded swiftly and Noel and his re-inforcements of a dozen men struck off over the rough scrub early the next morning, following the trail the messenger had taken. They warily skirted those settlements Noel had not succeeded in wooing, and were careful to avoid the parties of traders and travellers they sometimes spotted. Noel did not want a skirmish if he could avoid it.

They camped overnight on a low plateau, an elevated slab of igneous rock, bristling with good defensive positions. Fires were not lit and there were only cold rations. Noel even forwent his customary pipe. They slept badly under chill-night stars and set out, stiff-boned and weary, first thing the next morning. Noel used the throbbing in his damaged shoulder to remind him why he was out here. The two 'Rs': revenge and retribution.

They made good time under a lightening sky and were within the Khan's territories before the sun had produced much more than shadows as long and narrow as lances. Twenty minutes from the village, Noel spotted the snapping banners of the warlord's riders. It was a welcoming committee. Noel stopped and had his men draw up into another defensive position, but the Persians approached under a flag of truce. Behind it came the headman himself, flanked by copper-faced bodyguards.

The Khan was a young man with a straggly beard, ridiculously slender next to his burly, weathered retinue. Noel had been surprised by his youth on their previous meeting, but knew he had a reputation as a fine fighter, like his father before him, although he had not been blessed with his forebear's brains. With this one, it was always going to be about money.

'Salaam, Captain Noel.'

'Salaam, Rais Ali. It is good to see you again.'

'And you. You will join me for something to eat and drink shortly?'

'That would be most welcome, Rais Ali. But should we conclude our business first?'

Ali bowed slightly. 'As you wish.' He grinned. 'You English are always so impatient.'

Noel laughed at this. 'We like to do business, then relax. With you, it is the other way round.'

'Very well.'

'You have something to sell, I hear.'

'At the right price. I am thinking of five thousand sovereigns per man.'

Noel's face remained impassive. 'Major-General Sir Percy Cox knows what they are worth.'

The Khan inclined his head once more, accepting the truth in this. 'Of course he does. As do I.'

'I can offer you a thousand each.' He made sure his voice was rich with regret, as if he were letting down a friend, but his hands were tied.

The Khan looked horrified and, with a subtle movement of his legs, contrived to make his horse buck and kick, as if it, too, was outraged at the insulting offer. He brought it to heel with a snap of his reins. 'That will hardly pay for me to feed the guards.'

'You could feed your guards, your wives, your mistresses, your many sons and your animals for that.'

Rais Ali's head moved from side to side. 'For a few months, perhaps. Three thousand a man.'

'Two, Rais Ali. Six thousand in total.'

There was a heartbeat of a pause and Noel knew he had him. But there was still a low punch to come. 'Very well. And for the bags?'

'The bags?'

'The Germans' luggage. We have only talked about the men. Not their belongings.' The Khan clicked his fingers and one of his warriors passed a piece of paper across to Noel.

By now, the sun was up, and the heat was beginning to prickle the Englishman beneath his uniform. What he read on the documents, however, made his sweat run cold. 'Are there many of these?'

'A whole case full. And a wireless.'

'A what?'

'A wireless to Berlin.'

This, Noel knew, was impossible. No wireless existed out there that could raise Berlin, not since they confiscated the one at the German consulate in Bushire. It must be bluff on Wassmuss's part, to pretend he had a direct mandate from the Kaiser. Reluctantly, Noel said: 'Two thousand for the bags.' He pre-empted the Khan by adding: 'My final offer.'

The boyish face looked even younger when it was allowed to break into an enormous grin of victory. 'Then let us drink and eat, Captain Noel.'

The two parties formed into one and rode towards the walled village, its mud walls glowing a fiery orange in the new sun. They were half a mile away when they heard a great wail rise up from within the fortress. There came the sound of gunshots, a stutter of sharp little cracks. The enormous wooden gate swung back on its hinges and a rider emerged, whipping his horse on, yelling as he came, the machine-gun flow of words indecipherable even to the Englishman's well-tuned ears.

'What's he saying?' Noel asked, a feeling of foreboding descending on him.

The Khan turned pale and dragged at his beard. 'He is saying he's gone.' The man let out a curse. 'I should have put him in chains.'

'Who has gone?'

Rais Ali glared at Noel as if this debacle was his fault. His idea of British fair play had meant that Wassmuss had remained unshackled. And in his mind, the Khan had already spent the eight thousand sovereigns. He had built himself his new tower and taken another wife. 'Wassmuss,' he spat. 'Wilhelm Wassmuss has escaped.'

Five

Cairo

Upon his return from the fringe of the Western Desert, Lawrence presented his papers to the sentry at the gate of Cairo's mighty Citadel, which the British used as barracks, quartermasters' stores, mortuary and gaol. Waved through, he parked the Clyno next to the prison section of the great warren and extracted his map case from the panniers. Then he headed up the worn stone steps to interview his captive.

As always, Lawrence had to pass through a sequence of locked doors, each one guarded by a British soldier, until he reached the cool inner sanctum known as the 'conversation' rooms. There were windows here, but they were dim slits high in the walls, which were so thick the sun could not heat the interior above comfortably cool. That was the best thing about the former dungeons; against that, the air was inevitably fouled by the stink of old sweat, fresh rat droppings and the ever-present whiff of fumigating powder.

Interrogation Room Six contained a long wooden table, chipped and scratched by the fingernails of hundreds of anxious prisoners, and four metal chairs. A pitcher of water was on the table, covered with a muslin cloth weighted with beads. A few tired flies circled the bare bulb.

Lawrence sat and waited until the guard brought in his prisoner. The moon-faced, clean-shaven Tariq was immaculately dressed in full Turkish uniform, right up to his cloth-covered *kabalk*, which resembled a solar topee. The fact that his outfit had been tailored in Germany indicated he was an officer of some standing in the Ottoman army, which also explained why he was beardless, facial hair being discouraged among the higher ranks. Lawrence stood up and returned the smart salute and they both sat. Lawrence could feel the man's eyes roving over his own tarnished buttons and badly polished boots, as if to ask: which one of us looks like the prisoner here?

Mustafa Tariq was born on the blurred border between Mesopotamia and Persia. He was one of many thousands of Arabs serving the Ottoman Empire and had been captured leading a platoon of Bicycle Infantry during the disastrous attempt by Djemal Pasha, the second most powerful military man in Turkey, to take the Suez Canal and ignite a Holy War against the British within Egypt.

What the Turkish invasion had really lacked, Lawrence knew, was the element of surprise. Trying to sneak up on the British with twenty-five thousand men, fourteen thousand camels, three thousand bicycles and, for morale purposes, a troop of whirling dervishes, hardly counted as a sound battle plan. They had been crushed and the Egyptians wisely decided that their own uprising could wait.

'Lieutenant,' the Arab began, his voice resonating with a sturdy power and confidence. 'I must complain, there are more fleas in my bed than there are grains of sand in Arabia. One day, I fear they will carry me out of here on their backs.'

Lawrence said softly: 'You can always be transferred back to Maadi.' This was a barbed-wire enclosure out in the scrub, where Turkish prisoners slept in vast bell tents, thirty or forty crammed together. 'I can arrange it for later today, if you so wish.'

Tariq recognised something in the tone. The man was not in the mood for the usual sparring they indulged in. The Arab dimmed the combativeness in his speech, as if turning down the wick on a gas mantle. 'What is wrong? You are sad today, Lawrence.'

'Some bad news,' he admitted. 'My brother.'

'Killed?'

'Yes. France.'

'I am sorry. I, too, have a brother. In Erzerum.'

Lawrence filed that away for future use. It was a Turkish stronghold that guarded the approaches to Constantinople itself. 'You are worried for him?'

'No. Erzerum is impregnable. But perhaps he is concerned for me. Sometimes it is worrying to be worried about.'

Lawrence smiled at this. He remembered how Frank would fret about him and how unsettling that was. 'You are a long way from the war now, Tariq. He has no need to be concerned.'

'And a long way from my family.'

There was a wife and a daughter at home, although Tariq rarely referred to them. 'And your back-pay. I heard it finally got through to most units.' Recent Turkish prisoners from Gallipoli had been taken with cash in their pockets, a sure sign the salary-wagons had arrived. Tariq's eyes looked comically sad. The Ottoman Empire was notoriously poor at paying its soldiers. 'I was owed thirty out of forty-eight months.'

Lawrence made a sympathetic noise. 'There's not much to spend it on here even if you'd got it. But you have been given an increased prisoner's allowance. Seven pounds a month.'

His eye narrowed, suspicious of a bribe. 'Just me, or the other officers?'

'Across the board, of course. We might arrange a trip to Davies Bryan.' This was Cairo's huge and, despite the war, still well-stocked department store. 'Or Au Petit Bazar. Under escort, I am afraid.'

'Of course.'

'Now I really do have some bad news.'

Tariq stiffened a little. 'Tell me.'

Lawrence extracted the Syrian newspaper *Al-Ra'i-Al-Am* – *Public Opinion* – from his map case and handed it over. 'I'll be a few minutes.'

As the door was closed behind him, Lawrence heard the first cry of anguish and anger from Tariq.

* * *

The Englishman returned fifteen minutes later, holding a tin mug with an inch of treacle-thick coffee in the bottom, which he handed to the Arab. The man flicked the newspaper. 'This is genuine?'

'I can take you out to buy an identical one if you wish. It is no forgery.'

Jamal Pasha, the man who had been defeated at the Suez Canal, Tariq's own former commanding officer, had blamed his 'spineless' Arab soldiers for the debacle. Now, he had ordered the hanging of Arab Nationalists in Damascus and had decimated the ranks of al-'Ahd, the Arab secret society. Lawrence suspected that many of those executed were originally from Mesopotamia or had served with Tariq. His prisoner's expression told him he had been correct: Jamal Pasha had executed some of Tariq's closest friends.

'This will carry on, you know. The Arabs will be persecuted into being second-class citizens, unless the Turks are thrown out of all Arab lands.'

Tariq wagged an accusatory finger at Lawrence. 'To be replaced by the British.'

'Tariq, the English have no designs on the Arab territories.'

'No? What about the oil?' His home village was not far from the crude-producing provinces of Mesopotamia.

'The days of simply taking what we want have gone. The British will trade, Tariq. You will sell the oil to us. You will get rich.'

'You think because a few of my friends are hanged by mistake, I will turn traitor?'

'Against the Ottomans? Is that being a traitor? You think

71

you are safe because you share a faith with the Turk? Perhaps.' Lawrence shook his head sadly. 'It is possible you will be spared.'

Despite recognising the artifice in the gesture, Tariq's curiosity got the better of him. 'Spared what?'

'We are getting reports from Anatolia about the Armenians. The Chaldean Christians. The Greek Christians. Millions dispossessed, thousands slaughtered. Hundreds of thousands in the case of the Armenians. The Turks are clearing out the troublesome minorities. The Arabs will be on that list somewhere.'

'So you say, Lawrence. So you say. Let me make inquiries of my own.'

Lawrence took a deep breath. The worst was over. Tariq would find out enough to convince him that the Turks were no longer to be trusted. 'Of course. You will have access to recent prisoners at Maadi, they will tell you the truth of it. You can move to a house there, under lighter guard, if you wish. A certain Dr Bitter, a German physician, has had his villa commandeered. It is not far from the Maadi POW camp. No bars, just your recognisance and a guard or two. And it is very comfortable.'

'You will not persuade me with comfort, Lawrence.'

He gave a little bow to acknowledge this. 'I will leave you to consider. One thing. You say you have no love for the Germans.'

'I do not.'

'But they are all over your country like the fleas across your mattress.'

72

Tariq involuntarily scratched under his arm.

'Of course, there are no fleas at Dr Bitter's—'

'Stop it! You are a djinn, tempting me. Leave me alone.'
But there was humour in the plea.

'The Germans.' Lawrence unrolled his map on the table.
It was the Middle East, from Egypt up to northern Syria, split
into its constituent kingdoms. 'Might just ruin everything.'

'It is a national trait.'

Now Lawrence whispered, as indeed a djinn might, speaking
softly in Tariq's ear as he waved his hand over the map like
a cheap conjurer. 'Our game is to take all of this from the
Ottoman Empire, right under the noses of the French and
the Russians. You know the Russians will try and create a new
Caliph, their Caliph, when the war is over. But imagine the
alternative, Tariq. Imagine if we roll all the way up to Syria
by way of the Hejaz in the name of the Sherif. Not the King,
not the British Empire. But the Sherif and his people. We
take back all Arabia for the Arabs, for Mecca. It could be a
beautiful alliance, bringing together Sunni and Shia Arabs in
unison. I know it's a big game, but it might just be the last
one worth playing before all war becomes a conflict of attri-
tion and bombing. It's a risk. But won't the French be mad
if we win through?'

'Furious. The French want Syria more than anything.'

'They'll have to go and whistle. We'll biff them out of all
hope there. Once we are in Damascus, they will be power-
less. It will belong to the Arabs.'

'And the tribes will support the British?'

'They would if the prize was right.'

'You realise you would have to bring together rivals who have hated each other so long that the origins of the feud are forgotten, even if the roll call of the dead isn't. You must get Hairith to ride with Howeitat.'

'I could do that.'

Tariq smiled at the man's confidence. He wasn't entirely sure he appreciated the scale of that undertaking. 'And Ibn Saud?'

Lawrence nodded at the man's perception. There were those who thought the British should support the more dynamic Saud as the King of Arabia, the new Caliph, not the aged Hussein in Mecca. 'We will back the Sherif. After all, is he not a descendant of the prophet? And he has four strong sons, two of whom, Abdullah and Feisal, have some fire in their belly.'

Tariq shook his head, as if trying to clear a tempting mirage. 'I almost believed this madman's fantasy for a moment. You talk a great war.'

'You should believe. And it is not just words. But we have a few problems in your homelands to deal with first. The Germans are here and here and here, aren't they?' Lawrence stabbed his finger across Tariq's birthplace and into Persia. 'Trying something similar?'

Tariq gave an exaggerated shrug of helplessness. 'I have not been home for months.'

'This has been happening for a year now, perhaps more. The Germans sunk their hooks into the tribes well before war was declared.' Now Lawrence played the shabby trump card he had extracted from another prisoner, one willing to trade snippets for cigarettes. 'And I do believe, Tariq, that you have so far neglected to mention you were more than just a bicycle-soldier. You were an Intelligence officer in the Pasha's army. You would have seen many, many signals in your time.'

Tariq didn't speak for a few minutes, and then nodded to acknowledge that Lawrence was correct.

'I had a report from a Captain Noel in Bushire of an ambush that took place in the name of someone called Woss Moss. Does that name mean anything to you?'

Tariq nodded and held out his hand. 'He is not alone, a group were sent out from Berlin to, as you say, foment trouble with the tribes.' Lawrence hesitated before he realised what the man wanted, and he passed the charcoal pencil in his top pocket across to the prisoner. Tariq wrote across his home-town the word Seiler. 'This one is a fool.' In the very centre of Persia, he scrawled 'Niedermayer', then drew an arrow, pointing east. 'Capable, but too ambitious. He is attempting to cover all of Afghanistan.'

Then, finally, from Basra through Bushire, down to Banda Abbas, Tariq wrote the last name, in bold capitals. 'This one, however, is different.'

Lawrence spun the chart to see what he had written. '*Wassmuss*?'

'Wilhelm Wassmuss. This one is clever. Mark my words, Lawrence, this one will be trouble unless watched very closely.'

Six

Persia

The first that Major Frederick O'Connor, the British Consulate at Shiraz, knew about the troubles that were about to rain down on his head was the distinctive boom of a field gun. It was barely light but he was already up, dealing with the Consulate's business at the coolest time of the day, when the building rattled under the shockwave of the discharge. 'Bloody fools,' he muttered.

The British had recently bought the Gendarmerie – the Swedish-officered peacekeeping force – a number of heavy artillery pieces to help subdue the tribes that plagued the 120-mile road to Bushire on the coast. Obviously, they were playing with them now, announcing the new day with a ceremonial discharge. He looked at the walnut grandfather clock. Five minutes to six. Idiots couldn't even do it on the hour.

At that point the window of the study shattered with a

terrifying crack, spraying him with glass shards, and he slid to the floor. He groped into his desk drawer and found his revolver. Already he could hear thumping footsteps above his head and shrieks. 'Boy!' he shouted.

Yusuf appeared at the door, his face etched with fright.

'What was that?'

'A bomb, sir.'

He meant a shell. 'In the courtyard?' Yusuf nodded. 'Any news about the telegraph?'

'Still broken, sir.'

'Damn.' The lines had been pulled down yet again a week ago. There went his hope for reinforcements. 'Get everyone downstairs, and keep them away from the windows.'

O'Connor waited until the servant had gone, then crossed to the door and bolted it. He opened the safe and carefully extracted the half-dozen gold bars from within and placed them on the floor. He walked across to the fireplace with the first ingot and swivelled out the six ornamental studs that were part of the thick over-mantle. Each came free, to reveal a cavity behind. O'Connor pushed the first bar into one of the empty spaces, and then slotted the stud back into place. He repeated the action five more times. The tight bundles of cash in the safe he stashed into specially formed hollow pockets in the fireplace's uprights, then closed the safe and re-locked it.

There was a hammering on the door and O'Connor coolly checked for any telltale signs of his subterfuge on the mantle before opening it. It was Simmons, his assistant, wild-eyed and badly dressed. O'Connor reached out to fasten the man's top button, but Simmons dashed his arm away. Simmons had a wife, O'Connor recalled, which always made these situations more fraught. That was why he always left his own wife behind in Dunwich. The man was only in his twenties, two decades younger than O'Connor, so he had to take that into account as well. 'There is a gendarme in the yard,' Simmons blurted.

'Swede?'

'Persian.'

'Bloody impudence.'

O'Connor fetched his pistol and went out to meet the man. He stepped over a sprinkling of rubble from the stray howitzer round. A sizable crater had scarred the yard and a rather handsome magnolia tree now lay at a desolate angle.

The chap sent to negotiate was not an officer as protocol suggested, but one of the locals, another poorly dressed man with badly wound puttees. He held a white flag in one hand, in the other a letter, which was trembling slightly.

'And what is the meaning of this outrage?' O'Connor barked. 'I demand to see the Qawam ul Mulk.' Not that the obese mayor of Shiraz could do much about anything. He was in the pocket of every ha'penny warlord for fifty miles around.

'Sir. The Qawam is hunting.'

'Oh, how damned convenient.'

'Please read the letter, sir.'

O'Connor examined the flat rooftops that overlooked the outer courtyard. Between the branches of the oaks, chenars and ash that shaded the area, he could see men moving about, and recognised the snout of one of the new machine guns. The Consulate was surrounded and out-gunned.

'How long are you giving us?' he asked.

'It's in the—'

O'Connor stepped forward, putting his face so close he could smell the sour-smoky aroma of the yoghurt the man had slurped for breakfast. The alarmed Persian shuffled back.

'How long?'

'Thirty minutes.'

O'Connor raised his pistol and the man waved the flag feebly, as if the major hadn't spotted he was under truce. 'Get out before I blow both of your eyes out of your head.'

O'Connor spun on his heel and ripped open the letter as he strode back to the house. It was in French. 'The Persian Patriots have decided that we should arrest you and the rest of the English colony.' O'Connor snorted. The 'colony' was one more than a baker's dozen: eight men, four women and two daughters. 'If you do not turn yourself over to our custody, we will have no option but to storm the Consulate. You have half an hour to consider your decision.'

He screwed the paper up into ball and tossed it back over his shoulder.

'Well?' asked Simmons, falling in beside him.

'Thirty minutes to surrender.'

'What shall we do?'

O'Connor stopped and looked the frightened young man in the eye. He stroked his moustache for a moment before he said. 'We have no way of getting a message out. They have field guns and machine guns. We have three revolvers and a rifle between us and a dozen Indian troopers next door, who, I suspect even now, are either dead or under lock and key. Plus we have the worry of the women. I'm all for a good scrap, Simmons, but not at those odds. We have thirty minutes to burn all the signals and code books.'

In the event, they had less than twenty before Svenson, the Swedish officer commanding the Shiraz garrison of the Gendarmerie, turned up with a dozen armed men and horses and donkeys for the journey. Once more, O'Connor strode out to meet him, the anger crackling off him like static electricity.

Svenson had the good grace to look embarrassed when he announced: 'No harm will come to you. You are to be removed to Bushire province. I must have your pistols.'

O'Connor handed his over and said: 'The other weapons are in the armoury next to the kitchen. And need I remind you that no harm will come to us if you just ride on.'

Svenson shrugged. 'Ride on? I cannot do that.'

'Whom do you represent?'

'The General Staff Of the Committee Of the Fighters For Persian Neutrality.'

O'Connor guffawed theatrically. 'Can you fight for neutrality? That's a rich one. Must tell the Swiss. Of course, Alighieri said that the hottest places in hell are reserved for those who, in time of great moral crises, retain their neutrality.'

The Swede gave a thin smile. 'Be that as it may, you must come with me.'

O'Connor wagged a finger in the man's face. 'You have been bought, Captain. Bought like a goat at market.'

Svenson ignored the jibe and said levelly: 'If you will bring as few items as possible, we must make good progress.'

'What about my troopers?'

'They are in the citadel, disarmed. They will be released when you are away from here.'

'And His Majesty's other subjects?'

'Already being gathered at the Bagh. I make it fourteen. Yourself, Mr and Mrs Simmons; Mr Ferguson and Mr Ayrton; Mr Smith the telegraph clerk and Mr Bossington, his assistant; Mrs Smith; Mr and Mrs Christmas; and Mr and Mrs Croft and their two daughters. Am I correct?'

'Yes.'

'Now, someone will accompany you while you gather your things.' He checked the pocket watch in his tunic. 'You have ten minutes. Then we search the building.'

'There is no gold, you know.'

'We aren't looking for gold.'

Then what? O'Connor wondered. But he wanted to get off the subject. 'Surely you can spare the daughters. The eldest Croft girl is just sixteen. She will be like an itch they need to scratch to your men. It will drive them insane with lust.'

'Please, Major, you are being melodramatic.'

'Am I? You must let them go, at the very least.'

The Swede shook his head with considerable finality. 'I am afraid I can't do that. I have my orders.'

'And those are?'

'To deliver all of you to Wilhelm Wassmuss.' He glanced at his fob watch. 'Eight minutes, Major.'

Seven

Egypt

Although Cairo was rightly described as a sprawling mess of a city, the British functioned, socially at least, within a tiny proscribed area. On any given night a circle one mile in diameter described from the Midan Ishmael Pasha would capture 90 per cent of the English officers, their wives and important civilians. They moved from tea at Groppi's (favouring the one on Sharia Adly Pasha, which had the garden, although it was more of a sunken stony courtyard) or Maison Gianola, to the vast complex of the Sporting Club on Gezira or the men-only Turf Club on Sharia al-Maghrabi, to the great rivals of Shepheard's and the Continental hotels or the Trocadero and the Poulet d'Or restaurants. There was shooting, racing, swimming and sports every day and a dance or cocktail party every night, so that, if you were a member of the elite, you were never short of entertainment. Or, Lawrence thought, the companionship of frightful bores. To him, regimental dinners, receptions and tea parties were all torture. Better a forced march through ten miles of desert with a haversack full of stones, than an hour at one of Cairo's 'top set' parties.

The Criterion was slightly different. At least the crowd there was cosmopolitan. Situated in the cool, breezy residential district of Zamalek, the northern portion of Gezira Island, it had been opened shortly after Kitchener, the prewar governor, had declared the Sporting Club closed to all non-British. His intentions, he had insisted, were not racially motivated; just that he felt it wrong that the most vocal anti-British Egyptian officers should use the bar of the Sporting Club as their meeting place. He did not like the idea of revolution being fuelled by his own stocks of bitter lemon and tonic water.

In riposte to what was seen as his pettiness, the Criterion had open membership. It couldn't match the splendour of the Sporting, with its hundred and fifty acres and four polo grounds and two racecourses, having room for just two tennis courts and a pool, but the covered verandah, with its wicker chairs and silent fans, was as capacious as Shepheard's and there was a splendid view over the embassy lawns that sloped down the eastern branch of the Nile. You could idle hours away watching the dhows, ibis, kites and bustards go about their business.

Although Lawrence was no regular at the Criterion, an invitation had arrived on his desk that he had decided to accept. The party was to celebrate the club's second birthday and, as usual, there would be a healthy mix of Greeks, Armenians,

Copts, Jews, Egyptians and, of course, British. At first the latter had boycotted it, but it soon became clear that the Criterion had one ace in its multiracial pack. It attracted, at least in the early part of every evening, the most beautiful unveiled girls in Cairo.

Lawrence left his Clyno under the watchful eye of the door staff, adjusted his uniform, and walked through the bar to the terrace. There was a considerable crush and he helped himself to a lemonade and skirted the babbling crowd, their laughter already fuelled by the free drink on offer. Boutros Salem, the senior partner in the Criterion, was noted as a generous host.

'Lawrence, Lawrence, come here.'

He was pulled into a small group which was pressed against the stone balustrade that separated the terrace from the gardens. The man who hailed him was Clarence Jepson, a major who considered it his unofficial role to act as the social welfare officer for the men in the Intelligence community.

'So glad you came. Considering everything,' he said. Jepson stood a good six inches taller than Lawrence and his uniform, though tailored, seemed to hang off his skeletal frame. He was one of those men who, at least in his twenties and thirties, found it impossible to put on pounds, no matter how much he ate. 'Desperately sorry to hear . . .' he began.

Lawrence saved him any more mumbling. 'Thank you. I appreciate it. It's not as if I am alone. There are too many of us already.'

Jepson's brow furrowed at the thought of all those he knew who had lost a school friend or relative on the Western Front. 'Quite so. Ghastly.' He cleared his throat. 'Let me introduce you to some other people. This is Mrs Emily Marchand. You know her husband, Tom? Foolish man let her out alone. Lieutenant T.E. Lawrence, the most brilliant map-maker in Cairo.' Lawrence smiled. Jepson only ever spoke in superlatives, everyone being the best, most wonderful, the extraordinary, and so forth.

Emily Marchand was wearing a simple white shift dress and white pleated sandals. The only jewellery she wore was a double string of pearls and a thick wedding band, the only make-up a trace of powder. She held out her hand and said in the softest American accent: 'How do you do, Lieutenant. My husband hasn't let me out.' She shot a glance at Jepson to let him know she disapproved of being considered at large under licence. 'He's in Alexandria. I don't care for it, so I stayed behind. We're with the Legation. So, Lieutenant, what shall we call you? Thomas Eric is that? Or Thomas Edison, perhaps?'

'Thomas Edward. But most people call me Lawrence. Or T.E. Or Lieutenant.'

She laughed. 'You English. Does your mother call you that, too?'

'No, she calls me Ned,' he confessed.

'Ned. I like that. Ned Lawrence.' She purred rather than said it.

Over her shoulder, Lawrence spotted the figure of Abdel Sawat moving through the crowd. He was sipping lime juice and was dressed in a pristine cream linen suit and polished brogues. As he caught Lawrence's eye he raised his glass. He had a smooth baby-fat face and the skin was so soft, Lawrence reckoned he could give most Western women tips in keeping themselves youthful in the harsh climate. He was nearly forty, but looked ten years younger. Soon, he would run to fat like his father and the attractive face would balloon and the chins multiply, but for the moment he looked the epitome of the suave, Anglophile Egyptian haute bourgeoisie.

'You know that chap?' asked Jepson in a disapproving tone.

'Abdel? I know who he is.'

'He's a bloody monster, that's who he is. David Buck borrowed some money from him when he was in some difficulties.' At the tables, no doubt, thought Lawrence, but said nothing. It was only when Westerners had run up embarrassing debts at the Sporting Club or the casino in Alex that they went to the Arab banks. Word was unlikely to get back to one's colleagues from the bazaar.

'Well, Buck couldn't pay back the scrip in time, and do you know what that bastard Abdel did? Lured him to his bank to discuss it over mint tea, then had him held down and had him buggered by six of his bloody Nubians. Don't get that at the Midland, eh?' There was a pause, when Jepson broke into grin. 'Buck said that it would have been a hell of a punishment if he hadn't gone to the school he did. It was just like a Friday night in the common room to him.'

Jepson roared with laughter and Lawrence saw Mrs Marchand's eyes sparkle, although her mouth feigned disapproval. It was a story more suitable for the men-only Long Bar at Shepheard's. It had the air of being well rehearsed at such places. It dawned on him that Jepson must have had a fair bit to drink already to risk the telling in mixed company.

'Excuse me,' Lawrence said and inclined his head. 'Mrs Marchand.'

'Go on, desert me,' she said tartly. 'Leave me to these eunuchs.' Jepson bristled at the slight. 'Come to tea sometime, Ned?'

Mrs Marchand was flirting, perhaps seriously, but more likely playfully. All the women did it, in a fashion that would shock at home and Americans, of course, were even more forward than the English in such matters. Lawrence was used to it. As the wags had it, the climate might rot the feet, but it also loosened the stays.

'Sometime,' he said evasively and made his goodbyes. He pushed his way through the clusters of people, well aware that most of the British at least were getting what they called 'squiffy'. It would be time to leave soon. Already the laughter was harsher and laced with vulgarity.

'*Assalaamu aleikum,*' he said to Abdel. Peace be upon you.

'And may Allah's blessings be on you, Lieutenant Lawrence,' he replied in English.

'I've just been hearing about your trick with the Nubians.'

Abdel smiled and raised one eyebrow. 'Me? I heard that was that old rogue Abbas. Or was it Wissas, the Copt banker? I can't keep up.' He sipped his lime juice. 'Do you believe all those stories?'

'Those stories and the telling of them stop the English going mad.'

Abdel made an exaggerated examination of the crowd. 'Oh, I don't think they do. There is very little that can stop that. But the stories, they are always at our expense,' he said. 'They all say the same: we lie, we cheat, we bugger. It will have to stop, one day.'

Lawrence nodded. Abdel was not a firebrand revolutionary, but he knew the Egyptian supported eventually seeing the back of both the British and the Turks. 'How's business?'

'I manage, you know.' There was a twinkle in his eye. 'And yours?'

'Oh, I manage, too. I managed to hear that there are Martini rifles heading for the city. Perhaps to arm the Egyptian Brotherhood.' He whispered the name. The revolutionary group was the new Bogey Man in town and he didn't want to scare the nervous horses around them. 'Have you heard anything about that?'

'Martinis? No. And how many of this so-called Brother-hood are actually Egyptians? Syrians, Armenians, Turks perhaps. Very few Egyptians. Others are using our good name to get rich or make mischief. Sometimes both. Are you familiar with the chap over there?'

Abdel pointed to a man with matinée idol looks, a sharp moustache, and oiled hair which had an almost mirror-finish. He was holding court with a group of Australian nurses. 'I know of him. Count Jacques Spaark, Sparkie to his friends, late of Brussels and, I do believe, the prison in Paris at Fresnes.'

Abdel filed this last snippet away. 'He wants me to under-write a shipment.'

'Of?'

'Croquet sets.'

Lawrence laughed. 'They are always croquet sets. It's the shape of the boxes. Easy to hide the rifles in without arousing too much suspicion. But I didn't think Sparkie was a gunrunner. Who is the end purchaser?'

Abdel looked pained. 'That he won't tell me.'

'Origin?'

'Or that.'

'Athens?' European weapons destined for the Levant and beyond usually passed through Piraeus.

'It is likely. But I do not deal in weapons, Lieutenant – Martinis, Mausers or otherwise. The trouble with guns, is they can be turned on the buyer or the seller. Or the middle-man.'

'Tell him no, then.'

Abdel nodded. 'I have already decided to. I just thought you should know.'

There would be a bill for this small service, Lawrence knew, but he simply said: '*Hallet el-baraka.*' Let blessings come down. The gold sovereigns would follow later.

'*Mabrouk aleik.*' May the blessings be yours.

'Lieutenant Lawrence, may I interrupt?'

'Of course.' A tiny spinster with a ferocious energy that belied her stature, Miss Devonshire was the sort of woman you could never stop interrupting whenever she desired to do so. Abdel excused himself and faded into the crowd.

'Just that the day after tomorrow I have permission to take a little group along to the Mausoleum of Qait Bay. I wondered if you would be interested in joining us?'

The Qait Bay was one of the most famous buildings in Cairo, but had been out of bounds since Lawrence had arrived in the city. Lawrence knew this was because British and Empire soldiers had been found measuring their boots against the twin impressions in the floor that were considered to be foot-prints of the Prophet. Miss Devonshire, though, was respected by the Egyptians as a genuinely enthusiastic Islamist and ran tours to various monuments, free of charge, two or three times a week. 'I'd be very interested. If I can get away. Which I can't promise. I'll do my best.'

'Excellent. And, I wonder, could I inveigle upon you to address next week's meeting of the Ladies' Archaeological Club?'

He smiled at her guile. 'I'm no great speaker, Miss Devonshire.'

'Just something on your work in Syria. Just as you told me. The dig, the walk, the robbery.'

Lawrence tried hard to recall which version of the incident with the footpads he had told her. He tended to change the details according to his audience. 'I'm not sure they'd be interested. I was roughed up a little, that was all.'

'Nonesense. It's very dramatic. And you were close to death, but for the farmer and his family.' Ah, that version. 'You can tell a story, Lieutenant, not like some of these boors. Please.'

'I'll give it serious consideration.'

'Thank you. And bring some slides, if you will. It will be great fun.' Clearly, she thought 'consideration' meant 'yes'.

After a handful of other conversations, Lawrence decided to slip away while he still had a free date in his diary. Excusing himself, he retrieved the Clyno and headed back across the Nile to GHQ, where he found Storrs at his desk. Debussy was playing softly on the gramophone while Storrs worked his way through his correspondence. The Browning pistol he had brought from London when war was declared was acting as a paperweight.

'Not going to the Criterion, sir?' asked Lawrence.

The man's moustache twitched in amusement. They both knew that Storrs shared Lawrence's dislike of social gatherings. There were those who described Ronald Storrs, number 2 in Intelligence in Cairo, as a difficult man to get to know, unless you took him on at tennis at the Sporting Club. Some claimed he was unscrupulous and untrustworthy. Lawrence found him straightforward and easy to understand: he loved the art of Islam, the music of the West, Coptic churches and artefacts, Italian paintings and the wines of France. He despised cant, deception and what he considered shallow intellects. He also craved routine: early start, lunch at the Turf, golf or tennis, more work, Turf, dinner, and opera. One reason he hated the war was that it occasionally upset the daily rhythm.

'You've been, have you?'

He nodded and Storrs looked suitably surprised that Lawrence should have attended a party.

'To see Abdel. He tells me Sparkie is going into the gun-running business.'

Storrs put down his pen and leaned back in his chair. 'Is he, indeed? On whose behalf?'

'Abdel says he doesn't know yet.'

'Those bloody Zionists, I'll wager.'

'Possibly. But why bring them here? Why not have them delivered straight to Palestine?'

Storrs knew he was blinded by his dislike of the clamour for a Jewish home state. He and Lawrence disagreed on the subject, the latter certain that there was a solution to the problem, whereas the Oriental Secretary foresaw all kinds of trouble. 'For use here, then? The Egyptian Brotherhood?'

'That's also a possibility. There was that attempt on the Giza armoury last month. Perhaps having failed there . . .' He let Storrs complete the thought.

'Why do you think there are guns coming in?'

'Opportunism. If something happens in the Middle East, a blow against the British, then the idea is to have the weapons for a spontaneous uprising. To succeed where Djemal Pasha and his dervishes failed. The Turks and the Germans will encourage any disaffection, arm any insurgency that will require us to keep troops here.'

'You'll keep an eye on this?'

'Yes, of course.'

Storrs fiddled with the pen on his desk. 'How are your family? How did they take the news?'

Lawrence hesitated, always wary of talking about his parents, just in case the truth came tumbling out. *My name isn't Lawrence at all, I have no right to it*, or some similar confession that his life, his background, was all an elaborate charade, dreamed up by Robert Chapman and Sarah Junner to cover their deviant union. 'I haven't had a reply from them yet. But my mother is suspicious of excessive grieving. She will believe Frank's soul is safe and that is all that matters.'

As chief censor, Storrs knew from reading her letters that Lawrence's mother was what might be termed a religious zealot;

he was glad Lawrence had rebelled against it. Fire-and-brimstone merchants unsettled him. The thought of an intense man like the lieutenant infused with God's fervour was quite alarming. 'Is that healthy? Bottling it up, I mean. We grieve for a purpose, surely?'

'My mother believes we grieve for ourselves, that it is a form of selfishness. Anyway, Frank wouldn't have wanted too much wailing and gnashing of teeth. He had no regrets, I'm sure. Xenophon said: *Excess of grief for the dead is madness; for it is an injury to the living, and the dead know it not.*'

'Is there anything you haven't got a damned quote for?'

It wasn't a genuine rebuke and Lawrence smirked. 'I doubt it, sir.'

Storrs shook his head at his stoicism. He wondered if the man really believed the epithet. He knew that Lawrence was capable of terrifying anger and prolonged depression. The death of a brother could surely trigger either. Work, Storrs was sure, was the best prophylactic in such cases. 'You moved this chap Tariq from the Citadel?'

'I did. He is installed at Herr Bitters. I like him. I think we are becoming friends.'

Storrs raised an eyebrow. 'Friends?' It was said with incredulity, as if Lawrence had admitted to liking Martians or pygmies.

'Yes.'

'You be careful, Lawrence. A few weeks ago he was trying to kill us all.'

'He was a Turk then. He's an Arab now.'

'Leopards and spots, Lawrence. Leopards and spots.

Anyhow,' he picked up a telegram and waved it in the air, 'we have some news about this fellow your' – Storrs made a show of clearing his throat, as if something was stuck in it – 'friend told you about in Persia. Wassmuss.'

Lawrence felt his senses sharpen. Over the past few weeks he had compiled every mention of the man, which he had passed on to Storrs, arguing that he was not the usual German agent and deserved special attention. 'Yes?'

'He's taken hostages. British hostages.'

Storrs had his interest now, and Lawrence leaned forward on the desk, balancing on his knuckles. 'Who?'

'O'Connor, the consul at Shiraz.'

'Well, by Arab mores, that's diplomacy.' Both men knew that diplomats in the East had always been considered hostages, human markers against misbehaviour. For hundreds of years it was commonplace for them to be executed, beaten or expelled when their country's action displeased the court. Being taken hostage was a relatively minor punishment by historical standards.

'You could argue that O'Connor was fair game. Being a military man and what have you. But there are a dozen others, including women and young girls. I don't have to tell you, it's not an easy country for a fit man, let alone females.'

'No.' Southern Persia was rumoured to be even bleaker than the most remote, hostile portions of Syria. 'What does Wassmuss want in exchange?'

'The two Germans captured with him. Out of the question, naturally.'

'Why?'

94

'We hanged them.'

'Ah.'

'Wassmuss doesn't know that, of course. But there is something else.'

'What's that?'

'His bags. Two steamers and a valise. He's willing to make some kind of trade for them, too.'

Lawrence looked puzzled, as Storrs had anticipated. 'They've been checked?'

'Of course. Nothing suspicious, other than some printed propaganda.'

'Does he think we are a damned left-luggage office? Where are they now?'

'London.'

'So what is so special about the luggage that he should take hostages against its return?'

'Quite frankly, Lawrence, we have no idea just yet. Perhaps he is short of undershirts. But regardless of his bags, look at what you say he has been doing. It's only a spark now, but that spark could begin a conflagration, an anti-British, anti-Christian revolt that might infect the whole Middle East and India. Such an uprising could lose us the war. I don't always see eye to eye with Kitchener, but we are agreed on one thing.'

'You sent my reports to Kitchener?'

'He *is* the Secretary for War,' said Storrs sarcastically. 'As I say, we are agreed on one thing. We need to stop this Wassmuss. Dead.'

Lawrence smiled and shook his head.

'What?'

'I'm hardly an assassin, sir.'

It was Storr's turn to grin at the thought of Lawrence the Killer. '"Stopped dead" is simply a turn of phrase. But don't you worry if it actually comes to that. You just work up a strategy and put it in one of your reports. London will find someone else to do the dirty work.' Storrs glanced over at the ivory chess set sitting on his sideboard. 'Now. Fancy a game while we talk?'

Lawrence left the building with a much-needed lift in his spirits at the thought of London and Cairo instigating some action against this Wassmuss, even if he was to play no physical part in it. It wasn't the big blow against the Ottomans he had outlined to Tariq, but it was an important beginning, because if the Germans managed to pre-empt the idea of a native revolt, it could undo everything. True, Wassmuss was just one man, a single German agent at large. But Lawrence knew from his study of the history of conflicts, under the tutelage of Hogarth that, even in the grandest of wars, one man could make a difference.

As a bonus, he had thrashed Storrs at chess, winning three games to one, leaving the man tetchy and ill-humoured. Storrs was a good attacking player and sly when need be, but his strategy was weak. All you had to do was hold your nerve and counter-attack him with a cool head. That usually panicked him into ill-considered moves.

As he emerged through the gates, Lawrence spotted the huddled form of Munir, the street boy, sitting on the kerb opposite, his knees drawn up to his chest, a knitted cap on his head. He stared with his inexpressive brown eyes and watched as Lawrence pulled the bike out through the gates. Perhaps, the Englishman thought, he was silently bemoaning the revenue lost by not being there when Lawrence had arrived. When there was no Munir, he always parked the bike within the compound.

'Munir. Where do you live?'

Munir glanced over his shoulder, as if he expected another lad of the same name to be hovering there. He turned back, confused.

'Yes, you. Where do you live?'

'Darb al-Ahmar.'

This was hardly the best address in town, a nest as much as a district, a jumble of narrow alleys and makeshift shacks, not far from the Citadel. 'Hop on, I'll give you a ride.'

It took a second for this to sink in but the boy's face split into a grin. He ran across the street, ducked under a gharry's nag without breaking stride, hitched up his grubby *galabiyya* and straddled the pillion. Lawrence warned him to hold on and he felt the boy's thin, undernourished arms slide round him and the hands grip each other.

'Ready?'

'Yes! Yes.'

Lawrence opened the throttle as much as he dared, the rear tyre squealed and tossed a bucket full of grit into the air. The boy whooped in delight as they negotiated the streets, Lawrence pushing as fast as practicable, swooping and swerving in an exaggerated waltz. At one point Munir raised his arms in excitement and was nearly gone.

'Don't let go!' Lawrence warned him over his shoulder.

At that time of the evening the road to the Citadel, Sharia al-Qala, provided an exhilaratingly straight, uncluttered run and Lawrence took the bike up close to top speed, before swooping round and approaching the slum from the south. He could hear the boy panting with excitement in his ear.

'Where to?' he yelled as they entered the first of the high-sided crooked alleys of the district.

'Here.'

'I'll take you to your house.'

'Here, please.' Even over the clatter of the engine, Lawrence was aware of a note of pleading in his voice. He pulled the bike to one side, scattering rats from a pile of garbage. The sun had not seemed to penetrate the passageway, and the air was both chill and unpleasantly fetid. 'All right. See you tomorrow. *Inshaallah*.'

The boy hesitated, glancing up the lane towards his home. He was nervous about being seen with an 'English', because Darb was home to some of the most radical Egyptian nation-alists. Lawrence thought that if he had to live in such a place, he would be a rebel too. The boy rubbed his hands nervously on his *galabiyya*.

The rules of hospitality demanded a meeting with his family, endless glasses of mint tea and some simple sweets or pastries. At least, they would if Lawrence wasn't a British soldier. He could see the conflict on the boy's face, the desire to boast about the ride, the worry about turning up with a man in the wrong uniform. 'It's all right; I know why you can't take me. I am not offended. Salaam, Munir.'

The boy stepped forward, and Lawrence could smell the musky aroma of the street on him. He delivered the information he had in lieu of the tea and cakes at his home. 'They know you are after the guns that are coming from Persia.'

Persia? Lawrence felt a ripple of apprehension. 'Who knows?'

'Some men.' Munir was backing away, and gave his last offering. 'They say you are causing too much trouble. Since the felucca.'

The seizure of the Indian rifles by the British marines had clearly hurt someone, either politically or financially. Possibly both. Before Lawrence could quiz him further the lad had sprinted off, ducking into a side passage. Lawrence felt other eyes on him, and became aware of the beggars and the destitute, squatting in the doorways or prostrate on nests of rotting straw. On one of the *mashrabiyya*-screened balconies overhead he saw movement in the spaces between the complex patterns. A gaunt, hollow-eyed man carrying two live chickens hawked and spat as he passed on his way. Filthy water splashed on to the street a few yards away, and a pair of bold rats strolled down over the dirt to resume gnawing at the rubbish. This was not his place, not dressed as he was. He turned the bike and drove back to his billet at the Savoy, troubled by what Munir had divulged.

Eight

Cairo

Shortly after dawn, while the city could still breathe, Lawrence went for a ride around the city, taking the Clyno out to the Eastern Desert, past the vast cemetery known as The City of the Dead, before returning to GHQ at seven-thirty, late in the morning for him. Astonishingly, the day remained fresh and clear, the breeze continuing to scour the city and cut the heat and the thought of immersing himself in the suffocating sarcophagus of the Map Room for hours on end made his heart sink. Munir was in place, knees drawn up to his chest. Lawrence let the bike idle in neutral and, still sitting astride it, asked: 'Are you game for another ride?'

The other urchins watched curiously as Munir stood, walked over and, very solemnly, as if he were doing his duty, threw his leg over the bike. Lawrence puttered down the street in an equally unhurried manner.

'Where to?' he asked the lad. 'It's your country.'

'Across the river. Then north. I show you.'

'Just a second.'

Lawrence ducked the bike under a line of washing into an alley, peeled off his tunic and pulled the white Arab top back on. Less conspicuous that way, he reasoned.

The pair crossed on to Zamalik and on over to the west bank. There, with taps on his shoulder, Munir guided Lawrence north along the river – even *it* seemed invigorated by the weather; the water had lost its drab brownness and seemed to sparkle and dance in the sunlight. A pair of eights was out rowing, the soldiers pulling themselves through the usual clutter of dhows and lighters, sweat glistening on their shoulders.

The suburbs fell away and they rode on, the rising sun beating down with increasing violence, their bodies cooled by the slipstream. Lawrence was aware of the lad giving yelps of pleasure as they roared past the other traffic, sometimes slaloming between carts and camels.

After a few more miles, the boy indicated a low cluster of houses off to their left.

'My father's village.'

Close up, Lawrence could see that much of it had been abandoned. There were sections of roof missing on many dwellings, and the mud walls had crumbled. Some windows had been bricked up, others had collapsed as the supporting lintel gave way, and the wall above had sunk like a bad soufflé.

Lawrence knew what had happened. Many of the inhabitants, mostly the young and the vigorous, had been seduced by the lure of the city and had left their village to rot. There were a handful of children kicking in the dirt and half a dozen donkeys. He rode into a depressing, arid square, the centre of what must once have been a lively little community, and killed the engine. The children had disappeared, suddenly taking fright or, more likely, summoned by mothers or grand-mothers. A cock bugled in the distance, but there were no other sounds, other than the ticking of the Clyno's exhaust cooling down.

Munir let out a high-pitched whistle, so sharp it hurt Lawrence's ear.

A door squeaked open and in the shadows he could make out the leathery face of an old man. He peered out, and then raised a hand in greeting. Munir leapt off the bike, ran over, and indulged in what appeared to be an argument for several minutes. Eventually he turned back and gave a wide grin and flashed a thumbs-up sign at Lawrence. He had bested the old man.

He returned holding a large iron key. 'Come.'

Lawrence looked at the Clyno apprehensively. In a country where a double-decker bus could disappear under the nose of its guards, as had happened at the Alexandria docks, it was best to take no chances.

'It will be safe. Old Bes will look after it. You didn't see the rifle in the window when we approached?'

He shook his head.

'If we hear a warning shot, someone has tried to steal your bike. Come with me please.'

They walked to the rear of the village, passed a derelict

café decorated with chipped tin signs, into streets where the earth was desperately uneven, until the boy came to the place he was looking for. It was a two-storey building, flat roofed, and looked to be in better condition than most. The door was wood, studded with metal, a prominent hand of Fatima in the centre. A black dog, its coat gritty with dust, lounged on the brick step and the lad used the side of his sandal to kick it away. It slunk off without protest in search of other shade. Munir inserted the key into the lock and the door squealed on unoiled hinges as it swung back.

It was gloomy inside, the only light entering from high windows, and it took a few moments before Lawrence's eyes adjusted.

The double-height, barn-like room was empty, apart from one item, lying on a bed of old straw and rotten cloth. It was a stone column, marked with deep scores and what appeared to be dates, as well as some Roman numerals. It was a simple, quotidian device, but somehow beautiful.

'A nilometer,' said Lawrence.

'Yes. Our nilometer. The village's.'

Lawrence knelt down and touched it, running his hands over the cool surface. Nilometers varied from simple posts or columns – like this one – to a complex series of steps, but they had always performed the same task: recording the height of the summer flood. The one he was most familiar with was an octagonal column in the well on Roda Island.

'How old is this?' He stroked the stone; it was cold to the touch, like marble.

'We do not know,' Munir replied, then added: '*Min zamaan*. From long ago.'

Lawrence pushed his fingers into some of the grooves and repeated what Pliny had once written: '"Twelve ells for hunger, thirteen sufficiency, fifteen security, sixteen abundance." You could predict the future using one of these, Munir. From the level of the water, you knew whether good times or starvation lay ahead. Have you ever had it looked at?'

'You are looking at it.'

Lawrence laughed. 'Yes, but I am no expert.'

'Bes says they will take it away and put it in a museum.'

Lawrence stroked it once more and inspected the jagged edge at the base. It was perhaps eight feet long, but it had once been much taller. 'Very likely. But what use is it here?'

'Bes says one day, the villagers will come back and will need it again. He is keeping it for then.'

'Hence the rifle?'

'Yes.' Munir laughed. 'I know he is mad. The dams have stopped the big floods. But Bes says the dams won't last.'

Lawrence nodded. 'He's probably right.'

Munir looked puzzled.

'Nothing lasts for ever,' said Lawrence. 'But the Aswan will outlast us, I am afraid.'

'Will it outlast the British in Egypt?'

Lawrence smiled. 'What do you think?'

Munir kicked at the dirt on the floor, raising motes into the beams of sunlight bleeding in through the high windows.

'I think the British should come as visitors to a country that is ruled by Egyptians.'

Lawrence stood and ruffled his hair; it was surprisingly soft between his fingers. 'Would they let me in as a visitor?'

'Oh, yes. You before anyone. But not some of your friends.'

Lawrence hooted at this, before switching tack. 'Who are they, Munir? Who is bringing guns from Persia?'

Munir struck the pose of hurt innocence all Egyptian males were so skilled at. 'I overheard them, after – in a café.'

After I had reported to them, is what he had been about to say, Lawrence thought. He did not want to embarrass the boy. Munir had to scratch a living in a hostile city as best he could, and spying on the comings and goings of British officers was one way of doing so.

'Can you get me some names? Or dates of delivery?' he asked. Before Munir could answer, Lawrence added in English: 'Could you think about getting me some names? I don't want to put you in any difficulty.'

The boy gave a cautious nod.

'Good.' Lawrence pointed at the nilometer. 'And thank you for showing me this.' He tapped his watch. 'I'd better get to work.'

Munir nodded once more and said solemnly: 'Yes, me too.'

That night Lawrence's eyes snapped open in the early hours of the morning. He could hear his heart thudding in his ears, beating at double-speed of its own accord. He lay there in the dark, trying to hear something above the long, lazy squeaks of the fan he had left on. It was late enough that the nightly party downstairs, always audible as a low rumble of drunken conversation and laughter interspersed with the tinkle of breaking glasses, had run out of steam. The Savoy appeared to be slumbering, a rare respite from the demands of the British.

But something had woken him.

Lawrence threw back the single sheet that covered him, and swung his legs off the bed. His eyes were drawn towards the door. In the blackness he could see a shape, a pale patch of something, close to the door jamb.

It moved.

As his eyes grew accustomed to the gloom, he saw the object twitch and he became aware that it wasn't only the ineffectual fan squeaking. The creature on the floor was emitting a high-pitched squeal.

The next noise chilled his heart. The wail of a newborn baby filled his ears and drained his insides. He leapt over to the desk and clicked on the lamp as there came a second, pitiful cry, louder than the first.

The image of a blood-smeared foetus, plucked from its mother, struggling to cling on to the precipice of life, filled his brain. He shook his head to clear the image and forced his sleep-gummed eyes to focus.

A second's worth of relief flooded to him when he finally made sense of the bundle of flesh. It was no abandoned child. The comfort, though, was quickly replaced by a horror that made his stomach heave.

It was a cat. A cat that had been skinned. Its raw flesh left globules of blood on the rug as it tried to stagger upright, then fell down, causing more squeals.

The creature was behaving like a drunk. It dawned on him that was exactly what it was. The poor thing had been drugged, skinned, and then dumped in his room to regain consciousness.

The animal yelled pitifully once more, as its befuddled brain was pricked with messages of agony from all over its tiny, emaciated body.

'For God's sake,' he said, wanting to close his eyes.

The front paws began to claw at the carpet, ripping up threads as it dragged itself forward, leaving a smear of clear fluid after it.

Lawrence backed away until he hit the bookshelf and spun around. He grabbed a copy of Pryce Jones's mail order catalogue, the heaviest item there, took four long strides forward, raised it above his head and brought it down on the animal with all his might, falling to his knees as he did so. The skull crushed easily, cracking like an eggshell. There was one twitch and it was still.

Lawrence rolled the dead animal up in the rug and placed it by the door. A skinned cat was a warning in certain parts of the Levant. Keep out of our business, it said. You have ruffled feathers. Well, it was to be expected, perhaps. Secrets could not be kept in Cairo. But Lawrence would not have anticipated this particular caution in Egypt, where, although no longer sacred, cats were still held in some esteem.

He sat down on the bed, uncovered the water jug and

helped himself to a large glass. He cursed the perpetrators for their cruelty, at the same time swearing it would take more than a tortured feral mammal to scare him off finding out about the rifles coming from Persia.

Nine

Persia

The road to Bushire from Shiraz was notoriously steep and treacherous and the progress was much slower than the Swede had suggested. The carriage in which three of the women were travelling was particularly vulnerable to problems, splintering a wheel over rocks, and breaking a spring fording a dry riverbed. The Persians, however, were equally adept at running repairs, and always managed to have it moving within the hour.

The path took them firstly over the Range of the Hag, passing beneath cave-riddled peaks that ran to over ten thousand feet. The party of hostages were in shadow most of the time, hemmed in by sheer slopes, folded and creased and etched by wind and snowmelt. Some of Hag's outcrops did, indeed, resemble the profiles of old crones, while the cliffs were fluted in regular rows, so neat and precise they looked as if they had been groomed with God's comb.

Even when they did emerge into the sun, there was a biting cold in the thin air, and their breath came hard, until the path began a tortuous descent. Then it ran along a twisting valley of multi-hued rocks, decorated with extravagant striations and coruscating deposits of crystals.

O'Connor had always thought there was something intrinsically cruel about this place that infected the locals. He had ridden it before. The lack of vegetation meant the country had always reminded him of a flayed man, horribly deformed by the stripping of the outermost layer. Marco Polo talked of lush groves of trees in this part of the world; they were long gone, scoured away by man or nature.

The roads in the central stretch were often suicidally straight, plunging up and over mountains rather than trying to follow contours round them. The animals had to be carefully nursed, because there were many places where a lethal fall beckoned. Little wonder this section was known as the Cursed Range.

At lower levels, travel at the hottest time of day was almost impossible, so they moved in the half-lights of dawn and dusk, a ghostly convoy through a brooding land. O'Connor was aware of watchers at almost every step, often ragged bands of armed tribesmen, scanning the party, as if calculating the odds of a successful attack. The carrion predator in the sky that followed them for miles on end was probably making similar assessments.

For most of the second day O'Connor sublimated his anger at their abduction and rode alongside the Swede. They swapped memories of Stockholm in summer – O'Connor had

110

visited once en route to Helsinki and Moscow – and the history of Persia.

Svenson had a low regard for the locals, considering them cowards. He explained that, whereas in Europe they celebrated the heroic, in Persia the true achievement was survival. Which is why there were even incantations to protect fleeing generals.

As the shadows lengthened into night on day two, a group of the gendarmes were released to return to Shiraz, their place taken by a fresh batch of Tangistani. There was no one uniform among these newcomers, but the commonest dress was a half-sleeved tunic with tightly sashed waist and thick felt hats shaped like cooking pots, worn at a jaunty angle. The face was often wrapped in a wide cloth band, leaving visible only eyes that were impossible to read. They were all well armed and, thought O'Connor, none of them looked particularly cowardly to him, no matter what Svenson's opinion.

By the third night, the group was still not halfway towards Bushire. Svenson had chosen a caravanserai that consisted of a half-dozen tents occupying a side valley. There was a small spring there, and the women were allowed to set up a screen and make their toilet as best they could. Mrs Smith, a woman in her fifties who had settled in Shiraz with her late husband, was suffering. The heat affected her tremendously and she had developed a scratchy cough up on the Hag. Like the other women, she would sleep in makeshift canopies erected around the cart, with a Swedish lieutenant on guard duty, but O'Connor knew she needed better.

O'Connor and the other men's ablutions were equally lacking. They relieved themselves in a patch of the thorny plants that reminded him of a series of Gorgon's heads, with leaves like thick serpents. They were then given a meagre handful of sulphurous water each to try and shift some of the dust from their faces. It was a paltry effort and left them all smelling of rotten eggs.

The Englishmen were separated from each other and assigned two to a tent, with a Tangistan guard in each one. Simmons and O'Connor were given a semi-circular bubble of felt, its inside greasy with smoke; the atmosphere was what O'Connor's father would have called fowsty: hot, humid and slightly rancid. Dinner was yoghurt, cold rice and fried kidneys, prepared over a communal fire outside. The meat was oddly textured, full of gristly white tubules, and he doubted the women would eat it. The water they were given to drink contained the now customary whiff of brimstone.

O'Connor made sure he was at the opposite end of the tent from the guard before he spoke to Simmons. He glanced over at the Tangistan, who, once he had eaten his own food, had taken a gnarled black cheroot from his backpack and lit it. The smoke didn't improve the atmosphere, but it seemed to distract him. The man settled down into his *abba*, the camel-hair coat they affected, for his shift of duty.

'Game of cards?' O'Connor asked Simmons.

The younger man shrugged. 'Not really. Don't feel up to it. Hope you don't mind—'

'Game of cards,' O'Connor repeated forcefully, making sure his subordinate knew this wasn't a request.

Simmons tried to sound positive when he said: 'Splendid idea.'

O'Connor produced the two packs of cards he had taken from the Residence. 'Bit short handed for bridge. Let's try whist.'

He dealt out the cards straight on to the floor, away from the filthy blankets they were meant to make their bed with. 'Now, one thing the British Diplomatic Corps should have taught you is how to whisper.'

Simmons had the good sense not to glance at the guard. 'I doubt he speaks English.'

'I doubt he can speak after smoking that filthy thing. But never underestimate these people. Might have gone to Marlborough for all we know.'

Simmons laughed at the thought. 'What's trumps?'

'Hearts. We'll play it German style. For the face-up card. Listen, I think I've got that Svenson coming round. Did you see his expression when the Tangistan took over from some of his gendarmes? He's nearly outnumbered now.'

Simmons played a trump. 'Mine, I think. So what do you propose?'

So the man had no clubs. 'Well, he says he is to rendezvous with Wassmuss just outside Bushire. We have to get the women away before then. Mrs Smith is grievously poorly. I'm no medical man, but I fear her lungs have gone. I am not sure she will make it. Svenson has agreed it would be the right thing to do to let her and the others go, and hang Wassmuss. That's my trick, I believe.'

'Yes. You think we'll be able to do it? Get the women out without trouble? It would be a relief, especially for the young girls.'

'Let's hope they don't have any special plans for them,' O'Connor said quietly.

'They don't. The women will be freed at Chahgudak and allowed to proceed to Bushire. The Tangistan do not wage war on women and children. Nor does the Kaiser.'

Both Englishmen froze, unable to place the voice. Then they realised with dismay that the dirty vagabond of a guard had spoken, and in clear, accentless English.

'You, I am afraid, will be our guests until the two Germans and their luggage are returned.'

The confiscated baggage. That's what they had been searching the consulate for, not the gold. There was something in the bags that the Germans had abandoned that was worth taking hostages for. But what?

The man unwound the cloth from his face, revealing swarthy skin and an incongruously shaded beard; it was blond, but shot through with ginger. Set deep in the head were startlingly blue eyes, and a lock of fair hair fell over his forehead. There was nothing unusual about blue eyes and blond hair in central Persia – after all, this was where the Aryans had settled – but O'Connor knew immediately this particular specimen was Wilhelm Wassmuss himself.

Ten

On the morning after his discovery of the poor mutilated animal, Lawrence walked to the hammam behind the Savoy. He paid the attendant to turn away any other customers and stripped off. For an hour he sat and steamed in the hot room, breathing in the scalding air, trying to purge the smell of the dead cat from his passages. Afterwards, he plunged into icy water, waiting until his skin turned blue and his teeth chattered before he hauled himself out. He perched on the marble bench, shivering, and used pumice to rub at his fingertips, trying to banish the lingering sensation of the skinned flesh they had touched.

Eventually the elderly attendant indicated he should lie down on the slab. The man uttered a low prayer and then began to massage his back and shoulders.

The bony fingers seemed to penetrate each joint, finding the nerves and ganglia, pressing until Lawrence thought he must cry out. Instead, he bit his lip and let blood fill his mouth.

'Too hard?' the man asked after ten minutes.

Lawrence swivelled his head and smiled. 'Not hard enough.'

The man grunted as he pressed and pummelled with increased vigour. As the hands moved down his body, inflaming one sensory nexus after another, Lawrence realised the sights and the steely grip and the scouring pad of the attendant were driving out sounds of the tortured animal. He began to feel like a bag of fossilised bones, to be tossed one way or another, extinct, dead and useless. Slowly, Lawrence allowed himself to get lost in the healing pain.

Late that day, his shoulder muscles aching from the old man's kneading, Lawrence steeled himself to write to his parents, as he promised he would each week. He sat at the desk, immobile for a full fifteen minutes, before he could bring himself to start.

It seemed pointless to talk about Frank any longer and futile to express his concerns about Will joining the air force. He had no place lecturing his brother about being foolhardy, not after his own adventures in France and Syria and Sinai. Like Frank, like Ned, Will would want to engage with the war, even if it meant his death.

Security prevented him from discussing the intrigue in the city. '*I am working hard to stop arms being smuggled into the city, some of which may well originate in Persia.*' That certainly wasn't appropriate.

What about Wassmuss? He could hardly write: '*Mother, there is a German who is operating in Persia, possibly the same one looting our arms, who might cause the destruction of the British*

116

Empire.' Was that an exaggeration? Possibly not: if an Arab revolt could blast a hole in the Ottoman Empire, a similar Muslim uprising might puncture the British below the water-line. Storrs and Kitchener were right, the German's version of the revolt must be stifled, the man halted before any real damage was done.

But such speculation had to remain unwritten.

Nor could he tell of the plan he had discussed with Tariq. A scheme to ignite the Arabs, from soft city-dwellers to the fearsome Bedu, from warlike Howeitat to the proud Druse, all rising against the Turks, thereby drawing German attention – and supplies – away from the Western Front. All it needed was someone to convince Sherif Hussein in Mecca that the Arabs' future was in their own hands, that they could grasp history by the scruff of its neck if they took their opportunity now. If they did nothing, the Euro-peans would continue to divide and subdivide their king-doms into puppet regimes and colonies. Damascus was the goal. But that particular dream, too, had to remain secret for now.

In the end, Lawrence settled for doing what he always did in such an impossible situation.

He lied.

June 1915

There is nothing happening here except great talk and the continual supply of all sorts of things to the Mediterranean Expedition. Nothing I could describe as exciting ever seems to

117

occur in this city. Everything here very hot and unpleasant. Map-total is now 140,000, and still growing.

It is non-stop drawing, and overseeing the drawing of maps: overseeing printing and packing of same: sitting in an office coding and decoding telegrams, interviewing prisoners, writing reports, and giving information from 9 a.m. till 7 p.m. After that feed and read, and then go to bed. We do daily wires to Athens, Gallipoli, and Petrograd: and receive five times what we send, all in cypher, which is slow work, though we have a good staff dealing with them. Newcombe, MacDonnell and myself are Intelligence, Captain Cosens, Lord Anglesey, Lord Hartington and Prince Alexander of Battenburg do the ciphering and deciphering with us; that's all we are, with a Colonel Clayton who does Egyptian Foreign Politics in command of us.

We do no internal work: have little to do with Egyptians, or police or anything of that sort. That's all done by the Ministry of the Interior. We have only war work: European Turkey, Asia Minor, Syria, Mesopotamia, Persia, Arabia, Sinai, and Tripoli; we all dabble in them all. One learns a lot of geography, some people's names, and little else. No news from Syria; the country is quite at peace, which is a relief. Persia, though—

Lawrence stopped himself. How had that slipped into his thoughts? Wassmuss, creeping up behind him, like a footpad? He put a line through the last two words, making them illegible, and continued.

To be honest, I'm sick of pens, ink and paper: and have no wish ever to send off another telegram. I have made a friend of a local guide who has taken me to one or two interesting places. Otherwise, I think I shall be nailed up with my charts for all eternity, like some pharaoh or high priest. I envy Will his flying; what it must be soar over the land. I fully intend to try it as soon as possible. Anything is better than the slavery of the pen and the crippling boredom of inaction.

Ned

He reread the letter when he had finished. The crippling boredom of inaction. That part, at least, was true. It was what he feared most. Something told him, however, that he would soon have no concerns on that score. If nothing else, Persia would save him from that.

Eleven

Persia

As he had promised, Wassmuss allowed the women to continue on to Bushire. At the village where they parted company, a fly-blown speck called Chahgudak, there were tearful scenes and promises that each would never be out of the others' hearts or thoughts.

O'Connor was just pleased to see the back of the young girls who, although they hadn't suffered undue attention, were by far the most vulnerable of the party, excepting the increasingly frail Mrs Smith.

The last leg of the journey had been frustrating for O'Connor. Once Wassmuss had revealed himself in the tent, he had expected the man to have the good manners to travel and converse with the whites in the group. But no, after he had replaced the gendarmes with the Tangistani escort, he had faded in among them. With their scarves pulled tightly over their faces and their hats yanked down to their eyebrows, it was hard to tell one of these rogues from the other. Only occasionally did he glimpse a set of piercing blue eyes that he was sure belonged to the German, but the man often wheeled his horse away and slunk back into anonymity of the Persian pack.

O'Connor gleaned what he could from Mrs Christmas who had known the German before the war. She told him he was polite, erudite, given to spending days away in the wilderness, able to speak excellent English, reasonable French and good Arabic and Persian as well as his native tongue. He was a good hand at bridge, and generous with any supplies of European food and drink which came to the German Consulate. There were rumours of a dalliance with a native woman, but O'Connor knew enough about remote posting not to give that too much credence. Envy and slander were often behind such stories.

O'Connor watched the small convoy of horses, mules and wagons containing the women and its escort of four warriors with white flags, head off west to Bushire. Simmons sat staring as the figures shrunk to dots, the silver streak of a tear staining his cheek.

'You'll see her again,' O'Connor said to his deputy.

'But when?'

The sound of hoof beats made them both turn. A string of riders was heading for them, urging their horses on. As they came closer, O'Connor realised it was a race. The leader was standing in the stirrups and slapping his horse's flank with the flat of a sword blade. Above the hammering of the gallop, they could hear whoops and squeals and curses.

The men crossed an invisible finishing line, and the winner whipped out a pistol and fired into the air four times. O'Connor tightened his rein and patted his horse's neck as it skittered on tiptoes.

Their Tangistani escort parted to let the victor through to him. He had a broad grin on his heavily bearded face and he acknowledged the small bows the other horsemen were making as he passed among them.

'Sir,' he said in passable English when he reached O'Connor. 'You are the Khan of this group?'

'If by that you mean am I the senior officer present, then the answer is yes.'

'Very good. I am Zair Khidair, the Khan of Ahram, and you are to be our guests for a few weeks.'

O'Connor looked around the sea of covered faces and said, 'I want to speak to Wilhelm Wassmuss.'

'Woss Moss?' The Khan looked surprised by the request. 'He is not here. He has headed north. There is much work to do up there. You did not notice he had left?'

O'Connor felt very foolish when he said: 'He never told us he was leaving.'

'He never rests. He comes, he goes. Perhaps he has gone to consult Kaiser Hajji.'

'The Kaiser? To Berlin?'

'On his radio,' the Khan said, shaking his head at the Englishman's foolishness. 'He speaks on the radio.'

'That's nonsense,' O'Connor spluttered.

'You will see him, perhaps, in a few days.'

'Where are you taking us?'

He pointed across the scrubby plain, down towards the south. 'To the fortress at Ahram. I am your slave, you must make my home your home.'

O'Connor had to grant him this: it was a damned polite way of telling them they were his prisoners.

The fortress was nothing quite so grand as it sounded. To O'Connor it looked like a shrunken Norman castle, with a castellated tower at each corner of the mud walls, topped by deer antlers, and a large, squarer keep in the middle, which resembled, to his eyes, a brick-red version of the White Tower at the Tower of London.

A market, goat pens, stables, chicken runs and dwellings filled the space around the central fortress. Veiled women looked away as they rode in and naked children stood and stared, open-mouthed. The men made what were clearly caustic comments, and several spat on the ground. Even the old, laid out on wooden divans, waiting for death, struggled on to one elbow to inspect the Europeans, but their milky eyes displayed no reaction.

After they had dismounted, the Khan showed the bleary Englishmen to their rooms. There were two available for them to share, a bedroom laid out with a dozen clean blankets and a day room, with cushions and a long, low table, where meals were to be taken. The quarters were cool and dim, the light diffused by heavily barred windows. There was no running water, of course, but jugs of the local sulphur-laced variety would be provided for washing every day and a quantity of the precious, clearer spring version for drinking.

'I hope you will comfortable enough,' said Zair. He sniffed the air. 'I think you need to bathe. It has been a long trip.' O'Connor thought this a bloody cheek, coming from a man who stank of fermented goat's milk, yoghurt and badly cured animal hides. 'But first, some refreshment.'

The Khan clapped his hands twice and a tray full of black tea arrived, borne by a manservant so dark he had to be African. Each prisoner took a cup and drank, scouring the taste of the trail from his mouth. There were plates of dates, mulberries, walnuts and salted almonds, which they fell upon. Zair seemed pleased that his hospitality was appreciated.

'Can we write to our women?' Simmons asked the Khan.

'Yes. But Woss Moss must read anything you write. You will be taken out to the streams shortly for bathing. Two at a time, under guard. Please choose the order among yourselves. You will be comfortable and, once they agree to the exchange, you can look forward to seeing your women again. *Ma'zerat meekhaaham*. Until later.'

After he had gone the pitiful group of men clustered around O'Connor, demanding he predict the future, like some cheap end-of-the-pier clairvoyant. Finally, he had to raise his voice and order silence. They sulked like scolded schoolboys.

'Gentlemen, the British government will not abandon us –'

'But they will not trade us. They do not succumb to black-mail. You have said this many times.'

It was Simmons who had spoken and O'Connor fixed him with a steely stare. 'Perhaps not. But I swear to you that, even now, forces are gathering that will ensure our freedom. In the meantime, we must make the best of the situation presented to us.'

Croft the date-trader was far calmer. He was relieved to have shed the burden of his wife and daughters. 'What do you propose we do, Major?'

'We treat this as an opportunity. The Persians generally see hostages as enforced guests rather than common prisoners. They will accede to any reasonable request for books or materials. So, I suggest we better ourselves. All of us have skills we can pass on to others. Languages, story-telling, card games, painting. We share our resources, we concentrate our minds.'

'I don't understand,' said Mr Christmas.

'For instance, does anyone here speak Italian?'

'I have some,' admitted Mr Smith, the telegraph operator.

'Excellent!' declared O'Connor. 'Then I shall learn Italian.'

Twelve

Cairo

The runner brought a note saying that Mrs Marchand was waiting for Lieutenant Lawrence in the lobby and expected to see him shortly. Lawrence puzzled over it until he remembered the visit to see the Mausoleum of Qait Bay. He had told Miss Devonshire that he was interested, and then duly put it from his mind. He was interested. But not as a companion to Mrs Marchand.

He put away the map he had created of Southern Persia which charted Wassmuss's reported movements, changed out of his pumps, grabbed his cap, and headed through the corridors to the GHQ's entrance lobby, his mind full of half-formed excuses, none of which quite had the strength to stagger upright into something convincing.

Mrs Marchand was pacing the marble floor, parasol in hand, dressed in a tight-fitting jacket, belted at the waist with a full matching skirt. Her hair was drawn back under a wide-brimmed hat and she had on sensible, thick-soled boots. She was fully prepared for a day walking around tombs and ruins.

'Really, Ned,' she boomed in her loud American voice. 'You are a disgrace keeping a girl waiting like this.'

'I—'

'Three o'clock sharp, you said.'

It was fortunate that there were no other British officers to hear this exchange. Word would get around. But it was the long lunch, and only Egyptian guards and a few clerks remained at their posts. 'I did?'

'You know you did. Miss Devonshire and the others are waiting.'

'I can't,' Lawrence said, the slightest of stutters in his voice. 'Not today.'

'Why on earth not?'

Why on earth not? His brain repeated.

'Because I have to inspect a site this afternoon.'

Mrs Marchand pinched her lips and looked like a stern nanny, or, far worse, his mother after he had accidentally blasphemed. 'Well you might have let us know.'

Lawrence lowered his head, although he knew he was not guilty. He was being what the Americans called railroaded. 'I do apologise.'

'Where is this site?'

'I can't say. It's classified for the moment. Something to do with the Suez problem a while back.'

'An arms cache?'

'No.'

'An enemy stronghold?'

'I really can't say.'

'How interesting.' Her eyes sparked. 'Can I come along? We could take my gharry.'

'What about Miss Devonshire?'

'She'll understand.'

He found his head shaking even before he had formulated an answer. 'It's way out in the desert. Too far for a horse and carriage.'

She stuck her lower lip out and struck a sullen note. 'And how are you getting there?'

'Motorbike.' Before she could come back once more, he added, 'With my native guide on the back.'

She prodded him in the chest with the parasol and he winced. 'Are you being straight with me, Ned?'

'Please don't call me Ned. It's a family name. It sounds silly out here.'

'What nonsense. It's a perfectly fine name and I shall call you Ned if I want to. It's better than Tee-Ee, that's just stupid. As if you can't make up your mind what you want to be called.' She took a breath and some of the anger than had flushed her cheeks seemed to subside. 'So, I can't tempt you from classified nonsense to an afternoon at a mausoleum followed by tea and cakes at Groppi's?'

Oh Lord, no, you can't. Lawrence shook his head. 'Sorry.'

'Hhhmm.'

She eyed him up and down and appeared to file him

under 'waste of effort' and turned on the heel of her lace-up boots.

'Some other time, perhaps?' he offered to her back.

Her head flicked around and she gave him a mirthless smile. 'I think not, Ned. There are no second chances with the Marchands.'

This was excellent news, but he really didn't want to upset Miss Devonshire. He would do the talk for her Ladies' Archaeological Club as recompense. He also didn't want to be caught out in a lie. If he simply went back to the office, he could be certain that word of it would, somehow, leak back to Mrs Marchand and she would subsequently make sure that Miss Devonshire knew of his squirming treachery. Lawrence waited until he was sure she had left the building and that her gharry had driven off before he stepped outside into the blistering sun. He walked across to where Munir was sitting and summoned over the *kirkaday* seller, who poured him a glass of the hibiscus drink.

After a few sips, Lawrence asked. 'Munir, do you know any other interesting sites?'

'Sites?'

He switched to Arabic. 'Ruins, tombs. Something out of the ordinary, special, where tourists don't go.'

The lad thought for a moment, conscious of the many eyes watching him, wondering what this exchange could possibly be about, what kind of transaction could pass between an English officer and a street boy.

'There is one where people don't like to go, sir.'

'Call me Lawrence, Munir. And why is that?'

The boy gave one of his impish grins. 'Bats!'

Lawrence finished his drink and handed the glass and a coin to the vendor. 'How splendid. Let's take a look.'

The tomb lay in the desert beyond the so-called 'step' pyramids and it was easy to see why it was little visited. Sitting in a stony depression, its apex barely poking above the ground, it was virtually invisible. Lawrence also thought that a colony of bats was not the only reason for the site's neglect. Its perfect geometry was long ruined. At some point half of the outer stone had been looted, leaving the rest as precarious as a stack of children's building blocks, seemingly teetering on the point of collapse.

Once they had stopped and Lawrence had walked around it, Munir sensed his unease. 'It is quite safe. My father used to bring me here. He said the blocks are so heavy, they won't move.'

Lawrence reached out and touched the powdery stone's surface. Apart from this dusty outer layer, it seemed solid enough.

He fetched a flashlight from his panniers. 'If your father says it is safe, that's good enough for me.'

Lawrence located the entrance and ducked in, walking at a crouch for several yards before the chamber opened up. He inhaled the stale air of the single room with its sharp undertow of ammonia and flicked on his torch. As his beam cut across the empty space he heard the rustle of leathery wings from above. A soft, hazy light hugged the eves, the sunlight finding

130

its oblique way through fissures in the exterior, but it was hardly enough to illuminate the chamber's floor. He knew better than to shine the torch directly at the bats, which were probably naked belly tomb bats, first described by French explorers and early archaeologists. Sudden light was a sure way to panic them and, although these night-flyers held little terror for him, he had no desire to provoke them unnecessarily.

He was aware of the boy close behind him. 'Who does your father think was buried here?'

'He said, perhaps, a high priest.'

The interior was larger than it had seemed from the outside, and a series of rough steps led down to the actual burial chamber. There was no sarcophagus or plinth, just splinters of stone and pottery, mostly obscured by the splatter of bat dung. The walls were disappointingly bare of any markings. No hieroglyphics or murals glistened in the torch beam, no long-neglected scenes from ancient life, just a few faint scratches which looked to be twentieth century, some intrepid tourists marking their adventure with a set of initials.

And yet, despite its lack of ornamentation or treasure, there was a resonance about the place, a tangible sense of history. If it was a priest, he left something behind, an echo of distant awe, for Lawrence was aware that his heart was beating faster than normal. The dangling animals above rustled like paper once more, as if they, too, sensed some unspecified unease.

Lawrence took a few of the steps down and stopped. The boy bumped into him. 'What is it?'

He shone the torch on the ground and, at the foot of the stairs, he caught sight of a thin ribbon of material, almost obscured by the droppings. He bent down and picked it up and rubbed it between his fingers.

'Mummy wrapping?' the boy asked.

'Silk,' Lawrence said. The fabric had been found in tombs going back to the tenth century BC, and it was strong and resilient and almost rot-proof. It was impossible to know what it had been used for, but it was easy to guess where it had come from, traded perhaps a dozen times, in China, Mongolia, Persia, Syria, passed along like a relay baton until it reached Egypt, where its fabulous cost would make it the preserve of the wealthy and the God-like. 'It might have well been someone important who was buried here.'

Then the boy gave an involuntary shudder and he heard the same spasm pass through the hanging mammals. The air became alive with a kind of electrical twittering. 'What's that?'

Lawrence wasn't sure. He dropped the cloth, held out his hand and shone the light on to his palm. A fine dusting of sand covered it. More grains rained down in a delicate stream, until the lines on his skin were filled.

He touched Munir's hair and, instead of the softness he expected, he felt the grittiness of ancient, weathered stone.

He looked upwards, and the grains filled his eyes. He blinked them away.

'I think we'd better leave. Come on.'

Lawrence took the steps just as he felt the first rumble of the tremor vibrate through his legs. With a noise like a thousand hand claps the bats exploded into action and the space about them was filled with the snap of skin as panicked wings thrashed the air.

The boy let out a frightened yell and Lawrence turned and scooped him up, taking the last three steps in one leap. His boots slithered on the bat guano, before he ducked and plunged headlong down the tunnel towards the bright, ragged rectangle of daylight that marked the exit.

They both heard the howling of a new wind from outside. A wall of air punched down the access tunnel, like a fist pushing them back, and Lawrence found himself struggling to make headway.

The boy yelped in fear. Lawrence swung him behind his body, shielding him from the stinging sand funnelling into the corridor. Already, the floor had disappeared under the influx. 'Hold on to my top.'

The outline of the entrance began to blur as the tremor built. Lawrence made sure the boy had a firm grip of his shirt and worked up the slope, one heavy step at a time. The ground rippled beneath him and the air pressure increased. His feet were losing purchase on the fine sand. Lawrence found himself taking two steps backwards. Munir made another small, frightened sound.

If the pyramid collapsed, Lawrence knew they were done for. Each weathered block weighed several hundredweight. They'd be killed instantly or trapped and injured, to die of thirst or heat or blood loss.

Lawrence summoned one last enormous effort, lowering his head and raising his shoulders like a scrum-half, and charged for the outside, dragging Munir behind him.

Although there was no physical barrier, the final few yards were like forcing open a heavy vault door with no counterweight. Feet still sliding, he found a purchase for his fingers between the ancient blocks and he pulled himself and the boy forward, hand over hand, grateful for the upper body strength he had cultivated so carefully. His nails began to tear, but he forced the fingertips deeper into the crevices and, with one final jerk, yanked them free of the pyramid.

They burst out into a filthy spiral of dust that danced about them, moaning and shrieking. Lawrence could see very little, apart from the shape of the Clyno, which had been plucked off its stand and tossed aside by the disturbance.

Then, even the motorbike was lost to view as a fast rotating curtain of brown air enveloped them. Lawrence felt himself buffeted to one side, then the other, and for a second his feet left the ground.

He pulled off his jacket, put it over Munir's head and pushed the lad to the earth.

There were larger stones at the base of the whirlwind, caught on the atmospheric merry-go-round. They rolled and flew into them. Lawrence felt a rock bounce off his cheek with a sharp crack. He bit his lower lip.

The boy wriggled beneath him and Lawrence yelled: 'Don't move!' Even though he had spoken through clenched teeth, sand invaded his mouth and coated his tongue.

The ground gave two heaves, bucking like an unbroken horse, lifting them clear by a few inches, before they crashed down on to earth that became still once more.

The cyclone gave them a farewell swipe and moved on, leaving nothing but a whistling in their ears. Lawrence kept them where they were, his breathing hard, but it seemed the thing had passed. As the dust haze thinned, a shamefaced sun reappeared slowly from behind the thinning mist.

A cloud of bats that had fled the tomb in terror were circling the pyramid's top, disorientated and confused by the growing light until, one by one, they found the crevices that led them back into the comfort of the darkness.

Lawrence stood, brushed the sand from his body and pushed the half-buried bike upright, checking for signs of oil or petrol leaks. Apart from a tear-streak dribbling from the fuel tank's filler, there was no apparent damage.

He turned and looked at Munir, who appeared to have been slathered in dusty grease paint. Lawrence guessed he looked the same, because both burst out laughing at the spectre confronting them.

Lawrence fetched a canteen of water from the bike, took a mouthful and spat the debris from his mouth. He let Munir do the same. Then he poured a pool into his left hand and rubbed it on to Munir's face, gently removing the layer of dust. He repeated it until the young lad under the grimy carapace reappeared.

When he had finished, Munir cleaned Lawrence's face, splashing capfuls on to and into his scratchy eyes, saving just enough for them to have a last mouthful each.

The Englishman then sat down and examined the tomb. It lay undisturbed, the slant and cast of the stones identical to when they had arrived. The storm devil and the tremor had left it unscathed. 'Looks as if your father was right,' said Lawrence.

The boy shook his head and a look of retrospective fear flashed across his face. 'I made that up. My father always told me not to go in, it was unsafe. It was me who always thought it wouldn't move.'

Lawrence put a hand on his shoulder to show there were no hard feelings: 'Then, my young friend, it looks like *you* were right.' The boy looked at the ground. 'What is the matter?'

'I am sorry about what my father did.'

'Your father?'

Munir brought his head up and fixed Lawrence with a determined gaze. 'It was wrong.'

Lawrence felt a sinking in his stomach. 'What did he do?'

'I think he sent you a warning. Bes told him about the visit to the nilometer. He does not like me seeing you . . . he thinks . . .' The eyes flicked down once more. 'He does not like the British.'

'I'm not always terribly keen on them myself.' Lawrence pulled the boy close. Munir's father had skinned the cat. Lawrence had thought angry gunrunners had mutilated the poor creature. It turned out to be an over-protective father. He gave a mirthless laugh at his stupidity.

'What is it?'

'Nothing. It's just that sometimes things work out for the best for all the wrong reasons.'

Munir gave him a quizzical look. 'I don't understand.'

Lawrence stood and brushed more dust off his clothes. 'No matter. We should get back. But Munir . . .'

'Yes, Lawrence?'

'I won't ask you to lie. But in future don't tell your father about our trips together unless you have to.'

'Yes, Lawrence.' The name came out oddly, more like Orrance, but he didn't try to correct the boy. It wasn't as if it was even his real name anyway.

Thirteen

Persia

Major O'Connor could see the rescue party approaching from his elevated perch on top of Ahram's keep. It was a string of tiny ants on the desert floor, riding out towards them. He shaded his eyes against the new sun and tried to make out the group's strength. Mounted sepoys, for certain, and what looked like a gun carriage at the rear. But how many men? More than twenty, less than forty, he estimated.

O'Connor began to wave his arms and shout, but his voice barely projected over the walls. It was half drowned out by the bleating of animals in the pens below.

He scanned the grey expanse of the desert. It was a trap, he knew, but he had no idea how it was to be sprung. A messenger had appeared the previous evening, with news that a rescue mission had been launched from the garrison at Bushire. The Khan had informed them of this with great glee, and his mocking tone could only mean one thing. Now he knew they were coming, he would have a surprise waiting for them. 'Please, Major, you wake the babies.'

He turned around and was confronted with Zair, the Khan, and his ever-present retinue of lackeys. He was wearing an irritating smile that O'Connor would happily have wiped off his face. 'What are you going to do?' he demanded of the supercilious young man.

'What do you think. Do you think I am going to let them blast my walls down?'

'Where are your men?'

Zair made a great show of placing a hand on his brow and studying the landscape. 'They should be there somewhere.'

'Shouldn't you be leading them?'

'And risk capture and barter? Would you like some field glasses, perhaps?'

'So I can watch your monstrous plan more closely?'

'You should look and learn.'

O'Connor was torn for a moment, but eventually said: 'Very well.'

Zair sent a runner downstairs to fetch the glasses and the boy returned with a fine pair of Rodenstocks. Reluctantly, O'Connor took them and focused them on the troop of soldiers. They leapt into sharp relief and he turned the wheel, they were so close he could see the lead captain's moustache. He did a quick headcount. Thirty-two in all, four British bluejacket officers, the rest sepoys. They were riding at a brisk pace, eyes on the target, with rifles in scabbards, unclipped for a fast draw. A compact howitzer was being pulled by two horses at the rear of the column. It was the desert equivalent of a gunship, come to shake some walls and knock heads together.

O'Connor tried to manoeuvre himself so that the sun would flare off the lens, but the Khan tut-tutted and placed a hand on his shoulder. 'Please. No signalling.'

The major returned to studying the seemingly featureless waste around the unsuspecting soldiers. He lowered the glasses and demanded of the Khan: 'Where the bloody hell are they?'

'Watch.'

Another few minutes passed and O'Connor could feel the sun burning his face now, but he found it impossible to turn away from the unfolding disaster. Then, without warning, there came a puff of smoke, drifting into the clear air. The boom of the field gun reached him a moment later. A pillar of shale and dirt exploded at the side of the sepoys, a rain of stones sweeping over them, and he saw one rider thrown to the ground. The animals began to panic, dancing as if they were on hot coals.

O'Connor saw another cloud of smoke and he finally located the guns, cleverly located in a thicket of acacia. As he watched them, he was aware of more movement nearby, on the edge of his field of vision. From a fold in the landscape that created a small depression, he saw men and horses spring from the very earth. The Tangistani and their mounts had been lying under large blankets that had been covered in earth and pebbles. These they shook off as the animals staggered to their feet.

More cannon shells exploded among the beleaguered sepoys, and a horse was sliced almost in two. Its rider had apparently vanished, vapourised by the detonation.

The shelling stopped and the Tangistani cavalry, around fifteen men in all, launched themselves at the decimated party. They could gallop at full speed, O'Connor noted, and still fire their rifles with considerable accuracy. It was a horribly impressive feat.

'For God's sake turn around,' O'Connor pleaded under his breath. 'Turn around while you can.'

But the remaining sepoys and their officers pulled their horses down and began to make a spirited, if foolish, defence, firing volleys that took out a number of the Tangistan attackers.

Wisely, the Persians swung away and the field guns began again, zeroed in with sickening accuracy. Now, as the wind shifted, the major could hear the terrible braying and whining of dying horses as the explosives and shrapnel did their work.

Unable to watch any longer, O'Connor threw the field glasses at the Khan, turned and walked down his quarters. There would be no rescue that day.

Back at GHQ Lawrence received a uncharacteristically brusque welcome from Stewart Newcombe, who was waiting at his station in the map room.

'Lawrence, where the bloody hell have you been?'

'Out.'

'Out?'

'Gathering intelligence,' Lawrence said, rearranging his papers.

'Storrs is looking for you. Got a bee in his bonnet. Something to do with Persia.'

Lawrence stopped what he was doing. 'Wassmuss?'

Newcombe knew all about Lawrence's fascination with the German and his aims. Much as he liked him, he thought Lawrence could bore for the Empire on the subject of native uprisings. 'I think so. Yes. Something about . . .' Newcombe ran a hand through his hair.

'Something about what? The hostages?'

Newcombe nodded. 'There's been a massacre.'

Once a week the prisoners were allowed outside the gates of the fortress with a Tangistani escort. They walked to the north, following a well-worn path for half a mile, until they came to a small stream, shaded by ancient boulders. The water that pooled in their shadows was hot enough to send vapour curling into the air, and it smelled strongly of sulphur, but otherwise it was clean and relatively free flowing.

O'Connor and Simmons quickly undressed and, while the guards chatted and smoked, submerged themselves up to their necks in the tributary.

After they had been immersed for five minutes, a third guard appeared, said something to the men that started them laughing and gave each of them a neat 'tailor made' cigarette. They eagerly pinched out their crudely rolled cheroots and lit up. Even above the brimstone, O'Connor could smell the distinctive aroma of a German Turkish tobacco mix.

'Wassmuss,' he shouted.

The newcomer turned, walked across and crouched down on a rock. 'Cigarette?'

'No, thank you.'

'I'll take you up on that if you don't mind,' said Simmons eagerly.

'Schwarze tobacco,' he warned.

'Well, I'm all out of English.'

O'Connor had counselled Simmons to ration himself, as they had no idea how long they might be held. They were now in their sixth week; his deputy had ripped through his supply of Red Hussars in two. The major still had a decent stash of tobacco for his pipe; he would have to be pretty desperate to smoke the local cheroots. He hoped it didn't come to that. At one pipe a day, he had enough for another six weeks. After the abortive rescue attempt, he was debating whether to extend the interval to one every other day.

As Simmons lit up, O'Connor studied the German. He wore grubby breeches, a loose shirt with sash, into which he had thrust a Mauser machine pistol, an ugly but effective weapon. He had a fuller beard than O'Connor remembered, but, on close inspection, it was slightly better trimmed than the wild whiskers genuine Persians cultivated. His blue eyes were just as piercing as he recalled, but there were deep, dark crescents under them. It didn't need a medical man to know that the German was tired.

'You butchered those soldiers the other day, Wassmuss. You'll pay for that.'

The German sucked deep on the cigarette and exhaled the smoke through his nose. When he spoke, O'Connor was once more surprised by his effortless command of English. 'I was not here. But I admit to having devised the plan as a precaution. I told the Khan they would send a rescue party. And there they were, coming with flowers and chocolates for me. That was what was in the gun carriage, wasn't it? Although the sweets must have melted, the flowers wilted, because all I found were sets of leg irons. Perhaps *they* were for me.' His eyes twinkled. 'What do you think, Major?'

'It was damned cowardly. An ambush.'

Wassmuss looked both pained and surprised. 'Major, am I meant to take on the British in head-to-head combat? They have a trained army, I have –' He jerked a thumb over his shoulder at the guards, who smoked on, oblivious to the veiled insult. 'So I have to adapt to their methods and strengths. Hit and run. It's war, Major, but a different kind of war. No drums, no colours, no formations. It is a change you should get used to, because out here, it is the only way to fight. How do you defeat an army when there is no army to defeat? Do you think the Tangistani would have ridden in like that, in a perfect column, almost announcing themselves at the door? No. The first you would have known was when they kicked the door down.'

O'Connor could see the German was making sense, even if he didn't approve. 'Were they all killed?' he demanded.

'No. One officer and ten sepoys survived. They were allowed to return to Bushire with a simple message: Stop trying to rescue them. Give me my baggage and my colleagues and you can have them.'

'I told you before, your bags will have gone to London.'

Wassmuss flicked the remains of the cigarette to his left, away from the stream. 'Then they will just have to come back. I do believe there are ships which leave England every so often.' Wassmuss stood and stretched. 'I have to go. I must ride on. More hearts and minds to win.'

'To buy, you mean.'

Wassmuss shook his head. 'The best of them do it for me, not the money.'

'So you'd like to think. What do you hope to achieve here?'

'Freedom for these people. I have promised.'

'Then you will have to break that promise. You have no control over what governments will or won't do once this war is over.' O'Connor slapped the water. 'What if there is oil under here? Then they will come, regardless of what you promised.'

He nodded. 'There is a saying in India: when two elephants fight, it is the grass that suffers most. These people are the grass but we Germans will do right by them. I have to believe that.' He cleared his throat. 'You are being treated well by the Khan?'

'I asked about some Italian books. The Khan said permission was needed from you. I could have them sent from Bushire, where there is an Italian community. Under truce, of course.'

'Only if I inspect the books first.'

'For files or knives or an escape plan? It's over thirty miles to Bushire through flat, open land. How far would we get before your army of ghosts hunt us down? You have the upper hand.'

145

'Perhaps. And perhaps you are a very devious man, Major.'

'If I were a devious man, I wouldn't be in this position.'

Wassmuss threw back his head and laughed, then slapped his thigh. 'How true. What are these books?'

'There are just three of them. *Rascaldate Sul Fuoco*, *La Parta Bianca* and *Di Questa Lettera*.'

Wassmuss considered for a moment and, under water, O'Connor crossed his fingers, something he hadn't done since he was a child. 'As you wish. You may write a letter asking for them. But also request newspapers, as recent as possible. I want to see how the war is going.' O'Connor suddenly had a sense of the man's loneliness, far from home, among savage, capricious people, with no fellow countrymen to converse with and no up-to-date knowledge of how his country was faring in the great conflict. 'Not that they will tell me the truth.'

'No. That's not a commodity you turn to newspapers for these days.'

'I will tell the Khan about your books. Perhaps next time I call, we shall have dinner together.'

'I can practise my Italian on you,' said O'Connor.

'Alas, that's one language I have never mastered. But Arabic or Persian, perhaps. Keep well, gentlemen.'

O'Connor let out his breath. His gamble had paid off.

'Well done in getting the books,' said Simmons. 'That will keep you busy.'

O'Connor smiled and lowered his voice to a hoarse whisper. 'What books? No such books exist either in Italian or any other language.'

Simmons furrowed his brow. 'Then why the blazes did you ask for them?'

But O'Connor, tired of the man's dimwittedness, declined to answer and clambered out of the water to dry himself off in the sun, enjoying the sensation of finally having scored his first victory. Soon, Cairo would know all about this man Wassmuss and it could do something about him once and for all.

Fourteen

Cairo

Even after he had read the account of the ill-conceived rescue attempt at Ahram, Lawrence was forced towards a further grudging admiration for this German Wilhelm Wassmuss. His tactics were fluid and flawless. He could generate enough men for a head-on confrontation or, as he had been doing, mobile units that could attack hard and then melt away into the mountains and deserts of Persia.

Apart from the massacred sepoys, other signals from Bushire and Basra told of attacks on the British residence in the south and that Bushire port itself was locked down tight. The man was offering a gold sovereign for every British weapon brought to him. That gave him an ever-growing stock of rifles and pistols. Even the daily patrol from Bushire had been abandoned, because of the number of casualties, caused by the bounty on the soldiers' weapons. The British had a port, but nowhere to go with anything landed at it. It was guerrilla warfare. It was the kind of war Lawrence advocated, Arab against Turk. And it was being turned against the British Empire.

He shared these musings with Tariq, his Ottoman Arab prisoner, as they walked out of the compound of Dr Bitter's house at Maadi. It was their seventh meeting since the move from the Citadel and the formalities had gone, rubbed away like soft limestone to reveal the bedrock underneath: two men, unsure of the other still, not yet friends, but moving in that direction.

In the far distance was the wired POW compound, and the despondent figures of its internees could be seen at the fence, shuffling a few yards before turning and retracing the groove in the earth. They were like big cats trapped in a zoo, pacing the same stretch of stockade over and over again.

It was early evening, the brightness of the day fading to a dark saffron. The bars and cafés of Cairo would be filling up now, the best tables in Groppi's garden would have been staked out by the Europeans, having a quick gin and tonic either before a tardy return to work or as a prelude to a long, dissolute evening.

'I have written to Kitchener, through Hogarth.' Lawrence had already explained about his old tutor – who had the ear of the highest level of government where Arabia was concerned – and how Lawrence hoped he would come to Cairo. 'I have told him we must act against Wassmuss now, not wait for further developments.'

'I think you are right to be worried. I did warn you he was the one to watch,' said Tariq. 'If Wassmuss can spread his message of insurrection, then perhaps there will be more and more mutinies against the British. Tying up more and more troops.'

'Including Egypt?'

'This time, I think, perhaps. If the Egyptians sensed a weakness. And if there were the guns.'

Lawrence nodded but said nothing. Recently a shipment of Lee-Enfields had turned up at Port Said, with no telltale marks to show they were Sold Out of Service. And was it coincidence that Wassmuss was buying every gun his natives could get their hands on? Possibly, but those guns were coming from somewhere; if not Persia, then the slaughterhouse at Gallipoli. Perhaps both.

As they strode towards the desert, Tariq nodded towards the parked Clyno and the thin figure crouched beside it. 'Who is the boy?'

'He minds the bike.'

Tariq looked at Lawrence with a furrowed brow. 'And you take him with you?'

'The way one might a lock and chain. Only it's simpler.'

Tariq did not like the idea of an urchin who could be bought for a few piasters witnessing their conversations, but said nothing.

'Have you thought about what we spoke of?'

The prisoner stroked his face. A beard was appearing, a symbol of the sloughing of Tariq's Turkish skin. The disillusioned Ottoman officer would fade away as the bristles thickened, replaced, Lawrence hoped, by a proud Arab. Already, out of uniform, it was hard to recall the smart, German-dressed martinet whom he had interviewed at the Citadel.

They had reached the edge of the habitation by the time Tariq spoke again. Shadows were growing and the green-tinged dusk was gathering around them. 'I have seen your soldiers—'

'They aren't my soldiers, Tariq. Never mistake me for a soldier. I just wear the uniform because it makes my life easier.'

'Like the boy?'

'Like the boy makes life easier.'

'The British soldiers play a game similar to the one we used to play as children, before I knew better. We used to use sticks and lamp oil. They use petrol. We gambled with stones and simple toys. They use money.'

'What is it?'

'You find a scorpion, an aggressive one, and place it in a circle of petrol or sticks. You set fire to the circle. Someone begins to count. You watch the animal run this way and that, trying to find a way out through the flames. It cannot. Still, they count. The heat begins to attack the creature's shell. Its movements become more frantic. It is now, ten, twelve seconds. Then the scorpion realises it cannot escape, that it is about to boil in its shell. So, slowly, it brings its tail over until its stinger finds what it knows to be a vulnerable place. And it stings itself to death. The winner is the one who calculated how long from the lighting of the flame until death.'

The first stars showed themselves, little stabs of silver against a darkening sky. 'Your point being?'

'You are like the scorpion, Lawrence. Trapped here in Cairo, looking for a way out. Careful you don't go the way of the scorpion and sting yourself to death.'

'I don't follow.' The first hint of a night chill came off the desert and Lawrence relished the cool feel on his clammy neck. It was one of the advantages for those who lived out here; sometimes the suffocating, infuriating heat of the day was cut as darkness fell, while the city sweltered on through the night.

'You are desperate to see a chance in this Wassmuss. And perhaps your eagerness will get you killed.'

'Tariq, it is time I asked you a question. An important one.'

'Yes, Lawrence.' He said it as if this were no surprise.

'Will you help us? The British? Can you find it in you to do that? I don't mean like this, but out in the field, where you can do some real good.'

'No. I will not help the British.' The finality in Tariq's words surprised Lawrence.

'I am sorry to hear that.'

'But you. That is different. You I will help. If what you told me is true. If we ride on Damascus for the Arabs.'

Lawrence doubted that the powers would let him take part in such an undertaking, so he phrased his reply carefully: 'One day soon, the Arabs will ride on Damascus, I promise.'

Tariq slapped the shorter man on the back. 'Then I will help you, Lawrence. When do we begin? Now?'

Lawrence let out his breath in relief and looked at his watch. 'No, not right now. First of all, I have to face something far more terrifying than Wassmuss or an Arab Revolt.'

'What is that?'

'I have to address the Cairo Ladies' Archaeological Club.'

Fifteen

Persia

When O'Connor's request for the three Italian books finally reached Bushire it was passed on to Captain Edward Noel of the Political Department, the officer who had let Wassmuss escape captivity by failing to insist that he was shackled. Chagrined by the whole incident, he had become even more obsessed with the German, to the point where his exasperated superior officer had arranged to transfer him to Cox's staff at Basra in a month's time. The last straw had, apparently, been the debacle of the ambush at Ahram. Never mind that Noel had cautioned against such a head-on confrontation and had presented a stealthier alternative. He hadn't even been on the dawn raid, but still, everything to do with Wassmuss was now laid at his door. Because, the unspoken admonishment went, if you hadn't been such a gentleman about the ball and chain . . .

It had been a rare miscalculation for Noel. The captain

was a man who had twice, before the war, bicycled from England to India, on the grounds that friends said it was impossible. He spoke fluent Persian and had, for the most part, a good rapport with the locals. The abortive raid had told him one thing: Wassmuss might be German, but he could only be tackled if one treated him not as one would a European, but as a very wily brigand. That would be the key to his downfall. What Noel couldn't quite work out was how to bring this about single-handed.

As an Intelligence officer, Noel had the luxury of his own office in Bushire barracks, mostly so he could read signals and go about his 'shadowy' work – as regular soldiers thought of it – in some degree of privacy. It was here the message from O'Connor was delivered.

Noel examined the three pieces of paper, with their widely spaced sentences and tiny writing, asking for British newspapers and three Italian books. *Rascaldate Sul Fuoco*, *La Parta Bianca* and *Di Questa Lettera*. He'd checked and re-checked for any hidden code or cipher, letter repetition or reversed words, but there was nothing from the *Cryptologist's Handbook* in there. It was just a letter. What was O'Connor playing at with these books? Did he think they were a municipal lending library? 'Sergeant!'

Sergeant Ross entered Noel's tiny space. Ross, a ruddy-faced Welshman, cultivated an air of long-suffering, of impossible tasks done before breakfast, more daunting ones by tea. 'Sir?'

'Speak Italian, Ross?

'No, sir.'

'Know anyone who does?'

'There's a lady in town who gives lessons, sir. French and Italian.'

Noel wondered if that was a euphemism, but, after examining the impassive expression on Ross's hangdog face, he decided it wasn't.

'And you know where she is?'

'Sir.'

Noel scribbled the titles on to a fresh piece of paper, loath to let the original out of his sight just yet. 'Can you take this to her and ask if she knows where we could possibly get these three volumes. If she has any of them on her shelves, tell her we will gladly reimburse her for them.'

'Yes, sir.'

Noel went about setting his affairs in order ready for the transfer. He wrote to his parents, telling them about the move to Basra in four weeks. He sent requests for his itemised mess bill and made a note to settle some minor gambling debts. All the time his eyes went to the map and the red circle around the fortress of Ahram. Basra was a long way north of where the German was operating, but he hoped he wasn't finished with Wassmuss just yet.

Half an hour later there was a knock at the door and Ross entered with a striking, dark-haired woman in tow. She was past marrying age, quite short, but had a finely boned face and dark eyes that were wide with amusement. Noel leapt to his feet.

'This is Signora Ponti, Captain.'

A widow, then. Noel bowed and held out his hand. She brushed his palm. 'Signora, how do you do? You received our request?'

'I did, I did. And I hope I can help. Unfortunately, they are not books I have,' she replied.

'Ah, well. Perhaps he'd just like a selection in Italian.'

'You do not speak the language?'

'No, I'm afraid not, marvellous though it is.'

She gave him a smile. 'It is marvellous. Let me show you. *Rascaldate Sul Fuoco.*' She pronounced the phrase with a suggestive ripeness. 'Is lovely, no?'

'Signora,' he began, not having the time for ad hoc tuition.

'Heat Over the Fire.'

Noel stopped his next objection dead in its tracks. 'I beg your pardon?'

'*La Parta Bianca.* The White Part.' She paused, the smile still playing over her lips.

'Go on, please.'

'*Di Questa Lettera.* Of this letter.'

He put it all together. 'Heat over the fire the white part of this letter. Well, I'll be damned. Excuse my language, signora.' Now he laughed out loud. 'Well, thank you so much. Sergeant, if there is anything Signora Ponti needs, food, provisions, supplies, will you make sure she gets them?'

After they had gone, Noel removed the glass flue from one of the kerosene lamps and lit the wick. He held the note to the flame and watched as an ethereal writing materialised. *You are a good man, Major O'Connor. I apologise for anything I may have said that indicated otherwise.* At last, he could send good news to Cairo. Now, he thought, we have you, Wilhelm Wassmuss.

Sixteen

Cairo

'. . . and I am sure you will want to join me in thanking Lieutenant Lawrence for his most illuminating talk and slide-show. There will be refreshments served next door and I am certain the lieutenant will be pleased to answer any questions you might have.'

The Cairo Ladies' Archaeological Club met in a changing roster of private houses. The one that night was a villa on Gezira, overlooking the moored houseboats. It lasted two hours, as Lawrence was cajoled into progressing from Syria, to his mission to Sinai just before hostilities erupted, where he had struggled to mask the fact he had been OGB – On Government Business – with Newcombe.

When he finally tore himself away from the meeting, Lawrence wondered if he had gone too far, revealed too much of himself in the talk. It was impossible for him not to, once he began to re-imagine the sights and smells of the Carchemish camp. He had told them of how he had stood up to a Turk who beat one of the boys, which won him the respect of the locals, and how he instituted the gunshot signals to indicate a find. The exuberant locals loved the reward of firing into the air. It might have been childish, and pricey in ammunition, but it was highly effective in motivating the diggers.

He'd shown the ladies pictures of Dahoum, not just at Carchemish but posing beside the Byzantine cistern at Biz Berein in the Sinai, and knew he had allowed warmth to creep into his voice when he talked about how he had befriended him and of the raised eyebrows he had caused when he had brought him back to Oxford. The image of the Arab boy with flowing robes racing around the collegiate streets on a bicycle causing ladies in tearooms to drop scones in amazement raised a polite laugh or two.

Lawrence had also described for them the occasion when Gertrude Bell, the legendary Arabist and desert explorer, famous for her impersonations of a boy goatherd to hide her sexuality from the more belligerent tribes, had visited him at Carchemish. Because he sometimes affected the red sash of the local bachelors, the diggers had assumed she had come with a proposal of marriage. He told the ladies that the Syrians had consoled him when she departed without any announcement of engagement by claiming that she had been far too plain for him anyway. This drew smiles and gasps of horror in equal measure. Miss Bell, it transpired, was a hero to many of them in the room.

As Lawrence hurried from the garden into the road, where

the carriages were waiting, he saw Munir leap to his feet and beckon him over, but at the same time, there was a tug on his sleeve.

'Ned.'

It was Mrs Marchand, the persistent American.

'Ah, hello.'

There was a dry chill in the air, and so many stars in the sky that looking up gave you vertigo. Lawrence pulled his coat around him and examined the heavens. 'Cold tonight.'

'Yes.' But she would not be distracted. 'That was quite a little show in there.'

He wasn't sure that this was a compliment, but he took it as such. 'Thank you.'

Munir was still hopping up and down in agitation and Mrs Marchand glanced over at him. 'Is that the new Dahoum?'

'Don't be ridiculous,' he snapped. 'Of course it isn't. People aren't quite so interchangeable, you know.'

Mrs Marchand put her head to one side and examined him quizzically. Lawrence heard the predatory whine of a mosquito in his ear and was desperate to be on his away. 'I meant, your guide and yardstick.'

He had explained Dahoum's presence in most of the photographs by the need for human scale, to appreciate the size and scope of some of the monuments. 'He minds my motorcycle.'

'Are you still in touch with Dahoum?'

It wasn't his real name. 'Dahoum' meant 'the dark one', but he was in no hurry to share that intimacy with Mrs Marchand. He was actually called Salim Ahmed and he had been no more than fifteen – the lad wasn't sure of his own age – when they met. Although unschooled, he was not unintelligent, a quick learner and with a great sense of mischievousness. Lawrence had liked him, and been happy in his company. He knew what people thought and his own sense of mischief did little to disabuse them of whatever pictures they cared to paint. He knew the truth of the matter. 'He is caretaker of the dig, still.'

'Is he safe?'

'Yes. Syria is calm for the moment. Thank God.'

'Will you see him again?'

'One day, I hope. I want to return to Syria, yes.' With the present for the boy of a liberating army, he almost added. A free Syria, a liberated Damascus under an Arab flag, that would be a gift worth bringing.

Mrs Marchand was silent for a moment, then said: 'I think I understand you more after tonight.'

Lawrence couldn't stifle his laugh entirely.

'What is it?'

'When you get full enlightenment, perhaps you'd let me know. I'm not sure I understand myself that much.'

'You'd better go. I think the new Dahoum is fit to burst. Good night, Lieutenant.'

Munir was indeed still hopping from foot to foot and beckoning frantically. Lawrence heard the voices of other women emerging from the house behind him and he touched his cap. 'Good night, Mrs Marchand.'

Lawrence strode across the road and hissed: 'What is it for goodness' sake?'

'Come.'

'Come where?'

'Guns. Lots of guns.'

They bumped northwest out of the city for more than forty minutes. The Clyno's feeble headlight picked out the army's mile markers that delineated the stony track from the rest of the desert, but many were missing, snapped by a truck or snatched by a storm. Staying on the path was more a case of following the ruts of carts and the compacted imprints of many camel's hooves more than anything else. Behind them, there was only the swirl of dust, ahead an inky blackness beyond the unsteady beam from his headlamp. Lawrence could taste sand and the tang of salt. This whole area was alien to him, uncharted territory. He had put his trust in the boy entirely.

It was a good job he loved this feeling.

It was a mix of isolation, disorientation and danger, a heady concoction, specially formulated, it seemed, for a discerning few. Many men would look into the featureless night, and think of the foolishness of following a native into the unknown and feel fear. Lawrence, on the other hand, felt a spark of elation. He was cast adrift. Nobody knew he was out here, but one young boy. Were he to die, his desiccated corpse might not be found for weeks or months. Or, with its bones picked clean by vultures, and scattered by wild dogs, it might never be located.

It was, Lawrence knew, a frail, fleeting moment, as transitory, he imagined, as sexual gratification, the opium pipe or the decanter of whisky. But while it was there, he drank deep, not questioning Munir, just feeling the miles fall away behind him, taking him deeper into that special place, where he was weightless and untouchable, where not even Mrs Marchand could find him.

He was aware of the hills to the left of him closing in, dark humps like paper cut-outs held against a star-rich sky. Munir tapped him on the shoulder and he pulled over, the air thrumming from the chugging engine. He cut it and a silence enshrouded them.

'We walk now. Quietly.' His teeth were chattering and Lawrence offered him his outer coat, but the boy refused.

Lawrence used the torch sparingly, and on several occasions Munir hissed in alarm at him when he did so. Finally, Lawrence could wait no longer. 'Where are we going?'

'Markiz.'

This hardly helped, as he had no idea whether this was a village or a landmark, but he plodded on, treading as carefully as he could, wincing at every scattering of scree or tumble of rock. After twenty minutes, Munir slowed and his footfall became even softer. Lawrence moved in behind him, mimicking his actions. Then, the boy dropped to all fours, scuttling up a looming hillside like a primate, before freezing at the top, as if suddenly petrified.

Lawrence spent a careful two minutes joining him on the ridge. Below, there was nothing. No light shone, no campfire blazed, there was only the velvet fuzz of a darkness softened by a sliver of moon and the stars.

But then a camel snorted. A man broke wind and laughed softly to himself. There was a curse from a second man.

Lawrence felt a crushing pain in his chest and realised he couldn't breathe. He emptied his lungs, slowly, and filled them again. It was odd, he thought, how at moments like this the entire epidermis becomes itchy, yelling out to be scratched. The nose twitches with stored-up sneezes, the scalp prickles, the throat dries and rasps and demands a hack.

Lawrence ignored his body's silent rebellion, concentrating on the invisible men below.

He wasn't sure how long had passed before they heard the first smudged echo of a truck approaching, ghostly snatches of its gears grinding and whining, till the sound solidified into that of an engine. Lorries were still relatively rare, most Egyptians relying on four-legged transport. Which meant this most likely belonged to the British Army. It had come from the north, judging by the direction of its approach, perhaps from Alexandria. A lot of contraband leaked from the famously porous warehouses of the port.

Munir placed a hand on his shoulder and pressed the Englishman further down into the stony soil. Headlights appeared, sweeping the sky and grazing their hillock as the truck bounced through the hollows and humps of its approach.

The yellowy beams picked out a group of four Arabs at the foot of the slope below their hiding place. The quartet had made camp, and tied alongside them were three mules and six camels. The men stood up, casually unslinging their rifles. The vehicle came to a halt, its raucous engine still running, the rattling of its pushrods and tappets filling the night.

They heard rather than saw the cab doors open and two men step out. The pair walked into the illuminated patch and greetings were exchanged. Lawrence recognised one of the men as Spaark, the Belgian from the Criterion nightclub.

Two other figures appeared, carrying an oblong wooden box between them. Lawrence could tell what was within. Rifles. British Lee Enfields taken from the secure armoury at Alexandria. He didn't get to see any more because his foot twitched involuntarily and dislodged a rock. It clacked down behind them in a series of percussive cracks.

As luck would have it, a camel stamped the ground at the same time, partially masking his folly, but the combination unnerved the men, and heads began to spin and he heard the unmistakable snick of a round being pushed into a breech chamber.

Munir tugged desperately at his back, but Lawrence didn't need any encouragement. As if treading on gossamer webs, they propelled themselves backwards and disappeared into the night. It wasn't until they were fifteen minutes away from the truck, his chest painful once more from the effort of shallow breathing, that Lawrence spoke, and even then his voice was a coarse whisper.

'How did you know?'

Munir pulled his ear. 'I listened. They talk in front of me sometimes, in the coffee shops, like I do not exist or as if I have no ears. Did I do well?'

Lawrence slapped him on the back. 'You did very well.'

'What does it tell you?'

A great deal, he thought, but he said: 'That you are my friend. That I can trust you.'

The boy's teeth were just visible in the darkness as he smiled.

* * *

The next morning Lawrence's first action was to place an order with Clayton for a small-calibre Beretta pistol. The boy deserved a present, but he could not give him anything too ostentatious. Better a weapon, a sure sign of status, but also something that might be potentially useful to him. He would teach him to shoot in the desert. Not that the Italian pistol could match the Colt, but he could tutor him on the effective range and how to use it quickly and lethally. Just in case. The lad had embarked on a dangerous path and the least Lawrence could do was protect him as best he could.

He also knew he had to take it slowly. If he appeared too keen to pump Munir for information, he would frighten the boy, as he might a jittery stallion. If he could turn Munir completely, make him his spy in the coffee houses, he would learn about more than just gun shipments. Of course he had to do so without attracting the wrath of the father. He could live without seeing another skinless feline. Money might help smooth matters, as long as it was handled with sensitivity. He didn't want the parents to think he was paying for the use of the lad.

In the late morning Storrs brought him a visitor, Harry St John Bridger Philby, another famous Arabian explorer like Gertrude Bell, albeit one with a reputation for arrogance coupled with a fearsome temper. Philby had been in England settling his wife Dora and son and was on his way back to serve with Sir Percy Cox in Mesopotamia. Philby told him he had spent the journey reading all the dispatches and reports on the concept of an Arab revolt. He was therefore well aware of Lawrence's position. Equally, Lawrence knew from

INTRUSIVE signals that Philby was agitating for a very different solution to the Arab question.

Lawrence began, though, with pleasantries. He knew what was important to men like Philby: continuing the family line. Such considerations were beyond Lawrence, given his own fractured lineage, but nevertheless he said: 'Congratulations on the boy.'

'Thank you,' replied Philby.

'What have you called him?' Lawrence enquired, trying to sound like he cared.

'Harold Adrian Russell. But we call him Kim.'

Lawrence knew Philby Senior had served in the Punjab, so the source was obvious. 'After Kipling?'

'Of course.'

Philby scanned the map Lawrence had been working on, a rendering of central and northern Arabia. He had been annotating it with the latest estimates of the strength of the Turks at various towns along the Hejaz railway. Philby put his finger on Mecca. 'Thing is, Lawrence, all this about Hussein starting an Arab revolt is nonsense. The man must be eighty.'

'Not yet seventy. And he has sons,' Lawrence calmly reminded him.

'Softened by exposure to the Turks. They are not warriors. You met any of them?'

Lawrence was forced to admit he hadn't.

'I've spoken with Feisal. Impressive in his way, but no real stomach for a fight. All hot air.' His hand hovered over the map, until he swept a palm over the remote Najd region and jabbed at Riyadh. 'The Wahabi, that is where our money and effort should go. Ibn Saud and his people are proper warriors.'

'I disagree,' said Lawrence. 'Oh, they can fight. They do little else. But they are extremists. Zealots might be a better word. They even dislike music. I distrust religious fanatics of any hue. And the Hashemites will never follow them. I feel we should put our weight behind Hussein.'

Philby studied him for a long time in silence, before he said: 'Well, thank the Lord it's not up to people like you, eh?'

Lawrence stroked his forehead and massaged his temples for a few minutes after Philby had left before he felt strong enough to return to his annotations.

Lawrence, although irritated by his encounter with Philby – how could the man think the Saudis would unite the Arabs? – was comforted by a communication from Captain Noel in Bushire. He was in coded contact with the hostages, right under Wassmuss's nose. So, the German wasn't infallible after all. The thought cheered him immensely, taking the sour edge off his encounter with Harry Philby.

It was still light when he emerged from GHQ that evening. He scanned the street, but there was no sign of the Clyno or the boy. He asked some of the ragged hangers-on near the gate if they had seen anything, but each just shrugged, staring back at him with unreadable eyes. The corporal of the guard told him nobody had noticed anything untoward. 'Little bleeder's had it away. You can't trust the gyppos. Last you'll see of that bike, I'm afraid, sir. Should've parked it in the compound, sir.'

Apprehension flapped in Lawrence's stomach. 'I need another one, quick.'

'Sir?'

Lawrence leaned in close, pushing on to tiptoes to make his point more forcefully. 'Who else has a motorbike, Corporal?'

'Here? I dunno, sir.'

At that moment, a Signals messenger astride a BSA turned into the gate and paused to show his papers. Lawrence was on him in a second, holding the handlebars so they could not be turned, then he reached down and flipped the fuel cock. The engine stuttered and died. 'Sergeant, I am commandeering this motorcycle.'

The man pushed up his sand-splattered goggles. 'Like hell you are, sir.'

'In the name of Colonel Clayton.'

The rider shook his head violently from side to side. 'I have my orders—'

Lawrence's blow caught the man on the side of the head and he was swung partly out of the seat. Lawrence completed his dismounting by throwing his body weight against him. The stunned messenger crashed to the ground in a cloud of dust.

The sergeant, unsure of how to intervene in this unsightly scuffle, unslung his rifle. Lawrence glared at him and yelled: 'Get out of my way. Get this man seen to.'

He manhandled the bike around, reset the fuel switch and kicked the start pedal. The warm engine caught first time. Behind him, the messenger was already struggling to his feet, a series of curses issuing from him. Lawrence opened the throttle and the bike pulled him into the street. He could worry about the repercussions of his 'requisition' later.

Lawrence wasn't sure whether it was instinct or blind desperation that charted his course. His first stop was the alley where he had dropped the boy the night he had given him a lift home. An agitated Lawrence leapt off the bike, pulled it on to the stand and walked to the beggar who had been watching them so intently that evening. The man lay on his straw, pushing hard into the rough wall of the passage, hoping to make himself invisible.

'The boy Munir. Where does he live?' Lawrence demanded.

A pair of milky eyes stared at him. 'Boy?'

Lawrence reached down and yanked the beggar to his feet. The man's bones clacked like a marionette's limbs. 'The boy I gave a ride to. You saw us.' Despite the foul breath, Lawrence pulled him closer. 'Tell me or I'll snap your spine.'

'Up the alley. Blue door. Eye of Horus on it.'

Lawrence let him collapse back on to his filthy straw. 'Watch the bike. If it disappears, so do you.'

He found the door, which was open, and barged in through the bead curtains. The room was tiny, occupied by two women and a young man. The women screamed and covered their faces. From another room next door, a baby cried in alarm.

Lawrence squared up to the young man who, despite the panic in his eyes, had stepped to block his way as the women scurried off to the baby. 'I am looking for Munir.'

The lad was taller than Lawrence, but reed-thin. He tried his best to puff out his scrawny chest. 'He is not here.'

'His father?'

'He has left for Alexandria.'

'You are?'

'His brother.'

Lawrence grabbed the lad's upper arms, holding him firm. 'I am worried something has happened to him.'

'To Munir? What kind of thing?'

'That his father may be punishing him.'

'My father has work. He is out of the city since this morning. Munir is not here,' the brother repeated. The baby in the adjoining room gave another desperate wail. 'Go. Please.'

'If he comes back tell him to come and find me.'

'Leave.'

Lawrence did as requested. As he stepped back out into the street he heard the brother, his voice suddenly brave. 'If anything has happened to him, it will be your fault for not leaving him alone. You will pay.'

Next, he rode to the village with the nilometer, where Bes, the old guardian, took a wild pot-shot at him. Once Lawrence had disarmed him, he extracted a familiar reply. No Munir. He forced the guardian to show him the room with the monument, but it was as they had left it days before.

Finally, he took the BSA south to the ruined pyramid that sat concealed in a forlorn hollow in the desert, and there he found his young friend.

His murderers had bound his hands and legs, and then lifted him, stomach-down, on to a sharpened stake. The idea was that the body weight would press the flesh on to the point, slowly penetrating the vital organs.

The progress of the featherweight boy had been too slow, it seemed, for they had tied sacks of rocks to his wrists and ankles to assist gravity. The increased mass had helped propel the spike though his body, so that its blackened tip protruded through the split skin next to Munir's spine. In the beam of Lawrence's flashlight, the blood surrounding it was still red. It hadn't been very long since this happened.

Lawrence couldn't bring himself to look at Munir's face. He put his shoulder underneath the slender ribcage, and his hands on the lad's thighs and heaved. Lawrence tried shut out the horrible noises the body made as it came free by humming a fragment of a tune. Even so, it didn't entirely shield him from the sound of tissue slithering on wood. He wrapped his jacket around the torso to hide the great hole in it. Then he looked at the boy's features in the torchlight, closing the eyes and stroking the still-warm face until some of the traces of his final agony were removed.

Impalement was an old Egyptian method of execution, which was believed to bind the spirit – the *ba* – and the body to the place of execution, making it impossible for the soul to move to the next world.

Lawrence wrestled the spike from its pit in the tomb's floor yelling at the top of his voice as it came free, his cry disturbing the bats above. He laid out Munir in the centre of the chamber, folding his arms across his chest in repose. Still kneeling, he struggled for a few moments to remember an appropriate verse from the Koran. In the end Lawrence muttered: 'We all came from God, and we will all return to God again. Knowledge of the Hour of Resurrection belongs to God; it is He who sends down rain and He who knows what is hidden in the womb. No soul knows what it will reap tomorrow, and no soul knows in what land it will die.' The words were like ashes in his mouth. Lawrence touched the lad's forehead one last time and went outside.

He had no idea how long he sat on the sand, but eventually the sun began to slide below the horizon, the shadows grew longer and the fierceness of the burning air abated.

Then, Lawrence set about gathering the displaced stones that littered the area around the old pyramid and began to block the access tunnel. He rolled in the larger boulders first, finding a strength to move even the most stubborn. Then he found dozens of other rocks, ranging from fist- to head-sized, to fill in the gaps. Within an hour, he had sealed up Munir's final resting place. It was dark by the time he returned to Cairo.

Seventeen

Cairo

Most of the soldiers and sightseers who came to see the Muski, Cairo's bazaar, which took up a huge proportion of the Gamaliyya medieval quarter, only dipped a toe into its daunting labyrinth. Had they walked a hundred more yards down one of its alleys, they would have found themselves almost exclusively among locals, hundreds of them per tiny street, it seemed, crowding the coffee shops, the public scribes, the fortune tellers and bartering at the stalls. It smelled of sweet spices and rank meat, aromatic coffee and human sweat. Strangers call it chaotic, but that is just their way of expressing ignorance for the intricate layout. Those who came regularly soon discovered a pattern to its apparent anarchy.

Lawrence, dressed in a white *galabiyya* with a simple gold motif around the neck, pushed his way through the crowds, expertly finding the gaps between the bodies and the occasional

173

animal, careful where he stepped, for the ancient floor was slick with various fluids and effluents. The unwary could plunge knee deep into an old drain, or turn an ankle in a pothole.

Lawrence passed through the street of the bowl-makers, where the hammers beat sonorously on brass, and that of the silver and gold merchants, where finer tools tapped delicately on bangles and brooches. Then there were the locksmiths, a street where he loved to linger, watching the old men hunched over blackened vices, listening to the rasp of tiny files and admiring the glittering rain of brass filings sprinkling on to the cloth that prevented the metal being wasted. It was said that the locksmiths could duplicate any mechanism in the world, from the simplest padlock to the mightiest Chubb; Lawrence could well believe it.

It took him fifteen minutes of threading through cork-screwed streets to reach the coffee shop he wanted, a dark, cave-like establishment next to a carpet shop. He hesitated for a second before entering, re-positioning the hard, rect-angular parcel he had under his arm. The young merchant next door, sensing an opportunity, flicked open his rugs for Lawrence's inspection. 'Come. Just look. Tea, sir? Best price.' The tired, familiar phrases tumbled from his mouth.

Lawrence shook his head. 'They are indeed beautiful, but I am here to see Abdel.'

The lad looked disappointed and, just as deftly as he had laid them out, removed his wares from sight.

Lawrence stepped inside the gloomy coffee shop, waited a moment for his eyes to adjust, and then moved between the tables, ignoring the inquisitive looks he was attracting. He parted a beaded curtain into the rear and crossed the tiled courtyard, aware of a young woman scuttling from his sight, and pushed open a heavy blue door. He was in a corridor, the walls lined with silk; a similar material, but more diaphanous, hung from the ceiling. The cloying smell of perfume was strong. He clattered through a second barrier of beads and passed through it into Abdel's banking hall. It was decorated with carpets even more fabulous than the ones he had just been shown, the colours still intact after hundreds of years, saved from fading by the room's permanent half-light. The floor was covered in cushions and Abdel himself sat on a low ottoman facing him. On the *tabliah*, the low brass table in front of him, were stacks of money, Egyptian and English pounds and US dollars, as well as Indian rupees.

'*Allah ma'ak*,' he said, as he gathered up the cash and slipped it into a satchel. '*Meet ahlan wa sahlan.*' Welcome a hundred times.

'*Allah yittawil omrak*,' Lawrence replied.

Abdel was dressed in an elaborate *galabiyya*, blue and silver, with small jewels sewn into the fabric that caught the light from the oil lamps. Around his neck was a heavy gold chain, worn like a badge of office. He looked a very different man from the slightly dissolute character who patrolled the Criterion in his linen suits. 'You are very welcome, Lieutenant Lawrence. Please.' He indicated Lawrence should sit, and he folded himself down on to a cushion. The Englishman placed the parcel between his feet, and both men made a great play of ignoring it.

Abdel's servant appeared and cups were produced. The man

poured the hot brew from a *kanaka*, a long-handled copper pot, straight off the charcoal in the ante-room, which was separated from the business area by a heavy damask curtain that shimmered between gold and silver. The coffee dispensed, the lackey disappeared and returned with plates of baklava and dates.

As a sign of his trust in his host, Lawrence picked up his cup first and sipped, careful not to burn his lips. He nodded appreciatively. 'You serve excellent coffee.'

A nod in return. 'Try the dates. From Siwa. You have been?'

'No.'

'You must. Finest dates in Egypt. But also the place itself, it sits at the edge of the great depression. Beautiful and terrible.' Abdel told a story about his time lost in the sands and Lawrence listened and laughed at the punch line, when the Egyptian revealed he had merely been one sand dune away from a village and had never realised it. Lawrence sensed it was a fabrication. He offered his own story, a version of his time in Syria and the arrival of a plain Englishwoman whom the locals wanted him to marry. He did not mention Gertrude Bell by name this time.

'You are not married?' asked Abdel.

Lawrence shook his head. 'It is not for me. I find the whole idea . . .' he struggled for a while. 'Comical.'

'Comical? Yes. It is so funny I have done it three times now.' Abdel smiled good-naturedly.

The servant set up a *shisheh* on the table between them. He fussed as he set about preparing it for smoking, feeding a block of tobacco into the bowl of water. Lawrence watched him carefully while Abdel detailed his matrimonial history.

Lawrence didn't like smoking any more than he liked alcohol, and for the same reason. He did not want his body in thrall to any kind of drug with its insistent demands. But he also accepted that at least a few puffs were expected and the first mouthfuls of cool, sweet smoke were quite pleasant. However, he knew that the tobacco was sometimes adulterated with hashish to help make the client more compliant.

Eventually, when the flames had been stoked, he took the mouthpiece and inhaled a kind of gaseous honey. No hashish. He handed the mouthpiece over to Abdel.

'You know the price of tobacco now? Outrageous. Everything is going up, up, up. I can hardly afford to smoke any longer.'

Lawrence gave a sympathetic sigh. 'Prices will come down again when the war is over.' It often took months in transit before soldiers finally arrived at their camps in Egypt. During that time they had accumulated significant back pay, which they were issued at Cairo. So, the soldiers took the tram into town and helped fuel the inflation that was crippling the poorer Cairenes. Which was, of course, most of them.

'*Inshaalah*,' Abdel said after he had taken a draw on the pipe. He offered it back, but Lawrence held up his palm to show he'd had enough. Already his mouth tasted stale, the sweetness turned bitter and dry. He took some more coffee.

Protocol suggested another twenty minutes of stories and discussion, but Lawrence didn't have the patience that day to play the circling and feinting games of Eastern business. Instead, he took the parcel and placed it on the table. Abdel's eyes flicked down to it.

'You have not come for a loan, then?'

They both smiled, knowing that that would never be the case. 'No. For you. A gift.'

Abdel put down the mouthpiece of the *shisheh* and took the parcel, which was bound in plain brown paper, held with string. His dexterous fingers unravelled the knot and he extracted a rosewood box. He laid it down on the table and admired the wood's high, glossy sheen. Then he lifted the lid and a sly grin spread slowly over his face.

'A Colt?'

'No,' said Lawrence. 'Something finer.'

Abdel lifted out the revolver and turned it over in his hand. 'It is a cowboy gun, no?'

'Yes, but not a Peacemaker. It's a Schofield, chambered for the short Smith & Wesson .45. Don't try and use the longer cartridge.' He mimed snapping a stick. 'Break it.'

Abdel fiddled with the lever and seemed startled when the gun hinged open, to reveal the six-shot cylinder.

'The spent cartridges automatically eject. It was used by US cavalrymen because they could reload in under half a minute. Which gave it an advantage over the Colt.'

'It's beautiful. Have you fired it?'

'Once or twice. This gun came from Buffalo Bill Cody when he was in London. He handed out a few as gifts. My brother bought it. He gave it to me. Now it is yours. This was the kind of gun used by Frank and Jesse James, Cole and Jim Younger, John Wesley Hardin, Bob Ford, Texas Jack Omohundro, Pat Garrett, and Virgil Earp. You know these people?'

Lawrence knew he did; the showing of some of 'Bronco Billy' Anderson's moving pictures at the Rameses Theatre had sparked a fascination with all things Western in Cairo just before the war. The news that a print of Tom Mix's *The Man From Texas* was on its way had been the talk of the middle-class coffee houses for months. And Abdel was the kind of man who made it his business to keep abreast of every trend in town.

'I do, I do. You must come to my house. At Bulaq Dacrour.' This was one of the swankier suburbs of Cairo. 'I have a range there. We shall fire it together.' He began the elaborate wishing of blessings in return for the gift, but Lawrence stopped him.

'Who killed him, Abdel?'

The banker took one last loving look at the weapon and placed it back in the box. He opened his mouth to speak and Lawrence could tell he had his shrug of ignorance and innocence all ready.

'I know you know who I mean. If a motorcycle goes missing, you would know about that, because you would hear where it was on offer. You would then get to know the story and would know about the boy. You know he is dead, don't you?'

Abdel inclined his head to acknowledge the truth and Lawrence felt bile burn his insides. 'And how?'

'As God is my witness, no.'

'It wasn't pretty, Abdel. It was barbaric. He was impaled.'

The eyes flicked downwards. 'I am sorry.'

'Why would someone do that to him?'

'It is a dangerous role you have chosen. Friend to Egypt, loyal to your country. You move easily in the bazaar one moment, then raid feluccas the next –'

'I don't want a critique of my actions, Abdel. I want to know who killed Munir. Was it his father?'

Abdel looked shocked.

Lawrence told him about the skinned cat. 'Could he have gone one step further? Because he was friends with a British soldier?'

The Egyptian shook his head. 'I doubt that. If that were the case, it would be you who was on a stake, not a precious son. The warning was for you, not him.'

'So?'

Abdel pursed his lips, weighing up how much to divulge. 'The people you seek. I cannot name,' he said with regret. Lawrence waited. There was more. 'But I can tell you they work for the Belgian.'

'Sparkie?' Lawrence pressed him. 'Jacques Spaark?'

'Yes. I told you, he was planning to bring guns in. These people, they arrange the transport, the storage. You must have asked too many questions, perhaps found one too many cases of contraband.'

'But why the boy?'

'He, too, played a dangerous game. The two-faced spy. If they suspected his loyalty had moved, from them to you, well . . .' He made a sucking noise through his teeth.

Lawrence felt his molars grinding as he moved his jaw. If he hadn't given Munir the ride home or visited the nilometer or gone out to the desert to watch a nefarious transaction, the youngster might still be alive, minding his Clyno even as they spoke.

'I am sorry.'

180

Lawrence turned his head and blinked until the tears had gone and his eyes had stopped stinging.

'You liked him?' The enquiry was soft and delicate, but he could tell Abdel was wondering why it was worth crying over a street urchin. Scores of these children died every day, if not murdered then by disease, malnutrition or accidents in the workshops they slaved in.

'He was just a lad,' snapped Lawrence. 'It is unfair that knowing me should cause his death. And especially that particular kind of death.'

'When East meets West, it seems there must always be tears.'

Lawrence stood and, not forgetting himself, bowed. 'I don't accept that. It is a trite sentiment.'

'Lawrence,' he said, as the Englishman turned to go. 'I shall treasure the revolver. But please, don't do anything foolish. It's Cairo. Such things happen. As I always say, even better than cotton, the Egyptians are most clever at weaving wiles.'

'It was Aeschylus who said that. And I hope you are a better banker than philosopher, Abdel.'

Eighteen

Lawrence ignored the note at the desk of the Savoy requesting his presence at GHQ immediately. The bike incident, he supposed. Well, he had returned it: what more did they want? Still, he checked the lobby carefully for any representatives of the many police forces that operated within Cairo and, satisfied, took the stairs to his room. In the corridor, he waited outside, ear to the door. He listened for signs of someone within, a scraped chair, a cough or scratch, and sniffed the air for recent cigarette smoke. After ten minutes, he was fairly sure the room was empty and entered. There was the lingering trace of an unfamiliar smell. Cigarette smoke. He would have to be quick.

He had twice in recent days thought about Gertrude Bell and he took out his notepaper to write to her. There were few women he trusted and even fewer he admired. The species seemed fundamentally flawed to him, even his dear mother, who, along with his father, had conspired to ruin his life with their devious deceptions. Miss Bell, though, deserved to be proposed as a shining example of an exception to her sex's capriciousness.

She had crossed vast deserts, travelled alone, with local guides, had transformed herself into a herder's boy to fool even the great Ibn Saud. She climbed mountains for pleasure, pushing herself to her physical limits, and was one the best fencing blades in London. What was there not to admire there? She was the kind of woman, perhaps the only woman, whose knowledge of Arabia should be put to use in Cairo, Athens and Basra. She was wasted in London. David Hogarth, the Keeper of the Ashmolean, and now working his way up the ranks of military intelligence, should be able to help bring her on board. Lawrence would welcome a like-minded soul in the city.

Savoy Hotel,
Cairo

Dear Gerty,

I hope this finds you well. I hear you are involved in the Red Cross in London. That's very admirable, but I can't help but think your skills lie elsewhere. You should be here, or in Mesopotamia, especially, because there isn't a man to match you in knowledge of that part of the world. To be frank, I could also do with your help. I seem to have got myself into a bit of a situation and find myself in need of support. And you recall how difficult it is for me to ask for that from our time in Syria. How much simpler things seemed then, me with my red sash, you with your (fully deserved) disdain for our methods. What I wouldn't give to be back there, if I could just click my fingers. [REMOVED BY CENSOR] I am afraid I might have made rather a mess of things here. [REMOVED BY CENSOR] I am not sure I am that kind of person, not yet.

I am wondering if we can combine two things. Kitchener knows about my curiosity about this man W's luggage. [REMOVED BY CENSOR] Why has he gone to such great lengths to procure its return? I wonder if he can send a 'porter' with it for me to inspect it. [REMOVED BY CENSOR] What do you think?

As soon as you have completed your Red Cross business, why not contact Hogarth? He'll steer you right.

Things are afoot with him, I am certain, and I am equally sure he would be thrilled to have an offer from you. It would be marvellous to see you and even more wonderful to have that brain of yours applied to this situation.

I bought you a nobleman's ivory seal the other day. It's probably the only one you'll get from me this year, which is almost its only virtue. One wouldn't have bought it anywhere else, but in Cairo it was refreshing.

You'll have to come and collect it, though.

Your Dear Boy

TEL

Once he had finished the letter he took it down to reception and passed it to the concierge for posting. Then he caught a gharry to the Citadel, where he intended to spend the night in anonymity, occupying one of the bunks kept for soldiers in transit, just in case GHQ or the police came looking for him. For the moment, Lawrence was a fugitive in his own city.

Nineteen

Cairo

By popular consent, over the course of spring and summer 1915, Shepheard's gradually lost its pre-eminence as the finest hotel in Cairo. The influx of fresh officers meant that the terrace was often overcrowded, such that, despite the ornamental balustrade and pillars and the palm trees, it resembled Crewe Railway Station. The oriental salon inside was also subject to various high jinks, with drunken young men decorating the prominent breasts of the carved caryatids at the foot of the stairs – howling as if they were the first to ever think of such a thing – and sliding down the banisters.

Still, it continued to attract those who liked gossip and intrigue and to parade themselves to their fellow Europeans.

Lawrence, in uniform, sat across the street from the hotel in one of the larger cafés, hidden behind a copy of *Al-Ahram*. The lunch crowd were gathering on the terrace, drifting over

186

to their places in twos or threes, a good half-hour earlier than was usual. It was ninety in the shade; work was taking second place to long lunches, iced drinks, shaded verandahs and early G&Ts.

He saw Jepson from the Intelligence Section strolling down the street and snapped his paper back in position to cover his face. The people at GHQ were still looking for him, leaving increasingly exasperated messages at his usual haunts. He doubted there was any formal proceedings being taken as yet. You were given three days latitude before an unexplained AWOL became the more serious charge of desertion; he still had a few hours left.

Lawrence had just ordered a second coffee when he saw Count Jacques Spaark approaching Shepheard's. He was dressed in immaculate off-white linen, a black cane swinging at his side, a straw Panama on his head. He looked very dapper and, Lawrence noted, very pleased with himself. He was even whistling: the jaunty refrain of 'The Man Who Broke the Bank at Monte Carlo' drifted across the street.

Lawrence reached inside his jacket and checked that the Colt was in place and easily extracted. He had test fired it before he came to the café; he could feel the residual heat of its barrel through his undershirt and against his skin.

His gaze followed Sparkie as he moved past the doorman, up the stairs, through the tables and to one of the corner spots. There, two other Europeans stood to greet him. Hands were shaken, hats removed, drinks ordered. Within moments Sparkie's friends were guffawing at something the entertaining Belgian had said.

Give them a few minutes, Lawrence thought. Let them have their fun for a little longer. He forced himself to sip the fresh coffee, pleased that his hand was steady as he lifted the tiny cup to his mouth.

Lawrence checked his bill and left the appropriate coins and tip. He stood, adjusting the gun with his elbow to ensure it didn't slip from his waistband. He rolled up the newspaper and placed it under his arm, so his hand could discreetly rest on the weapon. Then he began the short walk across the road, pausing only for a passing gharry, his eyes never leaving the back of Sparkie's head.

The doorman saluted Lawrence as he mounted the steps. Lawrence returned it with a perfunctory poke at his cap's peak. The terrace was more crowded than it had appeared, with the tables pushed closer together than usual. As he squeezed between them, he upset a glass of lemonade, causing a bark of protest. He ignored it.

Sparkie turned to see what the commotion was, and his eyes met Lawrence's. The latter knew that Sparkie could read what was in them, because he began to rise to his feet. The Belgian's head moved quickly as he looked left and right for a way out.

There was none. He was cornered.

The Belgian was taller than Lawrence and in decent physical shape, but the Englishman had a steam of fury driving him forward. Lawrence jerked the gun from beneath his jacket, losing a button as he did so. There was a gasp from the nearest diners as the Colt appeared. Lawrence covered the last three feet in one bound, grabbed Sparkie's cravat and, cradling the butt of the pistol in his fist, landed a terrible blow between the Belgian's eyes. The man catapulted back into one of the pillars and there was a hollow ringing sound as his skull bounced off the metal.

Voices began to swirl around Lawrence and someone was yelling in his ear. He calmly raised the Colt and took aim at Spaark. The two dining companions scattered, upsetting more tables in their haste to get clear.

Lawrence held his right arm out straight and cocked the hammer of the automatic with his thumb. Just the lightest pull on the trigger was needed now. The Belgian was still leaning against the cast-iron pillar, his eyes shut. Lawrence's front sight hovered at the centre of his forehead. It would be a clean death, far cleaner than Munir's. More merciful than a murderer deserved.

The head slumped forward and Spaark began to slide down to the wooden floor.

'No,' shouted Lawrence, but the gunrunner continued to crumple, until he was coiled at the base of the pillar.

Lawrence had followed his downward progress with the barrel of the weapon, so it was still pointed at Sparkie's head, but he knew it was useless. He could not shoot an unarmed, unconscious man and the Belgian was out cold.

'Grab him!' someone exclaimed. 'Get the gun.'

Then, a shout of recognition. 'Lawrence! Good God, man!'

Rough hands grabbed Lawrence's arms and pulled him backwards. The pistol was twisted from his hands. 'Let's get you out of here before you are put on a charge. What the blazes are you doing? Have you gone troppo?'

The anger draining from him, his limbs growing heavy, Lawrence allowed himself to be dragged off the terrace and ejected from the hotel, where two military policemen bundled him away. The Shepheard's terrace slowly returned to normal, the diners pleased to have witnessed such an extraordinary scene, thrilled that they had a juicy story to take along to drinks that evening.

Following the fracas at Shepheard's, Lawrence was summoned before Colonel Gilbert Clayton, his commanding officer. Ronald Storrs sat in on the meeting. It was late afternoon, but still the outside temperature had climbed to over a hundred in the shade. Each of the three men in the room was sweating profusely despite the fans thumping away over their heads. It made for a tetchy, disagreeable atmosphere.

The colonel and Lawrence did not always see eye to eye. Bertie Clayton knew that the Arab question had to be addressed, and had long believed in a revolt against the Turks. However, he thought Lawrence's concept of a pan-Arab state dangerously romantic. 'You cannot alter the ways of centuries in a few years,' he liked to say to him. 'It would always be a nation of factions, Sunni against Shi'ite, tribe against tribe, brother against brother. Worse than Ireland.'

Still, Clayton's disagreements were usually amiable, but today he had left his geniality at home. The colonel launched straight into Lawrence with an attack on his dress, pointing to his stomach: 'Do that button up, man.' Lawrence showed the colonel that there was no fastening to be made, the button recently lost. 'Look at you. I don't understand, Lieutenant, what you thought you were doing. We work in Intelligence, lad, which behoves us to display some kind of discretion and, dare I say it, secrecy. To start public brawls—'

'It wasn't a brawl, sir. That implies two people were involved. The Belgian never got a punch in.'

Lawrence saw Storrs begin to smirk before he remembered himself. The Oriental Secretary ran a hand over his thinning hair and picked fluff from his tie.

Clayton leaned forward across his desk and narrowed his eyes. 'You can be very insubordinate, Lawrence.'

'That's not my intention, sir.'

'Then were you intending to shoot the Belgian?'

'It was at the back of my mind, sir. It stayed there, though.'

'So, you believe this Spaark to be an agent of the enemy.'

'Sir.'

'So, as a general rule, we should punch every known Turk spy on the nose, should we? Or perhaps just shoot them where they sit?'

'No, sir, it's not a recommended course of action.'

Clayton let his voice rise to full exasperation. 'So why did on earth you do it?'

'Personal reasons.'

Now the tone cracked. 'What?'

'He killed one of my informants.'

'A European? An Englishman?'

'Egyptian, sir.'

The noise he made showed how much he valued the life

of an Egyptian snitch. 'So, you thought it was worth exposing us for that, did you?'

'Yes, sir, I did. I wanted Spaark to know we were on to him. In retrospect, it might not have been a wisest course of action.'

The colonel leaned back and his voice became softer. 'Lawrence, I know you have been under some strain—'

'Not at all, sir. If you are referring to my brother, I am over that.'

Clayton shook his head. 'Are you suggesting that the death of your brother affected you less than the killing of an Egyptian?'

'They were not comparable, sir.'

'You're telling me. Lawrence, I want you to stop this running around Cairo pretending to be something you are not. Understand? You are an officer of the British Army. Your behaviour has been tolerated because Storrs here keeps telling me you are a genius. I've met geniuses in my time. It is another word for selfish, self-centred and dangerous people. You will confine yourself to reports, bulletins and map work.'

'I have some leave due, sir.'

Clayton's voice boomed with emphasis. 'Reports, bulletins and map work till I say otherwise. Understood?'

'Yes, sir.'

'And I want all of those letters you write to come through the censor. I know you've been bypassing the system by using the concierge at the Savoy.'

'Only for personal—'

'There is no personal correspondence in wartime. I have

had the last batch intercepted and forwarded here and censored. I know you've been prattling on to Hogarth and Bell and your other comrades-in-arms about the situation. Stop it now. And forget this Spaark business. It is no longer your concern. Captain Ford is taking over your duties with prisoners and contacts. Is that clear?'

Lawrence snapped back: 'It is, sir. Maps, reports and no more Spaarks from me.'

Clayton examined his face, looking once more for signs of disrespect, but it was like a china mask. 'Dismissed.'

As he left the room, stepping into the cooler marble of the corridor, Lawrence hesitated. Nobody looked his way, not the guards, the clerks or the Egyptian messengers. Eyes were downcast, mundane reports suddenly as riveting as any shilling shocker. All had heard the dressing down and, if they hadn't, word would soon get around. Cairo was more gossipy than the Garrick or Harcourt's at Westminster. Lawrence's indulgence had come to an end and his status was badly damaged.

He unsnapped his top button and walked off whistling 'Alexander's Ragtime Band', until hissed into silence by a major. He switched to a piece of Elgar. With the forced jauntiness of the condemned man, Lawrence ambled off to begin his sentence in the oppressive torpor of the map room.

Part Two

Twenty

Kent, England, 1915

The Rolls-Royce glided smoothly down the beech-lined drive of Broome Park. The chauffeur who had picked Quinn up from Canterbury station slowed the car to negotiate a sharp bend in the driveway. Here, a cunning gap in the trees allowed the visitor to appreciate the full splendour of the house. Quinn was a little disappointed, not with the theatre of the mansion's sudden appearance, but with the building itself. It was certainly imposing, a large brick-built mansion, but the roofline was so cluttered with gables and pediments, it looked more Dutch than English. And, since his time in South Africa, Quinn had harboured highly disagreeable feelings about anything with a Dutch or German heritage. He had always assumed the Secretary of War shared that view.

The Rolls slowed to a halt on the semi-circle of well-groomed gravel before the house. The driver opened the door for him and a manservant with tremendous white whiskers appeared at the entrance and nodded solemnly. Quinn was expected.

'If you'll follow me, sir.'

The interior of Broome Park was, as Quinn had anticipated, artfully crammed with foreign artefacts. Rugs and tapestries hung on the panelled walls, and a dozen enormous urns, amphorae and vases sat on the terrazzo floor. The Secretary had always been a voracious collector and a formidable customer. Rumour had it that whole streets in Karachi, Calcutta and Cairo would shut up shop on the mere rumour of his approach. He could browbeat and bully any merchant into parting with his finest items at cost or, often, less.

There came the frantic tap-tap of nails on a hard surface and three cocker spaniels burst from the rear of the house, yapping as they came.

'Gentlemen!' Whiskers scolded and, like admonished schoolchildren, the three dogs slithered to a halt. Tails wagged and tongues lolled expectantly and once their coats were ruffled, they slunk away once more. The Secretary had always loved dogs, more so than people, some said.

Whiskers threw open the door to a drawing room and announced in sonorous tones: 'Captain Harold Quinn.'

The room was light and airy, thanks to a large bay window that overlooked the grounds. There was less furniture in here, although two exquisite silk screens caught Quinn's eye. The Secretary for War was sitting behind a vast Regency desk, hardly an inch of it left uncovered by a spray of files and correspondence. As Quinn entered, the Secretary rose to his feet, and Quinn tried his best not to look too shocked at his former CO's appearance.

It was recognisably the same face that still stared from a million recruiting posters, the familiar wide-set eyes, apparently cold and hostile, although Quinn knew the forbidding aspect of his gaze was caused by glare-damage from the desert sun. His great moustache was a mixture of white and yellow from cigar smoke and no longer seemed the impenetrable barrier that it once was. Like the man himself, it looked droopy, tired and worn.

'Quinn!' Lord Horatio Herbert Kitchener held out his hand and Quinn took it. There was nothing feeble about the grip.

'Sir.'

'Can we get you something? Tea?'

Quinn turned to Whiskers. 'A glass of water, please.'

'Sit down, Harry, sit down. You look well.'

'You look tired, sir.'

Kitchener fixed him with those eyes and Quinn suddenly felt hot under his newly starched collar. Then the Secretary laughed. 'Never one to mince his words. I am tired, man. You can imagine why.'

'Sir.'

The war, as everybody knew, was not going well. The Germans had recently used chlorine gas at Ypres for the first time, an unwelcome escalation in the horror. Then there were the landings at the Dardanelles, a bold stroke that had slid into serious misadventure, with talk of many thousands of colonial troops slaughtered. And now there were Zeppelins over London, bombing the suburbs.

'Been in Liverpool, I hear? After the Fenians?'

Quinn related the story of his latest undercover mission for Vernon Kell, or 'K', his superior at MO5, the 'home' division of the Secret Service Bureau, knowing the Secretary would enjoy such an escapade. It was, just for him, an expansive version, colouring the incidents with an unusual number of adjectives and well-placed profanities and blasphemies, as well as a gunfight that would rival one of Tom Mix's Westerns. It seemed to relax the Secretary and he poured himself a whisky. Quinn refused to join him as politely as he could manage. He only drank at the far end of any mission, not the outset.

'Well, I'm sorry to drag you away from such high excitement. But it gave me the chance to have one last look at this old place. Sold, y'know. To some American.'

'That's a shame, sir. I know what it means to you.'

'We all have to make sacrifices.'

Now, Quinn sensed, they were getting to the nub, the part where Quinn discovered what his particular sacrifice would be. 'How can I be of assistance, sir?'

His water finally arrived and he drank. Whiskers asked if Quinn would be staying for luncheon and Kitchener, without referring to his guest, said he would. After he had gone, Quinn waited for the Secretary for War to continue. He knew his ex-CO wasn't a man for small talk. He sorted through the papers on his desk until he had isolated three documents. 'Harry, we have a problem. We have many problems, but this one might have your name etched on it. It concerns Bushire, Persia. You know it, I believe?'

'Somewhat,' Quinn replied, his insides twisting into a knot. Kitchener knew very well he was familiar with it. He had helped pick up the pieces after Quinn had come back from that godforsaken country, a miserable, broken man. It was Kitchener who had eased him into the Secret Service Bureau, saving him from the pit. 'As a civilian.'

Kitchener tossed one of the files over the table. 'I'll get you to read that after lunch. It's a dispatch from a fella called Noel. Captain Edward Noel. Political Officer. It concerns an attack on a number of British soldiers.' Kitchener grimaced. 'Quite barbaric. One of them was staked out in the desert and left to die. We have two soldiers and an engineer hideously murdered, then the party sent to investigate their disappearance also came under attack. Captain Noel survived; he says it was Tangistani tribesmen from Ahram. A bad lot.'

Quinn nodded.

'Particularly when they are armed with German machine guns. And Mauser rifles.'

Quinn recalled the locals carrying a rag-tag collection of weaponry, much of it highly antiquated or village-made. A Martini rifle was the best they could hope for in his day. 'The Hun are supplying them?'

'Indeed. According to Lawrence—' He spotted the quizzical look on Quinn's face. 'Chap in Cairo. GHQ. Good man. He thinks they swap the tribes' Martini-Henrys or Martini-Enfields for a modern Mauser. Then they ship the older weapons to places in the Middle East, places where they hope to cause us trouble. Such as Egypt.' Quinn knew Kitchener still had a soft spot for the country of the Pharoahs, not least because it had provided some of his finest antique pieces.

'Who is behind this? The Germans themselves or the Turks?'

'There is a name which keeps cropping up. Woss Moss.' He pronounced the opening consonant as a 'V'. 'Ring any bells?'

'Woss Moss? No.'

'They are mispronouncing it. Think Wassmuss.'

Quinn couldn't quite believe what he was hearing. 'Willie Wassmuss?'

'You know him, then?' Quinn shook his head and could see Kitchener was disappointed. 'Damn.' He stroked his moustache. 'Thought you'd know him.'

'Heard of him. Some of the women at the British consulate were rather taken with him. Quite dashing, so they said, and amenable. Good hand at bridge. He'd gone back to Germany by the time I had arrived.'

The Secretary made a grunting sound. Quinn wasn't sure whether this was because Kitchener had never been much of a bridge player or because the thought of there being a decent German was ridiculous. 'Well, he's not amenable any longer. He's a lot more trouble than that.'

'How so?'

Kitchener passed over another folder. Held within it was a series of crude, block-printed handbills.

'It's in Persian on that sheet. Arabic and Turkish on others.'

'How did you get this, sir?' Quinn asked him.

'A few months ago, Wassmuss was captured by a Khan sympathetic to us and held at the behest of Captain Noel. Wassmuss escaped by feigning sickness for his horse. But he was forced to leave all his baggage and his two companions. They've been dealt with; the luggage has been shipped here. Much of it was full of leaflets like that one. Incendiary stuff, I think you'll agree.'

'I never learned to read Arabic,' Quinn confessed. 'Or Persian.'

Kitchener glared at him, as if disappointed by the admission. 'Nor me. But, of course, I consulted a man who did. Would you like a summary?'

'If you wouldn't mind.'

'Hold on to your hat,' the Secretary for War said. 'Because you may be surprised to learn that the Kaiser has converted to Islam.'

Quinn had to smile at the thought.

'Not only that, he has made the hajj to Mecca.'

'Then he's a resourceful chap,' Quinn said, knowing this was ridiculous misdirection on the German's part.

Kitchener tapped the table with a forefinger to emphasise his point. 'These leaflets have been spread across Persia and Mesopotamia, along with doctored photographs of Kaiser Wilhelm wearing the sacred green turban of the hajji. I know it is hard to believe, but they have convinced many of the tribes that Germany is their true friend. Especially with Kaiser Hajji in power.'

'Slippery.'

'What we are worried about is that this man Wassmuss will

start a fire that will sweep across Persia, to Afghanistan and, eventually, threaten India.'

'Is that possible?'

'Lawrence thinks so. And Gertrude Bell.' Quinn nodded to show he knew of her. 'And John Buchan. The writer. You've heard of him? Well, he's not just a scribbler. Fine mind for intrigue. He says there is a dry wind blowing through the East and the parched grasses await the spark. Flowery, but accurate. And Hogarth, he's taken a look. Says he agrees with Lawrence. Of course, we all know that the war will be won or lost in Europe. No doubt about that. But if we have to drain manpower from the front to shore up the East, even for a few weeks, it might just weaken us enough to allow a German breakthrough. And then . . .' He cleared his throat and picked up a wickedly pointed letter-opener, which he turned over in his hands. 'Harry, it might seem the British Empire is built on solid granite, but believe you me, it sits on the most porous of sand at the moment and the right action in the East could wash away its foundations.'

'Is it really that serious?' Quinn asked. 'Persia is something of a backwater. A few rifles—'

'It is not just the rifles. He is preaching Jehad.' Kitchener spat the word. 'You know what that is? Holy war against the infidel. And because they believe the Kaiser has converted, that doesn't mean against Germany. It means against us. If it takes hold in Mesopotamia, there are the oil fields to consider. Lose the oil, we lose the damned Navy. Lose the ships, we lose the war.'

The British navy had converted from coal to oil in 1909

and much of the fuel came out of the refinery at Abadan, the port just below Basra in Mesopotamia. It was worryingly close to Persia.

Quinn knew that Kitchener already had something in mind for him. He had best show willing, even if it might involve a trip back to Persia. 'How can I help?'

'We are returning the bags. With a chaperone. I hope you'll agree to be the messenger who returns this apparently precious cargo to Persia.' Kitchener leaned forward over the desk and steamed in like a Dreadnought. 'Let me spell it out for you, Harry. Wassmuss can't be allowed to continue and I don't want him a martyr locked up in prison, where they might take more hostages to try and free him. I want you to deal with him in the appropriate manner at the first opportunity.' He gave a thrust with his letter-opener, as if spearing an opponent. 'Make no mistake, Harry. We would dearly love to know why he values his bloody bags so highly, and we will attempt to discover the reason, but ultimately, we want Wassmuss dead.' He flicked the pile of reports on his desk. 'All these people, they talk a good war, but men like Lawrence aren't up to the job. Too intellectual. It needs someone who knows what has to be done and will do it without flinching. And we think that man is you.'

Twenty-one

London

Billy Stubbs, the one-eyed old soldier who ran Whitehall Court apartments for the Secret Service Bureau, knocked on Quinn's door at seven-thirty on the day after his audience with Kitchener and delivered him two boiled eggs, tea and a copy of *The Times*. Quinn had been up till past midnight poring over maps of southern Persia, reading signals and dipping into a John Buchan book called *Prester John* and was sound asleep.

'You're spoiling me, Stubbs,' Quinn said as the batman laid out the tray. He sat up in the bed, wondering if it was the new curtains that gave the room an odd, silvery glow,

Stubbs noticed his puzzled expression. 'Strangest thing, sir, there's a fog.'

The batman whisked back the drapes, and, sure enough, instead of daylight there was a soft, diffused glow, the feeble rays of a defeated sun.

'At this time of year?'

'People are saying it's the Zeps, sir. A new secret weapon. To paralyse London.'

'Or it could just be the weather.'

Stubbs raised a sceptical eyebrow. He always preferred to believe the worst.

The bell to the apartment block rang and while Stubbs went off to investigate, Quinn tucked into his breakfast. He had just decapitated the second egg when the voice tube squawked. He unplugged it and heard Stubbs's cold, mechanical voice, not all of the effect due to the instrument. 'There is a Mrs Wake downstairs in the hall, sir.' His voice dropped to a croak. 'Said she is expected.' He pictured Stubbs in the little cubicle where the voice tube was situated, making sure he wasn't overheard. He would be treating the situation as if it were an invasion of vermin.

'Thank you, Stubbs.'

'Trouble, sir?' Stubbs asked knowingly.

'Not the kind you're obviously thinking of. Business.'

'She's one of us?' There was horror in his voice.

'A friend of the service.'

Stubbs made a growling noise that Quinn interpreted as a perfectly understandable dismay that any woman should be involved in espionage, even on the fringes of MO5.

'Would you please ask Mrs Wake to wait for me; tell her I shall be along shortly.'

'Very well, sir.'

After dressing, he found Mrs Wake pacing the hallway impatiently. The woman was somewhere around thirty, but he had never been very good at estimating women's ages. He usually settled for 'older than me' or 'younger than me', and he reckoned Mrs Wake scraped into the latter category. Just. She was dressed in the current fashion of pastel stripe, with a high frilly collar under her chin and a fulsome skirt that reached to her ankles. She was pretty enough under her hat, but her face was knitted into an expression of alarming intensity.

'We're late, Captain,' she admonished him with a wag of her gloved finger. 'And the streets are choked. There have been developments. We must hurry.'

Quinn, who did not appreciate being told to hurry by anyone, least of all a woman, followed her out into a city swamped in an ethereal half-light. He could smell sulphur and the bitterness of a nearby brewery. His throat began to constrict. He didn't, however, forget his manners and he opened the rear of the Wolseley car for Mrs Wake, then climbed in the other side and slammed the door, pulling his scarf up to his mouth to filter as many of the fumes as possible. Mrs Wake adjusted her skirts then tapped on the glass partition and the driver pulled away.

The car's acetylene lamps barely penetrated the fog and progress was slow, with the driver cursing as worried cyclists and spooked horses seemed to lurch through the impenetrable wall of smoke. Buses and trams passed like leviathans, grumbling on imperiously. If it was a secret weapon aimed at crippling London, it was rather a good one.

'This is very strange,' Quinn said, leaning forward and pulling back the sliding partition. 'Quite odd.'

'Innit, sir?' replied the driver over his shoulder. 'Bit nerve wracking. I'm not Miss Bell's usual driver. More used to South London.'

'You're doing very well,' he offered.

'Thank you, sir.'

'Came on last night,' Mrs Wake said. 'Around two. We were in the middle of a WPS patrol and zip, in it rolled, like sea mist. It was after the Zeppelins had been over, too, so at first we thought it was poison gas. You can imagine the panic. But it's just an unseasonable peculiar.'

It wasn't the idea of a summer fog that surprised Quinn. 'You're WPS?'

'Yes.' It was said with a challenge: what of it, sir?

Quinn smiled at the thought of what Stubbs might say about that. The Women's Police Service patrolled cities at night looking for lewd and immoral behaviour, especially by wives and girlfriends whose husbands or sweethearts were at the front. Women, the WPS thought, were sliding into degeneracy while their menfolk died in the trenches. 'Must keep you busy.'

Her faced pinched with irritation. 'That's not why we do it, Captain Quinn.'

'No, I would imagine not. But people can get up to mighty mischief in a good fog.'

She glared at him and lapsed into silence once more and they spent the rest of the journey west through a muffled London staring out of their respective windows, each thinking the other an insufferable example of their sex.

Gertrude Bell's house on Sloane Street was typically English on the outside, right down to the window boxes and hanging baskets, although they contained strange, unfamiliar flowers and, in the case of the boxes, odd lumps of stone, giving them the appearance of miniature rock gardens. Inside, however, was much more exotic, akin to something from Richard Burton's travelogues. Marie, Miss Bell's French maid, showed them in and led Quinn to the day room at the rear of the house. Mrs Wake excused herself and retreated into the hallway. Quinn heard the sound of her feet on the polished wood treads of the staircase.

Quinn looked around the room for clues to the owner's personality. There was a low carved table with three books on it; one Miss Bell's own *The Desert and the Sown*, Hogarth's *The Penetration of Arabia*, and *Arabia Deserta* by Charles Doughty. The room was dominated by two huge well-stuffed red divan couches and, apart from two small hunting scenes and a rack of foils and an épée – did Miss Bell fence? – the walls were all but obscured by carpets. He examined one of them, finding himself lost in the swirls of colour and the menagerie of animals that skipped across it.

The voice over his shoulder made him start. 'Captain Quinn, sorry to have kept you waiting. Lovely, isn't it?' Miss Gertrude Bell had entered quietly, gliding on huge woollen slippers the size of a guardsman's bearskin. Apart from these strange balls of fur, she was dressed all in white, but for a string of black pearls, and her red hair was clipped up with a bizarre contraption of leather and bamboo. He guessed her to be in her mid-forties and quite striking for a woman of her age, although he could tell from the shadows under her eyes and a rather drawn expression that she had been through unhappy times or a recent illness.

'How do you do, Miss Bell? Yes, it's lovely,' he agreed, looking back at the wall hanging.

'An eighteenth-century copy of a seventeenth-century Keman. Indo-Persian, probably from Agra.'

'Too precious to just walk over, no doubt.'

Miss Bell gave a small cough and he looked down at his feet, where a fierce tiger stared back at him. He was standing on an equally striking rug.

'I think things of beauty should be used, not put in museums,' she said. 'Otherwise, look what happens. You get art galleries.'

Quinn fell into it when he asked: 'What's wrong with art galleries?'

'They are little more than zoos for paintings. Evolution did not spend millions of years for its beautiful products to be put into cages, Captain Quinn. Art was never painted to be put in a gallery. Nobody ever created a canvas with the desire to be hung in a room with two dozen other paintings clamouring for attention.' She pointed to a miniature of a Nabob above the mantelpiece. 'They are intended for homes, whether a humble apartment or a Maharajah's palace. I find museums and galleries most depressing. Context is everything, don't you find?' Before he could answer one way or another she said, 'Please sit. Farid will bring us some tea shortly.'

Quinn took a corner of the other divan. 'Mrs Wake said there were developments.'

'Indeed. Ah, Farid, there you are.'

Farid was a handsome lad with delicate features and lush, dark eyelashes heavy, it seemed, with kohl. He wore a long

white tunic and the baggy *sharwal* trousers with a low crotch,
a fringed silk scarf, casually knotted at the neck; his feet were
clad in curved Arabic slippers and his head covered by a *labbade*
felt hat around which a halo of elaborately wound cloth had
been created, so that it resembled an enormous French pastry.
He arrived carrying a heavy brass tray loaded with metal pots
and cups. Quinn caught the whiff of mint. He had hoped for
Typhoo. His appetite for mint tea had been severely curtailed
during his time in Persia, when he must have drunk an ocean
in the *Ta'arof*, the ritualised protracted formal conversation
that preceded even the most trivial business deal in that part
of the world. The sparring was accompanied by mint tea or
sweet, syrupy coffee and endless, tiny, featherlight pastries.
Quinn had always found it a trial.

Farid laid the tray on a thick teak coffee table and poured
each of them a cup each from a great height without, it
appeared, spilling a drop. Quinn accepted his drink and waited
until the servant had withdrawn before he asked: 'Is Mrs Wake
joining us?'

'No, she has some tasks to perform for me. She is a busy
woman. Quite striking, don't you think?'

'She seems very pleasant.'

She detected the hint of insincerity. 'No great eye for the
ladies, Mr Quinn?'

'Not married women.' At least, he thought, not busybody
ones like her.

'Oh, don't worry about that. Mr Wake went down on the
Titanic.'

'Good Lord.'

'Not sure Mrs Wake was too bothered. No, that's a terrible thing to say. I am a great admirer of men, Mr Quinn, but Joseph Wake was a fool. And not just in his choice of ship.'

'So Mrs Wake busies herself being a policewoman?'

'I hope you aren't one of those men who think society is falling apart because women drive ambulances and make bombs.' Her eyes had hardened, daring Quinn to confirm her suspicions.

'No, not at all.' He really didn't want to get into a discussion on the role of women. He knew his attitudes were most likely out of step with hers and wouldn't be changed in a hurry, no matter how many women threw themselves under racehorses. 'But Mrs Wake thinks that the moral fabric of the country is being ripped asunder, after dark.'

'Does she, indeed?' The sparkle in her voice suggested he'd missed something crucial about Mrs Wake, but he couldn't imagine what. A priggish widow, sour before her time, summed her up perfectly as far as he was concerned. 'You know Persia, I hear. What do you think of the country?'

'There is no beauty in Persia,' Quinn said quietly, quoting from memory, 'but in the name. There are some parts that offer a few sights, pleasant to the eye, but for the most part it burns and bakes and festers.'

'Very eloquent.'

'It wasn't me who said that,' he confessed.

'I should hope not. It's completely, utterly, stupidly false.' She said it with a force that took him aback. 'I'm sorry—'

'So you should be. It's an ignorant, doltish thing to quote. Do you know the poetry of Hafiz?'

213

'No.'

Her green eyes blazed for a second. 'Then you are not qualified to talk on beauty or on Persia.'

Quinn didn't answer. He knew he was more than qualified to comment on the cruelty of the place. What little faith he had in God or humanity had been extinguished there. He also knew when to fight and when to back down. He had rubbed at something raw and it was best left alone. 'Mrs Wake said there had been developments,' he repeated.

'Yes,' she confirmed. 'The German has nominated a place for the exchange of luggage.'

'Where?'

'A town called Dalak.'

Quinn shook his head. 'Then we say no. It's not a town, it's a death trap.'

'How so?'

'It's at the end of a long valley. One way in, one way out, easily sealed. Not Dalak.'

'Then where?'

'A place of our choosing.'

'I think you mean of your choosing, Mr Quinn. Although a large part of me wishes I could come with you and help.'

Oh, no you don't, he thought. Travelling with women, even one like Miss Bell, brought with it certain conventions and responsibilities that Quinn couldn't countenance. Not if he was to fulfil his mission.

He was more than a little relieved when she added: 'But the Red Cross Missing and Wounded Office needs me here for another few months.' Then she snapped at him: '*Safar*

214

Bekheir.' And waited for his non-existent response. 'I just wished you *bon voyage*. You don't speak Persian?'

'Nor Arabic.'

Her eyes rolled heavenwards. This woman expected a lot, Quinn thought. Or perhaps no more than she expected of herself. 'The Tangistan, Wassmuss's main allies, speak mostly Persian. It would be useful if you did too. And, of course, Arabic would be a bonus, although it defeated me, too, for some years. There are at least three sounds that are impossible for the European throat. For some time, I had to hold my tongue with a finger to get some of the pronunciation right, which is hardly a polite way to converse. But Persian, that is a lovely language. How long were you there?'

Quinn drank his tea. He didn't like speaking about his time in that country, but it seemed churlish to refuse to share this simple information. 'For a year. I had a position with Lyman Brothers. It didn't end well.'

'I'm sorry to hear that. Did Kitchener tell you about Lawrence?'

Quinn made to help himself to a refill of tea, but Farid was there in an instant, repeating his pouring from shoulder-height trick. 'He mentioned the man. Do you know him?'

She looked thoughtful for a second, as if she, too, was deciding how much to divulge to a stranger. 'I've met him, yes. At Carchemish in Syria some years ago. The digging methods were prehistoric, and they found very little, but Lawrence himself is an interesting boy, if a trifle eccentric. Used to wear Arab slippers and a red sash around his waist, to show he was a bachelor, as the locals did. Tremendous energy. He battered me with Byzantine, Roman, Crusader, Hittite and French architecture until I cried mercy. But he has a sense of mischief. You know, because of that blasted sash, the locals thought I had come as his prospective bride, but Lawrence told them after I had left he considered me too plain to marry!'

She let out a shriek of laughter and despite himself Quinn coloured slightly. It was a brave story for an unmarried woman of her age to tell against herself.

'Let me warn you of one thing. There are some who don't take to Lawrence. Yet I find him serious and intelligent and able to talk to me on an equal level, without either side being condescending. That is rare in an Englishman.' Her voice darkened. 'However, I know of those in Cairo who consider him belligerent and capable of sudden acts of violence. I myself sensed a strange inner turmoil I never got to the bottom of.'

Quinn didn't think this sounded at all promising. He was glad the man Lawrence wouldn't be coming to Persia. After all, he was a sifter of dirt, not a soldier.

'Now, tell me, Captain Quinn. Did you have a large break-fast?'

'Reasonably. Why?'

But Gertrude Bell just gave another of her puckish smiles.

Twenty-two

Farnborough, England, 1915

Captain Harold Quinn did not consider himself a feeble man. He had faced battle-hardened Boers, enraged water buffalo, armed Fenians and truculent Persian tribesmen – not to mention the time his wife jokingly tried to stab him with a letter opener and tripped, nearly piercing his heart – but already his stomach had cramped so hard he thought he might soil his underlinen. His bladder felt the size of a Zeppelin and he knew that if he spoke, his voice would sound more like one of those musical saws they played at the Gaiety, rather than anything recognisably human. He was very, very scared. Which was causing his companions no end of mirth.

The strange morning fog was long gone and it was a sparklingly clear day, the sky dotted with clouds that looked like fluffy scones. Quinn was standing with Miss Bell and Farid, the manservant, who stood five paces back from his mistress. Behind them were the hangars of the Royal Flying Corps, each containing a collection of biplanes and monoplanes, a jumble of various types, from antique Bleriots to a tattered Voisin. On the concrete stand next to the hangars stood a proud row of six of the new Scout Ds, ready for dispatch to the front.

But all eyes were on the plane already in the sky, which was twisting and turning like a startled gnat, the daredevil – another word for insane, Quinn thought – pilot almost standing it on its wing edge. It was a strange beast, a 'pusher', that is with the propeller at the rear of the fuselage, behind wings held together by a cat's cradle of wires.

'Marvellous. Marvellous.' A tall, lean man with his gaze fixed firmly on the sky walked around the perimeter towards them, commentating as if it were a cricket match. 'Very sharp there. Oh, well done. Well, done.'

Miss Bell held on to her hat as the plane twisted on its axis and dived towards the group, roaring over their heads in a stream of hot gas and fumes. Quinn was nonplussed to discover he was the only one who had ducked.

The newcomer, whose face seemed to be a mass of nervous ticks, announced himself in a high, fluting voice. 'Geoffrey DeHavilland.'

'It's quite splendid, DeHavilland,' said Miss Bell. 'Well done.'

'It'll have to be to last more than five minutes against the Fokkers,' said DeHavilland to her. 'And not everyone can fly an aircraft like that. Precious few, in fact.'

Quinn had been told by Miss Bell that the Airco BE2

currently acting like a circus tumbler was the great hope for the air battles to come, the match for the increasingly mythic 'interrupter' Fokkers that were blasting the RFC from the skies over France.

'Who is going up?' asked DeHavilland.

'Me,' Quinn croaked and he could see Miss Bell laughing at his untypical trepidation.

'It's great fun,' he said. 'You'll see things you wouldn't believe.'

Like my insides, Quinn thought glumly. Why was he there? When it became clear what was expected of him, he'd asked if this was really, really necessary and had been told it was. All would be explained in due course. He'd rather face a horde of the most villainous Tangistani than ride in a machine held together by twine and good hope.

DeHavilland clapped him on the shoulder. 'You couldn't have a better introduction than with Dickie Daniels.' Quinn assumed this was the pilot whose recklessness they were witnessing. 'Wonderful chap. It's so stupid they wouldn't let him back in the RFC after his accident.'

Accident? What accident? Quinn wanted to scream. Only pride stopped him grabbing DeHavilland by the lapels and demanding more information. As he watched, the BE2 finally stopped acting like it was suffering from an aeronautical version of St Vitus's dance and came in for an approach.

The plane touched down with a thump, bounced, and then spun towards them. This time Quinn held his nerve as it taxied to within twenty feet of them and then, at the last moment, flipped left, coming to a standstill. He could feel the heat from the engine, smell the fuel and hot metal. And something else. Quinn sniffed the air, trying to place it.

'Castor oil,' said DeHavilland. 'It's the lubricant. Brilliant stuff, but with the engine in front of the pilot, he gets covered in the stuff. And you know what happens if he swallows it? It being a cure for constipation, and all.'

It took a moment for Quinn to catch on and he curled his nose in disgust. 'Really?'

'Occupational hazard. Don't worry, engine's behind you on this one. Trousers'll be quite safe.'

The propeller seemed to stutter and the wooden blades slowly appeared from the blur. A mechanic ran forward and chocked the wheels. After busying himself with switches for a few seconds, the pilot nimbly hopped out, removed his helmet, and walked across to the spectators. Quinn scanned him for any obvious signs of damage from this 'accident' but he seemed quite fit on casual inspection.

Daniels was a shade under six feet, with a thick thatch of almost chocolate-brown hair, flattened from the pressure of his helmet. His face was covered with specks of dirt and insects, but everything else was dwarfed by a wide, dazzling grin. 'Well, that was fun. It's much better with the extra stays, no wing twist at all. Well, hardly any.' He addressed all this to DeHavilland before turning to the others, peeling off his right glove as he did so. 'I'm Dickie Daniels.' He shook hands with each of them. 'So, who is the sacrificial lamb?'

Quinn raised a finger.

'Excellent.' He reached over and took off Quinn's trilby, passing it to DeHavilland. 'You'll need some goggles and a helmet. I'll get them for you. And I'd empty your pockets, if I were you.'

'Right.' And my bladder, he thought, but it was too late for that. When he went off, Quinn turned to Miss Bell and snapped: 'I don't quite understand all this. I can't fly all the way to Persia.'

'You never know,' she said.

Daniels returned, whistling, and proffered the shiny goggles and helmet. 'Here you are, slip these on. Just give that wallet to Miss Bell, she looks trustworthy enough. Sure it'll still be there when you get back to earth.'

When I get back to earth? *If* I get back, Quinn thought glumly.

Reluctantly, he brought out the final item that might cause problems in the air, his SSB issue Smith & Wesson Pocket pistol. Miss Bell accepted it with a grimace, as if he were handing over a small black sphere with a fuse and the word 'bomb' written on it.

The plane was a proper full two-seater, with the observer sitting low down in the front and the pilot on a raised seat behind him. 'Normally, you'd have a machine gun, old boy,' Daniels said. 'But we'll pass on that today. Don't want you shooting up half of Hampshire in your excitement. Ready? Here.' He made a cradle with interlocked fingers for Quinn. As he stepped into it, he was virtually tossed into the cockpit.

The plane rocked and twisted with each movement he made. He felt like a rhinoceros sitting in a wicker chair, liable to crush it at any moment. He'd been in dugout canoes that felt more stable. It bounced even more when Daniels climbed in. 'Nice and snug?'

'Yes.' Quinn cleared his throat and tried again. 'Yes, fine.'

Daniels laughed. 'Look, there's nothing to it. Put that belt across you there. Fasten the buckle. Is it tight? Right-o. Look at your feet. The copper cylinder? Fire extinguisher. Just in case. All set? Contact!'

There was a pause where nothing happened. Quinn was aware of a high-pitched whine and the smell of castor oil was making him queasy. Then there came a bang, a stutter and a jerk. Noise overwhelmed him, and a gale seemed to be sucked into his face. Daniels squeezed his shoulder and he looked over at Miss Bell and the others. Arms were raised in something that looked much like a last goodbye.

'Bloody hell,' Quinn muttered to himself. 'Give me an army of Fenians any day.'

'What was that?'

'Nothing.'

'Right. Off we go.'

The machine started forward then swung round and back, yawing in a sickening fashion. Quinn risked turning round to look at Daniels, who was intent on the controls. Now the engine pitch intensified and the little plane rumbled over on to the grass.

As the speed was increased, he could see the buildings and nearest people start to blur, like they did from an express train. The engine noise became more and more frantic, until it sounded like it must explode. Now it was hard to focus, as hangars, houses and trees bled into each other, as if a kineto-scope had got jammed at the wrong rate of revolutions.

Then, the rumbling and juddering stopped and, with a slightly soggy leap, the plane left the ground, crabbing as it did so. Quinn had the unsettling sensation of moving through the air sideways. He gripped the rim of the fuselage in horror as the earth fell away. But with the smudging caused by the acceleration gone, everything locked back into focus.

There came the squeak of control levers and moving lines. Parts of the wing flapped about and the plane corrected itself. Now it was flying straight. Quinn decided to concentrate on the lip of the cockpit, not to look down or up. As they rose through the sky, invisible hands seemed to buffet the plane, pushing it this way and that.

'Only rough up to a thousand,' yelled Daniels. 'Soon clear it.'

A thousand what? Feet? Miles per hour? He became aware that the fabric on the wings rippled and snapped disconcertingly in the slipstream, like a living, breathing skin.

'Finest Irish linen,' yelled Daniels, reading his mind. 'Tough as old boots.'

Quinn closed his eyes and felt a prod on the back of his neck.

'Don't do that, old boy, you'll miss everything. Look down. Go on.'

Quinn's mouth was terribly dry but he peeked over the edge and almost snatched his head away in terror. The fields of the countryside were intricate multi-hued patches the size of a postage stamp and they were shrinking further as the

plane climbed up and up. The aerodrome resembled something from a model village; the church steeples were pointed
candlesnuffers and the people were no bigger than walking
full stops. Then something odd happened.

Quinn found himself laughing. And when he craned his
neck once more and looked at Daniels, he was laughing too,
in collusion.

'It's quite a sight, isn't it?'

The novice nodded, a childish excitement flooding through
him. Quinn's brain was telling him this was dangerous illu-
sionary madness, that it could only be sheer willpower which
was keeping the aeroplane aloft. But he felt stupidly safe, and
elated by his conquest of the sky. It was no scarier than a
ferris wheel or a coaster ride at a funfair. Or being an undercover spy.

'Turning.'

An unwelcome crushing fear returned as the wings dipped
and he felt as if they were about to flip over. But Daniels
coaxed the plane round gently until they were over the village
of Farnborough itself. It was amazing how you could see man's
impact on the landscape, the roads carved through hillsides,
the artificially straight hedgerows, and the ploughs at work
in the fields. It made him feel proud. Then something odd
caught his eye.

'What's that?' Quinn asked.

'What?'

'That blob. On the ground.'

'It's a shadow. Of a cloud.'

Of course it was. Quinn shook his head in disbelief. He

could spot them, right across the landscape now, irregular dark splashes of grey. And he could see birds, gliding through the air below him. He was higher than the birds in the sky!

'Turning again. You want to try some loops?'

Once more his aerial courage was revealed as fleeting. 'Not unless you want to see what I had for breakfast.' Now he understood Miss Bell's warning.

Daniels let the nose drop and Quinn felt his vitals push up through his body. Something rose in his throat and he waved his arms, silently pleading for mercy.

'You'll be all right. Mr DeHavilland builds a good machine.'

'I can see that. But I might have had enough now.'

'You sure?' Daniels sounded surprised. 'Only been up a few minutes.'

'Don't want to spoil me.'

Daniels let out a long laugh that merged with the thrum of the engines.

The landing seemed slow and ponderous right up to the very last moment when the ground rushed at them and Quinn was jolted so hard he bit his tongue. Now he was down safely, a tang of iron in his mouth not withstanding, he felt an even bigger rush of adrenaline, a heady delight that he had done it and survived. How many people in the country had experienced heavier-than-air flight, had seen the toytown world from above, who knew about cloud shadows? Not many. He was a member of a very elite band. And still alive, to boot.

As they taxied back to the hangar, Quinn said: 'Daniels, DeHavilland mentioned something about an accident. What kind of accident did you have?'

'Oh, that. Shot down while bombing the marshalling yards at Marville. Still got a bullet in the back somewhere, too tricky to remove. Managed to get back behind our lines, but the old girl was fatally wounded. I crash landed. Walked away, though. Always a bonus.'

'That's why they kept you out of the RFC? Because you wrecked an aeroplane?'

Daniels laughed. He put a hand to his mouth and spat out his teeth. 'Good Lord, no,' he said gummily, 'it's just that you can't fly in the RFC with false teeth. Which is why I work with Mr DeHavilland for the moment.'

They seemed to slither to a halt, and as the engine stopped Quinn became aware of a humming in his ears that felt like it was settling in for a good few hours. He lifted off the goggles and helmet and, as gracefully as he could manage, jumped down on to the solid ground once more. His limbs felt terribly heavy and he was aware that clenching his buttocks for the best part of twenty minutes had left a strange ache in his groin.

Miss Bell and DeHavilland applauded as Quinn walked on to the concrete hangar apron, and he gave a theatrical bow. He wasn't used to being the centre of attention, preferring work that was done in shadows, but he had to admit he had enjoyed the whole experience. He just had no desire to repeat it.

'Now,' he said to Miss Bell with as much force as he could muster. 'Perhaps you will tell me what all this little show has been about.'

* * *

After the flight, they adjourned to a small officers' mess, where Miss Bell took them to a discreet corner and Farid waited at the door. Neither DeHavilland nor Daniels joined them.

'You were wondering about the flying lesson. Kitchener's idea. It was just to demonstrate the power of the machine. So that you don't think what I am about to suggest is complete madness. I have to say, Daniels let you off pretty lightly. Usually gives new johnnies a good old shaking.'

'I think he thought I might do something unpleasant in his cockpit.'

'Quite. Anyway, it was no idle joyride, Captain. There are two complete examples of DeHavilland's plane already crated up, on the high seas en route to Persia as we speak. They will eventually join up with Mesopotamia Half-Flight of 30th Squadron, Royal Flying Corps. Which left Melbourne some weeks ago. This will eventually be the backbone of the Royal Desert Corps. And believe you me, they'll take pilots with dentures.'

'What has this got to do with Wassmuss?'

'What do you think?' she asked

Quinn barely managed to keep his tongue civil. He wasn't used to such dances around the facts. 'I'm damned if I know.'

'We cannot land you from the sea at Bushire.' That pointed 'we' told Quinn all he needed to know. Thanks to Kitchener, this woman was now his spymaster. Or, more accurately, spymistress. 'It is locked in tight by Tangistan, with machine guns and, thanks to the gendarmes, our own field guns. But we can at Banda Abbas and then we can fly you to Jam – queer name, but it's a real place – to rendezvous with someone who will fill you in on the situation.'

'Fly? By air.'

'Of course by air,' Miss Bell confirmed. 'The first time a British force, conventional or otherwise, has ever been moved into position by aircraft. Exciting, eh?'

Not the word Quinn would have chosen. He could well believe Kitchener was behind all this. The man loved anything new-fangled. As a young officer he'd once almost been court-martialled for hitching a ride in a French observation balloon over a battlefield. 'It seems a remarkable amount of effort. Couldn't we just take a team of horses? Or camels?'

Miss Bell laughed at that. 'It'll take days – weeks, compared to aircraft. Don't worry, there will be fine horses when you get to Jam, and friendly faces.'

Quinn, used to working alone these past months, was instantly suspicious. 'What friendly faces?'

'Captain Edward Noel.'

'The man who let Wassmuss escape?' Quinn sneered.

'Never underestimate a soldier's desire to make good on such a setback. Noel is one of our best men. He will be ready with intelligence, horses, camels, guides and a strategy for exchange. And once that has happened, he can get you close enough to Wassmuss to, um, fulfil your mission. We have one more piece of essential preparation before you go off to meet with Lawrence and let him examine the luggage.'

Quinn voiced a question that had been nagging at him for some time. 'What exactly does this Lawrence think he can discover that cryptology and security sections can't?'

Miss Bell sighed. 'That is no concern of yours. You will be stopping off in Cairo for a few days anyway en route to Persia.

There is no harm in letting Lawrence take a look. But first, we must complete your preparation.' Her eyes sparkled with amusement. 'You need to learn some Arabic and Persian if you are to be of use to us.'

'I don't have much time.'

'You will on board the ship.'

Quinn imagined long days locked in his cabin, struggling to master a foreign tongue. 'I shall do my best.'

'You shall also have a tutor,' she beamed. 'I know a superb one. You'll be pleased to hear that Mrs Wake is fluent in both languages.'

Quinn felt his heart plunge into his boots.

Twenty-three

At sea

The SS *Medina* was an M-Class Peninsular & Oriental Steam Navigation Company vessel that had been used to take King George V and Queen Mary to Bombay, Calcutta and Delhi in 1911, where the king was proclaimed Emperor of India. Now, refitted with three classes and steerage, it ploughed the Tilbury-Lisbon-Gibraltar-Malta-Cairo-Karachi-Bombay route.

Although travelling on the ship as a civilian, Quinn had been told that War Office rules applied to men appointed On Special Duty: officers went First Class, warrant officers and sergeants Second, and other ranks Third Class. As a captain, he was entitled to First, as was Mrs Wake, at Gertrude Bell's insistence. Her argument was irrefutable; there was no way she could give lessons with the restrictions that separated the classes on board, so hang the expense.

Still, the Bay of Biscay made no exceptions or exclusion for any class: all were equally queasy by the second day. There was a vile swell running that didn't seem able to settle. Every time the ship's captain thought he had its measure, the wind and the current appeared to shift, with the result that the ship wallowed its way south.

Quinn spent much of it on deck, even when the day darkened and brought a stinging rain squall, because he found the heat of the cabin and the faint aroma of tar and oil upset his stomach more than the bite of salt and spray on his face.

When the vessel finally slipped from the grip of the worst of the weather and had settled into a relatively calm passage, Mrs Wake appeared on the promenade deck after breakfast. She carried a white parasol and wore a hat tied under her chin, double protection against any sun darkening her skin. The rest of her was encased in a high-necked silk blouse and a deep plum-coloured woollen skirt. She seemed fresh-faced and rested, and looked as if she had been for a stroll in St James's Park, rather than confined to her cabin for the best part of four days.

'Captain Quinn, how are you enjoying our voyage?'

'Mrs Wake.' His hand went to his head, ready to raise his hat before he realised he didn't have one on. It was a strange, naked feeling. 'I feared you'd fallen overboard.'

'Feared or hoped?'

Quinn banged the rail melodramatically. 'I would have demanded we turn around and scour the oceans.'

'How gallant.'

He looked out at the surging Atlantic, imagining being a

lost speck out there. 'Well, Miss Bell insisted you carry the banker's draft. So I'd have had to have found you.'

'How practical.'

Quinn wasn't entirely joking about the importance of the money. In Cairo she would visit the Anglo-Egyptian bank, where she would be furnished with six thousand pounds' worth of gold sovereigns to help smooth his way in Persia. Britain may have come off the Gold Standard when war was declared, but its sovereigns and half-sovereigns were still the universal lubricant when it came to commerce, bribery and war. He had calculated that his purse would weigh one hundred and eight pounds; a mule load. A mule worth murdering for, he reminded himself.

She, too, looked out at the churning grey-green Atlantic and pictured a soul lost in its pitiless vastness. 'Little chance of finding anyone out there, with or without a banker's draft, I would imagine.'

'Yes. I was sorry to hear about your husband. Has it not made you rather disinclined to be . . .' He indicated the expanse of ocean.

'I avoid routes with icebergs,' she said tartly. 'As he should have. We are behind with your lessons, Captain. I suppose you've forgotten everything we did?'

'Of course not. *Man englesi hastam.*'

One quizzical eyebrow went up independent of the other – an interesting little trick, Quinn thought. 'I don't think they'll have any trouble spotting you are English.'

'I have kept to my studies, Mrs Wake.' He pulled out a small, crimson leather-bound volume he had bought at Henry

Sotheran's and read the gold lettering on the spine. '*From the Gulf to the Caspian* by Sir William Dunderforce-Wake. Riveting stuff. Any relation?'

'No.'

'So how do you know Persian?'

'I was born in Persia. In Tehran. And I revisited before my marriage.'

'And is that where you met Miss Bell? On your travels?'

'She came to talk to us, at Oxford.' She glanced down at the polished rail and rubbed at the accumulated salt. 'I think I showed off my Persian, somewhat.'

'I'll wager that took her aback.'

She flushed slightly. 'It was the most terrible boasting on my part. I'm mortified to even think of it. Well, she asked me to write to her and I've been a kind of unofficial assistant for some time now. She's a marvellous woman. I know she might seem somewhat odd to a man like you.' Before he could ask what that was, she added: 'With a military background, I mean. Not the most socially progressive part of England, is it? The Army?'

'No.'

Quinn didn't bother to elaborate on the fact that, originally, it was not his choice of career. But second sons did not have much say in such matters. His eldest brother, a profligate wastrel though he was and remained, had inherited the family farm in Suffolk.

'So, Mr Quinn. Back to Persian. Shall we say half an hour? In the First Class Card Room; it's free at this time of day. It's—'

'I know where it is.'

'Good. I've been thinking. Perhaps we should try some hypnosis. To speed up the learning.'

Quinn laughed.

'What?'

'Doesn't that belong in the music halls?'

She looked as if he had just uttered a blasphemy. 'My uncle was a magician and hypnotist.'

Quinn tried hard not to sneer. 'And you think it works?'

'I don't think it is all the sham you clearly think it is. I'll show you. Give me a coin,' she demanded.

Quinn took out a halfpenny and passed it over. 'I can see you are a gambling man, ready to risk a small fortune. I was rather hoping for a half-sovereign.'

He shrugged. 'Let's start with a ha'penny till I know you better.'

She examined it carefully for distinguishing marks. 'Look, this is ghosted slightly. You can see Britannia on the King's head.' He looked again and, sure enough, the images had blurred together. 'It's a common problem. So, just to be certain you recognise it again, there is a notch opposite the King's nose. See?'

'Yes.'

Mrs Wake pulled back her arm and flung the coin as far as she could, and it disappeared into the swell, so insignificant Quinn couldn't even see a splash.

'There.'

'Well, that cost me. And you wanted a half-sovereign.'

From her bag she fetched her purse, rummaged around

and extracted a small velvet bag. She passed it across to Quinn; he could feel the coin between his fingers. 'No, I don't believe it.'

'Look inside.'

He slid out the disc on to his palm and, sure enough, there was the ghosted halfpenny with the telltale nick.

'My uncle taught me that magic is about believing. Just like hypnotism. Does it work? Yes, if you believe hard enough. I shall go and fetch my books from my cabin.'

'I'll be along shortly. I think I'll have a pipe.' And try and figure out what that was all about, you peculiar woman, he said to himself. He fished in his pocket for his briar and pouch. He'd sworn he would give it up once they reached Egypt; he didn't want to be a slave to the rough cut while On Special Duty in the desert.

Quinn realised Mrs Wake was lingering. Her voice dropped and she took a step back towards him. 'By the way, I saw something very odd.'

'What was that?'

'I think Farid is on this voyage. He seems to have spirited his way onboard.'

'Farid? The manservant? Are you certain? Miss Bell said nothing about him coming along.'

'No, but that isn't unusual for Gerty.'

'Where did you see him?'

'Not long before I came up here. There is a gate where First and Second meet, and I saw someone lurking there. That headdress, it's pretty distinctive, especially in Second.'

'Yes. You might expect it in Third, I suppose.' That was

where the servants and those of the coloured races habitually travelled. 'What did you do?'

'I went across, and I am sure it was him, but he scuttled away when he saw me.'

'You must know him, though? To speak to?'

'Not really. He appears with tea, drives the car – very well, I might add – and sometimes accompanies Miss Bell to openings and events. Always causes a stir. But he isn't the most talkative man I have ever met.'

'Would he even have a passport?' Servants, wives and children always travelled on their master's – or in this case mistress's – passport; it was rare for anyone in service to have their own documents.

'It's possible, I suppose. Gerty is quite liberal on such things.'

'Do you think Miss Bell has sent him to keep an eye on us? In case anything improper occurs?'

She frowned at him. 'I don't think you have anything to worry about there, Mr Quinn.'

As she left, he shook his head in despair at the scheme Kitchener had pitched him into. Mrs Wake with her parlour tricks and superciliousness; Wassmuss, his bafflingly valuable luggage sitting in the hold marked Not Wanted On Voyage, and Lawrence, the strange archaeologist.

An unholy trinity, if ever he had encountered one. And he made four.

Quinn left the rail and headed for his cabin, trying to banish unwelcome thoughts of horses and apocalypse.

Twenty-four

Cairo, 1915

It was that fleeting moment of the day that Dahoum, Lawrence's young friend in Syria, had called the House of Two Lights. Twilight was just fading, leaving the sky a deepening indigo that had not yet thickened to black. This was when the wicked djinns appeared, the invisible devils that would whisper of worries and cares into the unsuspecting person's ear. They would plant the doubts that would grow into terrible uncertainties, the images that would populate the nightmares ahead. Just before dawn, if you were lucky, the other djinns would come to blow such concerns away, to leave you positive for the day ahead. But, Dahoum claimed, if you ever woke at three in the morning, sweating, with your palpitating heart gripped by an unnamed, unknowable fear, the Djinns of the Two Lights had been at work.

Lawrence was sitting cross-legged on a small hill on the

very edge of the suburbs of Bulaq Dacrour, on the western side of the Nile. It was not to be confused with the great warren of Bulaq, which occupied the eastern bank, north of the Egyptian museum and the Kasr el Nil Barracks. Out here, a permanent cooling breeze seemed to blow on the fortunate few, the mud houses had given way to shacks, then country lanes, followed by crowded villages and their surrounding fields, until larger, swankier houses had appeared, shaded by date palms, walled off from the scruffy lean-tos of the homeless that dotted the landscape out towards the desert.

Lawrence could just make out some of the dispossessed below, to the right, and smell the *molokkiyya* soup they were brewing up on the open fire. The residents of Bulaq Dacrour instigated a pogrom every few months to purge these streets of the great unwashed and, for a while, it worked. But slowly they crept back, imperceptibly at first till, finally, the scales were tipped once more and another cleansing began. It was, thought Lawrence, not unlike a dog with its fleas.

Now, the last of the twilight djinns had disappeared, although not the cloying heat, which had hardly dropped with the sun. The stars were out, a big-faced moon was rising and the lights were appearing in the windows of the villas that formed this small community. Each one was worth many thousands of Egyptian pounds, and each had been built a decent distance from the other. Privacy was what your money, hard earned or not, bought out here. If he strained his ears, Lawrence could just about hear the expensive trickle of running water from the courtyards, the splash of a swimmer in a pool, and before the cooking smells had overpowered it, the scent of rose petals and camomile scattered over footpaths. Within these villas lived Cairo's merchants, bankers, wealthy Egyptians, Greeks, Armenians, Copts and Jews and even the occasional Englishman, all in cosseted splendour. Only the dregs of Cairene society outside occasionally ruined the paradise created within.

Lawrence stood and slithered down the hill on a cascade of stones and dirt. 'Who is there?' came an alarmed voice from the darkness.

'A friend. Enjoy your soup.'

A pause. 'You will take some with us?'

'Not today, brother. Allah's blessings be with you.'

'And with you.'

'*Eid mubarak*,' Lawrence said, and heard the good wishes repeated.

He spoke some lines to himself, plucked from the Rubaiyat:

'Now Ramadan is past, Shawwal comes back,
and feast and song and joy no more we lack;
the wine-skin carriers throng the streets and cry,
here comes the porter with his precious pack.'

The next day would be Eid ul-Fitr, marking the end of Ramadan, which that year had occupied most of July. There would be parties, prayers, visits to relatives and Cairo would slowly return to normal. The British held their own quiet celebrations, in that the local waiters and servants would no longer seem quite so sullen when they plied their betters with food and drink during daylight hours.

To test himself, Lawrence had fallen in with the tradition

of Ramadan and not eaten between dawn and sunset. At first it had been difficult, but he enjoyed the experience of self-denial and the sweet, gratifying taste of the first bites after darkness had fallen.

Lawrence strode past his replacement motorcycle, a fine and robust 500cc single Triumph, and walked on through the dusty landscape, hopping over the slimy streams of effluent that snaked lazily across the earth. He skirted past an ugly brick-built villa, two storeys high and not one inch showing the slightest concern with local architectural history or conventions. It was the kind of home he expected to find in the affluent suburbs of London, trumpeting the owner's wealth and good taste. Here, it just looked barbarous and vulgar. He turned the corner of this displaced monster and there, furthest away from the city, right on the edge of the desert, where a few spluttering fires betrayed other camps of the dispossessed, was the house he sought.

The entrance was a solid, blue door housed deep within an elaborate curved arch. Enough light escaped the barred slit windows which pierced the walls at intervals for him to just make out the two big Nubians standing outside. They stiffened when they heard the scuffling of his approach. All they could most likely see was a slight figure, dressed mostly in dark colours, drifting towards them.

'*Salaam. Izzayyak?*'

No reply came, so Lawrence opened up his arms to show he came in peace and had no hidden weapons.

'Stop.'

He did as he was told and one of the men trotted over and

patted every inch of his body. Satisfied he was unencumbered with lethal devices of any description, the man said: 'What is your business here?'

'I am here to see Abdel.'

This guardian of the gate looked him up and down in the thin light and could see enough not to be impressed. 'The master is not in. He will do business in the Turkish Bazaar as usual, tomorrow.'

'Tell him Spaark sent me. I will wait here while you do so. Rude though it is.'

The man scowled at him, strode over and banged the door three times. It opened a crack and then wider as he slid his bulk inside.

Lawrence stayed where he was, stock-still; his arms remained outstretched in the position he had adopted for the search, his head on one side as if he had simply nodded off. The other guard shuffled and grunted in discomfort, unnerved by this strange, unexpected visitor and his Christ-like pose.

The first Nubian returned and grunted at him: 'Come.'

Lawrence let his aching arms drop, bowed to the other guard and followed the big man in. As he expected, the court-yard was dazzling. There were three fountains on the path to the house, placed at intervals along the mosaic, each water feature bigger than the last. Trees had been carefully trained to bend in shade over every passage, so the sun would not trouble the owner or his guests. The air was rich with blossom and spices and soft background music played.

Inside it was all cool marble, stone and tile, with large circumference wicker fans churning the air, sofas that ran the length of the walls, another fountain, this one tricked out with coloured lights, and a semi-circle of round brass tables, each containing a bowl of a different delicacy.

A *safragi* in a taboush bowed low and asked Lawrence to make himself at home. His master would be no more than two minutes. Would he care for a drink?

Lawrence thought it best to refuse, even after the man pressed him. The irritation at his unexpected guest's rudeness was hardly noticeable as the *safragi* wafted out of the room.

Abdel, of course, kept him waiting twenty minutes before he bustled in through a heavily beaded curtain, robes flowing, offering profuse apologies. 'My dear Lieutenant Lawrence. Why did you not send a runner to say you were coming?'

'I didn't know myself until quite recently.'

His face collapsed into a mask of calamity. 'You have not been offered a drink?' Abdel's head spun around, as if looking for a serf to beat.

'I was. Most graciously. I refused.'

'A sherbet?'

'No. Thank you.'

'Then please sit, at least.'

Lawrence did so, helped himself to some pistachios, the plainest snack on offer, then crossed his legs and spread out his arms along the back of the divan. 'This is a very nice house.'

'This, pah. It was my father's. He was the clever one. All I do is stand still compared to him.'

'I doubt your father put the generator in. Or the gramophone.'

Abdel smiled. 'I have made a few small improvements, it is true.' He rearranged his robes as he sat. 'The guard said something about Spaark.'

'The guard also searched me. Thoroughly. Now they watch.'

Abdel followed Lawrence's gaze to the bulky shape lurking just beyond the bead curtain. 'You will forgive an old man's suspicions.'

'I would if you were old, Abdel. Or feeble. You could break me like a matchstick. If you had cause to.'

He clicked his finger and the silhouette disappeared. 'Do I have any reason to?'

Lawrence shook his head. 'We are friends here. Valued clients of each other.' Abdel nodded. 'Forgive me for not bringing a gift. I thought, for once, it might be inappropriate.' Lawrence knew Abdel would suspect any fruit or sweets to have been adulterated. It was just how his mind worked. And how he kept alive in the world of business in Cairo.

'I think your last gift will cover you for several visits. I am still embarrassed by it.'

Lawrence waved his hand to dismiss the revolver as a trifle.

'You have not been heard of much for two or three weeks, or is it more? Not since . . .' Abdel put his head back and snorted with laughter. 'Not since you hit Spaark. That, I didn't expect.'

'I am in a place we English call the doghouse, Abdel. It is not a good place to be.'

'It does not sound it. Because of Spaark?'

'Partly.' Lawrence cleared his throat and carefully put his

hands together, fingertips touching. There was motorbike oil under the nails, as usual. 'He isn't coming, Abdel. Spaark won't be here tonight.'

Now there was a flicker of consternation over the Egyptian's fleshy face, replaced by curiosity. 'You have killed him?'

Lawrence shook his head. 'That's not really my job, Abdel. I am just a mapmaker.'

'Too modest, Lawrence. You were always more than that. So what of Spaark?'

'You were expecting him here, with either the guns, or the details of where you can get the guns. Don't disagree with me. I am not sure I have all this entirely right. You killed the lad—'

'Lawrence—'

'You killed the boy,' he repeated forcefully. 'Or had him killed by some tame sadists. Don't insult me by denying it.'

The Egyptian glared, confident of his invulnerability. 'Why should I deny it?'

'He was my friend.'

'Your catamite,' he spat. 'I saw your tears.'

Lawrence sighed.

'They say you had boys in Syria.' The man's visage had now twisted into distaste.

'They say lots of things about me. Some of them are even true.'

'Including that?'

Lawrence rolled his eyes in contempt. Abdel was not the only one who wouldn't, or couldn't understand, the freedom, the joy, of being with young people who haven't yet been smothered by a society's rules and regulations, its taboos and castes, who still had something of the free spirit about them. Better a few hours with such a person, no matter how lowly, than a lifetime of cocktail parties and dinners with his so-called betters.

Lawrence did his best to keep his anger under control as he spoke. 'That wasn't why you killed him, was it? If that were a crime, half of your friends in Cairo would be in the City of the Dead by now. No doubt you knew Munir was feeding me information about the guns. You killed the boy to make me angry. You knew I would come to you to find out who did it. You tell me it is Spaark. Sparkie then becomes persona non grata, as we say, with the British. So, if he were found dead, double-crossed in a gunrunning deal, would we care? No. Would we encourage the Cairo police to investigate? Unlikely. You get the guns for free, and a potential competitor is wiped out into the bargain.'

Abdel had returned to his old equitable self. The beaming smile demonstrated that he knew Lawrence had nothing on him. 'All very fanciful. And lies, lies, lies. I would not repeat such a thing in the Bazaar. You might ruin my reputation.'

'There was just one tiny flaw in the plan, Abdel. Sparkie was one of ours. Or should I say, is one of mine. Always has been. A good agent. He even took a hefty punch from me without too much complaint, although we had practised it a few times to make it more convincing.'

The whole thing had been a charade, from the terrace of Shepheard's to the very vocal dressing-down of Lawrence by Colonel Clayton, which could be heard booming along the corridors of GHQ. 'Of course, we knew that news of our fight would confirm that he was no friend of mine.'

Abdel crossed his legs twice, a sure sign of his discomfort. 'Sparkie worked for the British?'

'No, not the British,' Lawrence corrected. 'For me. There are no guns coming, Abdel. Not from Spaark. And the case he gave you as a sample? The one I saw him deliver in the desert? The pins are brittle. Ten or fifteen rounds is all they'll manage before they jam.'

Abdel laughed once more. 'So I am swindled? Ah, such is business, Lawrence. I only paid a deposit. A few hundred. You think you can put me out of business with this one Belgian?' He couldn't resist a boast. 'You have no idea how my roots have spread. No idea at all.'

'Perhaps not, but I hear things. Your name is being whispered far and wide, Abdel. I congratulate you.' Lawrence stood, taking the Egyptian by surprise. Manners insisted the host struggled to his feet as well. 'But you know the saying: an egg thief becomes a camel thief? You are growing from eggs to camels. Moving from hashish to guns, that is not what we want to see. Bringing guns – British guns – from Greece and Persia? Foolish. Trying to manipulate the British? Stupid. They are slow sometimes, incompetent even, but sooner or later they are prodded into action. You have made yourself dangerous to them and that is not good. Besides, you have to answer for the boy, Abdel.'

His eyes widened with mirth. 'Some gutter boy? Me? I could eat a dozen of their hearts every day and not have to answer, you know that.'

246

'You have to answer to me. I am taking you to the Citadel.'

'You are?' Abdel put his head back and roared with laughter. 'You stupid little man.'

Abdel clapped his hands together. Lawrence heard the clack of the bead curtain as it was parted by somebody. The Egyptian turned, a finger pointing at Lawrence. 'Take this—'

The words died on his lips.

Captain Harold Cornelius Quinn was standing where the guard should have been, pistol in his hand, knees bent slightly, balancing on the balls of his feet.

Abdel's head snapped around and he glared at Lawrence, before turning back to Quinn. Then he did something very foolish.

'No!' Lawrence cried when he realised what was about to happen. The banker made only a small movement, something he might have thought better of. He didn't get the chance.

Quinn's arm moved up in a smooth, fast arc and he squeezed the trigger as soon as it came level. The bullet entered the Egyptian's right temple, blowing out a red breath of blood, brain and bone from the far side. Abdel swayed for a second, then appeared to fold into his robes as he crumpled. His face made a loud slap on the hard floor.

A lesser man might have died there and then, but the Egyptian began to thrash around, leaving a smear of cranial matter on the tiles. He tried to shout for help. The sound wasn't human.

'For God's sake,' cried Lawrence, putting his hands over his ears.

Two more bullets entered the Egyptian, the first in the

chest, the second leaving a black crater where his right eye had once been.

Lawrence felt vomit curdle in his stomach and burn his throat. Then he remembered the boy and the feel of cooling skin as he stroked Munir's contorted face. The nausea quickly subsided.

The door to the garden opened and Tariq, the former Ottoman soldier, stepped through. He had a knife in his hand, the blade glistening with fresh blood. He was shaking his head with regret. 'I had to kill one of the Nubians.'

Lawrence looked over at Quinn, who shook his head and patted the pocket that held his lead-filled cosh. 'Mine are just down. They'll live.'

Lawrence shrugged. Abdel's Nubian bodyguards were in all likelihood the ones who had put the boy on the stake. He could shed no tears there.

He looked at Abdel, sprawled across his own tiles, the vibrant glaze now darkening as the blood seeped across them.

The lieutenant gave a sigh of regret. 'We were to bring him alive.'

Quinn crouched down, pulled open Abdel's long tunic and extracted a small pistol. He tossed it to Lawrence. It was a compact Beretta, just like the one he had wanted to buy for Munir. Abdel had made the mistake of moving his hand towards it, which Quinn had interpreted as a hostile act.

Quinn stood. 'We should go.'

'Go?' Lawrence asked. 'What about the others?'

'The servants will already have fled. The bodyguards will as soon as they awake. What we have here is a business deal gone wrong. A hazard of his chosen occupation. There will be others to pick up his contacts and debtors, with regret and an insallah.'

'You are a quick learner, Captain Quinn.'

Quinn bent down and scooped up the three ejected brass casings from the automatic pistol he had used and pocketed them. He looked down at the dead body and gave a bleak smile. 'There appears to be a lot to learn about you, Lawrence.'

Twenty-five

Mrs Wake had invited Quinn to dinner that night, a very modern and emancipated act, even booking the table in her name rather than his. She knew the captain was to ship out for Persia with Wassmuss's peculiarly valuable luggage and sovereigns the next day and that Lieutenant Lawrence had asked Quinn to help him with a 'small matter' before he left, but she wanted to say goodbye properly. She was not surprised when he was a little late, but she was by his demeanour. He was back to the distant, somewhat prickly and incommunicative man she remembered from before the voyage.

The grill room at the Continental was packed with uniformed soldiers and Quinn had reverted to wearing army khakis. Civvies were too conspicuous in that town. Mrs Wake was dressed in a peg-top skirt and another of her high-button blouses with long sleeves. It seemed even dowdier in Cairo than London; Quinn had noticed women's fashions in the tropics were far racier, and brighter, than at home.

'Are you all right?' she asked. 'You look quite pale.'

'I'm fine. I'll have a brandy.' He ordered one from the waiter and managed a smile at her. It was a poor, ragged attempt.

'You're not coming down with something?'

'No.'

'There's a lot of malaria about, so I'm told. Perhaps you should have a gin and tonic instead.'

'I'm fine.'

'And did you see Lawrence?'

'I did.'

His brandy came and he knocked it back in two big gulps and ordered another.

'Harry,' she said. 'Take it easy. Please.'

The two weeks on the ship had passed quickly, but there had still been time for him to become 'Harry', although she remained 'Mrs Wake'.

She frowned at him as he gulped more alcohol. 'Shall we order? Or is it to be a liquid dinner?'

Quinn forced himself to look at the menu, even though he wasn't hungry. He chose soup and roast chicken. Surprisingly, Mrs Wake followed his lead.

'I think Lawrence is an interesting chap. Gerty likes him.'

'Gerty is welcome to him.'

'Clearly, this isn't an evening for social niceties. I made a terrible mistake. Forgive me.'

Her chair scraped loudly on the floor and he could see other diners look over their shoulders at them. Two guardsmen glared at him, and he felt his dander rise. Then he realised

251

Mrs Wake was a whisker from leaving and he spoke quickly. 'I apologise. I truly do. Stay. Please.'

Mrs Wake shuffled her chair back in and disarmed the concerned guardsmen with a dazzling grin. They returned to their coffee and cigars.

'I—' Quinn struggled for words. *It is always the same after I have killed a man.* No, that wouldn't help. *I don't like being duped into murder.* No, nor that. 'Why is nothing as straightforward as it seems?'

'Do you mean Lawrence?'

'People. Yes, Lawrence. Kitchener. Miss Bell. Always some hidden agenda.'

'You might as well add me to the list.'

'You?'

'Me.' She leaned forward. 'I have a confession to make, Harry.'

'Yes?'

'About the Women's Police Service.'

She paused while the waiter served them both soup.

'You weren't ever in it?' he suggested. 'It was all an elaborate joke?'

'No. I was – am – a member. But I was in it for K.'

His somewhat alcohol-befuddled brain asked: 'Kay who?'

'K,' she said as softly as she could manage over the conversation and subtle clash of cutlery and crockery. 'Vernon Kell.' Vernon Kell was the head of MO5, and Quinn's boss.

His brows knitted together in confusion. 'I don't—'

'Where do you think the WPS gets its funding? From

MO5. It's perfect, a whole network of nosey women, gossiping about all and sundry. All you need is one agent per branch and you have a ready source of intelligence. Especially in the ports. It's worked brilliantly—'

But he wasn't listening to the justification for the organisation. A wave of sobriety had washed over him. 'You're a spy as well?'

'Was. And we prefer the word "agent".'

Quinn always thought this a prissy distinction. 'And did Miss Bell know?'

'Know? Of course. She suggested me.'

'She has the ear of K? As well as Kitchener?'

'Miss Bell knows everybody and has the ear of them all. She is a trusted member of the Intelligence community.' Mrs Wake caught the attention of a passing waiter. 'Can I have a glass of white wine, please. Do you have any German?' She almost mimed the final word.

The man shrugged expansively. 'No, it is not allowed.'

'Pity, it travels much better than French, I find. And don't offer me Algerian. Do you have a Greek moschofilero? That's the one that's similar to a gewürztraminer.'

'Yes, ma'am, I believe we do.'

Quinn waited for the waiter to absent himself. 'Well, I'll be blowed.' He took some soup.

'You'll be blowed because I am fussy about my wine or because of what I've just told you? That K has hired women?'

He tried not to sound like a stuffy old colonel when he said: 'It's very progressive of him.'

'Progressive, my Aunt Fanny. He knows that there are

certain situations where women are more useful than men. And we can go places you men can't.'

'Why didn't you tell me?' he asked.

'Tell you what?'

'That you were a spy.'

'I just have.'

'Earlier,' he insisted. 'Why didn't you mention it earlier, on the ship?'

She looked exasperated. 'Because I'm an agent. We don't just advertise our profession to all and sundry. I shouldn't have to tell you that.'

Damned women. What was K thinking of? They tie you up in knots. 'Does this mean you are not Mrs Wake?'

'It says so on my passport.'

'And I've got one somewhere that says I'm the Duke of Wellington.'

She gave him that smile, turned to maximum sweetness and part of him wanted to dash the remains of his brandy in her face. It seemed everyone was determined to make a fool of him. 'Put it this way, Harry. There was a Mr Wake on the *Titanic* manifest. But he wasn't my husband.' Before he could comment, she added: 'Widows have more freedom of movement, more leeway to form, um, attachments than single women. Mrs Wake has been very good to me.'

'Is it your real name?'

'Dunderforce-Wake. I was a little taken aback when you produced that memoir.'

'I see.' She was the daughter of the author of *From the Gulf to the Caspian*. 'You speak Persian because—'

'My father spent ten years there, yes. Appalling book, by the way. I think I get one line. "A bonny daughter" or some such.'

'I didn't notice.'

'My point entirely.' She took a breath and let it out. When she spoke again, she had softened her voice. 'Look, you'll be off to the port tomorrow. With the gold sovereigns. That's the end of my responsibility. I probably won't see you again. I just wanted to say: good luck.'

Quinn scooped up the brandy bowl and they clinked glasses. 'Yes, thank you.'

'Despite your occasional boorishness, I have enjoyed our time together.' Quinn tried to untangle the conflicting sentiments in that sentence, but failed. 'You know, I half wish I was going with you,' she added.

Not another, he thought. Before he could reply there was a commotion at the door, and a cry of protest from the maître d'. Military police had moved in and were striding across the room, much to the disgust and annoyance of everyone in the restaurant. The wave of anger at such a crass intrusion over dinner was followed by one of relief as the big, burly sergeant walked past the other tables and presented himself at Quinn and Mrs Wake's station. Quinn knew the easiest exit was behind him and that he could draw his gun and shoot the man dead before the policeman could react. He was also now sober enough to realise that this probably wasn't the wisest course of action.

'Captain Savage?' the military policeman asked.

It took a fraction of second for Quinn to remember his

alias. He cursed the residual fog of the brandy. 'Indeed. You have the advantage of me.'

'Sergeant Drake.' The man fingered the pouch containing his handcuffs on his belt, suggesting there was a choice of ways to perform this unsavoury task. 'I'm sorry, sir, but you are under arrest. If you will come with me . . .'

'On what charge, might I ask?'

Drake lowered his voice, but in the hushed atmosphere of the grill room, where diners had suddenly discovered the ability to cut, chew and swallow in absolute pin-dropping silence, it must have carried. 'Murder, sir.'

Twenty-six

There was a holding facility to the north of Shepheard's Hotel, next to the Railway Station. Quinn was relieved of his pistol and ferried there in a staff car, flanked by two young MPs, with Sergeant Drake in the front next to the driver. A fourth member of the arresting party had remained with a horrified Mrs Wake to ensure she did not create what they called a 'spectacle'. Quinn's ears still burned red with fury at the humiliation of being paraded through the dining room, down the stairs to the lobby and across the terrace. His captors had crowded him as he was taken away, but at least they had spared him the handcuffs.

The escort, of course, said nothing, so Quinn kept quiet, too. He was led to rear of the Military Police facility and shown into a cell that stank of stale urine and the comatose New Zealander who lay snoring on the stone bench.

'Shouldn't take long, sir. To arrange some transport for you.'

'Where to?' he asked.

'You are to be interned at Maadi, sir, pending a court martial. Be more comfortable than here.'

Quinn looked at the snuffling Kiwi, a string of saliva drooling from his mouth, and nodded.

'I'll rustle up some tea.'

Quinn moved the New Zealander's feet and sat. He stoked up a pipe and, after some effort, got it going. It helped kill the stench that was coming from the enamel latrine bucket in the corner.

So, what exactly had gone wrong? How did they make the link from Abdel to him so quickly? Someone must have talked. And he suspected that someone was Lieutenant bloody Lawrence. Get Quinn banged up and he could take his place on the mission to Wassmuss. Was that the game? It had a horriby plausible ring about it, that was for sure. Lawrence considered this whole matter his pet budgerigar, it seemed. Getting Quinn out of the way was a clever precursor to offering to complete the mission himself.

The man has ambitions, Quinn thought, and his ruthless-ness in pursuing them was now very apparent. First, get Quinn to kill the man who murdered his young friend, then use that to frame him for the murder, clearing the way for Lawrence to go after his arch-rival in Persia. It was a very, very neat package. Apart from the fact that no dirt-digger and pen-pusher like Lawrence was up to such a job. Quinn had seen him go green around the gills when Abdel had been dealt with. It was laughable. In fact, he decided, it was so beyond the bounds of reason, he must have got it all wrong.

Perhaps, even now, Lawrence himself was being hauled off to a cell.

Tea arrived within ten minutes, in a chipped white enamel mug from the same school as the latrine bucket. The tea didn't taste of much, but it was hot and sweet. Quinn drank it, hoping to shift the last of the alcohol fug from his brain, eager to be thinking clear and straight.

After half an hour Drake returned, his face serious. 'Ready for you now. Transport's outside. I've no need to 'cuff you, have I, sir?'

'None.'

'Thank you, Captain Savage. I hope it goes well with you.'

The man had to be the most civil MP he had ever met. Normally they were selected for their closeness to the simian. 'Thank you, Sergeant.'

The scruffy canvas-sided lorry shuddered at idle, its fumes belching into the still Cairo night from the tailpipe and a hole in the fat Maxim silencer. The tailgate was already dropped down and, as he went to climb up, hands grabbed him under his arms and hoisted him inside. The gate rattled closed, a fist was banged on the wooden slats of the frame, and the truck jerked forward with a harsh grind of the gears.

He grabbed one of the hanging straps and looked around in the gloom and came face to face with a mirror image.

The man was not exactly identical, but certainly, if you glanced at him together with Quinn in the semi-light, you would have trouble distinguishing them. He was also dressed in identical kit.

'Evening, sir,' the man said. The uniform might suggest officer, but the voice was anything but. 'You all right?'

The man on Quinn's left slid along the slat bench and pulled him down next to him. 'Sorry if we gave you a scare.'

'Lawrence,' he said. He looked around at his other companions. There was Tariq, in the uniform of an Egyptian officer, and, most startling of all, Farid, dressed as he had been at Miss Bell's, with that great spiral of a turban atop his head and the silk scarf at his neck, now pulled up to cover the lower part of his face, masking the fumes from the leaky exhaust. The only addition to his wardrobe was a stubby knife in a sheath hanging from his belt. He nodded his head, the disc of wound material exaggerating the movement. Quinn turned back to Lawrence.

'What the hell is going on?'

The lieutenant pointed to Quinn's doppelganger. 'Captain Savage, meet Captain Savage. Or he will be, the moment you hand over your documents. Corporal Codling, here, is going to be tried in your place.'

'And probably swing for you, sir,' the impostor said with remarkable cheerfulness.

'What?'

'Well,' explained Lawrence, 'in order to set an example, to show the life of an Egyptian is every bit as valuable as an Englishman – although nobody in the city actually believes that – Captain Savage will be tried by court martial and executed.' He looked at Corporal Codling. 'Probably shot, old boy. More dignified. And easier to fake. A little bullet trick.'

'I don't understand.'

260

'The story will be that Savage, in the short time he was in Cairo, amassed debts, and financed himself through Arab bankers. Unable to pay Abdel, he killed him and one of his servants. Now he must pay the price. Give him your papers.'

Quinn did as he was told. 'So you are—'

'A corporal who got into a spot of bother, sir. Who, I am told by my superiors, will come out of this intact.' His voice changed and modulated and out came the trim tones of privilege. 'As long as I can carry this little deception off, fool a few fellow officers. Shouldn't be difficult, most of those chaps have nothing but wool between their ears.'

It was quite a remarkable transformation. Even his facial expression had changed, his chin had become firmer and his eyes somehow more arrogant.

'And he'll be considerably richer,' added Lawrence. 'Oh, the trial will be reported in the newspapers along with the execution and Captain Savage will be no more. But then, he never was, was he?'

'I suppose not. Look, my other documents, my other identities, are in my hotel room.'

'Already cleared out and en route to the ship. Along with Wassmuss's vexing luggage.'

'What ship?'

'HMS *Hardinge*, bound for Banda Abbas on the south Persian coast. Sorry to have dragged you away from dinner. Mrs Wake, was it?'

Quinn just nodded and glanced over his right shoulder, out through the thrumming canvas flap at the rear, and the almost empty Cairo streets rushing by. He cursed himself for his boorish behaviour earlier that night. The last memory Mrs Wake would have of him would be a man who couldn't take his drink.

And he'd never even said goodbye to her properly.

'One other thing, Captain,' said Lawrence. 'About Persia.'

What else could there be? 'Yes?'

Lawrence's face broke into a boyish smile. 'I'm coming with you.'

Twenty-seven

COVER LETTER WRITTEN TO FAMILY BY TEL TO ACCOUNT FOR HIS ABSENCE ON SPECIAL DUTY IN PERSIA, AUGUST–SEPTEMBER 1915:

Military Intelligence Office
Athens

19.8.15

This is only a scribble as there is a post going. Athens is very hot, and the glare of sun very bad. Otherwise not too dull. I am in office there from 9 a.m. (when shops open) till 7 p.m. (when shops shut): so I have so far bought nothing, and seen nothing, except the Acropolis from the window. A longer letter soon, but don't worry if it's a while. I have a great deal to do and nothing much to report. I don't want to bore you with more letters about trying to make bricks without straw!

N

Twenty-eight

At sea

The glass bottle seemed to quiver for a moment before exploding into fine powder. The next one along on the handrail shattered into five jagged pieces that tumbled into the white-flecked sea and were gone. Two more glass containers were smashed by .45 bullets before the shooter was satisfied and the firing stopped, leaving the deck filled with the fumes of the Colt's discharges.

Lawrence bent down and scooped up the cartridge cases.

'Keeping your eye in?' asked Quinn from the shade of a bulkhead.

Lawrence looked over as he pocketed the last casing. 'Something like that.'

'There's one thing I'd like to ask—' Quinn began.

Lawrence raised a hand to silence him. 'Not at the moment.' He walked off, disappearing rapidly down a gangway. Quinn moved to the rail where the bottles had stood and tried hard to ignore the stabs of anger at the rudeness of the intelligence officer. He spoke, it seemed, when he felt he had something to say or the other party something to offer, otherwise Lawrence remained silent. And there were people who thought Quinn taciturn.

Quinn had quickly discovered there was little to do on a voyage to Persia. There was no First Class band or card rooms with the navy, no deck games or predatory spinsters of the kind who drifted through the public rooms of the P&O ship. The landscape on shore was depressingly monotonous, ribbons of sand and palm trees, with tiny fishing communities, for mile after mile. Their ship, HMS *Hardinge*, was hardly the pride of the Royal Navy. It was not even part of the RN: it had been loaned from the Royal Indian Marine. Equipped with four- and six-inch guns and powerful searchlights for sweeping unfriendly shores it was, along with another ship, the *Fox*, the dogsbody of the Red Sea and the Persian Gulf. Conditions on board were hot and cramped, even in the officers' quarters, but the ship had one advantage: *Hardinge* was very fast, even if top speed did set up a teeth-loosening vibration throughout the ship.

Once they had left Port Said, Lawrence disappeared for long periods of time and came back sweating and exhilarated. Quinn wondered for a few days what on earth he was up to. It transpired that he had volunteered to help stoke the *Hardinge*: the ship was still coal-powered. Quinn went down to see him one evening. It was like a flame-licked medieval vision of Hades, a dark cavern of glistening torsos, shovelling for all they were worth, whipped on by a truculent chief stoker. Quinn left them to it.

Three days after the target practice he had witnessed, just as afternoon was sliding into evening, he found Lawrence standing under the barrels of the ship's six-inch guns. The inky waters flashed and foamed at the bow as the *Hardinge* knifed northeast at more than twenty knots.

'How is it down there?' Quinn asked. 'In the belly of this beast?'

Lawrence remained silent for a few moments, as if wondering whether to engage. Quinn was quite prepared for him to remain silent or slope off after a brusque reply. This time Lawrence answered. 'It's a place to think. The robotic routine of repetitive labour. It somehow frees the mind. I am sorry if I have seemed distant. I have had much to consider.'

'Wassmuss?'

'And Arabia. Mecca. Hejaz. Damascus. Anyway, I have done my thinking for now. You wanted to know what it's like down there? One's first impression is that you have been set among the vilest creatures of the world. It is like a zoo with no bars. Then, gradually, the personalities appear and you begin to see people. Real people, some fascinating. They really are among the foulest-mouthed men on God's earth, however. I have learned a whole new vocabulary of terms for women's various openings.' He gave a theatrical shudder. 'And so obsessed with sex.'

'The same as men everywhere.'

'Really? I've never met any reasonable man who cared so much as a biscuit for it.'

Quinn smiled. 'Most men care a whole tin of Huntley and Palmers, I'm afraid, given the right circumstances.'

'Well, one comes across them, I suppose. Just that there seem to be so many more important considerations.'

'What decided you to come along, Lawrence?' Quinn asked.

There was another lengthy pause, and Lawrence levered himself back and forth from the rail, as if he were performing vertical push-ups.

'Simple, really. It is best I desert Cairo for a while, until the vacuum Abdel leaves is filled. There will be those who see my hand in it, despite our little smoke screen. And, of course, to prevent the flow of weapons, British weapons, into Egypt. To stop Wassmuss and his war of propaganda.'

Quinn said nothing for the moment. Lawrence had kept the Wassmuss luggage he had brought from London for five days. He, too, had drawn a blank. Quinn had always thought Lawrence's insistence on examining it might turn out to be pure hubris; he had been proved correct. Perhaps, in the end, Wassmuss simply had a sentimental attachment to his baggage.

'You don't believe me?' Lawrence asked, interpreting the lack of response as doubt.

'I do. Kitchener said the same thing. It is vital that a man like Wassmuss is removed from this war. But I'm not sure I believe that is your only motive in coming to find Wassmuss.'

Lawrence stopped his push-ups. He didn't address the question, but said: 'I know what your orders are.'

Quinn scratched his cheek and stayed silent.

'And I've seen you at work, remember. I am sure you can do it.'

Again, Quinn waited. There was a codicil to be attached.

'But when we do find Wassmuss, I'd like you to stay your hand for the time being.'

'Why should I do that?'

'For me.'

Quinn couldn't help smiling at the presumption.

'Not indefinitely. Just long enough to let me speak to the man.'

Quinn shook his head. As he had suspected, Lawrence was more than a little curious about Wassmuss. A straight kill was not on his agenda. 'As you say, I have my orders.'

'I understand that. But if you can. It's important to me.'

'Why?' he repeated.

'It just is. Our whole mission might hinge on a few words. Trust me.'

Quinn, unable to promise to do any such thing, changed the subject.

'Where are Tariq and Farid? I haven't seen them since we came on board.'

'With the serving staff, of course. Can't have natives with the officers. Empire'd crumble within hours.'

'And what's Farid doing here exactly?'

'He knows the country. The tracks, the villages, the wells. He has maps, not all of them written down. He can lead us to water, if need be. That's invaluable.'

'We're flying in, not crossing the desert.'

'You need to be prepared for every eventuality, Quinn. I

am no soldier' – Quinn didn't argue – 'but I thought you of all people would appreciate that; after all, you know how unpredictable the desert can be. But for a man who has already seen Persia, you don't speak much of it.'

Quinn listened to the thrum-thrum of the engine and the hissing of the bow wake. 'I have a wife there.'

'Really?'

Quinn managed a taut smile at the surprise in Lawrence's voice. 'People do, you know.'

'I didn't mean that. Just . . . well, you don't give much away, Captain Quinn. What happened? Is she local?'

'No. When I say I have a wife there, I mean, I left her in the country. She was called Kate. She died. That's all there is to it. God took her but left me here.'

Quinn stoked up his pipe, while Lawrence went back to examining the stars. They had the awkward air of two men who had said too much, far more than they were used to saying.

Still picking out constellations, Lawrence said softly: 'I am truly sorry. About your wife.'

There was no brooking the sincerity in the words. So Quinn said: 'Thank you.'

'Tell me, why did you agree to come back to Persia if you loathe the place so?'

Quinn didn't hesitate. 'For Kitchener. I owed him, I suppose. He's saved me twice. Once from a hanging in South Africa and again after Persia. It was him who got me into this business, dragged me up by my boot heels. It's why I couldn't refuse this mission.'

'And he probably knows that,' added Lawrence.

'He probably does, the old fox.' With what he hoped was a gentle touch, Quinn steered the conversation around to the subject that had been bothering him all this time. 'You lost a friend recently, I believe.'

Lawrence turned to him, his eyes hard to read. 'A friend?'

'When I was in the kitchen I heard you talking to Abdel. About a boy.' Quinn knocked out the pipe on the railing and watched the wind catch the sparks and dance them along the side and over the deck. 'I thought we were taking Abdel out of circulation because of gunrunning. Not because of a local lad.'

'Munir used to look after my motorcycle in Cairo. And, yes, we became friends, or would have. And I don't mean in the sense of what the Greeks called *paiderastia*. Or maybe I do, in its more innocent sense of mentor and pupil. Like Hogarth and myself. But they used this poor, harmless lad to get to me, to make me angry. That made me even more furious. But I didn't intend for Abdel to die.'

'Are you sure?'

'I didn't tell you to shoot him.'

'But you engineered a situation where I might. Can you tell me that it wasn't at the back of your mind?'

Another group of officers appeared on deck, their voices thick with the spirit of the wardroom. Quinn and Lawrence moved away from the rail.

Eventually, after a lengthy consideration, Lawrence replied. 'No. I can't say that for certain.'

Quinn gave his pipe one final tap against a bulkhead and slipped it into his top pocket. For some reason he couldn't quite fathom, he felt a sense of relief. 'That's the only answer that would have satisfied me. Goodnight, Lawrence.'

Twenty-nine

Persia

The air across the port of Banda Abbas, Britain's toehold on the southern coast of Persia, hung dim with dust from the movement of men, horses, mules, camels and lorry. It was as if every inhabitant suffered from chronic restlessness, greeting each day with a plan to move stores here, trudge there, create havoc here. Lawrence looked upon the port with ill-concealed disgust. Even a cursory glance showed things were not run efficiently, that barges were moored too far out and had to be served by lighters, rather than unloaded with gangways, that the system of emptying and filling the vessels was woefully unsystematic. The soldiers, too, seemed either ill disciplined or badly used, as they appeared to spend most of their time getting in each other's way.

Lawrence spent some time scribbling furiously in his notebook, his eye picking out a hundred ways to improve the infrastructure and the efficiency of this outpost of the Empire.

Banda might be neglected, he thought, but there was no excuse for such slovenliness. People mistook his own lack of smartness for just that, but it was really a way of showing his discomfort at having to wear any uniform, of being classified as a mere soldier. In all other respects he wanted the military to run smoothly, well lubricated and slick. What he saw in Bandas was far from that.

After reporting to the officer in charge of the port, a harassed Lieutenant Commander, who was overwhelmed by the arrival of five thousand Indian troops bound for Basra, Kut and then, it was hoped, up the Tigris to Baghdad. To the CO, the arrival of four extra bodies from Cairo was neither here nor there, so Lawrence's small force was quickly dismissed. The group commandeered two mule-drawn AT carts to transport them through the dusk, out to the aeroplanes that would fly them north to their rendezvous with Captain Noel, the intelligence officer currently playing cat to Wassmuss's mouse.

It was a twenty-minute, bone-aching ride through to the aerodrome and it was, thought Quinn, a far cry from Farnborough. The runway was a strip of stony ground that had been painstakingly cleared of the larger rocks and raked over. This was surrounded by a sea of tents, each one sporting a campfire, wafting the smell of unfamiliar food over them. The strip had been hemmed in by those five thousand Indian troops en route to Mesopotamia, or Irak, as Lawrence liked to call it. There were sepoys as far as the eye could see. Having such a concentration of troops at either end of the runway would make take-off and landing a hazardous business, whether you were in the aircraft or on the ground.

Not that such a consideration mattered, because no heavier-than-air machine was going to take off in the near future. In one of the bell tents lay Dickie Daniels, the pilot. His right leg was smashed, his left eye covered by a patch, the sheen of a fever on his forehead.

Outside, Daniels's Airco lay twisted on the ground, like a piece of paper crumpled and tossed aside by giant hands. The second Airco was also down to its component parts, a collection of wooden ribs and struts, so that, in the cold, brittle light of the new moon, it looked like something from an elephant's graveyard.

'Bloody bad show, sorry,' said Daniels when they located him.

'What happened?' asked Quinn.

Daniels grimaced as he tried to push himself up the cot-bed. His damaged limb was hidden under a cotton sheet, and a metal cage kept the material from his skin. The slightest movement caused him pain but, nevertheless, he was determined to sit up straighter. Quinn and Lawrence took an arm each and helped him.

'Thank you. It's the heat that does for the aircraft. Makes for thin air. Can't get any lift except at dawn and dusk. Otherwise the engines just struggle away to no real avail. But worse than that, in the heat of the day, the glue melts, and the plane starts to come apart. I thought perhaps it reset just as hard when it cooled, but then the undercarriage went as I came in. Snapped clean off. Rogers, my observer, was killed . . . my pins aren't too clever.'

'Is there a doctor?'

Daniels nodded. 'Yes, naval chap, very good. Comes every

day. Wants to ship me to Cairo or Karachi. Told him to bugger off. Look, I've ordered some better adhesive and high-tensile screws from the Australians at Basra. They found the same problem flying in the outback, you see, and have this demon sticky. Probably mixed from kangaroo spoors, but who cares, as long as it works? When that arrives, we can put the other Airco back together. I'll be right as rain in a few weeks—'

'We haven't got a few weeks,' said Lawrence glumly. 'I'm needed back in Cairo. And we've work to do here prior to that.'

Daniels looked crestfallen. 'Sorry.'

'It's not your fault,' said Quinn. 'And you are in no fit state—'

'Me?' Daniels laughed, an act that caused him some discomfort. 'Not the first time this has happened. I was six foot four when I took up flying. Barely make six foot now.'

'Can I have a word?' asked Lawrence, motioning to Quinn that they might step outside.

Excusing themselves, they walked out into the chill of the night, where Farid sat at his habitual station on their considerable stack of luggage, a rifle across his thighs. Lawrence indicated Quinn should stay where he was and walked over to their companion and there was a hurried, whispered conversation.

'That's torn it, as you English say.'

Quinn spun round. It was Tariq, a cheroot between his teeth, and a mat under his arm. He had taken himself off to pray when they arrived at the airfield.

'The planes?'

275

Tariq nodded. 'I always thought it was crazy plan. I have seen flying fever with the Turks. Aeroplanes are like some new toy the generals want, but they can't quite understand what it is for or how it works. So they try it for everything. One day, they'll realise, ah, THIS is what it's best at. How many centuries did it take to perfect the cavalry charge? They are rushing things. That is my opinion.'

'What do you suggest?'

'For us? Horses, mules, camels. Things that are not glued together.' He pointed at the indistinct hump of the Airco wreckage. 'Ever seen legs fall off a donkey?'

Quinn laughed and they fell silent. The smoke of the crude cigar made his nose twitch, so he set about lighting a pipe. The last one, he swore, until he was back home.

In the distance were the winking lights of the port, where the army had its main garrison and, scattered around that, the softer glow of the locals' fires. Up above, a sprinkle of stars winked down on them, the clear sky sucking the day's warmth from the earth. Quinn pulled his jacket tighter, wondering what the hell they could do now.

Lawrence broke away from his conversation after slapping Farid on the back and strode over to Quinn.

'I need some of your sovereigns, please.'

'What for?' Quinn asked.

Lawrence didn't answer directly, but thought for a moment. 'I think a hundred should do it.'

'A hundred?' It was a small fortune.

'It's not your money, man. Give me the key to the box.'

'Not till you tell me why.'

Lawrence shook his head. 'You'll see. Just ask Dickie who is the best mechanic in this godforsaken place, will you, and tell that man we need him for a morning tomorrow. You might want to get that luggage moved under cover. And sleep with it. Tariq here will help, eh?'

Tariq gave a mocking bow. 'Oh yes, I have travelled over the ocean for just such a task.'

Lawrence smirked at the sarcasm. 'Be quiet. Farid!'

The Arab tossed the rifle across and Lawrence caught it. He handed it to Quinn.

'Keep it close at hand. Don't worry, Farid and I will be back before dawn.' There was mischief in his smile that worried Quinn. 'Now, one hundred sovereigns, if you please.'

It was well before sunrise when someone tugged at the outside of the bell tent that held the luggage. Half dozing on the cases, Quinn jerked fully wake and grabbed the Lee Enfield, snaking his hand around it and resting his index finger on the trigger guard.

He blinked away the incipient sleep. 'Lawrence? That you?'

'Is that Captain Quinn?'

'Who is that? Identify yourself.'

'I'm looking for Captain Quinn. I do believe he's hereabouts. Can I come in? Bloody cold out here.'

Quinn worked the bolt and put one round into the chamber. 'Enter. But do it very, very slowly.'

The flap snapped back and a shadowy figure slipped inside. Quinn said: 'There's a lamp down to your left, if you care to light it.'

'Of course. Had the devil of a job finding you, old chap.'

'Can you identify yourself, please?'

The man rattled a box of Swan Vestas to check there were matches within and took off the glass flue. 'Apologies. Should have said. Captain Edward Noel. I'm the Political Officer at Bushire.'

The man who failed to restrain Wassmuss and thus caused all these problems in the first place, thought Quinn. 'You're a long way from home. Weren't you meant to meet us at Jam?'

The light spluttered on and Quinn could see the man was streaked with dirt. He had the smell of the road on him too, and of the native rags he was wearing. 'We've been riding for four days.'

'We?'

'Me and a few tame natives.'

'How on earth did you know we were already here?'

'I told you, I'm the Political Officer.'

'You were meant to meet us at Jam,' Quinn repeated. 'At the airstrip.'

'Sticky situation at Jam, if you'll pardon the expression.' He gave a bark of a laugh. 'There is no airstrip at Jam, old boy. Well, there was, but it is now in rebel hands. That's why I came to warn you, before you took off. Glad we made it in time.'

'Well, you could have saved your strength. We won't be taking off.' He explained about the aircraft. As he spoke, Noel squatted down and inscribed patterns on the dirt floor.

'I hope you don't mind me saying this, Quinn, but you've gone off a bit half-cock all round, don't you think?'

278

Quinn bristled at the presumption of the man. 'Our mission is to execute the exchange without being taken prisoner ourselves. It is quite simple.'

'Nothing is simple in this country. And to rely on machines, aeroplanes in particular, is madness. Persia will break anything it can. If you don't pay careful attention, it will break you, too.'

He didn't reply, but Quinn knew only too well what the man meant. It had broken him once. He had watched his wife die of cholera, slowly, in agony, fading from view before his eyes, like an old photograph bleaching in sunlight. Some part of him had certainly snapped then.

'Where's this chap Lawrence? I hear he's hitched a ride with you?'

Quinn laid the rifle down, although, by force of habit, it still pointed in Noel's direction. 'I have no idea where he is.'

'Or what he's doing? No, thought not. Who exactly is in charge here?'

'Well, we both outrank him, theoretically.'

Noel clearly didn't like the sound of that. 'What do you mean, theoretically?'

'You'll see.'

'Explain yourself, man.' Four days in the saddle had clearly left him irritable.

'Well, he's a bit of a character.'

'Is he, indeed? Look, Quinn, I am in touch with the hostages. Stroke of luck, really. O'Connor is a good, robust man and he engineered a hidden code. But some of the others . . . according to O'Connor, they don't seem to have the stamina for much longer in captivity. It's best we do this as straightforwardly as possible. Oh, I know you'd like to see this Wassmuss get his comeuppance. We all would. He is responsible, indirectly, for the deaths of some good men. And he has Bushire nailed down pretty tight. But first, we do the exchange and get O'Connor and the others out. Then we deal with the German. Agreed?'

That suited Quinn. A kill after the hostages were safe was a satisfactory plan. 'Agreed.'

Just then there came a parping sound that made them both jump. They scrambled to their feet and stumbled out into the first inklings of dawn. Twin beams of light blinded them, and Quinn shaded his eyes. He ducked out of the glare and could just make out the imposing shape of an open-topped automobile. As he got closer, he could see Farid behind the wheel and Lawrence, now dressed in native garb, beside him. It would need to be a gloriously bright sunrise to rival the great smile across the Englishman's face. 'Get in, Quinn, it's marvellous.'

Quinn and Noel exchanged glances. Quinn asked: 'Where on earth did you get that?'

Quinn had rarely heard Lawrence sound so happy. 'Well, it was meant to be unloaded from the *Hardinge* in Karachi for some nabob or other. But, don't you know, someone misread the manifest and, well, here it is.' So that was where the sovereigns had gone. He'd bribed the stevedores. 'Shame to let it go to waste. I said we'd get it back in one piece.' A suspicion came into his voice. 'Hello, who is this?'

'Captain Noel. Political Officer. Bushire,' Quinn explained as the stranger stepped into the light.

Lawrence brightened. 'The man who can tell us all about our quarry.'

'Lieutenant—'

'Call me Lawrence. Or T.E. I don't think we should stand on rank or ceremony.'

'Lieutenant—' Noel tried again, but Lawrence was already out of the car, running his fingers over the fine coachwork.

'Seats four plus luggage. Farid soon got the hang of it. Tricky advance and retard, apparently. But we should all learn to drive it, just in case.' It was Quinn's turn to try and interrupt, but Lawrence was in a state close to rapture. 'Runs beautifully. Bit thirsty on the old juice, have to take plenty with us. Look at that craftsmanship. Beautiful. Marvellous Rolls, wonderful Royce, I say.'

'It's two hundred miles to Bushire,' Noel said scathingly. 'Over some of the worst roads in the world. Across the Maarifa Heights. And the nearest petrol is God alone knows where. It's an awful drive.'

Quinn knew from experience that Lawrence did not respond well to being told something was beyond him. Lawrence banged the bonnet of the car with enthusiasm. 'And this, my dear chap, is a Rolls-Royce. I'll call it *The Green Ray*. What do you think?'

'I think it's insanity of the highest order.'

Lawrence looked crestfallen. 'As you like.' He thought for a moment. 'What about *The Green Mist*, then?'

The newcomer gave a groan and Quinn suppressed a laugh

at the man's expression of frustration. As Quinn turned his head to hide his smile, he could have sworn he caught a sly wink from Lawrence, but it could have been a trick of the light.

Thirty

The finest mechanic at the Banda air base was a Scot called Jimmy McCain. Over breakfast, bemused that a group of officers should lower themselves to enter the men's mess tent, he listened to Lawrence laying out what he required. Quinn and Noel were present, too, keen to hear what he had in mind, leaving Farid and Tariq to keep watch over the luggage.

'Lovely motor car,' said McCain as he shovelled scrambled eggs into his mouth. 'More suited to a Sunday parade, though.'

'Nonsense,' said Lawrence, stirring sugar into his vile coffee. 'They are built for the worst country estates imaginable. And Indian roads. They use them as armoured cars in France.'

'This isn't France,' the mechanic warned, taking a gulp of tea.

'And the Duke of Westminster has a battery of armoured cars in the Western desert, operating against the Sanussi.' This was a fanatically religious, anti-British tribe causing sporadic trouble by opportunistic raiding.

McCain sniffed. 'Aye, but specially built for the desert, those ones.'

'True. Which is why I want the springs on this stiffened. Can you do that?'

McCain shrugged. 'Easily enough.'

'And I want you to salvage the gun ring from the Airco.'

That had the mechanic's attention. 'Why would you want to do that?'

Lawrence took a sip of the coffee. The sugar hadn't helped. Now it was vile and sweet. 'Because I want a Lewis placed on the back of the Rolls. So a passenger can stand up and fire.'

McCain grinned and wiped grease from his mouth. 'Well, that might do a little damage to the bodywork. Y'know, fixing the supports on.'

'Don't fret about that. Can you do it?'

McCain took another slurp of tea, and all leaned forward to hear his reply. 'If I was you, Lieutenant, I'd also have something rigged up so you have a forward-facing machine gun. Operated by the passenger in the front.'

'Two guns? Excellent.'

'Have to ask the Wingco about all this.'

'Leave him to me, Corporal.' Lawrence beamed. Quinn had no doubt that after fifteen minutes in his company the Wingco would offer to hold the welding torch and turn the starting handle. He was beginning to appreciate that, when he wanted something, Lawrence normally found the appropriate strategy to get the job done.

'Also,' added McCain, nodding towards the tent where

Farid and Tariq stood guard. 'You have a mighty lot of luggage. Yon car has a big back end, but you could do with a rack on the back.'

'And you can do all this?'

'I might. But, as I say, it's up to the Wingco. It's not exactly regulation. And I'd be doing it on ma own time.'

Lawrence turned and looked at Quinn. 'Captain Quinn, I think we need that magic box of yours once more.'

'And, although I can do the donkey work, there is someone else worth talking to. Young Sam Rollins. That man knows engines. You appreciate they detune these machines? To make them smooth at parade speed. Sam Rollins can get you more power out of that beastie if you wish.'

'More horsepower?' Lawrence's eyes blazed at the thought. 'Oh we wish, we wish, Corporal McCain. Bring me this Sam Rollins.'

By mid-morning the sun had bleached out the surroundings till they seemed to inhabit a monochrome world. Even the dark distant mountains, so richly purple at dawn, glowed white and featureless. A hot wind was blowing from the north, and Quinn remembered all too well the smell and taste of the desert dust, the sensation of slow suffocation it brought.

Most of the movement in the landscape came from the buzzards, rising and falling in slow spirals, and occasionally a kite joined them hovering in space, eyes fixed for any movement on the earth. The majority of the soldiers, tranquillised by the building heat, had crept into whatever shadows they could find.

The Rolls-Royce had been wheeled under a canvas canopy and the Scot got to work in its shade. Sam Rollins, meanwhile, busied himself with the enormous engine and its bird's nest of wires and cables.

Noel and his Tangistans had set up a makeshift camp close by and soon the air was filled with the smell of their bread. At the luggage tent, Quinn found Farid inside, his rifle at the ready. Quinn tried his Persian. 'Can I get you some water?'

Farid's voice was soft and low through the loose scarf he habitually wore across his lower face to keep out the all-pervasive dust and the flies that liked to suck at the lips, and Quinn had to strain to hear the reply. 'That would be most kind, sir.'

'No need for the formality. I'll do a shift later. So you can get some lunch.'

'It is no problem, sir. Tariq will do his share.'

'I insist.'

Farid switched back to English. 'You have good Persian, sir.'

'Thank you.'

From the officer's mess tent, Quinn fetched a container of water, which he placed at Farid's side. The air under the canvas was thick and treacly, hard to breathe. Quinn sat, folding his legs under him. 'Where are you from, Farid?'

'Gahar, sir.'

'I don't know it.'

'Few do.'

'But Miss Bell does? Is that where she found you?'

'I was in Tehran when she hired me.' Farid lowered the scarf and drank, sipping slowly, savouring the taste of the water.

'You missed prayers to guard this.'

He wiped his mouth and raised the protective scarf again. 'I am Christian, sir. From a Christian village. I belong to the Assyrian Church.'

'Forgive me, I assumed too much.'

The lad shrugged. It was nothing to him. 'All travellers have to adapt. Sometimes it is better to be Muslim when travelling. Then I am a Muslim. Where did you learn the language?'

'I had a teacher.'

'A good teacher, I think, sir. But you have been here before, so Lawrence says.'

'Yes. Before the war.'

'Were you a spy then?'

Quinn stood and shook his head. 'No. I bought dates for the British.'

For some reason they both found this funny and began laughing. 'Lyman Brothers?'

Quinn nodded.

'But you don't like this place?' Farid asked.

'Is it that obvious?'

The Persian nodded. 'I can see it in your face, sir. Why?'

Quinn helped himself to some water. 'I have a wife buried at Bushire.'

Farid lowered his head. 'I am sorry, sir. What was her name?'

For some reason Quinn couldn't quite grasp, telling him Kate's name was a step too far. That was for his friends. And he had precious few of those. 'It doesn't matter.'

'I understand. You will see her? The grave?'

'No.'

'Why not, sir?'

Quinn shook his head. 'It's just a coffin in the earth. It's not her in there.'

'No, she is in heaven, sir.'

Quinn stood, knowing it was foolish to try and argue with such a childish sentiment. 'I will see you later. For a turn at guarding. No arguments.'

The boy nodded, staring at Quinn with his dark eyes, in a way that he found disconcertingly direct, much like his questions.

As he stepped outside, Quinn almost bumped into Noel and Lawrence, deep in conversation. He made to join them, but Lawrence said: 'Check on the Rolls, will you, Captain? I think Tariq is more used to changing bicycle chains than dealing with automobiles.'

Lawrence made sure Quinn was out of earshot before he asked: 'So, Captain Noel, tell me about Wassmuss. Why do they follow him?'

Lawrence and Noel quickly crossed over the blisteringly hot stones of the airstrip, past mechanics dismantling the remaining sections of the crashed Airco. Ahead was a series of boulders that would offer some shade for their conversation. Noel shooed flies from his face as he spoke. 'Hard to say. The man has charisma, but it isn't that alone. I think they believe what he says.'

'Which is?'

'Not too much. No huge, grand promises, as far as I can gather.'

'A cruel man?'

Noel looked shocked. 'Why do you say that?'

'What happened to the telegraph party?' asked Lawrence. 'Was that not cruel and barbarous?'

'That was the Khan of Ahram.'

'Under the auspices of this German.'

Noel shrugged. 'Certainly. But I am sure you appreciate that some of the tribes in this part of the world are a cruel and barbarous people by our standards. But rarely by their own measure. Wassmuss understands this. I think one of his strengths is he does not interfere with their way of fighting. If traditionally they loot, he lets them loot . . .'

'And if they rape?'

'They don't.'

'But if they did?'

Noel spoke quietly. 'Then they will.'

'And if they take no prisoners?'

Noel considered for a moment. 'Then there will be no prisoners. The tribes will fight in their own way no matter what. Interfere with tradition, you get resentment. Resentment begets dissatisfaction. Dissatisfaction is the father of desertion. In the end, the undertaking will fall apart.'

'So not a cruel man?'

'A realist. Do not bring your European ways to the campfire, I think that's his point of view. Work with the material you have, no matter how crude.'

'What about this way of fighting?' asked Lawrence. 'Do you approve?'

'It's not a case of approving,' the captain replied almost tetchily. 'The question is, does it work? Wassmuss is not an army. He is an influence, an idea, a thing intangible, invulnerable, without front or back, drifting about like gas. He is a lethal vapour and as hard to kill. And when you try and catch that vapour, he has a secret weapon.'

'What's that?'

Noel spread his arms, taking in the scrub and the jagged blue-tinged hills. 'The land, the desert, the mountains. It's worth a whole battalion of regular troops, perhaps more, because it is scary, inhospitable and will kill you if you make a mistake. It's the greatest ally of all.'

They reached the nearest rock formation, sat in its meagre shadow, and drank from their flasks. Lawrence poured some water over his head. 'Interesting.'

'Yes. Now, you will travel in uniform?' Noel asked.

'Native garb, like this,' Lawrence tugged at his tunic and pointed at Noel's, 'and like you. Khaki is thick, itchy and you sweat more than necessary. Arab and Tangistan dress is cleaner, more comfortable.'

'I agree.' Noel's voice dropped once more, and he sounded concerned. 'But the Rolls is madness, Lawrence.'

'You think?' He had a twinkle in his eye. 'Fun, though.'

'Fun?' He made the word sound vulgar and distasteful. 'Not

when you break down in the desert. Not when all your petrol has evaporated.'

'What are you saying?'

'I'm saying, give it up. Come with me and my men. There are good horses to be had here and baggage camels. We can avoid the rebels easily enough. I did on the way down.' He took out a folding linen map and laid it across a flat stone. 'And make an exchange here. Or here. On this escarpment. You could survey the whole countryside from there. Wassmuss would have no chance of springing any surprise.'

'Sounds interesting. But I still want to take the Rolls. *The Green Mist* cost us a lot of money to hire. Shame to waste it.'

Noel shook is head in dismay. 'Then there is only this road. It is bad, but the others are worse. I have mules. Why don't you load up the baggage with us? And fuel. We can go ahead today and meet you . . .' His finger hovered over the map. 'Here. Lars.'

'You would take spare fuel for us?'

'And any other parts you needed. And all the bags.'

Lawrence raised his palm at that. 'The Wassmuss bags stay with me.'

A flash of frustration distorted Noel's features.

'I know you and he have history, Captain. And you want to make good.' Or arrange your own exchange to expurgate your blemished reputation, he thought. 'But this is my mission.'

'And Captain Quinn's,' Noel reminded him.

'And Captain Quinn's,' Lawrence agreed. 'Who has welcomed me onboard as an equal player.'

'I took those bags in the first place, if you recall,' Noel said bitterly.

'Forgive me, but you lost Wassmuss in the process.'

'Will that always be held against me?'

'Not when you deliver him to Bushire.'

'You'll turn him over to me?'

'Once Quinn and I have finished with him, yes.' Of course, it might be a body he would be taking, but he thought it best not to labour that point. Lawrence, wanting no more discussion on the matter, moved back out into the sunlight, as if anxious to leave. 'Shall we see how they are getting on with the conversion? I doubt we'll be ready to leave until tomorrow at the earliest. Perhaps the next day.' He stood and looked at the sky, his eyes narrowed to painful slits by the glare. 'And then I'll wait until the worst of the day is done before setting off. The Rolls won't like the midday sun.'

From beneath the folds of his clothes Noel produced his pocket watch. 'I cannot keep the Tangistan here that long. We could leave today, clear the road for you. We'll be waiting with fuel and more supplies at Lars.'

'Excellent idea. I'll see you are properly victualised.'

They began their walk back. 'You are sure about this Rolls-Royce madness? After what this country did to the aeroplanes?'

'I won't be moved on the Rolls, Noel. I have a choice, I can sit here and wait for the plane to be fixed, or I can get off my backside and get cracking. Given the choice between inaction and action, I will always take the latter. I appreciate your offer to help me. But I have a Rolls-Royce. I am going to use it.'

292

Noel sounded sorrowful when he replied: 'I suspected as much.' Then: '*Vis consili expers mole ruit sua.*'

It was Horace, and Lawrence knew it well. '*Force without wisdom fails under its own weight.* Well, God grant us wisdom, then.' But it wasn't the familiar words, but the delivery of them that suddenly made Lawrence uneasy.

Noel and his Tangistans were ready to move by the middle of the afternoon. They made for a stirring sight, looking completely at home in the hostile landscape, their faces masked, their rifles slung casually over their shoulders, the horses subtly decorated with silver and copper that flashed in the sun.

After a series of elaborate farewells, Lawrence, Tariq, Farid and Quinn watched them leave. The proud riders moved among the tents with their mounts' heads held high, the front legs high-stepping and the bewildered sepoys watched what appeared to be a squadron of bandits pass among them in silence. As they reached the edge of the encampment, the party gave a sudden spurt. Soon, they were lost in the shifting wall of fine dust the hooves flicked from the earth.

'I'm glad they're on our side,' said Quinn when the shimmering horizon finally took all trace of them.

Lawrence gave a little snort. 'I don't think they are.'

'What?' asked Quinn.

'They're not,' replied Lawrence, his doubt hardening to certainty.

'Not what?'

'On our side.'

He heard a little gasp from Tariq. 'Are you sure, Lawrence?'

'I wasn't. I think I am now.' Lawrence cursed under his breath. 'What a fool.'

Quinn turned to Tariq, hoping for more sense. 'Can you explain?'

'Lawrence does not think that was your Captain Noel.'

'Then who in blazes . . . ?' he began, but he knew the answer even before he reached the end of the sentence. It faded to a low groan.

Lawrence saw the realisation dawn on Quinn's face and put him out of his misery. 'That's right. I think we've just had our first encounter with Wilhelm Wassmuss.'

Thirty-one

Over the next few hours Lawrence worked alongside McCain and Rollins, sweating over the car that was being transformed into *The Green Mist*, bolting and welding on struts and braces, impervious to the hot sparks which landed on his naked torso. Farid, Tariq and Quinn helped fetch and carry. A guard from the Indian regiment had been posted on the luggage while they laboured, just in case Wassmuss tried to sneak back and snatch his belongings.

'When did you know that it was the German?' Quinn demanded of the former Ottoman soldier.

'Seconds before you did,' Tariq replied. 'I could see it in Lawrence's eyes.'

'And what tipped him the wink?'

Tariq shrugged. 'You'll have to ask Lawrence that.'

'And why didn't Wassmuss try and take his bags by force?'

Tariq considered this. 'I suspect he didn't know before he

arrived that five thousand sepoys had shipped in. Even Wassmuss might not have liked those odds.'

Quinn strode over and leaned on the car. Despite the canopy covering most it, the metal was too hot to touch for any length of time. He stepped back. 'Lawrence.'

He was in the rear of the vehicle, screwing something to the floor. 'Pass me a wrench. Three quarters.'

Quinn knelt down and sorted through the tools that had been tossed on to the ground, picking them up gingerly and dropping them as soon as he could. Those that had no shade were white hot from the sun; those that had been in shadow were merely blistering. He found the right one and used his sleeve to pass it to Lawrence. The man grabbed it without flinching. 'Thanks. Nearly done. Lost a bit of room in the back because of the support for the gun mount.'

'When did you know it was Wassmuss?' Quinn demanded.

Lawrence looked up at him and considered the question. 'Quite late on. Out at the rock I got my first suspicion that something wasn't right. But I dismissed it as foolishness on my part. Yet...'

'What?'

'Why didn't I let him take the bags? Or go with him to Lars? Why wasn't I straight with him about our intended route? It was as if some animal part of my brain, a deep instinct, knew something wasn't right, whereas the higher centres accepted him at face value. Curious.'

Quinn couldn't hide his exasperation. 'But, but—'

'Yes. I know what you are thinking.'

'It could be all over now.'

'Perhaps. But by the time I listened to my inner doubts it was too late. There is, though, one other thing to consider. What if we had acted and arrested Wassmuss, if that is who he was? This isn't the place for a confrontation. We out-numbered his men, but they were strong fighters. No matter how we did it, there would have been bloodshed. And who is to say what instructions he left about the hostages if he didn't return? It could be he had left word for them to be slaugh-tered if he was captured. Arresting him would not necessarily have got us O'Connor.'

Quinn had to concede this was a good point.

Lawrence sighed. 'It's done now. This is the hand we are dealt. What say you we pick it up and play with it?' Before he could reply, Lawrence straightened and drew the back of his hand across his grease-streaked forehead. 'Farid! Get the Lewis, will you?'

Quinn moved back and appreciated for the first time what they had done to the once handsome car. It had sprouted an ugly tower of metal in the rear and a folding metal screen with holes at the front, which could be lifted to protect the glass. The previously immaculate coachwork was scuffed and scratched where they had been careless with wrenches, span-ners and drills. The bonnet was covered in dusty footprints and there were burn marks in the upholstery. 'Dear God, the nabob isn't going to be best pleased with this.'

'Not unless he plans to go tiger hunting in it.'

'Lawrence, what do we do now?'

He had anticipated the question. 'Wassmuss was very courageous coming here. Quite a little show. I admire him

297

for it. Now, he is waiting out there for us, to take us when there aren't five thousand onlookers. The thing is, we have one card up our sleeve.'

'Which is?'

'He doesn't know we know it was him. Doesn't, I hope, even suspect.'

'So you have a plan.'

Farid struggled over with a machine gun, which had a grooved, circular magazine on the top of it. It was a fearsome weapon, able to do a lot of damage with its ninety-seven rounds. Lawrence said: 'McCain. Give him a hand, will you?' He turned back to Quinn. 'We have to change the game. Get the upper hand once more. And that means rescuing the hostages without giving up the bags.'

'And how do you suggest we do that?' Quinn prompted.

Lawrence stepped out of the car, crouched down, and began to scrawl in the grit of the arid soil. 'We are here. Correct? Lars is here. Is that right?'

'I don't know,' Quinn admitted. 'I never got this far south.'

Lawrence looked up and summoned Tariq with a wave of his hand. 'Lars, here, yes?'

The Arab nodded. 'Yes.'

Farid left McCain to fix the Lewis to the gun ring and stepped down from the car to join them.

Lawrence squinted up at Quinn. 'This is where Wassmuss will be waiting for us. He thinks we will be coming this way. But Farid knows a second road that can carry an automobile, don't you?' The servant confirmed this. 'It is called the Zoroastrian Way. They used to use it to take the dead from Bastak and Garash to a Tower of Silence, where they were laid out for the predators to strip. They are long gone, the Zoroastrians, and for years it has been a smuggler's path. Hence its other name, the Gun Road. It runs here.' He traced a straight line and then stabbed the dirt. 'To Ahram. With *The Green Mist*, we can be there, free the hostages and be away before Wassmuss realises he's been duped. What do you think?'

'The Rolls only carries four,' Quinn said, trying not to state the obvious. 'We are going to storm a fortress with four of us?'

'And the element of surprise.'

'I'd rather have the element of a battalion. And how do we get them back here?'

'We don't. We only have to get them to Bushire. Here.' Another mark in the earth. 'A thirty-mile run across flat, open country.'

Open country meant no cover, no hiding, that any pursuer could find you without difficulty and hunt you down. 'Am I the only one who thinks this somewhat . . . misguided?'

Tariq remained impassive; Farid shrugged. Lawrence stood and pronounced. 'Wassmuss said something very interesting, about striking like vapour and then disappearing. That's what we'll be doing.'

Quinn wondered if they were confusing his hesitation for cowardice. Nevertheless, he said: 'And that's what I am worried about, Lawrence. Four of us. Disappearing like vapour.'

Lawrence sighed. 'Go on, tell him, Farid.'

The lad spoke in that low, soft voice of his. 'The village of

Deh Now is about twenty miles from Ahram, sir. The Khan of Deh Now, he hates the Khan of Ahram. He would welcome any chance to attack the fortress. But the Khan of Ahram—'

'Zair Khidair,' said Quinn, to remind them they weren't dealing with a complete ingénu.

'Yes. He has had modern weapons from the Germans.'

Lawrence leapt in. 'Which made him strong enough to repulse any attack. But our boot will contain gold and guns and there are warriors at Deh Now ready to use both of them.'

'At least forty, perhaps more,' confirmed Tariq. 'According to my old reports.'

Lawrence grabbed a cloth and wiped his body, before pulling on a shirt, which he misbuttoned on the first attempt. He re-did two of the buttons, then left the shirt flapping open. 'So, you see, Quinn, four become forty, just like that.' He clicked his fingers. 'And we have this' – he slapped the side of the Rolls – 'up our sleeves. And, of course, their great tactician, Wassmuss, will be cooling his heels at Lars, waiting for us to toddle up to his gate. Once we have the hostages, we can invite Wassmuss to come and get his baggage at our convenience. Not his. Now, we should begin loading and change into more suitable clothes.'

'Why?' asked Quinn. 'The conversion isn't finished.'

'The windscreen isn't strong enough to take a gun mount without more struts. And we haven't got time to do it now, not without losing our advantage. We'll have to make do. We'll take a second Lewis in the boot. Wassmuss thinks we aren't leaving for another day at least; we must play to that.'

'So when are we leaving?'

Lawrence looked up at the sun and shaded his eyes. 'I'd say in about an hour.'

Quinn turned on his heels, putting distance between them at a cracking pace.

'Where are you going, Captain?' demanded Lawrence.

Against his better judgement, Quinn found himself blurting out an answer. 'To write a letter.'

Thirty-two

There were those who claimed the Rolls-Royce to be the finest motor car in the world, Quinn knew, and this one was going to have to live up to that accolade. It was to be conveyance, workhorse and war-horse combined. Shovels, fuel, ammunition, water, blankets (for giving the wheels purchase in case of sinking into soft sand), water, spare wheels, tools, rifles, water, the rest of the sovereigns, pistols, food, water: the poor car creaked and groaned as more and more provisions and necessities were loaded on to her. When there was no more room in the boot or the rack, Lawrence and McCain improvised further racks along the side. It meant the doors could not be opened, so that all four riders had to clamber in over the sills.

Lawrence had Rollins run the engine up to temperature, listening intently as he revved it until the tappets clacked with the valve bounce. 'Good job, Sam. Very smooth.'

'Thank you, sir,' said the mechanic.

'Where did you learn about cars?'

'I worked for Sunbeam before all this.'

'Did you? You know, the Duke of Westminster has a brigade of armoured cars in the Western Desert. Short of good drivers and mechanics and I'll wager it'd be more exciting that Banda. I could approve any request for a transfer, if that would help.'

Sam thanked him profusely and set about re-checking every bolt and clip beneath the bonnet. This, thought Quinn, would be as reliable a Rolls engine as human hands could manage.

Quinn watched Lawrence carefully that morning as he dealt with the various soldiers and airmen he needed to help him perfect the car and its cargo. Here was a yet another version of the man; one with quiet authority, a sense of purpose, praising and chiding where appropriate. There were no obscure quotes, no lengthy silences while he was lost in contemplation. Lawrence had said he was no soldier. Perhaps not, but Quinn was beginning to appreciate that, beneath the many layers that he habitually wrapped himself in, there might just be a leader.

In reality it was another three hours, not one, before Lawrence told them that departure was imminent, just as Quinn could feel the first grudging drop in the day's temperature. Daniels came out of his tent, hobbling over on crutches.

'For God's sake, man,' said Quinn. 'You shouldn't be up.'

'Just come to wish you good luck.' He nodded at the car and laughed. 'You'll need it in that. And you were worried about my aeroplanes. No accounting for some people. I hope we can get some glue and see you up there. I'm sorry it didn't work out.'

Lawrence came across to shake hands.

'Well, I admire your commitment to improvisation, Lawrence.'

'Circumstances rule men; men do not rule circumstances,' Lawrence replied. 'Herodotus.'

Daniels's face furrowed. 'Didn't he kill all the firstborn?'

'No, that was Herod—' Lawrence began before he realised he was being teased. He smiled and added: 'See you in Bushire, perhaps.'

'Perhaps. But you'll need these for the road.'

Daniels's batman appeared with four pairs of brand new flying goggles, smelling of leather and canvas.

'And I've put some bully beef in with your rations. You're bound to get tired of eating like a native.'

'Thank you,' said Lawrence, accepting the goggles and tossing a pair to each of the others in turn.

'And take this if you will.' Daniels unfurled a striped scarf.

'Balliol. Thank you. But I'm a Jesus man,' Lawrence said.

'It's the closest you'll get to Oxford out here,' Daniels said. 'Take it, please.'

Lawrence looked slightly embarrassed as he accepted the gift. 'Thank you. It will keep me warm at night. Right, let's see what this beauty can offer us.'

Tariq turned the starting handle according to Rollins's instructions and the engine caught on the third turn. Lawrence climbed in the front, next to Farid, Quinn positioned himself behind the driver and Tariq was beneath the Lewis gun, which had been lashed so that it couldn't spin on the mount. One good pull on the cord would free it, however.

With first gear engaged, the car gave a jerk forward, and then moved smoothly over the ground. Daniels raised a crutch in farewell and Lawrence gave a brief wave of his new purple and black neck warmer before turning back and facing forward. On his lap he unfolded a map and made an X at the starting point.

Quinn slumped down in his seat, trying to remain calm. He felt like Persia was a savage animal that had taken one bite from him and, having acquired the taste for his flesh, had come back for more. The bleakness of the scorched land ahead gave him no cause for optimism.

'Who was it you write your letter to?' Tariq asked Quinn over the din of the car.

Quinn was noncommittal. He regretted the outburst where he had revealed his intention to put pen to paper. 'A friend.'

Tariq nodded. 'Is always nice to know.'

'What is?'

'That someone is worrying about you. That someone will mourn you if you don't come back.'

'I'll come back,' Quinn replied, huffily. 'That was why I wrote the letter.'

Tariq said nothing, and just slid a piece of silken cloth over his mouth as the Rolls crossed on to the dusty track that was the road out of Banda Abbas. A column of smoke seemed to surround them, coiling up into the air. Quinn tapped Lawrence on the shoulder. 'There's no way we can sneak up on anyone in this.'

The Englishman nodded. 'Farid says the road surface

becomes firmer later, less muck to throw up. But you are right. Some of the tribesmen are bound to spot us.'

'And come looking,' said Farid.

Tariq joined in. 'Be warned. We may encounter bandits or a scout party from one of the villages that thrives on the pickings from travellers. If they approach in single file, that is good. If they spread out in a line or semicircle, that is bad. And if they make to reach for gifts . . .'

'What?' asked Quinn as the sentence tailed off.

Tariq reached up and tapped the Lewis gun. 'Shoot them.'

The weight of the vehicle and the stiffened suspension made for a harsh, juddery ride. Quinn shoved a piece of his head-dress into his mouth after his teeth had clashed together for the fourth time. Nobody spoke apart from Lawrence. Every so often he consulted a map and shouted out a snippet of information. At one point he consulted his compass, which flashed bright in the low rays of the sun.

'This is why I was robbed in Syria. This is what they were after,' he yelled. 'It is a cheap French one, but I polished it so that it shone like gold. They beat me for it and then threw it back on my broken body when they discovered it was but poor metal and elbow grease. There's a lesson in there somewhere.'

The land was rising as they drove, imperceptibly at first, then with an increasing gradient. Although the car itself was shuddering and bumping badly, the engine showed little sign of strain. There was more than adequate power under the bonnet for decent progress. However, Farid twice insisted they stop and remove large boulders blocking their way, rather than driving over them, to protect the steering arms. 'They strengthen them on the armoured cars, I would think,' he explained. 'Corporal Sam warned me these are fragile.'

Most of the surroundings were leached to a sandy beige, but on the low hills to their right were splashes of colour, a ribbon of green here, the lonely flame of a few flowers there. When he first arrived in Persia, Quinn had wondered how anyone could survive, let alone thrive in lands such as these. But they could and did and the glimpse of a few lonely sheep silhouetted on a crest told him that men were not too far away. Perhaps Tariq was right, horses or camels would have been better than the Rolls; they tended to pass with less disruption.

He wasn't alone in scanning the horizons. Both Lawrence and Tariq were rarely still. Lawrence sometimes took off his goggles and used a pair of binoculars, although Quinn couldn't imagine how he could focus given the tossing about they were suffering. Once Lawrence made them stop to examine a series of stone pillars, which he quickly sketched with a few easy strokes and filled in the shape of the hills behind them. It was a simple but startlingly effective record, thought Quinn.

'Look,' he said. Lawrence strode across to a circular base of mud bricks, which looked as if they had melted in the sun. 'I'll wager this was a signal tower. They were all over this region.'

He looked up as if he could visualise the long vanished, soaring structure still piercing the sky, its oily flames sending warning to the others in the chain.

'I wish I had two months here, a year even,' Lawrence said, almost to himself. He turned to Quinn, his right arm pointing directly north, past the mauve-tinged cliffs that appeared to bar their way. 'You know what great palaces lie over there? Of the travels of Chardin or Fryer?'

'No,' said Quinn truthfully. The heat was pulsing off the sandy ground in waves, making him feel nauseous. He took some water. The glow of the engine, coupled with the sun, made the inside of the vehicle a crucible and he'd sweated several bowlfuls of fluid. He knew they had to be careful not to dehydrate. No sooner had he licked his lips than flies landed around his mouth to steal some of his saliva. He shooed them away and pulled up his neckscarf.

Lawrence sounded wistful as he took the canteen. 'Yonder lie Pasargadae and Paarsa, which the Greeks called Persepolis, Darius's showcase, destroyed by Alexander, both built when Persia ruled the known world, neither excavated. It would take a lifetime to tease out their secrets.' He let out a sigh. 'That would be a life worth living.'

'Meanwhile, we have this life to waste. We should go on.'

Lawrence smiled at him. 'Sad, but true.' He slaked his own thirst. 'You know, Quinn, I'm glad they sent you. It is comforting to have a real soldier along.'

At first he thought the man was joshing him, but apparently not. Quinn wasn't sure how to respond. As usual, Lawrence had wrong-footed him. So he held out his hand and it was taken in a mighty grip. 'I don't know how you talked us into this. You are quite mad, you know.'

It was not meant maliciously, and Lawrence smiled as he

nodded. 'You are not the first to say that. In my family we prefer to think of it as being different.'

There're more like you? Quinn thought, but kept quiet.

As they continued, the higher range to their left began to close in on the road, and Farid had to slow down for more rock falls and erratic boulders, again insisting on rolling them out of the way if there was no way round them. The sun was almost touching the crests of the hills now, and the earth glowed a rich tangerine. Without warning, Farid swerved to the right so that the radiator faced into the cooling wind and they came to a halt. The Arab switched off the engine. Quinn pulled off the goggles and attempted to remove some of the grit from his ears.

Farid pointed at a gash in the foothills to the northwest. 'That is the road, sir.'

Lawrence stood and stretched, shaking the dust from his clothing. 'Is there anywhere suitable to make camp tonight?'

'Another hour.'

Tariq said: 'It will be dark soon.'

'Then we press on. Captain? Need anything?'

Quinn shook his head, but he had caught sight of Farid flexing his aching biceps. 'Want me to drive? Must be a strain on the arms.'

'No, thank you. Tomorrow,' said Farid. 'Perhaps.'

The goggles were repositioned and after another mile and a half the Arab led them up a cone of scree, the wheels spinning on the shifting surface, and on to a path that ran along the floor of a high valley. The first mile was narrow, but quickly fanned out as the hills retreated. Surprisingly, the smugglers' route was compacted sand and shale and gave a far smoother ride than the open plain they had just crossed. Quinn plucked out his tooth-guard.

Night came on in a rush and they were running on the acetylene lights when Farid came upon an area of limestone paving dotted with thin blades of fresh grass which looked like black spines in the headlamps. There was water there, a thin trickle running off the mountains. Farid found a small natural amphitheatre in the hillside into which he backed the Rolls. Again, the precious engine and cooling system were positioned to take advantage of any breeze.

Farid and Lawrence lit two oil lamps and set about excavating a fire pit, while Quinn walked away to stretch his limbs and relieve himself, before sitting on a boulder to watch the shooting stars flare across the sky. The River of Lights, as he recalled, was the Tangistan name for the Milky Way.

After a while, he became aware of Tariq sitting next to him. He hadn't heard his approach only because, he hoped, he had been too engrossed in the celestial *son et lumière*. Now his senses snapped back to fully alert. From beyond the car came the soft sound of shared laughter from Lawrence and Farid.

Tariq spoke to Quinn in English. 'You know the stars?'

'No,' he admitted as he craned his neck once more. 'You?'

'You live in this land, you must know the stars. My home is that way. Look, see the cluster of four?'

'Yes.'

'We call them the Four *Dokhtar*.'

'Daughters?'

'That is one meaning. The other is virgins. They would lead me home.'

'Is that why you are here? To go home?'

Tariq passed him some water. It was warm in his mouth, hardly refreshing at all. He held it for a few seconds before swallowing. 'I am here because Lawrence asked me to be here.'

'Why would you follow him?'

'Why would you?'

Before Quinn could answer, Lawrence appeared, announcing that dinner was served. The meal was rice balls, pressed together with fatty meat, and bread followed by dates and almonds. The temperature plummeted as if pushed over a cliff edge and, after washing in the meagre stream – heeding Farid's warning to watch for snakes – they bedded down in sleeping bags around the Rolls-Royce. Before he turned in Farid laid a blanket on the Rolls's engine to prevent, he said, dew damage. 'Or it will never start in the morning.'

Tariq suggested Quinn lay at the rear of the car, out of the wind, the way Arabs always slept in the lee of their kneeling camel. 'But at least this machine won't keep you awake with its chewing,' he laughed.

Quinn went straight to sleep but woke in the night, shivering with cold, certain he could hear voices, whispering. He listened hard, but then decided it was the slow groaning of desert rocks contracting as the temperature fell. He put his fingers in his ears, pulled his knees up to his chest, and drifted off once more into confused, turbulent dreams.

Quinn was woken with a rough shake while it was still dark. The two storm lamps were burning brightly. Farid was kneeling beside him, fresh faced and wide-awake in the glow, a thick, sweet coffee in his hand. It took a flustered moment for Quinn to realise this wasn't part of the dreams. The air was sparklingly cold and he could see the rolling clouds of his breath. The ground was covered in tiny glass beads, as was his sleeping bag. He touched one of the miniature jewels and it dissolved. Dew. He moistened his lips with the precious liquid. 'What time is it?'

'Four, sir,' the lad replied, handing him the cardamom-flavoured coffee. 'Or just after. We drive for six hours, then rest. You want to try the car, sir?'

'Driving? Yes. Give me a minute.' He waited for life to come to his stiff limbs. The numbness told him it had been frighteningly cold in the deep of night, and this during summer. In winter, a night in the open in these mountains meant death by exposure.

Once Quinn had revived his circulation, it took them less than a quarter of an hour to strike camp, by which time the sun had appeared, its amber light flaming off the rocks, giving the world a golden lustre. Fool's gold, thought Quinn. Such a sun was no friend of travellers.

Farid gave Quinn a quick lesson in the controls and they set off, slowly at first, as Quinn got used to the feel of the wheel and the advanced-retard mechanism for the timing of the spark. There was a tremendous outpouring of heat from the engine into the driver's well, which made Quinn's calves burn and his feet felt like they might catch fire. But Farid had said nothing and so he, too, kept quiet about his discomfort.

Now Farid sat under the gun, with Tariq behind Quinn,

while Lawrence remained in the front seat, only his goggles visible after he wrapped his headdress around his face and the Balliol scarf around his neck. As they drove on, skirting the malformed rock formations that sometimes protruded on to the path, Lawrence scribbled in a red notebook.

'How long will this take?' Quinn shouted.

Lawrence consulted his pages. 'We should be at Deh Now late tomorrow if there are no mishaps. Then, we move against Ahram the next day.'

'Won't they just kill the hostages the moment we appear?'

'If they get to see us,' Lawrence replied. 'Even then . . .'

'You don't know Persian ways very well, do you, Captain Quinn?' said Tariq.

Quinn risked turning his head for moment. 'About as well as you understand the English.'

Tariq roared. 'But, Captain, there is nobody on God's earth who does that, save another Englishman.'

Lawrence and Quinn exchanged amused glances. The former went back to his notebook. *Sometimes not even then*, Quinn thought.

After two hours, Lawrence declared that he would relieve Quinn. They stopped for a water break and Quinn walked around in a large circle, massaging each arm in turn in an attempt to get rid of the tingling caused by the constant vibration. Noticing his discomfort, Farid came over to him, grabbed a wrist and began to shake the arm, as if he were flicking out a rug, hard enough for Quinn to think it might pop from its socket.

'Careful, it's not that well attached.'

'I'll be careful, sir.' Farid glanced over his shoulder, and spoke in a conspiratorial whisper. 'Lawrence is curious to know who you sent your letter to. He says a man like you has no friends.'

Quinn shook his head. 'Lawrence knows nothing about me.'

'I think he does. He says you are a sad man.' Farid switched to rippling the other arm.

'I think the lieutenant should stick to—'

Quinn stopped when he saw the boy's eyes widen in alarm. The lad let go of his hand and raced across to Lawrence. Quinn glanced over his shoulder and saw it too. The telltale dust signature of riders. They no longer had the Gun Road to themselves.

Lawrence had also spotted the newcomers. 'Quinn. Take point, please.'

Quinn quickly fetched a Lee Enfield rifle from the Rolls. He checked the magazine and ratcheted a cartridge into the breech, then cradled it in his arms, the barrel pointing over his left shoulder towards the sky. It gave the appearance of non-aggression, but could be brought to bear in less than a second if need be. He felt a familiar little quiver in his belly.

It wasn't quite mid-morning, but already there was the dancing pool of a mirage across the path and it was a while before Quinn could make out the tribesmen as anything other than a single shifting, sinuous shape in the warped air. Whoever they were, they were coming from the direction of Abbas. Could they have been following them? It was possible, given the average speed of the Rolls.

The blurred mass solidified and separated into individual horsemen. Five, Quinn estimated. No, six, all positioned in a line across the path.

'Tariq,' said Lawrence. 'On the Lewis, if you please. Captain Quinn, I think you should move to greet our friends. Keep them at arm's length, away from the Rolls.'

Quinn turned to object and then shut his mouth. At a time like this, you didn't need two leaders. Besides, Lawrence was right: you made strangers stop where you wanted them to, not where they considered best.

Quinn walked twenty yards forward from his companions, shading his eyes against the glare as the men came on. 'Maybe they are just passing by,' he yelled over his shoulder.

Tariq kept his voice just loud enough to reach Quinn's ears. 'In which case they will come in single file, like I said, with the leader in front.'

As they came nearer, Quinn could see the riders were mottled with dust, but the horses looked fresher than the men. They had been changed recently. The group was within a few hundred yards when they slotted into a non-aggressive single file. Quinn raised an arm, as if in greeting, rather than an instruction to halt.

'Salaam.'

'Salaam,' replied the leader, reining his horse to a stop. He was a big man, dwarfing the animal he sat upon. He boasted a fine if unkempt beard, and above it a splendid aquiline nose and piercing green eyes. When he smiled there was a large gap between his front teeth. 'You are lost?' the man asked in Persian.

'No. Not lost. This is not a place to be lost.'

He nodded as if that were sage advice from a stranger. 'What brings an Englishman out here?'

So much for the language lessons and native garb, Quinn thought. Spotted in one. 'We are travellers.'

'We are map makers.' It was Lawrence, a large sheet of paper in one hand, and a sextant in the other, drawing level with Quinn, but around ten yards to his right. Now they could both see down the line of riders. 'We are to produce maps to this region.'

The Persian looked perplexed. 'What if we don't want maps? Maps will tell everyone about this road. This is our path. Why should you tell the world?'

Lawrence shrugged. 'It is progress.'

'For you, perhaps. Not for us.'

'You cannot hide away for ever.'

'How true and how terrible.' The leader bowed his head as if a great weight had fallen on him.

'Where are you from?' asked Lawrence.

The man pointed over his shoulder. 'Rostaq. Where are you going?'

'Only as far as Jam.'

'We go there too. Let us accompany you. As your *rafiq*.'

The word meant security or guide.

'We travel alone. We have much, much work to do,' Lawrence replied, as if he was genuinely sorry. 'We will slow you up.'

'Then Allah look after you. Allow us to give you gifts for

your journey.' He swivelled in his saddle and began to search in his bags.

Quinn saw that the linear grouping had subtly broken and each rider had taken his horse to either the left or right, giving each a clear line of fire. The fourth in the row was also reaching for something. As it came free of the scabbard, it was clear it wasn't any kind of gift.

Quinn shouldered the Lee Enfield and shot number four through the ear. The rifle the Persian had produced spun away out of his hands. He was dead well before he slumped to the earth.

Quinn worked the bolt and watched the cartridge, still wreathed in its cocoon of cordite fumes, fly away. He rammed the metal rod back.

Now he looked at the leader, who was bringing a revolver to bear on him.

Quinn squeezed off two more rounds in quick succession, the noise battering his ears. The front man arced over the rear of his mount, which reared in panic.

The brittle snap of the air around him told him fire was being returned.

Quinn took several paces to his left, to bring another of the party into his sights. He felt a bullet, far too close to his head. Had that man been a Boer, Quinn would have been dead. Quinn punished him for his inaccuracy.

To his right Lawrence had dropped the sextant and papers he had been holding to reveal a Colt .45 pistol. He was crouched down and had the gun in a solid two-handed grip. The slide was hammering back.

Then, the remaining raiders seem to jolt and jerk as one, their bodies twitching under the impact of shells. The horses bucked as blood spurted from their sides. Tariq was firing. The Lewis gun swept back and forth, scything through them with its heavy-calibre rounds. The earth threw up a cloud of dust as the bodies of men and their beasts fell heavily.

Quinn lowered the rifle, knowing any more shooting by him was unnecessary, but Lawrence carried on till his pistol was empty and the slide locked back.

The Lewis stopped after less than twenty seconds, its work done. Acrid smoke from its breech drifted over Quinn. He was grateful. It masked other smells.

Only two horses were left standing and they turned and galloped away, terrified. One of the fallen animals was twisting its head, the lips pulled back to show blood-flecked teeth, as it tried to find the strength to stagger to its feet. Quinn raised the Lee Enfield once more and shot it between the eyes. For the first time, he felt a tinge of regret. Men put themselves in harm's way; horses were put there through no fault of their own.

Quinn shook his head violently and swallowed hard until his ears popped. Now there was just a loud buzzing in there.

He checked his heart rate. It had fallen close to normal and his skin prickled with the chill of a post-combat shiver. In some people this triggered shock; with Quinn, it simply told him he was still alive.

Lawrence looked away from the carnage and down at his pistol, as if it had killed of its own accord.

'You all right?' Quinn asked.

'Yes.' But Lawrence's hands were shaky as he dropped the spent magazine and inserted a fresh one. First time, Quinn thought. It wasn't quite the same as shooting bottles off a ship's rail.

He glanced back at Tariq, who was still in place behind the Lewis. Farid was at the front of the car, examining a bullet hole in the machine.

'Thank God for the Lew—'

Quinn never finished the sentence because as he spoke, Tariq folded down in the seat, and Quinn could now see the dark stain on his chest. He'd been shot. Lawrence was at Quinn's heels as he sprinted across, vaulted into the rear and caught Tariq's head as it flopped.

'Damn, damn, damn,' said Lawrence, leaning into the back. Then one more time. 'Damn it all.'

Quinn laid Tariq down on the seat, covering his own tunic with dark blood as he did so. The man was beyond help. 'What a waste.'

Lawrence reached in and touched Tariq's forehead.

Quinn forced himself to think clearly. 'We must move on.'

Lawrence nodded his agreement. 'We must find someone to perform a proper burial for him.'

Quinn jumped out and unstrapped a spade from the side of the Rolls. 'We'll bury him here. You can say a few words.'

Lawrence's eyes widened. 'No. No Christian words.' He felt a flash of guilt, remembering Munir's inadequate burial. 'We find an imam, a village where they can do it properly.'

'Are you insane? Word gets around that we killed a group of believers on the road—'

'Word will get around how?' Lawrence demanded.

Quinn pointed south. 'The horses will tell their story. I don't know as much about these places as you, Lawrence, but I know nothing is harmless in this desert unless it is dead.' He thrust the spade in the direction of the fallen raiders. 'And even then I am not sure. I should have shot the horses. They will lead people here. People who want revenge.'

Lawrence had to admit that was very likely. 'Then we must get to a village soon.'

'And say what? Our friend shot himself in the chest? Can you bury him with all due ceremony, please?'

'Lawrence. Quinn.' It was Farid. He was kneeling down at the front of the Rolls, and they followed his gaze. A steady rain of rusty water was dribbling into the earth, staining it black.

Lawrence undid the bonnet stays and lifted the panel. 'Radiator,' he said after a moment.

Quinn peered into the dark heart of the machine. 'How bad?'

'In this climate any leak is bad.'

'Do we have a spare radiator?' Quinn asked, knowing the answer.

'No.' Lawrence managed a rueful smirk. 'You have to send to Derby.'

Quinn flicked a fly from his face. 'Can we fix it?'

Lawrence thrust his chin out, as he did when in thought. 'We can stuff a rag in it, perhaps.'

'Eggs, sir,' said Farid.

'Does that work?' asked Lawrence, with doubt in his voice.

320

'Does what work?' Quinn demanded.

'Breaking raw eggs into the system might patch it for a while.'

'Well, anything is worth a try. Do we have any eggs?'

'No.'

Quinn threw the spade to the ground. 'Marvellous.'

Farid spoke again. He was consulting an old oft-folded piece of paper, a crude map of the region, copied by hand. 'There is a village perhaps twelve miles on. There is water. There will be eggs, sir.'

'And maybe an imam,' said Lawrence. 'And a cemetery.'

Quinn thought for a moment. 'All right, you win.' He bent down and slotted the shovel back into place. 'But only because of the eggs.'

It was then he noticed Farid's fingers, streaked as if by dark nicotine. But he didn't smoke. 'Are you hurt?'

'It is nothing, sir.'

'Let me see.'

Farid stepped back but Quinn was much faster. He lifted the lad's left arm. There was a smear of deep red three inches below his armpit. 'We'll have to have a look at that.'

'Not now,' pleaded Farid. 'We must leave here.'

There was a cross-shaped shadow playing around them, the first vulture circling the site. The scent of the blood soaking into the warm earth must be strong, thought Quinn.

'All right. I'll top up the Rolls with water, Lawrence you drive. Farid, you go in the front with him. I'll go with—' He found he couldn't say his name. 'I'll go in the back.'

After he had refilled the radiator and secured the bonnet, Quinn climbed into rear and, as gently as he could, closed Tariq's eyes.

The village was set back in a side valley, away from the road, amid vegetated hillsides, where there was some meagre grazing for sheep and goats. Children and women fled before them as they limped in, a thin plume of steam issuing from the front of the Rolls. The Khan who emerged to meet them was a tall, elegant fifty-year-old with a grey-flecked beard; four armed men flanked him. Quinn kept his Lee Enfield across his lap, and he could see Lawrence's pistol next to the gear lever within easy reach.

'Leave this to me,' said Lawrence, who scrambled out with commendable agility. Somehow, the pistol went with him, concealed in the folds of his clothing. Quinn noticed he was in bare feet. He had driven the car with no boots or sandals on, his flesh pressed against the hot metal. And now he was walking over sharp stones as if it were the softest turf.

Quinn watched the expressions of the bodyguards as Lawrence explained what had happened. He didn't lie, he told how they had been set upon by bandits and been forced to defend themselves. Lawrence's voice was full of regret at the deaths. It was, Quinn realised, no performance.

The news of the attack didn't seem to surprise the Khan at all.

'It is a perilous road.'

The headman came over and looked in at Tariq. 'A fallen

warrior. He could have been buried where he fell,' the man said, to Quinn's dismay. 'But we will wash him and wrap him in a *kafan* and the imam will lead prayers.'

'Thank you,' Quinn said.

The Khan eyed the rifle on Quinn's lap warily. 'You will not need your weapons. You will be our guests. Whatever you require.'

'Thank you,' Lawrence said. 'Do you have any eggs?'

'I want Lawrence to look at it. Please, sir.'

They had been given a hut in which to rest from the hottest part of the day while the funeral was organised. Tariq was being washed and prepared by one of the Khan's wives. Now they had to see how badly Farid was injured. There was no furniture in the hut, just blankets and cushions, but Quinn had created a makeshift couch from the latter to examine the lad. It was gloomy and Lawrence was lighting two thick, squat candles that gave off greasy smoke.

'I've done field surgery,' Quinn protested.

'Lawrence will look. Please wait outside, sir.'

Quinn looked between the two, but Lawrence was saying nothing.

'If you wish.'

'Thank you, sir.'

Quinn emerged into the brightness of noon and made his way to the shade of the tree where they had left the car. Some of the bolder children were examining the Rolls, but backed away when they saw him come out.

'It's all right,' he said in Persian. 'Look but don't touch.'

323

Three of the boys stayed, walking around the machine, occasionally whispering, pointing and laughing like children anywhere. Quinn took the opportunity to refill the tanks with petrol, and they watched in amazement as he positioned the funnel and poured the liquid in, careful not to waste any.

'Does it eat as well as drink?' asked one of the lads.

Before he could answer another boy appeared, and tugged at his sleeve, and spoke in fractured English. 'Orrans says you must come.'

'Who?'

'Orrans. Your Khan.'

Quinn ignored the promotion. 'Lawrence.'

'Yes, Orrans. He said to say, your friend is shot.'

Farid was lying on the temporary couch, his head turned towards the doorway, while Lawrence knelt on his left side, having cut away part of the patient's tunic. There was a line of sweat glistening on Farid's upper lip. Quinn could see a sliver of exposed, white skin.

'How is it?' Quinn asked.

'It's a ricochet, I think,' replied Lawrence. 'The bullet seems to have skidded along the ribs and lodged just beneath the surface. If it had been a direct hit it would have penetrated further.'

'Can I see?'

'No need. I'm going to dig it out.'

'Use my knife, sir,' said Farid. 'It has done the job before.'

From beneath the folds of the young man's clothes,

Lawrence took the six-inch straight-bladed knife and examined it. He ran a thumb along it. The point and the edge were both sharp. 'This will do.'

Farid smiled bravely and held up his right hand to Quinn. He took it and felt the fingers burrow into his flesh. Quinn had grown used to thinking of him as almost a man, but now he could see the anxiety of a young boy on the shadowy face. He squeezed back in reassurance.

'Stay here,' Lawrence said. 'I'm going to sterilise this and get some clean water and dressings.'

Quinn knelt down on the earth and said: 'It'll be all right.'

'Not like poor Tariq, sir.'

'I know.' Quinn hesitated. 'Lawrence will blame himself.' The boy nodded his agreement. 'He shouldn't. In war, such things happen.'

'I am sure that is correct. But it was not easy for him, to kill those men. You are different. I watched you fire that rifle, sir. I have never seen a man fire so many shots in so short a time.'

'Practice. The Boers were even faster. And they could do it on horseback and still be accurate. It was a case of learning to fire like them or be killed by them.'

A tear squeezed from the corner of Farid's eye. When the young man spoke, the voice was rasping. 'How do you do this work you do, sir? Where so many men die?'

Quinn squeezed the hand once more. 'Shush. It helps if you don't talk or think about it.'

He wondered if there was any way of unearthing alcohol. He hadn't brought any and he was sure Lawrence wouldn't have any brandy about his person and the village, of course, would be dry. The only other anaesthetic he could think of was a swift blow to the jaw, and he doubted the lad would agree to that.

Lawrence returned with the water, blade and strips of clean cloth, but also a woman, her face all but hidden; she was carrying a carved wooden box. 'A nurse,' he announced. 'Well, the closest we'll get to one.' He inhaled sharply. 'Right, let's go.'

'Thank you for coming, sister,' Farid said in Persian to the newcomer. The woman gave a short, sharp nod. 'An *asu*?'

Another indication of the head.

Farid turned to Quinn and explained in English. 'A specialist in dressings and poultices. As opposed to an *ashifu*, who could tell me which god, spirit or devil has possessed me.'

'I think I know. The God of Mauser,' said Quinn.

Farid smiled. 'I think it was a Martini, sir.'

Lawrence cleared his throat. 'It's a bullet, wherever it came from. Let's get to work.' He looked up at Quinn and mouthed. 'Speak to him.'

Quinn shrugged, unsure of what to say.

Lawrence said, as casually as he could: 'Captain Quinn. You told me on the boat that Kitchener saved you from a hanging. I didn't ask you how.'

'Not now, Lawrence,' Quinn snapped.

Lawrence's eyes widened and he nodded to show he wanted Quinn to pick up the story, to distract Farid from the pain. 'Come. Everybody likes a narrow escape from the gallows.'

Quinn relented and spent a moment gathering his thoughts.

'I was serving with Kitchener. The Boers had had a grievance against the British since the abolition of slavery. The way they saw it, we freed the Bantu so they could burn their homesteads. It got worse when diamonds and gold were discovered. There was a dispute over who exactly owned the rights and who would be allowed to exploit it.'

'I don't understand,' said Farid. 'Are the Boers a tribe?'

'A white tribe, yes. A clever, resourceful tribe. We were fighting against Chris, Christian de Wet. To be honest, he was knocking seven bells out of us. They would raid army outposts and transports and disappear again. Kitchener thought there was only one way to stop them.'

Lawrence interrupted. 'This may sting, I'm just going to clean the wound.' He looked up at Quinn. 'Containment, am I right?'

'Containment,' Quinn confirmed. 'Cut off the guerrillas from their supply bases. Corral the women and children who were the support groups into camps. Concentration camps, they called them. Lawrence, what would you do against Wassmuss if you were in charge in Persia?'

The local woman began to pray softly to herself and from the box extracted a number of pungent herbs that she rubbed together in the palms of her hands. She lit a small candle and the scent of sulphur reached Quinn's nostrils; within a minute, the ever-present flies beat a retreat.

'In the long term, I would occupy the villages and the wells he uses to re-supply,' admitted Lawrence. 'Rather than chase around the country after him.'

'That was the plan in South Africa. It went wrong. The

327

camps became centres for disease. They were supplied by government agents who used it as a God-given opportunity to make profit. The British paid for first-class meat and the Boers got maggoty carcasses. I—'

'Be brave,' whispered Lawrence.

Farid's fingers spasmed and his nails cut into Quinn's flesh. The boy gave a small grunt of pain and the grip relaxed slightly.

'Go on with the story,' Lawrence prompted Quinn.

'I came across one land agent who was unloading food I wouldn't have fed to a dog. We got into an argument. He pulled a gun. I shot him.'

The patient hissed through clenched teeth. 'Self-defence, sir.'

'It's never self-defence when the man in question is well connected, both in South Africa and in the London clubs. He might have been the black sheep of the family, but they rallied round once he was dead. I was court-martialled. It was only because Kitchener intervened that . . . Well, I thought they would hang me.'

'That's when you came to Persia?' asked Lawrence.

Kate's father had been one of the partners in Lyman Brothers and also a friend of Kitchener's. The latter had told Quinn's prospective father-in-law the true story of the killing. Despite his disgrace, his courtship of Kate had been allowed, marriage approved and a position in Persia secured. After the ignominy of South Africa, finding Kate was like walking out of a swirling hailstorm into a clear, bright day. He couldn't share that feeling, and had never been able to. 'A while after my dishonourable discharge, yes.'

'I think you should visit your wife's grave, sir. It isn't right. To be so close. You must go there. Promise me, sir.'

Quinn shook his head, unable to do so.

'Got it!' Lawrence produced a tiny, misshapen ball of metal. 'Worst bit over, Farid. Farid?'

But Farid had passed out.

Thirty-three

The Rolls left the village in the late afternoon, the radiator full of egg whites with, in the front passenger seat, a heavily bandaged and poulticed Farid. Quinn was driving and a pensive Lawrence was ready to operate the Lewis if need be. The group felt grievously short-handed without Tariq. Quinn had not realised just how reassuring his presence had been. Now, the party felt curiously unbalanced. The funeral had been brief; the *salat-l-janazah*, the prayers, were said in the court-yard of the Khan's house, the grandest building in town. After-wards, the men of the community accompanied the body to the graveyard and watched as this stranger was interred, while the women prepared food.

When they left, Lawrence had given the nurse more money than she had ever seen and, embarrassed, had tried to give half back. He refused, much to Quinn's annoyance. Lawrence also paid over the odds to the Khan, the imam, the mourners and the caterers. Now their treasure trove was positively meagre. It was as if the man had no real idea of the value of the sovereigns.

As far as Quinn could tell, they had all parted as brothers. What the villagers would say when warriors appeared looking for the murderous infidels, he couldn't begin to imagine. Perhaps then they would recall Lawrence's generosity.

They travelled in silence, past scenery that seemed even more depressingly arid that usual. There was little joy in this landscape, little to cheer the eye. To break down here would be to throw yourself on the mercy of a country that had none to give. The only thing between them and immobility was a clutch of eggs.

The unlikely repair held, however, and the party stopped for the night next to a series of thin peaks, which looked like sugar twists re-cast in black stone. The earth around them was soft and pliable, but these half-dozen towers were diamond-hard, resistant to all that the region could throw at them. A storm blew up that night. The gale swirled between the dark columns, creating a moaning vortex. None of them slept well, and Farid groaned enough for Lawrence to re-check the dressing and the poultice the woman had applied at first light, before declaring himself satisfied.

They continued, struggling up a steady incline for most of the day, nursing both the damaged Rolls and Farid as gently as they could. They rested at midday beneath a rare but welcome tree, a gnarled, pugnacious specimen. They dined on some of the bully beef and biscuits donated by Daniels back at Banda.

That afternoon the road became rougher, the soil a bruised purple, and the surrounding hills even more grim. There were snaking bends to be negotiated, and the Rolls was chaperoned gingerly along the edge of a gorge.

Eventually, they crested the top of a rise and below them they could see the plain of Sefidar, glowing orange as the light dimmed. There were other hills and mountains criss-crossing it, some like the upended keels of massive boats, others saw-toothed and vicious-looking. There was also the tempting sparkle of rivers, a promise of limitless water; the sight caused an involuntary licking of parched lips. They were nearly at their destination when Lawrence pulled over so that they could take in the vista in more detail.

'One more night. We shall be there tomorrow, sir,' said Farid, wearily. He pointed to the right. 'That road would take us to Shiraz.' To call it a road was an exaggeration, but Quinn could make out the trace of a path. 'But only if we were on camels or mules. This one, which goes to Deh Now, should be better, unless the winter rains have been unkind. We should drive for a few more hours till the light goes. I am strong enough to take the wheel now, sir.'

They repositioned themselves, with Quinn beneath the Lewis gun, and began the slow descent towards the plain that ran all the way to the coast. Directly below them was a strange structure, a citadel built into the side of a pointed peak, with the remnants of a path that traced its way in a series of switch-backs from the bottom to a once-gated entrance, which now gaped open to all-comers. A few flecks of white showed the massive stones had once been painted.

'The Tower of Silence, sirs,' said Farid. He explained that it was where the Zoroastrians left their dead to be baked by the sun and stripped by vultures before the bones were placed in the ossuary.

Quinn had underestimated the size of the tower and it was dusk before they reached it. That night they made camp in the shadow of it, watching the bats stream out to feed as the day died all around them.

As he struggled for sleep, Quinn was aware once more of Lawrence and Farid in whispered conversation. At one point Lawrence rummaged in the Rolls and there was the sound of ripping and cutting. Quinn knew he should challenge him, demand an explanation for his continued subterfuge, but his muscles ached from the constant vibration and, despite a chill wind cooling his exposed face and nose, he fell into a deep, dreamless slumber. He didn't even notice the scorpions which came to inspect him, drawn by his body heat. They scuttled off as Farid, his conversations with Lawrence finished, expertly caught one of the larger arachnids on the end of a stick and flicked it out into the dark.

Deh Now was an unattractive sprawl of a village, largely built of mud from the nearby river and apparently populated mostly by scraggy dogs, half-starved camels and bony mules, but at its centre was a grand palace, constructed when the town had wealth and the Khan was a man of substance. The wealth had gone, along with the Khan's prestige, but the palace remained, its deep terracotta walls decorated with fantastical spiral motifs, albeit now chipped, weathered and worn.

The egg protein in the radiator had lost its consistency some twenty miles from the town, and they had had to coax the machine the last part of the journey, stopping frequently and letting the engine cool before they could risk topping up the radiator. They didn't need a cracked block at that stage. Fortunately, they were able to coast for a great many miles, letting gravity pull them down to the town.

It was a sad *Green Mist* that juddered into Deh Now in the late afternoon, its engine stammering with a misfire, its inhabitants red-eyed and weary. This time, the children and women didn't run and hide. They stayed framed in windows and doorways, silent and impassive. The women adjusted their face coverings, while some of their offspring pointed, their exclamations of wonder at the strangers stifled by a mother's kindly hand or a sharp gesture.

They parked the battered vehicle outside the gates to the Khan's palace and switched off the engine. For the first time it ran on, huffing and chuffing for a few seconds before stopping with a final, grateful tremor.

Lawrence said: 'I think you might be right. The nabob probably won't be wanting this Rolls now.'

Quinn stood so he was inside the gun ring and inches from the Lewis. Somewhere a goat bleated, but there was no other sound, apart from the buzzing of flies. Lawrence climbed down from the Rolls and looked up at the ramparts of the village's central fortress. 'Hello? Anybody home?'

The palace gates heaved back and a corpulent middle-aged man stepped through. He had on a simple white tunic, overlaid with a long, elaborate waistcoat in gold and blue. A small cohort of armed followers came with him.

'Greetings, Ghasanfar Es Dashti,' said Farid, standing and bowing his head. 'May the blessing of Allah be with you.'

The man peered through the gathering gloom. 'And with you, stranger.'

'But I am no stranger,' Farid laughed as he climbed down stiffly from the car. 'And I can still out-ride you.'

Quinn stayed manning the gun. He couldn't actually bow to show respect to the Khan without deserting his post, but he lowered his head, if not his eyes.

As Farid approached, Quinn could see the recognition in the Khan's eyes, but it was quickly replaced by horror. 'Little One. They didn't say it was you,' the headman exclaimed.

Farid stopped where he was. Then took an agitated step backwards. 'Who didn't?'

The clack of rifles being cocked was unmistakable and when Quinn looked back at the houses where the children had once stood staring at the strangers, they had been replaced by Tangistan warriors. Mauser barrels were now pointed at them, in place of fingers.

Anger flashed through him and he charged the machine gun, jerking the bolt back.

'Quinn, no!' Lawrence's yell froze his finger on the trigger. 'Don't. Please.'

Quinn realised he was right and gingerly let the mechanism close.

Another figure emerged from the gate, looking groomed

and relaxed. He performed a theatrical bow with a welcoming sweep of his arm. It was the man who had introduced himself as Captain Noel, but whom they now knew to be Wilhelm Wassmuss.

Thirty-four

Lawrence, Farid and Quinn were taken inside the fortress and separated into adjacent rooms, all smelling of damp earth and neglect. A lamp was lit and each was brought a bowl to wash in and a plate of food. Lawrence was about to take a particularly succulent date when he heard Farid's voice through the flaking walls.

'Don't eat. Whatever you do, don't eat. Water only.'

Lawrence examined the plate of food, picking over the fruit and nuts and pastries. Poisoned? There were easier ways to kill prisoners than that.

He drank some water and waited. Outside the window with its intricate, but strong, metal grill, the world had grown dark. A muezzin called. He could smell meat cooking, lamb he thought, and his stomach rumbled. But Lawrence had resisted worse temptations during Ramadan.

The room was furnished with a divan couch and a heavy wooden chair with an ornately carved back. The latter looked highly uncomfortable, but it was this he chose to sit in. He needed to keep his wits about him, because, so far, he thought, he had been behaving witlessly. He hoped the discomfort would keep him focused.

Losing Tariq had been a blow, although it probably wouldn't have helped them avoid this capture. But a good man was dead, a terrible price to pay. Lawrence had hoped to use him both in Persia and, later, to encourage other defections among Ottoman Arabs. And, he reminded himself, he had been, above all, a friend.

Frank. Munir. Tariq. The tally was rising.

There came the sound of bolts being slid back. The door opened outwards and in stepped the Khan. Lawrence, rudely, remained where he was.

The Khan indicated the pile of food. 'You don't eat.'

'No.'

The Khan walked over, picked up a handful of dates and popped one into his mouth, demonstrating they were un-adulterated. 'You must eat.'

'I am not hungry.'

The Khan looked agitated and stroked his beard. 'You must enjoy my hospitality. Please.'

'We are prisoners.'

The man smiled, apparently sincerely, as if Lawrence had merely got the wrong end of this particular stick. 'You are guests.'

'Then I'd like a walk outside.'

The Khan shrugged. 'I'm sorry . . .'

'You knew Farid, the Little One, from before.'

'Yes.'

'You know who he is?'

The Khan sounded shamefaced. 'Yes.'

'Yet you treat us like this.'

The Khan looked genuinely pained. 'I was only told you were infidels . . .'

'Take the food away.'

'You must eat—'

Lawrence stood and with a well-aimed kick flipped the heavy tray up into the air, sending the food skittering across the room. The metal disc boomed across the stone floor and then spun, humming as it did so, till, with a final clank, it came to rest. 'No.'

The man's face darkened and he left, squelching the fruit into the flagstones as he went. That was what Farid had meant. To refuse food from a Persian was both insulting and upsetting. It was a small and empty triumph, but it made Lawrence feel better.

Wassmuss came twenty minutes later, the Mauser machine pistol in his belt, an armed Tangistan hovering in the doorway. The German surveyed the room as if examining the handiwork of a petulant child who had soiled his nursery. 'You've upset the Khan,' he said.

'Not enough to be even remotely satisfying, I fear,' replied Lawrence.

'Do not push him too far. Or me.'

'What have I got to lose?'

'Your life and the lives of your companions.'

Lawrence sighed, as if this were of no consequence. 'Instinct may shun it, but reason calls the grave a gateway of peace.'

'I don't think you are ready for such peace just yet.'

'May I ask you a question?'

Wassmuss put a foot on the divan and rested his weight on his knee. 'Of course.'

Lawrence hated to admit ignorance of any topic, but he forced himself to make the enquiry. 'How did you get here? And how did you know we'd come this way?'

'I used logic. I thought like you would think. As I left, I suspected you were beginning to doubt me. It was not so hard to anticipate what you might do.'

Lawrence felt himself bristle at the slight. His capacity for small talk seemed suddenly exhausted. 'And how are the hostages?'

'In good health if not spirit. They feel bereft, wondering why their government has forsaken them.'

'It hasn't.'

Wassmuss laughed. 'Sending your party of four hardly qualifies as a gunship. Let me ask you a question. How did you tumble to me? How did you know it wasn't Noel at Banda?'

'The Latin quote. Horace.' Lawrence enjoyed the next moment. 'You still speak it with a German accent.'

'Really?' Wassmuss seemed disappointed. 'How thoughtless of me. And why didn't you detain me?'

Lawrence decided to be honest. 'Doubts set in, but certainty came too late. So, what do we do now, Wassmuss?'

'Well, by the spoils of war, it's my Rolls sitting out there. And my luggage in the first place. So perhaps I should use the hostages to free my two colleagues, now that I have no need to bargain for the bags.' Lawrence had all but forgotten the two Germans captured with Wassmuss. He didn't know of their fate, then. Nor had he taken a close look at the luggage. 'I'll sleep on it.'

Lawrence remained silent.

'By the way,' Wassmuss paused in the doorway. 'When I arrived, I had an interesting chat with the Khan. He told me all about Farid, the Little One. I was being frank when I said I thought bringing the Rolls-Royce was foolish, but that . . .'

Wassmuss shook his head, as if saddened by the quality of his opponent, and left the room.

Thirty-five

For the next thirty minutes, Lawrence paced his prison, raising motes of dust that danced around the yellow light of the lamp. Angry, accusatory voices filled his head, some familiar – Hogarth, Storrs, his mother, Dahoum – others from people he had yet to meet, such as Tariq's wife and child; an imagined chorus chanting abuse at him.

A wave of tiredness hit him and he realised he was burning up precious energy. It was no use fretting or becoming angry with himself. That would deplete his stamina as surely as running across the desert. Lawrence knew he could be no help to anyone if he was churned up, confused and self-lacerating. For the time being, at least, he needed clarity. In Wassmuss he was dealing with, at the very least, a competent strategist. It was up to him to be more than that, to raise the level of his own game.

It was time to prepare the combat that would surely come, once Wassmuss discovered Lawrence's deception.

From the mess on the floor he found a partly bruised pear and an orange. He washed the pear and devoured it, then consumed the orange more slowly. Then he lay down to get some rest.

He was vaguely aware of a cockerel rasping its way into the dawn, when the door was thrown back. Lawrence sat up, blinking in the gloom and rubbing the sleep from his eyes. Wassmuss was standing before him and the affability of the previous evening had evaporated.

'Get up and come with me.'

Lawrence swung off the divan and splashed some water on his face before following the German outside. Both Farid and Quinn were already in the corridor, still struggling with the fog of sleep. The trio was marched outside, into the courtyard of the palace where a few fingers of mist clung to the ground, curling over the dozens of items that lay on the earth, casting their long shadows in the milky sun.

It was the Rolls, dismembered. The wheels were off, the seats had been torn out and the leather upholstery sliced with blades and carelessly eviscerated. Bundles of padding lay discarded in piles. The doors had been unbolted, every canister had been emptied or split open and the bonnet panels had been removed to reveal the engine. The filter pans and hoses had all been ripped off.

'Thank goodness the nabob isn't here to see this,' said Lawrence dryly.

Wassmuss turned on him. 'You are playing dangerous games, Lawrence.'

'There is your luggage, as I told you.'

For a second he thought Wassmuss was going to strike him.

Wassmuss regained his composure and lowered his voice. 'Please don't be foolish.' He took Lawrence by the arm and walked him briskly over to where the bags lay. 'They are incomplete.'

'One valise and two trunks. It is what London sent.'

'The bags have been mutilated. The locks are missing.'

'The locks? Oh yes. Well, you can always get new ones. Although the clasp is rather damaged there—'

Wassmuss shouted. 'Where are the locks?'

'In London, I should imagine. They opened the cases.'

'Ari!' Wassmuss yelled at one of the guards. 'On my signal, shoot one of the two prisoners. I don't care which.'

Lawrence folded his arms over his chest. 'You won't do it.'

Wassmuss stepped up close. 'Watch me.'

Lawrence turned his back on the cases. In front of him, four guards surrounded his compatriots, three with a rifle, one of them – Ari, he supposed – with a heavy revolver. He had levelled it at Quinn's head. The Englishman had tensed slightly, no doubt weighing up whether he could break Ari's neck.

A minute passed and Lawrence felt the first sweat of the day run down his back.

'Well?' asked Wassmuss.

'Well, what?'

The German gave a heartfelt sigh to show his patience was being tested and his intelligence insulted. 'The locks were in place at Banda Abbas. I saw them, remember?'

344

Lawrence knew damned well he had. 'Really?'

'And they aren't now. Which rather suggests you removed them. And hid them.'

'Which also suggests I know how important they are.'

'I don't believe you do, Lawrence. How could you?'

'Perhaps I couldn't. But I know they are important to you. I used logic, you see, to follow how you would think.' Wassmuss's eyes narrowed in irritation. 'There was nothing else in those cases that was worth all this effort. So, if they are important to you, we can trade for O'Connor and our freedom. Can't we?'

Wassmuss became less agitated now the man had admitted to having his three locks. 'Where are they?'

'Buried on the trail. You'd never find them without me.'

'How far?'

Lawrence shook his head. Not a single clue would escape from his lips. And it was a long way back to Banda Abbas.

Wassmuss considered this for a few moments. 'The locks for the hostages?'

'Indeed.'

Wassmuss made a signal to his man with the revolver to lower it. Quinn slowly exhaled.

'On one condition.'

'What's that?' Lawrence asked, warily.

'You have breakfast and shut the Khan up.'

Lawrence laughed. 'We'll have breakfast and then we will go and get the hostages and then the locks.'

'The locks, then the hostages.'

'Both at the same time. An exchange.'

345

Wassmuss didn't consider for long. As they both knew, the German still had the upper hand: he had the men and the guns. 'I will send riders to fetch the hostages.'

'Just O'Connor. Let the others go. As a token of good faith. You don't want to drag them all out here. O'Connor alone is worth the trade, you know that. The others are just fellow travellers.'

The German looked nonplussed. 'And where is the profit in that for me?'

'My compliance. My word I will do as I promised and take you to your locks.'

Wassmuss nodded his assent and held out his hand. Lawrence could see the man was relieved, but was still unsure why, exactly. Perhaps because he did not have to kill a prisoner, because he was unburdening himself of the hostages or because of the fastenings, he couldn't be certain. Nevertheless, he took his grip and met the German's gaze. For a few seconds two pairs of blue, unblinking eyes locked on to each other till, as one, they released the handshake.

Forty-five minutes later, the Khan's hospitality taken, the party gathered in the courtyard on fresh horses.

'How long do you estimate to your hiding place?' Wassmuss asked Lawrence as they mounted.

'Seven or eight hours.'

'Then O'Connor will not be at the rendezvous until evening. I need your word you will try nothing foolish.'

Lawrence looked at the Tangistan escort, four of the strongest looking tribesmen. They stared back at him,

346

unblinking, as if pleading with him to do something 'foolish'. He turned to Wassmuss. 'You have my word I will lead you to the locks. You don't have to make me promise for every eventuality, otherwise we could be here for days.'

'Just in case, they have orders to fire if you break away from the group for any reason, unless you have my express permission.'

The baggage ponies were saddled with everything they would need for making camp and the group left the fortress and rode down the lumpy streets towards the road they had taken with the Rolls. Lawrence fell in next to Wassmuss, Quinn rode beside Farid, examining him at intervals for signs of distress, but he seemed to be fine.

'Sir,' Farid whispered. 'Did you manage to save any kind of weapon from the search?' They had been thoroughly patted down after their capture.

Quinn swivelled in the saddle, making sure the escort was out of earshot, but was then forced to admit: 'No. You?'

'I wish it was so, but no.'

They rode on in silence, mostly at a brisk trot, with short bursts of cantering. It was strange seeing the country in reverse, thought Quinn. The range they had traversed in the Rolls now looked like the bleached spine of a giant lizard, a series of linked, knobbly protuberances. Yet the path within had been much smoother than it would appear from the plain, like travelling along the spinal canal of the enormous reptile. No wonder the smugglers favoured it; any outsider would dismiss the chances of finding a fast road up there as non-existent.

Wassmuss called a rest halt just before midday. They

sheltered under a patch of thorn trees, and fed and watered the horses while the heat built and the world around them grew blurred by super-heated air.

The German passed around a water skin and chunks of bread and goat's cheese. Lawrence examined Farid's wound for seepage and seemed satisfied. Quinn spent the time wondering how to get the upper hand over a quartet of armed tribesmen and a wily German when they didn't have a single weapon between them. He could come up with no clear plan that wouldn't leave at least one of them dead. So he lay down and snoozed, lulled by the rhythm of crickets, the lazy chirp of a ground jay and, apparently arguing vehemently about how to improve the Spartan defence at Thermopylae, the low, angry voices of Lawrence and Wassmuss.

The sun had begun its descent towards the hills by the time they reached the Tower of Silence. Lawrence dismounted and examined the sparse tamarind bushes that marked the spot where they had made camp two nights before.

'It will take me some time,' said Lawrence. 'To retrieve the locks.'

'You marked the spot,' Wassmuss said. It wasn't a question. 'Please don't fool around.'

Lawrence put his hands on his hips. 'Even so, we wait.'

'What for?'

'The arrival of O'Connor. We do the exchange then.'

Wassmuss's fists clenched. 'You are an irritating man. What difference will it make?'

Lawrence spoke with irrefutable reasonableness. 'It has a

nice symmetry. We exchange the locks for the man. You go on your way.' He pointed up the slope of the hill towards the pathway that led to the southern coast. 'We head back to Banda. Everyone is happy. Wassmuss, you still have the guns, so why should you not be a little magnanimous?'

Wassmuss glared at Lawrence as if waiting for his face to betray some artifice in his plan. He pointed to Ari, the Tangistan guard, and said: 'Search them again. Just in case. Then we wait and get this over with and we can get rid of you all.'

Quinn and Lawrence exchanged glances. There was more than one way to interpret that sentence.

Thirty-six

Zair Khidair's approach was indicated by a smear of dust, barely visible on the dry plain below. Lawrence noticed the disturbance in the otherwise featureless expanse of rocky terrain, but said nothing. The three captives shared fruit and coffee under the alert eyes of the guards. When Lawrence walked away to relieve himself, Ari was up and with him before he had gone two paces.

'I'm going to enjoy killing him,' said Quinn when Lawrence returned. 'And Wassmuss.'

Lawrence ignored him and pointed at Farid's side. 'How is the wound?'

The lad raised his arm to show there was no stiffness. 'Good, thank you, sir.'

Quinn made to touch the lad's brow, but his head snapped back out of reach. 'No fever?' Quinn asked.

'No fever, sir.'

'They come,' announced one of the guards, pointing with

a spy-glass to the tiny whorl of a dust devil marking Zair Khidair and O'Connor's progress. Lawrence was surprised it had taken them so long to notice.

'About time,' snarled Wassmuss, looking at the sun. 'How many in total?'

The man put the telescope back to his eye. 'Four plus the English.'

'Which makes,' said Lawrence softly, 'eight Tangistani altogether.'

'And Wassmuss,' Quinn reminded him.

'Don't worry about Wassmuss,' Lawrence said.

'What do you have in mind?'

'Bourcet said that after strategy, improvisation is the general's greatest friend. The ability to improvise is the mark of the finest warriors.'

'In other words,' suggested Quinn, 'you don't know.'

'Precisely.'

Wassmuss strode over. 'Lawrence, you need to keep your part.'

'Of course. When I see it's O'Connor in the party,' said Lawrence evenly.

Wassmuss's eyes narrowed but he turned away without comment.

For the next twenty minutes, they all watched the quintet of horsemen approach. Wassmuss handed Lawrence a pair of binoculars when the arrivals reached the foothills and their accompanying dust cloud dissipated. He counted the four Tangistan and one Englishman, the latter riding stiffly and imperiously, as if it were a Sunday in Hyde Park or a parade;

the others displaying the easy movement of the long-distance desert rider. Lawrence was satisfied there was no way they could have substituted one of their own for O'Connor; that rod-backed form of horsemanship was developed over a lifetime.

'Shall we brew some coffee and welcome our guests?' Lawrence asked.

Quinn repeated it in Persian and the Tangistani, remembering their manners, set about remaking the fire. Or at least, two of them did. The others still cradled their weapons and stared at the prisoners.

As the party entered the camp, the captive group rose to its feet. A battered-looking O'Connor raised his right hand in greeting and said. 'Gentlemen. Am I pleased to see you. Major Frederick O'Connor, at your service.'

Lawrence approached and held up his hand. 'Lieutenant T.E. Lawrence. Military HQ, Cairo. My colleague Captain Harold Quinn and Farid. And I believe you know—'

'Wassmuss,' said O'Connor.

'*Buongiorno*,' said Wassmuss with an infuriating smile. '*Benvenuto*.'

O'Connor looked perplexed. 'You spoke Italian all along?'

'*Cosi cosi* . . . But enough to get the gist of the book titles. I apologise.' He gave a little bow. 'I read all your messages to Noel and all his back to you. But it was still a brilliant ploy on your part, Major. I congratulate you.' He turned to Zair. 'The other hostages are gone?'

The Khan nodded curtly and when he spoke, the manner was brusque. 'Yes, yes. To Bushire under escort and flag of truce. So, now we get the gold?'

Gold? thought Lawrence. *The man thinks Wassmuss is bartering for bullion, rather than the more esoteric goods he really requires.*

A small flicker of embarrassment crossed Wassmuss's features before he spoke. 'What we have is better than gold.'

Zair didn't seem convinced by this sentiment. 'What is better than gold?'

'Knowledge.' Before Zair could comment, he turned to Lawrence. 'So, Lieutenant, you have your man.' He held out an arm as if presenting O'Connor on stage.

Lawrence inclined his head. 'Yes. Well, I am sure the major would like to rest while we do this. Major?'

The Englishman dismounted and led his horse over to a shrub, where it nibbled cautiously amongst the spines. The escort remained mounted, but let their horses dip their heads to scavenge whatever they could from the rough ground.

The German prompted him again. 'Lawrence. If you will.'

'Wait.'

Wassmuss produced his Mauser C96 and inserted a clip of ammunition into the ugly weapon. He chambered a round to concentrate Lawrence's mind. 'Well?'

'Yes, yes,' the Englishman said. 'I need to pace it out. Give me a moment.'

Lawrence examined the stony earth until he had found a particular rock and began his measured strides. He headed for the copse of spindly trees that colonised the slopes beneath the Tower of Silence. He counted out loud as he did it, with Wassmuss at his shoulder, one pace behind as if he were a servant. 'Keep an eye on them!' the German shouted. 'How many paces?'

'Fifty.'

'No tricks, Lawrence.'

'I am fresh out of tricks, Wassmuss.'

'I wish I could believe that.'

They pushed their way through whip-like lower branches, some of which snicked at their flesh, the stubby thorns leaving their faces dotted with tiny globules of blood. 'Couldn't you have chosen somewhere more agreeable?'

'I needed somewhere nobody would stumble upon by accident.'

Wassmuss flinched as a barb opened a thin line along his cheek. 'You chose well, then.'

'Forty-nine. Fifty. Here.' He pointed at the earth.

'Out of the way.' Wassmuss pushed him roughly aside. 'I want to make sure you haven't buried anything else. Where?'

'The red stone.'

'Step back, please. More.' When he was sure that Lawrence was far enough away not to jump him, he knelt down, carefully resting the machine pistol within easy reach. The rust-coloured rock was the size of a thick pancake and reasonably heavy, and as Wassmuss heaved it aside he could see it concealed a pit, in which had been placed a bulky canvas sack. He snatched it out and peered inside. There were three combination locks within. 'Excellent. I think that concludes our business.'

'Just a little matter of letting us leave with O'Connor,' said Lawrence from behind him. 'Then, I need a bed and a good night's sleep.'

They retraced their steps through the thorny bushes.

As they emerged from the trees and back into the camp, Wassmuss held up the booty. 'We have it.'

Zair Khidair looked puzzled. 'That sack?' he asked in amazement. 'You said it was gold.'

'I said that it would get us much gold.'

The Khan shook his head. That wasn't what he recalled at all. 'Don't play word games with me, Woss Moss. I have fed and watered those people for months. They have cost me a small fortune. Then you tell me to let most of them go. I am left with just this one. What is in there that is worth all this trouble? Let me see.'

Reluctantly, Wassmuss handed over the bag and Zair looked within. His face was like a fist when he spoke. 'What do you take me for?'

'It will reap its reward in due course.'

The Khan leaned forward in his saddle and bared his teeth. 'It is always "in due course" isn't it? The British will be gone "in due course", the gold will come from Kaiser Hajji "in due course". When does this impossible time ever arrive?'

'It is here, now. You must believe me. This is what we have worked for.'

Zair was silent as he considered his options. He weighed the sack in his hands, as if unable to believe it didn't contain a fortune in precious metal.

'This changes very little. It seems to me, Woss Moss, that what we have done is exchange some not very high-grade hostages for some rather better ones.' He pointed at Lawrence and Quinn. 'These two unbelievers are from Cairo. Sent here to negotiate. They must be valuable men. And we know the major is a man of standing. So we can begin again, with a request for something decent. Not these . . . clasps.'

'No,' said Wassmuss firmly. Quinn could see the thought of starting the whole business over was hardly an attractive one. 'We have what we needed.'

Zair Khidair stood in his stirrups. He spoke with long pent-up fury. 'What? Do not say "no" to me, Woss Moss. I am the Sheik of Ahram, the Cock of the Tangistan. You are an infidel. Our paths converged for a while, but I now see we are heading for different destinations. The alliance with Ahram is at an end. Take your horse and go.' He pointed to the inhospitable land below the camp. 'If you come to my fortress again I will stake you out in the sun and watch your eyes burn out.'

Wassmuss, taken aback by the venom behind these words, looked at his Tangistan companions for support, but they remained impassive. They were no longer his men; the loan was over.

The Khan tutted. 'No, no. Their loyalty is to me. Always was. You merely borrowed them.'

'Lawrence.' It was Farid. All followed his gaze. Out on the plain was another rolling cloud.

Zair twisted round. 'Ah yes. A few friends. Some support, just in case things went against us.' He turned back to Wassmuss. 'Leave.'

'How can you do this? You won't be able to live with yourself for betraying a guest.' Wassmuss banged his chest to emphasise his sense of treachery. 'A friend.'

The Khan dismissed this with a wave of his hand. 'In this

country, man either eats well or sleeps well. I know which I prefer.'

Wassmuss, in turn, looked at Lawrence, his frustration evident in his expression. 'I'm sorry. It wasn't meant to end like this.'

Lawrence shrugged. 'One never knows how these things will end. Maybe we'll meet again.'

'Go,' the Khan repeated, and Wassmuss reluctantly walked to his horse.

'Get the hostages mounted.' Zair paused for a fraction of a second as he examined Farid closely. He pointed a long finger at him and scowled. 'That one is a Christian, I fear, and of no use. Kill him.'

Thirty-seven

Quinn looked at Lawrence for guidance, for the decisiveness he had shown on the gun road. The inexperienced lieutenant, though, seemed frozen by the Khan's words. Yet these first seconds were vital if anything was to be done. They couldn't let them bleed away.

Quinn's head spun to the nearest Tangistan, calculating how many steps before he could tackle him.

Too many.

The Khan sat, waiting for his word to be acted upon, a look of impatience on his face.

Only Wassmuss made a move, a step back, as if shocked by the order to kill Farid. But he was hardly going to help them, thought Quinn. The terrible realisation came into Quinn's mind that they had no edge, nothing to pull out of the magician's hat.

Still, he had to do something.

Quinn took a long stride forward, one he knew was about to cost him his life, heading for the man called Ari, who had made the first, tentative move to act on the Khan's instruction. He appeared happy at the thought of killing Farid. The expression did not last for long. As he extracted his revolver from his belt, he staggered, his eyes wide with shock. Blood flicked from his mouth as he opened it. Even from across the clearing, Quinn, still well short of grappling him, could see the handle of a familiar knife protruding from where Ari's Adam's apple had once been.

Farid's knife, the one Lawrence had used to cut out the bullet.

Ari hit the ground with a great, lifeless thump.

At the same moment, Lawrence flung his right arm around the neck of a second Tangistan, pinning him solid. In his left hand, Lawrence held his Colt .45 automatic.

How? Quinn asked himself.

Lawrence fired two shots in rapid succession, the aim perfect. Two guards went down.

There came the fearsome roar of another weapon. A Mauser machine pistol in automatic mode, a series of long rolling burps. Quinn watched the muzzle flash, waiting for the bullets to strike him, but it was the Tangistan behind him who was flung into the bushes by the impacts.

Lawrence chopped his captive hard in the neck with the butt of his pistol and let the man slump towards the ground.

During this one-sided fight, Zair and the two other riders had pulled their terrified horses round and sprinted away. Wassmuss raised the Mauser and squeezed on an empty chamber. Lawrence, still lowering his victim to the ground, yelled: 'Quinn!' and tossed the Colt to him. He had a better line of fire than Lawrence.

Quinn snatched it from the air and fired four shots in rapid succession at the retreating group, until one of the Tangistani fell out of his saddle, rolled along the ground and lay still. Freed from his weight, his horse surged past the others. Quinn fired again, but he no longer had the effective range to do further damage.

'Jesus, Mary and Joseph,' Quinn growled. 'What the hell happened there?'

Wassmuss calmly changed the clip in his Mauser. Quinn knew he was, at that moment, helpless. He levelled the Colt at the German's head and thumbed back the hammer.

'And whose side are you on?'

The German stopped what he was doing. 'For the moment, it looks like yours.'

'And why should that be?'

'He has no choice,' said Lawrence.

'*If* you are on our side . . . *If* . . . then a fat lot of good that thing is,' Quinn shouted, pointing at the machine-pistol. 'You should have shot Zair first. How fast does that magazine empty?'

Wassmuss kicked at one of the guards on the floor who appeared to have no chest left, just a grizzly hole. 'Best ask him,' he said. 'And Zair and his lieutenants were no immediate threat. They were not holding weapons. Can I finish reloading?'

'Very carefully,' advised Quinn, lowering the hammer on the pistol, but keeping it pointed at Wassmuss. When he had replaced the magazine, Wassmuss extracted a pair of binoculars from his saddlebags and focused them on the plains.

He settled on the other plume of dust, the second wave of Tangistani. 'Zair appears to have about a dozen friends on the way. It's my guess they won't hesitate to come after us.'

'I'm wounded, I believe.'

It was O'Connor, holding up a hand with one less finger than the other. It had been severed below the knuckle. 'Sorry. Instinct. Put my hand up to protect myself. Ring finger, too. Wife won't be best pleased.' He began to examine the ground around him. 'If I can find it I might be able to save the ring at least.'

Farid took his arm and said gently. 'Perhaps later, sir. We should bandage that wound first.'

O'Connor looked at him blankly before he nodded. 'Of course. Probably best.' He spoke as if he had a thorn to be removed.

It'll hurt like hell once the shock wears off, thought Quinn.

'We won't outrun Tangistani riders,' said Wassmuss. 'They've ridden me into the ground often enough.'

Quinn began to collect up the rifles. The guard Lawrence had pole-axed was still alive. He gave him a tap to the temple with the butt of a Lee Enfield. 'I don't suppose you can appeal to their better nature? After all, you were one of them until about five minutes ago.'

Wassmuss didn't reply.

'Suggestions?' asked Lawrence.

Quinn couldn't resist a jibe. 'I'm sure Bourcet says something on this matter, gentlemen.'

Farid tore a strip off one of the dead guard's tunics, inspected it for bloodstains or dirt, and wrapped it around O'Connor's hand. 'The bandage should be boiled, but that can wait.' He addressed Lawrence and Wassmuss. 'The Tower, sirs,' the lad suggested.

Lawrence nodded. 'The Tower. We can hold them off there.'

'Until when?' asked Quinn. 'Judgment Day?'

'Until something better presents itself,' said Wassmuss. 'With a Khan of the Tangistani against us, the whole country becomes hostile. As the man said, at the end of the day, we are infidels. They will always choose to help a brother.'

Quinn looked at Lawrence. 'Hold on. Are we going to listen to this man? This might be the right time for a parting of the ways.' Quinn slipped the safety off the Colt once more.

Wassmuss caught the movement and spoke calmly. 'If it was me in this situation, I wouldn't want to lose another rifle hand. Not just yet.'

From the corner of his eye, Quinn saw Lawrence nod at the wisdom of this. Quinn wasn't convinced. 'Better no rifle hand, than one we can't trust.'

'You can trust him,' said Lawrence firmly. 'Until I say otherwise.'

'If we are going to move, we must do so soon,' said O'Connor forcefully. 'They are no more than ten or fifteen minutes away.'

Even as he spoke, they heard the distant report of a rifle, as an enthusiastic rider fired a greeting into the air. The Khan had almost reached his friends.

'What about these two?' Wassmuss asked of a pair of guards who were still alive.

'Bind their wounds and bring them,' suggested Lawrence.

The two shots from the Colt Quinn was holding made the German leap back in shock. The prone men gave a twitch each and were dead. Wassmuss glared at Quinn.

'Quinn—' a shocked Lawrence began, but the assassin silenced him.

'One day, Lawrence, you'll discover that prisoners are a luxury you can't always afford.'

They mounted and took the horses up the winding path towards the ruined Tower of Silence, hooves clattering on the loose stone surface. It would be dark within two hours, Quinn thought, and it was likely the Tangistani would come for them then. Still, he had had no better suggestion, so decided to go along with it. At least they had five good rifles now, as well as the Colt pistol and the German's Mauser. But where did Wassmuss stand in all this? Could he really be trusted, or was Lawrence simply being fooled? And why had men died for a sack of fastenings?

'What are the locks, Wassmuss?' Quinn asked. 'That they are worth so much killing?'

Wassmuss shook his head heavily as if the burden were too great to share.

'A code,' said Lawrence from the rear of the group. 'The three cylinders make an encryption device, don't they?'

Wassmuss hesitated, taken aback that the Englishman knew why they were so important, and finally nodded.

'And if it was discovered you'd lost the device—' Lawrence began.

'Berlin would recall me immediately. In disgrace.'

'And now the Khan has them.'

'Yes. However, he has no idea what they are. And at least you haven't got them,' Wassmuss added with a hint of satisfaction. There came the distant echo of another rifle shot. 'Of course, all that is the least of our worries.'

At the Tower of Silence, the horses clopped into a circular courtyard of compressed red earth, surrounded on all sides by thick stone walls. It was clear from the holes in the masonry that there had once been several wooden floors, but they had rotted away, apart from two huge crossbeams at the very summit of the tower, which had once provided extra strengthening for the area where marbled slabs had stood for the laying out of the dead. There were, however, still two separate stone staircases that led to the upper ramparts, where a wide ledge would afford them a view over the surrounding countryside.

The base of the walls was punctuated by a series of deep, arched alcoves, which ran the entire circumference. They were around four foot high. A man could enter one if he stooped. There was a similar row one floor up and a third above that.

'The ossuaries,' Lawrence said, when he saw Quinn examining them.

'How shall we deploy?' asked Wassmuss.

'Farid, Quinn, take the door,' said Lawrence. 'The rest of us will go up top. Quinn, please give O'Connor a couple of rifles. You all right with that, Major?'

'It's not my trigger finger,' he snapped back. 'Course I am. I've been waiting for months to get my hands on a gun.'

He was staring at Wassmuss, so Lawrence said: 'Major, I'd rather you didn't take this personally.'

O'Connor shifted in the saddle and considered the request.

'It's Zair who is trying to kill us,' Lawrence reminded him. 'A truce is in order.'

The Major hesitated before he held out his uninjured hand to Wassmuss, who took it.

'Wassmuss?' asked Lawrence. 'Rifle?'

He held up his Mauser, to which he had attached a wooden shoulder stock, transforming it into a more accurate weapon.

'What about you?' the German asked.

Lawrence was already down from his horse. He walked across to the base of the walls and counted seven alcoves from the entrance. Then he ducked into the seventh arch and backed out, dragging a heavy object. It was the spare Lewis gun that had once been in the boot of the Rolls. Quinn had not even noticed it had gone. With it were three circular magazines. 'Couldn't sleep when we camped near here,' said Lawrence.

'How did you know we'd come back this way?' asked Quinn

'I didn't. But it seemed a reasonable enough precaution. There's some spare water in there, too, just in case.'

He went over to the wall and examined a rectangular stone plinth that butted against the stonework. It was covered with a rock the shape of a millstone. 'And there's a well here,' he announced. The locals would have ransacked the abandoned tower for any useful materials, be they wood or iron or pottery, but no man who lived in a desert country would foul a well. Whether they would live long enough to need this secondary water supply was another matter.

Lawrence heaved the Lewis on to his shoulders and began taking the stairs to the ramparts two at a time. O'Connor helped tether the horses and then followed him up. Wassmuss hung back, as if he wanted to get something off his chest.

'Turn up for the books,' offered Quinn. 'You being on our side now.'

'I wanted to say I am sorry. For this mess. It was not what I had hoped for. It was meant to be a straightforward exchange. Nobody was to die.'

Quinn had to admit he sounded sincere. Then he remembered. 'You had a gun put to my head.'

'Lawrence was right. I wouldn't have done it.'

'Well, whatever your motive, thank you for using that.' He nodded at the Mauser. 'But let me know when you are going to fire it again.'

'Why?'

'I want to make sure I am behind you next time. It's a good job there's no bullet to dig out of O'Connor. That number nine on the handle?' The numeral was embossed on the gun's 'broom handle' grip.

'Yes?'

'It means it carries nine-millimetre Parabellum, doesn't it?' The C96 was produced in a multitude of calibres. The number on the handle indicated what type of ammunition should be loaded, just to avoid embarrassing – and perhaps fatal – mistakes.

'Yes.'

'Well, if we find the bullet that took off O'Connor's finger, I suspect he might recognise it as not being Tangistani in origin.'

Wassmuss looked pained. 'You really think so?'

'I don't seem to recall them getting much of a shot in. Of course, it happened very quickly. The heat of battle and all that.'

'Then thank you for keeping quiet.'

'I don't want to give O'Connor any more of a reason to shoot you. Not yet.'

'I appreciate that.'

'After all, that's my job.'

Wassmuss examined Quinn's face for irony or levity, but there was none there. The German accepted that there would be a reckoning when this was done. Either that, or they would all be past caring about such things.

'Talking of heat of battle,' Quinn tapped the Colt pistol in his belt. 'Where did Lawrence magic this from?'

Wassmuss shrugged. 'I think I am moving beyond being surprised at anything he does.'

'I think I am too.'

Wassmuss gave a smile. 'No. You still have one surprise to come.' He slapped him on the shoulder in an unnerving gesture of familiarity. 'Good luck.'

Quinn and Farid sat either side of the doorway, amid the spongy splinters of the decayed gate. They could cover most of the approach road that way, at least while it was light. After dark, it would be a different matter.

'You used a rifle before?' Quinn asked.

Farid shook his head.

'It's very simple. It's all about being as smooth as you can possibly manage. Hold it hard against your shoulder, or the recoil will hurt like hell. You jerk the rifle around, you have to re-aim each time. So you try and pull the bolt back without snatching. Don't worry about being as quick as me. Better one good shot than three wild ones.'

Farid worked the bolt, but Quinn could see it was hard for him. The grating sound of the breech mechanism suggested the weapon had not been loved. He checked his own rifle. It had been carefully maintained and greased. 'Take this one. I think it's a slightly easier action.'

As he handed it over Quinn noticed Farid's hands were shaking. Post-skirmish shock was setting in. He'd seen it before. 'Are you all right?'

'Yes, sir.'

Quinn held on to Farid's rifle and felt the vibration through it. 'Was that the first time you have killed a man?'

'Yes.' The voice quivered. 'I am a guide, that is all.'

A guide handy with a knife, Quinn thought. 'I am very pleased you decided to start a new career today.'

Farid snorted. 'As what? Murderer?'

'Warrior.'

Now the lad laughed. 'Warrior? I come from a long line of linguists and travellers. Not warriors. It was a reflex, sir. That was all.'

'It was the right reflex. And staying alive in those situations is often no more than that. Where did the knife come from? You were searched.'

'Throw me a stone, sir.'

'What?'

'Throw me a stone, sir. A distinctive one.'

Quinn picked up a white-ish piece of chalk before he realised what it was. 'It's a bone, I think.'

'Perfect. Throw it over.'

Farid caught the object, examined it, and then flung it out, across the road and into the scrub.

'What was the point of that?'

From beneath his tunic, he produced a small pouch and tossed it back to Quinn.

'Hiding a knife is simple compared to that.'

Quinn felt the purse. He didn't need to look inside. He could feel the same metacarpal. 'I've seen that trick done before.'

'Really, sir?' Farid said. 'I was taught—'

The rest of the sentence was drowned by the distinctive burst of the Lewis gun from above.

Thirty-eight

Vanity brought me to this, Lawrence thought. The misplaced pride of a map-maker who thought he was a warrior, the foolishness of a desk-wallah convinced he could take on an experienced agent like Wassmuss man-to-man. Because of his arrogance, they were bottled up, trapped like chickens waiting for the fox.

Stop it, he told himself. *Deal with the situation, the future, not the road that led us here. That can wait.*

'How long till nightfall?' Lawrence asked.

'An hour,' said Wassmuss.

'At most,' added O'Connor.

They were spaced out around the rim of the tower facing the road. Wassmuss was using his binoculars to examine the approaching riders. Lawrence was looking across to the old camp, where the bodies had attracted circling vultures. Quite how the ugly, baggy-faced creatures always appeared within such a short space of time baffled Lawrence. He hadn't seen vultures all day and now, with the blood of the dead still warm, the predators had arrived, gliding on silent, finger-tipped wings.

'What are the Tangistani doing?' Lawrence asked, looking out at the plains.

Wassmuss lowered the glasses. 'Zair has reached the support group.'

'No hope that they are turning back to Ahram, I suppose?' asked O'Connor.

Wassmuss clamped the binoculars to his eyes once again. 'None. They come.'

'There is always the chance they won't look in here,' said Lawrence. It wasn't only the echo of the stones that made his words seem hollow and empty.

O'Connor said: 'We should keep our heads down just in case.'

Wassmuss sounded tired and defeated when he spoke, the burden of the last few hours crushing down on him. 'Let this be a lesson to you, Lawrence.'

'What lesson is that?'

'A hard-won one.' Wassmuss sounded glummer than ever. 'Never think the war in someone else's land is about you and what you want. I lost sight of that.'

Lawrence stood down from the parapet and pulled out his red notebook. In it he scribbled the events of the past few hours, with a mix of appropriate quotations and the occasional fragment of poetry or prose. He had been right about the significance of the locks, which was pleasing. Of course, if the Germans knew that one of their diplomatic codes – there were three in all – had gone missing, they would change it. Which would mean they would be useless to the British. There was still more to play for. Their lives, for one. He closed the book and stood.

A pale moon was rising over the hills. The bats hadn't stirred yet, but Lawrence could see some desert finches flitting among the trees, snatching at insects. The arid hills would come fully to life as soon as the darkness enveloped them.

'Two riders coming up your side,' warned Wassmuss.

Lawrence stood and watched the pair of Tangistani urge their horses on up the shale-strewn path. They had been sent to ascertain if it was occupied and the strength of the defence. By firing, Lawrence would confirm they were there. By not firing . . .

He heaved the Lewis on to the top of the stone wall. Oh, for the Rolls right now, to break out and plough them down. Or some swift racing camels, even. Something to tip the balance.

Still they came.

He squeezed the trigger. The gun skittered over the parapet, spewing bullets in every direction, but it had the desired effect; the riders turned and raced, heads down, for the shelter of the thickets where the bodies of their comrades still lay.

'Not easy to aim accurately,' said Wassmuss.

'Not at all,' agreed Lawrence ruefully.

There was no further movement. Although the Zoroastrians built their Towers on pinnacles of bare rock, the direction for correct construction dictated there should be plenty of vegetation in the surrounding countryside. Much of it had long since gone, but there was enough on the lower slopes to obscure exactly what Zair and his riders were up to.

As the light failed, the bats sallied forth from the alcoves, dark smudges against the walls, spiralling up and out of the tower before scattering jerkily in all directions, foraging far for their brief feeding frenzy. A slight breeze brought the murmur of distant prayers from the trees as the sun fell.

The moon he had cursed as a harbinger of night waxed full, bleeding its quicksilver light across the rugged hills. Harder to read, more deceptive than daylight, it would nevertheless make the Tangistani feel exposed, especially if they tried to take the main road by stealth. And that pathway's treacherous consistency meant that every footfall released a trickle of stones that would boom through the night's silence.

Thirty minutes passed. Through the filter of the trees they could see the flicker of a campfire, and smell food, but there was no sign of offensive action. There was another sound, that of earth sliding on metal. The Tangistani were burying the dead.

'One of you could risk sleeping,' said Lawrence eventually.

'Rather not,' muttered O'Connor. 'I'll get us some blankets from the horses.'

'Make sure Quinn and Farid have something. It will get cold.'

They listened to him make his way down the dished steps with ponderous caution.

Wassmuss produced a cigarette, put it in his mouth but, wisely, did not light it. 'You know, I thought I was becoming like them. Like the natives. That I thought as them, simply by donning their clothes and raiding a few supply trains with them. It is impossible for a German to become an Arab or a Tangistan or a Turkoman.'

'And an Englishman or Irishman, I fear.'

'The best we can hope for is impersonation.'

'The trick, I suppose,' replied Lawrence, 'is to make it a convincing one.'

There was a pause while Wassmuss considered this. 'Like your friend Farid has?'

'I thought that impersonation exceptional,' Lawrence insisted.

'Perhaps. Possibly too good. It nearly got him killed.'

'Farid is why you changed sides?' asked Lawrence, amused at the thought.

Wassmuss hesitated. 'Partly. I couldn't allow such an execution. No German officer could. But I also realised I was no longer in a strong position. I never would have thought Zair would turn on me. But, as I said, I put my goals before his. Or, at least, let him see my goals weren't necessarily the same as his.'

Lawrence could see the sense in the local man's tactics. 'It was the right thing for Zair to do. He thinks you are a spent force, Wassmuss. He's right. Then he would have been giving away his best chance of influencing the British by letting us all go. He might be a vicious, capricious warlord, but he isn't stupid.'

Another short silence followed. 'Lawrence?'

'Yes?'

'Quinn was wondering where the Colt came from. You were disarmed.'

There was no reply.

'It doesn't matter now. And I think we can forget we are enemies until we see how the night turns out. Don't you?'

Lawrence thought for a little longer before he spoke. 'I left it in one of the trees when I buried the locks. In the crook of a branch. I reached up and fetched it while you were bending down, getting the sack.'

'Ah. How sly. I thought you might have buried something with them. I did not think you might have left something above them. You aren't left-handed, are you?'

'No. Why do you ask?'

'During the scuffle. You fired that gun as if you were. Got two with two shots. It was impressive.'

It was telling that, in the confusion, Wassmuss had noticed such a detail. 'I practised on the cadet range day and night till I could fire equally well with either hand. Then did the same with archery. I'm good with a pistol, but I'm even better with a bow than a gun. As a child I was obsessed with knights, chivalry and heraldry. Probably because my own lineage is so murky.'

'How so?'

There came a small croak of a laugh. 'My crest has bars sinister. They are rather jolly ornaments.'

There was no response Wassmuss could think of to a man confessing his illegitimacy. It was bad enough in England, he knew, but could be overcome. In Germany, it was a stain that no amount of rubbing or reinvention could remove. 'I see. I'm sorry.'

Lawrence shrugged. 'It's of no consequence here, is it?'

'No. None.'

He had told few people that his parents' union was a sham. Every day he still thanked his mother's capricious God that Frank had never found out they were all bastards before he died.

'There are only two blankets,' said O'Connor as he puffed up the final few steps of the stairs. 'And not much food.'

'I don't need either. You share the victuals,' said Lawrence.

'Nonsense,' objected the major.

'No. I won't feel the hunger or the cold.'

O'Connor gave a grunt and made to move along to Wassmuss.

'How's the finger?'

O'Connor considered lying, but decided against it. 'What's left of it is throbbing like hell. I'd give another one up for a bottle of brandy.'

'And Quinn and Farid?' Lawrence asked him.

'Alert enough, but I told them to shut up. Yak, yak, like the bloody servants.'

Lawrence settled down for a sleepless night, knowing that he could go forty-eight hours without closing his eyes. It was something else he had practised. He was aware, though, that keeping watch in bright moonlight was a terrible strain on the eyes, that the patterns created by the mosaic of half-light and shadow played tricks on the febrile brain. If used cleverly, the moon could hide as much as it revealed.

Lawrence appreciated this just as the new sun washed a few tentative brushstrokes of light across the eastern sky. He had been trying to identify the rattles and squeaks coming from the direction of the Tangistan camp, as well as the accompanying groans of men and whinnying of packhorses.

It was only when he heard the ringing clash of well-machined metal parts slamming together that he realised what they had done under the guidance of the full moon. They had sent for artillery.

Thirty-nine

Somewhere in the far distance a jackal called, a series of crude yips and growls. Another answered with a long, low howl. 'It's almost light,' said Quinn, stifling a yawn. 'Perhaps those damned creatures will shut up then.'

It was the first time he had spoken in hours. His eyes were sandy from lack of sleep and the constant staring into the night. The bottomless black shadows never seemed to be still, figures and shapes were made and reformed within them, but so far they had always been just that. Imagined shapes, rather than flesh and blood. His muscles were stiff from inactivity, although the night had not been as cold as he had feared. The stones of the Tower of Silence appeared to store the day's heat and had bled it out slowly, tempering the worst of the chill.

'Why have they not attacked, sir?' Farid asked.

'Perhaps the Lewis scared them off.'

'I think not, sir. We have to face up to . . .' He let the thought die.

Quinn tried to sound reassuring. 'It's not over yet, lad.'

Farid took out a piece of paper and a stub of a pencil and wrote a few lines. Quinn wondered if it was his last will and testament. 'Sir, who did you send your letter to?'

He considered telling him, but thought better of it. 'Someone at home.'

'That's a long way from here, I think, sir.'

Quinn gave a rueful laugh. 'Isn't it just. Shush! Hear that?'

They listened to the soft rattle of chains and links and the squeak of bearings. 'What is it?'

'I don't know.'

'They are up to something, sir,' said Farid. 'That's why they didn't rush us. It would be honourable to die killing infidels. So they must have been saving themselves for something else.'

There was a tremble in the last few words.

Quinn didn't speak for another few minutes, scanning the landscape and its shadows, which were turning from solid black to shades of grey.

'Sir—'

'Quiet.'

Farid seemed to unfold from the ground in a single smooth movement sweeping up the rifle to his shoulder and firing, the report of his weapon lost in the first boom of a howitzer.

The shell didn't whistle as Lawrence expected, it whooshed and growled as it arced over their heads. It landed with a boom beyond the rear walls, and a rattle of rocks and stones and the crackle of falling branches followed. Lawrence felt a light rain of debris fall on to him. Then there came the crack of Lee Enfields from below. Quinn and Farid were engaging.

'Suppressing fire!' he cried.

The Lewis kicked and bucked in his hands, but he had the measure of it now, allowing the stream of bullets to rake in an arc from the thicket protecting the howitzer to the pathway up to the entrance, where he glimpsed the shape of at least one horseman.

All too soon the magazine ran dry and the firing pin clicked on to an empty chamber. Lawrence manhandled the disc off, while Wassmuss continued to fire. He wondered how much ammunition the German had. Not much, he suspected, and on automatic fire the Mauser was even greedier than the Lewis. Lawrence picked up the second-to-last of his precious magazines.

The next shell came over low and Lawrence felt the impact of the detonation this time, a hot fist driven into his kidneys. As he was pushed forward, the edge of the parapet drove the air from his lungs and the magazine skidded from his grip. Desperately he launched himself after it, but it spun over the stones and disappeared into the gloom below.

'Damn it!'

Whoever was aiming the artillery piece got the hang of the clinometer and the elevating wheel by the third shell. This time, Lawrence saw the muzzle flash and, in the strengthening light of morning, the puff of smoke. Again, the round flew over his head but dropped down on to the far wall. The entire structure shuddered under the explosion and a chunk of masonry came spinning at Lawrence, banging painfully into his forehead and drawing a thick stream of blood. He wiped it on to his sleeve. He shook his head to try and clear the ringing.

As the dust cleared, he could see O'Connor, hanging in a space where his walkway had once been, his legs kicking the air.

Before Lawrence could act, Wassmuss was round there, skidding to a halt and diving on to his stomach. He managed to grab the Englishman's wrists and pull him to safety. Both lay for a second, panting.

'All right?' shouted Lawrence, aware yet again of how dead his voice sounded to ears battered by the roar of bombardment.

A grey-faced O'Connor raised a hand. A trickle of blood was apparent beneath one nostril. The major pointed at his own ears. The concussion of a round at such proximity must have knocked them out completely.

'Lawrence!'

It was the muffled sound of Quinn, from below. 'Yes?'

'Flag of truce approaching.'

Lawrence dusted himself down and ran a hand through his hair, disloding the larger chunks of stone, and dabbed at his bleeding forehead once again. He peered though the grit-filled air across to O'Connor's side of the tower. One of the two big beams was twisted out of its support, and dangled down towards the floor at a perilous angle. It would be dislodged with one more shell. Below, the tethered horses whinnied in terror.

As he took the first few steps down the steps, Wassmuss strode around the parapet. 'Lawrence.'

He looked up at the dirt-smeared German. 'Yes?'

'If you can trade me for you and your people . . .'

Lawrence smiled. 'I don't think it is going to be that simple.'

'No,' came the reply. 'I fear not. But if you have the opportunity.'

Lawrence passed a chalk-faced Farid, standing behind Quinn, who was positioned just outside the gate, a rifle aimed at the rider. Lawrence strode out on to the shale, the clattering rocks slithering away under his feet. He tried his best to stand tall as he approached, but his ribs and head were aching and he wasn't sure he couldn't keep the pain from his face.

He did not recognise the rider; it was not Zair. Of course, he wouldn't come himself. White flags were no guarantee against one impetuous shot from a man like Quinn.

'Yes?' Lawrence tried to sound as if the man were an inconvenience, a trespasser on his land to be sent off with a flea in his ear. 'What can I do for you?'

The emissary leaned forward and patted his horse's neck. He was young, perhaps not yet twenty, although honey-filled pastries and sweet coffee had blackened his teeth. 'My master wishes to discuss the terms of surrender.'

'If he cares to stop shelling us, we will gladly accept his surrender.'

The man ignored this impudence. 'He will keep you and Wassmuss and let the others go.'

This surprised Lawrence. 'Free passage for the others?'

'Yes. Free passage.'

'And what of us?'

'You will be his guests.'

Lawrence thought about this. With the blood of his men spilt, there would need to be some kind of revenge by Zair. But he would also assume that he and Wassmuss were worth something to their respective governments. Lawrence doubted this was true. He was a junior Intelligence officer and Wassmuss an expendable agent provocateur. Neither government would negotiate with a native for a ransom of such men. But Zair would not appreciate that.

'I shall need to discuss this.'

The Tangistan nodded and glanced at the sun. 'You have five minutes.'

Lawrence backed slowly up the path, keeping his eye on the rider. It was an offer that deserved consideration, although there were many variables. Such as, would Zair keep his word and not just kill them all? But he could do that anyway with the howitzer. By blowing them up, there was no doubt he would be wasting what might be a prime opportunity to extort gold. Lawrence knew that Persians traditionally prided themselves on three things: riding well, using the bow with exceptional prowess and telling the truth. But was Zair a true son of Persia? Was his offer sincere?

As Lawrence reached the gate, Quinn hissed at him: 'I heard that. You can't do it.'

'I think it is a fair exchange.'

'They'll kill you, sir,' said Farid.

'Perhaps. Perhaps not. I think Zair is pragmatic to a fault.

Wassmuss,' he shouted up to the ramparts. 'Did you catch any of that?'

'Yes,' came the reply. 'We should let the others go. You and I can take our chances.'

Quinn shook his head and looked up at the German, who was peering over the edge of the walkway. 'Don't try and be martyrs.'

Lawrence scoffed at this. 'Martyrs? It's not that. Farid must be saved. Imagine Gerty's fury if he isn't. You must go to escort him. O'Connor has suffered enough, so he should be freed. As he says, Wassmuss and I can take our chances.'

Quinn dropped his voice. 'You forget what my job here is.'

'Your job has been superseded by other concerns.'

Quinn shook his head. 'That's not up to you. I am here for Lord Kitch—'

To Quinn's surprise, Lawrence grabbed his neck. His fingers were terrifyingly strong. 'You try and fulfil that mission and I'll kill you.'

Quinn pulled out his pistol and pressed it to Lawrence's head. The man didn't flinch.

'Stop it!' hissed Farid. 'What good will that do?'

The protagonists stared at each other, eyes unblinking.

'A fine display for the Tangistani,' Farid sneered. 'A great demonstration of our cohesion.'

Cohesion? thought Quinn. An interesting word for an Arab to use.

Farid stepped closer. 'Please.'

Quinn lowered the gun and felt the fingers loosen at his throat. When Lawrence spoke, it was soft enough to be for his ears only. 'Quinn, we are playing for bigger stakes than a simple assassination here. Wassmuss must live. Or we've been wasting our time. You have to trust me. Do you?' Those blue eyes seemed colder, angrier than ever. 'Can you do that?'

'Why, exactly?'

'Not for sentimental reasons. For the King. For England. For the young men dying in France. Men like my brother. For Tariq. You must be with me on this.'

Quinn felt some of his fury drain away. He had to assume Lawrence knew something he didn't. Eventually, he nodded his consent.

Lawrence began to speak quickly. 'Then there is a small task I need you to perform in Cairo while Wassmuss and I are prisoners. It involves going to the bazaar—'

''PLANE.' It was O'Connor again, croaking a half-swallowed word.

Lawrence glanced up at the major. 'Plain?'

O'Connor coughed dust from his throat and found his voice. 'AEROPLANE.'

'It's an aircraft.' It was Wassmuss speaking, confirming the sighting, a cruciform shape almost lost in the disc of the rising sun. Shortly afterwards they all heard the distinctive racket of an aero engine.

Lawrence hesitated, torn between accepting the terms of the surrender and running up to take a look. Wassmuss settled the matter for him. He raised the Lewis in the air and fired precious bullets into the sky as a signal to the pilot. The

Tangistan messenger, taking this as a termination of negoti-
ations, turned and galloped back to the camp.

Lawrence was breathless when he reached the top of the
ramparts, scanning the heavens for the machine, but it was
nowhere to be seen.

'Where the hell is it?'

The next shell must have had too much propellant charge
because, instead of being lobbed into the centre of the courtyard as he expected, it once more overshot the mark, throwing
up a harmless column of sandy dirt into the air. Lawrence
knew that their luck couldn't last. The gun's action would be
nicely familiar by now, the barrel warmed; the shells would
slide easily into the well-greased breech. Any minute now, he
thought, and we'll be blood, bone and dust.

The air thrummed with more noise and Lawrence covered
his ears, but it was no shell. The spindly shape of a biplane
whooshed across his vision and out over the plains, where it
began to make a rapid turn.

Quinn's voice came from the path below. 'Wave your scarf.'

'What?'

'The scarf. Wave it. Show you're English.'

'What if it's a Turkish craft?' asked Wassmuss, suddenly
doubting his own initial assumption.

'Ha!' Lawrence laughed. As he watched it swing through
the air, he knew from its shape this was no Ottoman aircraft.
It was an Airco pusher. And he suspected it was held together
with decent, heat-proof glue and long screws. 'It's British, my
friend. Not only that, I think the pilot went to Balliol.'

The Airco came roaring towards them, its propeller chewing

through the waxy morning air, the engine spraying out its mist of castor oil and Lawrence took the purple and black scarf and waved it over his head. As he did so, a round came from the howitzer and detonated in the courtyard.

The stonework funnelled the cruel blast upwards and Lawrence was lifted off his feet and slammed down on to his back. As the roaring subsided, he heard the creak of one of the giant beams breaking loose and crashing down. The whole structure became a bowl full of boiling dust and smoke. From the bottom of it came the shrieks of dying and maimed horses.

'Quinn? Farid?' Lawrence shouted down into the swirling mist.

There came another explosion that nearly tossed Lawrence down into the obscured courtyard. But this one had come from the hillside below, around the Tangistan positions. Wassmuss jerked Lawrence back to the parapet and pointed to the camp, to the spiral of black smoke coiling from it. The plane was making another run and Lawrence could see the observer clearly, clutching his bombs, ready to toss them into the thicket.

Lawrence cheered.

A volley of Tangistani rifle fire greeted the plane as it approached, but the pilot kept his nerve. The observer, however, appeared to panic and released the missiles well short of his target. Lawrence heard Wassmuss groan.

The tiny, wobbly cylinders, though, seemed to keep as much forward momentum as vertical and, willed on by the two men, they disappeared into the undergrowth.

The next detonation uprooted whole trees as it boiled into

the sky, and the shockwave almost dashed them off the ramparts. It was followed by a succession of smaller bangs and then another massive thump, a kettledrum to the other's snares, which sent flames leaping fifty feet into the sky. The air crackled as the corona of thin, dry branches vanished in a flash.

'My God. He must have caught an ammunition box.'

There was one final thud, and then silence, but for the snap of burning trees and the hum in their ears.

The aeroplane came back, passing low and slow, and the pilot raised his goggles and then an arm. It was Dickie Daniels.

They both watched the plane recede in the sky as it headed west, to the kind of country where a small aircraft might land safely.

'Lawrence! Wassmuss! O'Connor! For God's sake help me!'

The three men rushed down the stairs, choking their way through the cloud of debris. At the bottom, they found Farid, face spattered with blood, trying to move the enormous wooden stay off Quinn, who lay on his face, pinned by the ancient beam.

'I told him to stay out of here,' said Lawrence.

'He was trying to get the horses clear,' Farid explained.

Lawrence became aware of the plaintive whinnying of a wounded animal. Quinn would have been trying to get them to safety for practical, not sentimental reasons, to aid their escape.

Wassmuss knelt down and scooped away the earth and

rubble, making sure the trapped man had room to breath and checked for a pulse. It was wild and erratic.

Farid slipped his fingers under the massive beam and was straining to lift it. The veins in his neck were as thick as fingers.

'Stop that!' Lawrence said. 'Save your strength.'

'No!' he yelled, snatching off the hat and letting a knot of hair cascade free.

O'Connor gave the smallest gasp of surprise as the newly revealed woman knelt down.

'Harry, it's me. Mrs Wake.'

The eyes fluttered, but she couldn't be sure he understood.

'It's me. Elizabeth.'

It took some time before Quinn's damaged brain could make sense of that. Farid was Mrs Wake. Mrs Wake was Farid. He tried to recall the time he had seen them together. On the liner to Cairo? No. At Miss Bell's? Again, no. His cracked lips parted in a smile. What a fool. 'The trick—'

She knew he meant the one with the bone, which mimicked the one with the coin she had performed at sea. 'Yes, I did it on the ship, remember? Don't be angry with me. I had to become a man to come along.'

He managed a nod. 'The letter. I sent it . . .'

She leaned closer. 'Yes?'

'I sent it to you.'

A rattle of air escaped from his lungs on the final word. Mrs Wake blinked, stood and tried once more to move the beam. 'Help me.'

Lawrence gently grabbed her shoulders and eased her away.

'We do it together. If you are exhausted, you are no good to us. Just wait. Where is the pistol?'

She looked appalled and lowered her voice. 'What? No. He's not that hurt. You can't.'

'Where is the gun?' he demanded.

'By the doorway.'

Lawrence fetched the Colt and stumbled over the rubble, to where one of the injured horses lay. Its frantic cries were not helping. 'Sorry,' he said softly, and put a bullet into the animal's vast forehead, hoping for a clean kill. It thrashed twice, then became still, blinking once before the light went from its eyes.

'He'll die if we don't get him out,' Mrs Wake said softly as he returned. She pointed to Quinn. 'He's dying now, Lawrence.'

Lawrence said nothing in reply, but quickly positioned three of them at the end of the beam and allocated O'Connor the task of pulling Quinn free. 'On the count of four, gentlemen. One . . . two . . . three . . . heave.'

It was far heavier than he had thought, and Lawrence felt his sinews and muscles strain as he pushed. The beam barely gave at all and, after thirty futile seconds, the three of them staggered away. Lawrence breathed deeply and gathered his wits, before he said to Wassmuss. 'Go down to the camp. Every field gun and howitzer comes with at least one tin or a bucket of grease.'

'Grease?'

'For the shells and the breeches and the bearings,' Lawrence went on. 'Artillery runs on grease and oil. Fetch it.'

'Are you . . . ?'

'For God's sake, man,' Lawrence barked. 'Every second counts.'

Wassmuss left at a trot. Lawrence's tone instantly returned to normal. 'Farid, Mrs Wake, the alcove where I left the Lewis gun. There is water there. Can you get it, please.'

With only a moment's hesitation she struggled off over the stones to find it. Lawrence knelt down next to Quinn and stroked his forehead.

'We'll get you out soon.'

'Sorry. Didn't mean to get pinned.'

Lawrence watched the light in his eyes flicker like a guttering lamp wick. 'Wassmuss has gone to fetch something. Help slide you out. It will work. But I also needed to get rid of him rather urgently. I have to tell you why we must let him live. Or all this is in vain. So don't think you have failed if he doesn't die.'

'I don't understand.'

'He has to think we don't have the code.'

'And do we?'

Lawrence nodded. 'I took the locks to the Street of the Locksmiths in the Cairo Bazaar. They copied them to the last brass pin. They are still there, awaiting collection. I wasn't sure then what they were, but there was nothing else in the case it possibly could be.'

'Clever.' Quinn closed his eyes as pain shot through him. 'Feels like something's broken inside.'

'Just lie still.' Lawrence knew it might be more than broken. The blast from a shell could turn a man's innards to mush without leaving much of an external mark. He wondered at what stage Quinn had gone into the tower, if he had caught the full force of the shell. If so, pulling him free would do little good.

'And what about . . .' He gulped air. 'Farid being Mrs Wake? You knew all along?'

Lawrence admitted he had. He had known from the start and Wassmuss had discovered the truth from the Khan at Deh Now, where Miss Wake had used the disguise on her previous travels. It was why the German had acted to stop the execution by Zair's men: old fashioned chivalry. 'It's a Persian tradition. We are in lands where identity is not fixed, but a fluid commodity. One of its more attractive facets. Mrs Wake used it well.'

'Blind.'

'No, you weren't. You don't see what you are not looking for. And she's good at what she does. Like you. Like Miss Bell.' Gerty, the past master of such deception, had apparently tutored Mrs Wake in the art of passing yourself off as a local. Hadn't she herself fooled the wily Ibn Saud by presenting herself as a goatherd? And Mrs Wake had been so convincing, so skilled at the nuances of Farid, that Lawrence had even had to look twice, three times on occasion, to check he hadn't dreamt the whole charade.

'Lawrence,' Quinn croaked. He leaned in to catch his words. 'You are wasted behind a desk. You're a soldier. Not the usual kind, perhaps, but one all the same. I am sorry if I ever thought otherwise.'

'And you know, try as I might, I never thought you were

a hard-hearted assassin. You do your job. But you need to know what you do is right. You cared when you thought Abdel died for the wrong reasons. He didn't, but I appreciated your reasons for worrying that it was a personal matter. You are not lost to humanity, yet, Captain Quinn, much as you try to hide from it.'

The injured man managed another smile. 'Nor you, Lawrence.'

O'Connor was working his jaw up and down and was rewarded with a click like a snapping wishbone that kicked one ear back into play. 'He won't only get the grease, you know.' he said. 'Wassmuss, I mean. He'll be looking for his locks.'

'I know,' replied Lawrence, realising that O'Connor had not heard a word of what had passed between himself and Quinn. 'I know.'

'Was that what you wanted me to do in Cairo?' Quinn asked through gritted teeth. 'Pick up the duplicates of the locks?'

'Yes. And take them back to London. Which I would still like you to do, once you are fixed up.' He tried not to make the sentiment sound too hollow, but suspected he had failed.

Mrs Wake returned with the water, crouched down and poured a little on Quinn's lips. He groaned slightly. 'What's taking Wassmuss so long?' she demanded.

'Be patient,' said O'Connor.

'I said, I wanted to call on you.' It was Quinn, his voice a flickering shadow. 'In the letter.'

'Of course you can,' said Mrs Wake thinly. 'In fact, I insist.'

The responding smile was fleeting and insubstantial.

When a breathless Wassmuss did return, he looked wan and sick. Lawrence could imagine what the detonation of ammunition boxes would have done to the men and beasts. He wondered if Wassmuss had even been able to identify Zair, let alone claim his blessed codex system. But he did have a metal bucket of thick, gloopy grease. 'There are some horses still alive down there. Seriously skittish for the moment, I nearly got a hoof in the head. They were tethered away from the camp. They have some shrapnel wounds, but nothing too serious. They'll calm down.'

Lawrence nodded. That, too, was for later. 'Quinn.' He shook the pinioned man awake. 'We are going to pack grease round you as best we can. If we can even lift it a fraction of an inch, it might help O'Connor slide you out.'

Quinn nodded his understanding and they set to work, each taking handfuls and smearing the slimy material on every accessible surface from his waist down. 'It's useless,' said Mrs Wake. 'It needs to be on the top, where the timber is pressing on him.'

Lawrence said nothing. He tore off a strip of his tunic, wiped his hands on it and tossed it to Mrs Wake. 'Get the grease off your hands. You must get the best purchase you can.'

'Mrs Wake.'

It was Quinn. She knelt at his side and poured more water on his mouth. His tongue greedily licked his lips.

'Call me Elizabeth. We're just going to try and clear this—'

'No. It's no good. I can feel my insides are . . . I'm crushed.' Tears welled. 'I want you to do me a favour.'

'Anything. What is it?'

'Bury me with Kate.'

'Don't—'

'No. I understand now.' His eyes widened into great circles like an owl's. 'If there is a God, I cheated him by leaving Persia in the first place. All this, this whole thing was to get me back here, so I could end up where I should have been all along. With her.'

She squeezed his hand. It was clammy to the touch. 'You are talking such nonsense.'

'Bury me with Kate,' he repeated, the voice even weaker this time.

'We'll go to her grave together, Quinn. You remember the poem I taught you on the ship? *Kifa, nabki, min zikra habibin oua manzili, ala sikkat el'liqua.*'

Quinn, between short, sharp breaths, translated out loud. 'My friends, let's stop here and weep, in remembrance of my beloved, on her traces, here at the edge of the dune.'

'I taught you well, didn't I?'

'You did, you did. Thank you, Elizabeth.'

'Now just hold on and we'll lift. Just hold on.'

Mrs Wake ran round to the end of the beam and got herself into position. 'Come on, put your backs into it.'

But the others stood where they were, looking down at the body. Lawrence knew from the way Quinn's face had relaxed, the softening as the muscles had unknotted, that the pain had gone now, for ever.

'Come on. Push.'

'Just a moment,' Lawrence said.

Mrs Wake snarled her words. 'What the hell do you mean? Come on. Come on, damn you. Major O'Connor, are you ready?' She threw her shoulders against the beam, her teeth grinding as she urged her body on, summoning the strength of madness. With a loud creak, the stay lifted a tiny amount. O'Connor bent down and yanked at the body, helped by Lawrence. Gliding on the grease, Quinn came clear of the joist.

Mrs Wake let the great transverse drop and stood, staring at the still, small figure that wasn't moving. 'Oh, my Lord.'

Lawrence checked for a pulse, both in the neck and wrist. He held a hand over the mouth, hoping for the smallest of breaths. He peered into the eyes and flashed a finger across them. There was nothing. The pupils were fixed, the lungs still, the heart stopped.

She glared at each of them in turn, as if searching for someone to blame, before, eyes down, she strode out from the Tower of Silence, the repository of the dead, which had taken one last soul to the other side.

The oxygen seemed to have gone from Lawrence's body, and for a few moments he was unable to find his voice. He forced his constricted throat to relax. 'Mrs Wake—' he began.

She didn't look back. Lawrence wasn't sure what he could have offered in any case. More empty words.

Forty

Lawrence, O'Connor and Wassmuss tried their best to ignore the sound of weeping while they prepared Quinn for transport to Bushire, binding his ankles and strapping his arms to his side so he could be placed over a saddle. Once they had finished, they walked down the slope to fetch the horses, past the crumpled shape of Mrs Wake. Lawrence laid a hand on her shoulder and her fingers touched his, briefly.

She looked up, blinking away the film of moisture that covered her eyes. There was hate and anger in there. Lawrence held her gaze, watching the tussle of emotions in her and, after a few seconds, she simply nodded, accepting what had happened. Her eyes became slick once more and she looked down at her feet.

The men continued their gradual descent.

'Bad luck,' said O'Connor, breaking the pensive silence. 'Quinn.'

'Yes,' Lawrence agreed, although it seemed beyond mere

misfortune. Four set out from Banda. Two dead. A fifty per cent casualty rate was not what he had been anticipating. He felt as if each new death was a small chip off his soul, making him less human.

'Would Quinn have carried out his mission?' Wassmuss asked as they slithered down the path, his question breaking into Lawrence's thoughts.

Lawrence gave an honest answer. 'To kill you? I'm not sure. We'll never know.'

'And you?'

'I am no assassin.'

'Then I have to go now, you know. To leave you.'

O'Connor heard this and began to protest. Lawrence held up a hand to silence him. 'I realise that.'

'It was a temporary alliance, you and I. My future is still with the Tangistani. Even more so, now they have lost their Khan. Despite what happened here, they are good people, given the chance. We are the ones who don't belong, who create these situations, not them.' He cleared his throat and spat out the dust. 'Will you try and stop me?'

Lawrence shook his head. 'No.'

O'Connor made a disapproving grunt but kept his counsel.

Clouds of flies rose as they passed the shattered remains of the camp and the twisted and scattered lumps of metal that had once been a howitzer. Vultures reluctantly took to the air, angered by the interruption to their work, and circled patiently.

Wassmuss stopped and looked down at a severed foot, the stump still lividly red. 'You know it is a wicked death for a

Muslim,' Wassmuss said softly. 'To be blown apart. It means that come the day of resurrection on the Day of Judgment, there is no whole body to be revived.'

'They were happy to do the same to us,' O'Connor reminded him.

'That's different,' Lawrence said, intrigued by the revelation. 'We are infidels. We have no chance of seeing Allah anyway.'

Gingerly, with many soothing sounds, Wassmuss inspected the horses, which had been left in a hollow that had sheltered them from the worst of the blasts. Gently, he wiped a smear of blood from the flank of one and, after a few minutes of stroking, levered himself into the saddle. The animal shuddered and bucked slightly and its lips quivered as it neighed. Wassmuss leaned over and scratched behind its ears and spoke softly in his native tongue till it had calmed.

'You have your locks, I suppose?' Lawrence asked.

The German hesitated before nodding. His hand moved towards the Mauser.

Lawrence shook his head, indicating he wasn't going to try and take them.

'What will you do, Wassmuss?' asked O'Connor.

'I shall return to Ahram and report the death of their great Khan in a battle against the English.'

'In which you fought bravely at his side,' added Lawrence.

'Of course.' He indicated the scattered remains of the dead. 'There appears to be nobody left to contradict me.'

O'Connor frowned. 'Will they believe you?'

Wassmuss gave a tired smile.

'They'll believe him,' said Lawrence. He raised the Colt, aimed it carefully at Wassmuss's head and pulled the trigger. The pistol bucked in his hand as the slide whipped back, the ejected case spinning away into the bushes.

O'Connor flinched, his damaged ears ringing once more from the smack of compressed air.

The horses thrashed at the report, kicking up a cloud of dust and protesting loudly. The circling vultures closed their wingtips, letting the thermals carry them higher. The sound of the shot took its time dying away.

A dazed Wassmuss reached up to the side of his head and brought away a hand coated with blood. He swayed in the saddle, dizzy with shock.

'It's not as bad as it looks or feels,' said Lawrence. 'Ears always bleed profusely. You turn up without a scratch on you, and they'll be suspicious at Ahram. Now you have a warrior's wound, it looks as if you did your part.'

Wassmuss managed to laugh through the pain. He knew Lawrence was right; an unscathed survivor of a skirmish always created suspicion. 'I never thought I'd thank a man for shooting me.'

'It was a pleasure. But I'll need a favour in return. I'll need safe passage to Bushire. We have dead to bury.' He nodded at O'Connor. 'Wounded to treat. I don't want raiding parties from Ahram troubling us.'

'If it is within my power, you shall have it.'

'Thank you.'

'Major,' the German said, 'it was a pleasure meeting you.'

400

O'Connor gave a half-hearted salute.

Lawrence had one last item to deal with before he could let the man go. 'Wassmuss, there is something else you should know. Your colleagues.'

'Dead?' He didn't sound too surprised, just saddened.

'I am afraid so. You will be wasting your time taking more hostages.'

'I think my hostage-taking days are over.' Wassmuss gave a small bow. 'Goodbye, Lawrence.'

'Goodbye, Wassmuss.'

The bloodied German urged the horse forward and galloped off, keen to put distance between himself and his potential enemies, before they changed their minds about letting him ride away with the cypher.

'What now?' the major asked, when Wassmuss had disappeared from view.

'You are the ranking officer,' Lawrence reminded him.

O'Connor raised his eyebrows. 'I have a feeling that cuts little ice with you, Lawrence.'

'Perhaps not.'

Lawrence looked back up at the Tower of Silence. He could see the forlorn figure of Mrs Wake out on the road, retying her elaborate headdress, bringing Farid back to life once more. She would need that persona for a few more days, to ensure she got out of the country unmolested. 'Then I think it is the same as always, Major. The living have to pick up the pieces and move on to the next battle.'

He reached over and lifted O'Connor's damaged hand to examine it. The major winced. It was twice the size it should have been, puffy and purple. Both men knew that he could lose the arm unless it received attention soon. 'Although you might be *hors de combat* for the time being.'

Lawrence undid the horses, ignoring their agitation, took the reins of two of the animals and handed a second pair to O'Connor. 'We'll need one for Quinn.'

'Lead on.'

A distant storm was assembling in the east, the dark-fringed clouds coalescing, a mist already masking the horizon. They felt the air thicken around them. With the animals in tow, the two men trudged slowly back up the slope, each lost in their own thoughts. One of them was looking forward to a bath and a soft bed with cotton sheets after his months in captivity.

The second, however, was already calculating how best to put into practice all he had learned and seen these past few days and weeks. He knew that, from now on, every step of his way would be shadowed and weighted by an echo of the dead he had lost. The most he could hope for was to ensure that his fallen had not died in vain.

'*You are wasted behind a desk. You're a soldier.*'

He could live up to that, for Quinn's sake.

But Tariq? How to honour him?

By keeping his promise, the one made at Maadi, outside Dr Bitter's villa. *One day soon, the Arabs will ride on Damascus.*

It was what he had thought about during all those hours in the boiler room of HMS *Hardinge*. There, lost in the rhythm of the shovelling, he had conjured from the roaring flames an army of the desert – Hussein's sons, and himself, at its head

– riding north from Mecca, through Yenbo and Medina, taking Aqaba and Amman, blowing the Hejaz railway, pushing back the Turks, until they reached Deraa and then, finally, gloriously, Damascus.

It had been, as Tariq had once said, a crazy, cracked dream, a madman's vision. That didn't mean it was beyond him. It would not be easy. It would require guile and subterfuge to make sure he was in the vanguard of the campaign, to convince Storrs and Clayton that he should escape his desk and help raise the revolt. If that failed, he would be a devil, all teeth and claws, one they would do anything to be rid of from Cairo.

As he heaved Quinn's body over the saddle and secured his wrists to his ankles with twine, Lawrence determined that he would become one of those people who dreamt their most vivid dreams not at night, but during the day, as he had on the ship. The dreamers of the day were dangerous men, for they acted their dream with open eyes, overcoming every obstacle to make it possible. This he would do.

Epilogue

Two Years Later

Palestine, 1917

I

When Lawrence heard the goats, he knew there was trouble ahead. After leaving Rollins and the Wadi Umt gorge, the camel riders had headed east into rough, scrub country. He had arranged to meet with Auda at the three wells just beyond a village called Dariya, some fifty miles from the Hejaz railway.

The light was failing as they came within the village's grazing grounds. At first, Lawrence thought the dark lumps on the stony soil were dead men, but as he came closer he could see they were goats, already bloated from several hours lying under the vanishing sun. They had all been shot, some several times, apart from a number of pathetic, hungry kids, whose bleating Lawrence had heard. They were nuzzling up to their lifeless, putrefying mothers.

'Farraj!' he yelled.

The boy drew level with him.

'Pass the word. Weapons ready. But no firing unless I do.'

'Yes, Orrans.'

Lawrence unclipped the flap of the holster he carried slung around the pommel of Ghazala's saddle. In it was the Colt .45 he had used since Persia, now scuffed and scratched, but still reliable. He oiled the mechanism frequently, and as he stripped and reassembled the pistol, he always thought of Frank and Quinn and Tariq. When he fired it, he did so for them.

It was dusk as they passed to the south of Dariya village. The mud huts were unlit, brooding silhouettes against the deep blue sky. Daud, the other servant boy, voiced Lawrence's misgivings. 'No lights, Orrans. No cooking fires.'

'Ride on,' said Lawrence, the stench of charred wood reaching his nostrils.

With the village behind them, they could see there were glimmers of light around the three wells, but Lawrence called a halt a mile short. He dismounted and let Ghazala graze on the shrubs. Through binoculars he could see indistinct shapes moving around the campfires, but the gathering darkness had robbed him of detail. He could not tell if they were Arab, English or Turk.

Bandak, one of the Howeitat, asked: 'Shall we send scouts?'

Lawrence opened his mouth to speak, but it wasn't his voice they heard.

'I can tell you what they will find.'

The words came out of the gloom of twilight. Lawrence spun round, his arm automatically raising the Colt, even though he recognised the distinctive sibilance of the voice. It was Auda.

'You will find friends, Lawrence.' The chieftain emerged from the low bushes, pulling the hood of his *bisht*, the brown riding cloak, back from his face. His rifle was slung over his shoulder and his revolver in his belt. 'It is our camp. I heard your camels farting as they came a whole hour ago.'

Lawrence stepped forward and embraced him. 'I fear that was Bandak. Be grateful you only heard it.' Auda laughed, as Lawrence knew he would. He became serious. 'The village?'

Auda gave a slight shake of his head. 'None alive.'

'Turks.' It wasn't really a question.

'We caught up with the raiders at Ba'ma,' Auda said. There was pride when he added: 'But I remembered what you said, Lawrence. About gathering intelligence. We have two prisoners up there.' He pointed to the campfires burning at the wells.

'How many were in the party that sacked the village?'

'Thirty or forty.'

It was no good berating him. By his own standards, Auda had been merciful, saving a pair of them for Lawrence to interrogate. Besides, he didn't really have to ask what Auda had found in the village. Lawrence had witnessed atrocities perpetrated by both sides, come across scenes that would make Jesus himself into a vengeful monster, force Buddha to take up arms. The Turkish cavalry, in particular, were adept at thinking up fresh horrors.

'One more thing,' Auda added. 'Before they left, they dynamited the wells.'

To a Bedu, this violation of the desert code was as big an act of terror as slaughtering an entire village.

'And you need water?'

'We do. But in one of them, the charge did not explode, we think. It seems intact. But . . .'

'It might be booby trapped,' completed Lawrence. The Turks had a trick where they rigged up a trip wire that would detonate a mine when a bucket was lowered.

'Possibly.'

'Have you taken a look?' Lawrence asked.

'It was getting dark.' Auda smiled his toothless grin. 'Besides, Lawrence, you are Emir Dinamit, the king of explosives.'

Lawrence walked back to Ghazala and remounted. 'You know, Auda, the moment I clapped eyes on you, I knew you'd be trouble.'

He set off for the wells with the sound of Auda's laughter at his back.

II

Lawrence descended the flint-sided square water hole at first light. He had a rope tied around his waist, played out at the other end by his servants Farraj and Daud, whom he could trust not to let him fall.

Before his descent, he had interrogated the two Turkish prisoners, a sergeant and a captain. They had repeated the rumours that were surfacing all over the desert, whispers of a British betrayal and of French subterfuge. Auda had listened without comment, but Lawrence could tell the man was worried that this might be more than gossip.

He wasn't alone. To Lawrence, it had the ring of truth.

And if it was more substantial than rumour or propaganda, it could ruin everything.

It was ten months since Lawrence had travelled with Storrs to meet Emir Feisal, to discover why the Arab revolt, begun by his father, the Sherif of Mecca, on 10 June 1916 with a single rifle shot from his balcony, had stalled. The uprising had begun well, but had seemingly become mired in tribal politics. Unable to remain a frustrated bystander any longer, Lawrence had used every guile to be on the boat for Jeddah with Storrs's fact-finding mission.

'Are you all right, Lawrence?' Auda's voice rang from the stones as he shouted down the well.

'Yes. About a third of the way now.'

Lawrence had known even then that what the Arabs lacked was a wider view of the world, one that went beyond the next water hole, valley, and tribe. To the Bedu, disputes were parochial and personal, not international and political. The revolt didn't lack men, or arms, or – God help the Empire's coffers – gold. It was a want of ambition, the fire of idealism that was holding it back. But Lawrence couldn't give that directly. He had listened closely to what Wassmuss said. He could not lead. He had to inspire.

At Jeddah he had met one of Feisal's sons, Abdullah. He struck Lawrence as brave enough to lead the revolt, but lacking in vision and drive. So, Lawrence had ridden across a hundred and twenty miles of desert to Feisal's camp at Hamra, producing saddle sores the size of his fist. Blistered skin and lips added to his torture.

When he had arrived, Feisal, an imperious man in his early

thirties, had asked him how he liked his quarters. Lawrence had looked around the mud hut, and replied that he liked it well, but that it was far from Damascus. The words cut Feisal like a sword. Praise be to God, the Arab prince had replied, there are Turks nearer than that to kill. It was a good, robust reply. Lawrence knew he could work with this man.

Feisal was worldly enough to accept Lawrence's view that the revolt could not succeed without the northern tribes. Which meant, the prince said, they had to recruit Auda abu Tayi. Lawrence had heard whispers of him, not all of them reassuring. He was a legend among the Bedu, Feisal had counselled, but it was true he was wilful and sometimes greedy and duplicitous. But as a fighter, and a friend, there was none better. As an enemy, there was none worse.

And so he had proved.

Lawrence at that point remembered the parcel Rollins had given him, still in his saddlebags. He made a mental note to retrieve it as soon as he returned to the surface.

The ambient light began to fade and he descended into echoing gloom, aware of the occasional disturbance in the water below as he dislodged slivers of rock. His feet were finding easy purchase on the jagged walls, but he had to swing each foot out into the central space, probing for a trap, before he could rest his weight on it. His fingers were aching and bleeding by the time he stepped on the small ledge at the bottom.

Lawrence felt the chill of the water, and suppressed a shiver. From the bag over his shoulder he produced a candle and some matches. He screwed the candle into a flat brass holder and placed it on a jutting piece of stone at chest height. Then he lit the wick and stepped back while the light gathered strength.

'Lawrence.'

Auda sounded distorted and a long way away, but it wasn't just the depth of the well or the hard stones muffling his voice, it was the loud humming in Lawrence's ears.

'One moment.'

There was a small bundle of dynamite all right, but the fuse had extinguished at some point. Not wanting to waste any more explosive, the Turks had fallen back on another method of putting the well beyond use. Often, they used camels or horses or goats. Not this time. Floating face down in the water was the body of a baby, no more than two months old. It was naked, its skin the colour of a plum in the flickering flame, but unbroken, it seemed.

Lawrence carefully unknotted the rope from his waist and shouted up an instruction.

'What?' Auda came back. 'I didn't hear.'

'Send down a bucket. And put my riding cloak in it.'

While he waited, Lawrence inspected the explosive. It had fallen on to the rock shelf and lodged behind a stone, rather than rolling into the water, so it was still dry and could be used again. He plucked out the half-burned fuse and rammed it into a crevice.

Then he knelt and lifted out the stiff-limbed body, drying it with his sleeve. It was a little boy. He forced himself not to imagine too much, whether he was still alive when it happened, or if the mother had survived long enough to witness it.

The bucket arrived and Lawrence swaddled the child tightly

in his *bisht*. He gave him a soft kiss on the ice-cold forehead, remembering how Auda had said goodbye to Ali, then laid him in the leather bucket. He slid the dynamite, the instrument of the young one's demise, next to him. He put back his head and yelled. 'Bring it up. And Auda . . .'

'Yes?'

'Do nothing until I am with you again.'

Lawrence blew out the candle, repacked his bag and commenced the climb, moving fast now that he knew there were no traps to impede his progress. He was barely a third of the way up when he heard the flat sound of two shots from a revolver.

As he emerged into the bright morning, Farraj and Daud reached into the well-head and pulled him out. 'The water is clean,' he said. 'Fill up Auda's skins, then ours.'

The lads, who had seen the baby, looked doubtful.

'Throw away the first two buckets,' Lawrence improvised. The poor child hadn't been down there long enough to foul the supply, but the boys were bound to be squeamish about drinking it. 'The rest will be unsullied.'

Farraj, the brighter of the pair still seemed unconvinced, but nodded anyway. 'Yes, Orrans.'

'And Daud, when you have done that, dig a grave for the child. He might be young, but he died a warrior.'

'Yes, Orrans.'

A few yards from one of the ruined wells, Lawrence could see the two Turkish prisoners lying in the dust, both with the backs of their heads blown apart. Ah well, he reasoned, restraint was another virtue Auda had yet to discover.

Their executioner was on a rock nearby, smoking a cigarette. At his feet, the tiny bundle of the dead child. Outside, it seemed even smaller, its fate even crueller. Around Auda, his men were packing up, ready for the day's ride. 'I am sorry, Lawrence,' he said.

Apologies were something of a rarity from his lips. The Howeitat always thought the best form of defence was attack. It was why getting into arguments with them was such a risky business.

'For what?'

'For denying you the opportunity to kill them yourself. I was angry when I saw the baby and impatient.'

'No matter.' Lawrence would have liked a second interrogation, but they were clearly beyond that now. 'I have something for you.'

Lawrence walked to Ghazala, opened his saddlebags, and tossed the parcel Rollins had given him to Auda. The Arab opened it with great care, perhaps even suspicion. When he saw what was inside, though, he leapt to his feet, ran over and almost crushed the smaller man in his arms. Then he stepped back and slid the new dentures into his mouth, grinning and moving his head back so that the sun reflected off the single gold incisor. 'Much better than Turkish teeth.' He clacked them appreciatively and pointed in the direction of the distant railway. 'Now, Orrans,' he said, mimicking the servant boy's mispronunciation, 'shall we go and see how well they bite?'

'No.'

'No?' Auda sounded disappointed.

'Not me. I must leave you again. I have to go and see the man who delivered the teeth.'

Auda displayed his new dentures again. 'To thank him?'

'Perhaps, my friend. Perhaps.'

III

A volley of rifle fire greeted Lawrence and his bodyguard as they rode towards the forward encampment of the 54th (East Anglian) Division. The shots whistled harmlessly overhead, as intended, but Lawrence called a halt. He decided to ride on alone, while the others made camp. There were protests. He overrode them with some sharp words. He was Lawrence. He was used to being obeyed.

He pulled himself tall in Ghazala's tasselled saddle. It had been almost a week since he had left Auda. His eyes ached from the blindingly white mudflats they had crossed, his stomach from the brackish water of the last well and his soul from the stories he had heard everywhere of British perfidy. The last hurt more than any physical wound.

As his camel trotted into camp, several officers moved to block his way, swagger sticks at the ready, holsters unclipped, with a group of riflemen at their back. Some were very young, barely shaving, replacements for those lost at Gallipoli. They could only see a disreputable vagabond approaching, a 'rice-convert' perhaps, drawn by tempting rumours of free food or gold for any Arab who joined the revolt, even temporarily. Lawrence allowed his face covering to drop, and pushed back the cloth to show the blond hair beneath. He knew the power his contrary appearance had to shock and confuse.

He stopped twenty yards short of the man he had identified as the senior soldier. 'Colonel. Permission to enter camp, sir.'

The colonel was a ruddy-faced man with a toothbrush moustache who, Lawrence had to admit, was immaculately turned out. The glare from his buttons was almost as blinding as those mud flats.

'And you are?' the man demanded.

A voice from the left answered the question. 'Captain Lawrence. Welcome.'

The colonel turned and addressed the speaker, Major Edward Noel, who had emerged from his tent. 'Captain?' He asked in disbelief.

Noel nodded. 'And one of the finest in the British army.'

Lawrence inclined his head at the compliment. He made Ghazala kneel, swung a leg across and hopped out of the saddle. He strode across to his friend and embraced Noel, ignoring the disapproving stares at such a foreign gesture.

Noel turned to the colonel. Although, as a senior Intelligence officer, he knew of Lawrence's exploits, very few others had even heard of the captain, let alone his army. 'Sir. The captain leads a unit of Arab irregulars for General Allenby that has tied down Turks that would otherwise have been attacking the British forces across on the coast. He has also harassed the Hejaz railway for months now, again detaining units best employed elsewhere. Would you allow them to come near, better to water their animals and cook their food and possibly resupply?'

'Irregulars?' The colonel smiled, despite himself. It was a very apt description of Lawrence and his Arab robes. 'If you think so, Noel.'

'I do, sir.'

'Very well.' He turned to a corporal and instructed him to drive out and invite the camel corps to make camp closer.

'Tell them Orrans has said so,' Lawrence said to the corporal as he climbed into a Talbot staff car. 'Or they won't come. And don't believe a word the two boys say.'

Noel took Lawrence by the arm and led him towards his bell tent that had been pitched in the shadow of one of the tallest cliffs. Once inside the cool canvas room, Lawrence removed his headdress and sat in the folding chair next to Noel's portable writing bureau.

The major rang a small hand bell, and ordered tea and biscuits from an orderly. Even in some God-forsaken gorge, thought Lawrence, the British kept up appearances and routine.

Noel looked Lawrence up and down. He had grown scrawny, yet tough, like the Bedu themselves. The corners of his eyes were lined from sun and wind.

'You were harder to find than I thought, Major,' Lawrence admitted.

'Good. We are moving around to make the Turks think we are stronger in number than we really are.'

'Thank you for the teeth. You have a friend for life in Auda.'

'They fitted?'

'I'm not sure about that. But he looks even more terrifying now.'

'Good. You've seen Allenby?'

'No,' Lawrence replied. 'I wanted to see you first.'

'Me?'

'You are a man who knows things. A man I can trust.'

Noel felt flattered, although he wasn't sure why he deserved such an accolade. Lawrence and Noel had seen each other several times since the day when Daniels had bombed the Tangistani. Noel had been the bomber on the aeroplane. Once Lawrence had left Banda in the Rolls, the pilot had screwed together an Arco and had flown to Jam, to find the real Noel still waiting for Lawrence and Quinn to appear. The airstrip had not been, of course, in rebel hands at all. Wassmuss had been lying.

From there the pair had flown on to Deh Now, where they had cowed the Khan with a display of aerial bombardment. He had told them where to find Lawrence, Wassmuss and the others. After the destruction of the Tangistan artillery piece by the Airco, they had all met on the plains below the Tower of Silence; once he had taken O'Connor to Jam for treatment for his hand, Daniels had shuttled Lawrence, Farid and Quinn's body to Bushire. Lawrence had stayed just long enough to see Quinn interred with his wife before he shipped out for Cairo.

In the subsequent years, Noel had followed the Englishman's career with interest; their paths had crossed in both Kut and Jeddah and they had kept in touch. When Lawrence had needed to source Auda's false teeth, he knew Noel could assist him.

'You have done well,' Noel said. 'These past months.'

Lawrence's smile was small. 'At a price. Two hundred thousand pounds a month.'

'What?'

'That's how much the revolt costs us. A thousand camels for Feisel, gold for Auda to keep the Howeitat fighting. Two hundred thousand pounds. I hope it will be worth it.'

The tea and biscuits arrived and Lawrence nibbled on a digestive. He could smell the grease on his fingers from what seemed like a hundred meals of sheep head buried in rice, the liver or intestines glistening on the top of the gaping skull. He relished the dry, crumbly texture of the biscuit.

Noel did his best to reassure Lawrence. 'I wasn't exaggerating when I said your Arabs are tying the Turks in knots. They are spending a fortune repairing the railway. Thousands of troops are deployed protecting it. The Germans are having to keep an eye on the Turks, lest they make a settlement with us. Not to mention the gold and supplies flowing from Berlin to Constantinople, to keep Enver Pasha sweet.'

Lawrence shook his head. 'It sometimes feels like a sideshow. My nerves are going and my temper wearing thin.'

'Bad crossing of the flats?'

Lawrence laughed at Noel's perception. It had been a hard few days. 'Yes, it was.'

'Nothing a few nights' rest won't cure. By the by, there is a journalist looking for you. An American. Lowell Thomas. Has a cameraman in tow. He wants to film a raid.'

'How does he know about the raids?' Lawrence was well aware that it was a most secret war he was waging and he wanted it to remain that way.

'Allenby must have told him.'

'Thomas couldn't stomach it,' said Lawrence. He thought of the decimated Arab village and its goats, the baby in the well, the shattered skulls of Turkish prisoners. 'No journalist could. And the public isn't ready for the real story of this war.'

'They aren't ready for the truth about the trenches, either. He'll give them a yarn, something to celebrate. A hero. God knows we are short of those.'

Now Kitchener was gone – drowned at sea when the ship taking him to Russia had foundered off the Orkneys – the War Office had taken to eulogising the fighter pilots of the Royal Flying Corps, brave men such as Albert Ball. Unfortunately, every new ace seemed to be shot out of the sky within weeks of their canonisation, including Ball, VC, whom the Germans claimed had fallen victim to Von Richtofen.

Lawrence spoke ruefully. 'I am merely a liaison officer to the Arab forces. I am no hero.'

'Not yet. But perhaps this journalist could make you one. Think of the publicity for your cause.'

Lawrence gave a snort of contempt. 'I can imagine it. Vaudeville. As they say in Arabia, the magic will take over the magician. Besides, what have we achieved so far that is heroic?'

Noel took a deep breath. He knew that weariness did this to soldiers, how the sense of futility grew as fatigue set in. And the Garfa salt flats Lawrence had just traversed could suck the humour from the strongest of souls. 'You cannot see the context of your actions for the moment. You are too close, too bound up in the everyday. You never know what you have

421

achieved until after the event. Posterity judges, not contemporaries.'

Lawrence sat up straight, aware of a deeper context. 'What is it?'

Noel crossed to the writing bureau, rummaged through it and produced a piece of paper which he thrust at Lawrence. 'Read that. I could be court-martialled and shot for showing it to you, but read it.'

Lawrence did as instructed. It was a copy of a telegram:

NOT FOR CIRCULATION. Category V.

[Translated from German]

FROM: Zimmermann, Berlin

TO: Count J.V. Bernstorf, Washington

STATUS: Most Secret

Instructions for your approach to Mexican Government as follows:

We intend to begin on the first of February unrestricted submarine warfare. We shall endeavour in spite of this to keep the United States neutral. In the event of this not succeeding, we make Mexico a proposal of alliance on the following basis: make war together, make peace together, generous financial support and an understanding on our part that Mexico is to reconquer the lost territory in Texas, New Mexico and Arizona. The settlement in detail is left to you. You will inform the President of the above most secretly as soon as the outbreak of war with the United

States is certain and add the suggestion that he should, on his own initiative, invite Japan to immediate adherence and at the same time mediate between Japan and ourselves. Please call the President's attention to the fact that the ruthless employment of our submarines now offers the prospect of compelling England in a few months to make peace. ZIMMERMANN.

'What has this got to do with Arabia?' Lawrence asked after he had read it twice.

'Very little,' said Noel. 'But a lot to do with Persia. And a lot to do with you. That is a telegram sent to Washington by the Germans. Arthur Zimmermann is the Kaiser's Foreign Secretary. Von Bernstorf their US ambassador. It instructs him to approach the Mexicans with a view to supporting them in a war against the USA. Germany would supply money and arms to help distract the Americans from Europe. It was decoded in London using Wassmuss's lock cipher, which the embassy in the US is still using. The cipher you had copied in the bazaar. Once the contents of that telegram were released in the United States, opposition to entering the war evaporated. And because the Americans have promised men and materials, the war will be shortened. Millions of lives will be saved. All because you copied the locks. Because you outwitted Wassmuss.'

'Well, well.' Lawrence let his solemn face break into a slow smile at the unpredictability of it all. America in the war, thanks to three combination locks painstakingly duplicated in a filthy workshop in the bazaar.

'You must say nothing of this,' Noel counselled. 'The

Germans are still using rotary ciphers. They have no idea how we cracked this, have not traced it back to Wassmuss and his damned luggage.'

'And what of Willie?'

'Wassmuss? A spent force,' said Noel. 'His reputation never recovered from the loss of his ally the Khan of Ahram. He is somewhere on the Afghan border now, I hear. But he lives. Which, I am afraid, is no longer true of Dickie Daniels. Lost on patrol in Mesopotamia.'

'One by one they fall; great and strong and wise, they sleep deep the long sleep of death in gallant company.' As he spoke, Lawrence put his biscuit down. In the aftermath of their rescue, he had talked much about the use of the new air power in war with Daniels. The total destruction of the Tangistan howitzer at the Tower of Silence had made Lawrence appreciate just what potent support one or two aeroplanes could provide, especially for an unconventional army. 'How sad. I liked him. My brother Will, too, was lost over France. His first sortie as observer. Shot down.'

'I'm sorry to hear that.'

'Frank and now Will, both wasted. There are just three of us brothers left,' he said wearily. Three bastards of the Chapman line, masquerading as Lawrences, he thought. And then, out loud: 'Or perhaps two-and-a-half by the time the desert has finished with me.' Lawrence gulped some tea and washed it around his mouth. 'I have come to ask you a question.'

'If I know the answer—'

'You will,' Lawrence said quickly. 'A man like you will know.' He made an effort to keep his voice calm and steady, despite

the anger he felt. He thought back to what the Turkish prisoners had told him. 'I keep hearing rumours from the Turks
of an agreement between the French and the British.'

'Regarding?'

'A carving up of Arabia after the war.'

Noel shook his head. 'Politics, that's all.'

Lawrence stood. 'Yes, politics. I am leading these people
to Damascus with a promise of a kingdom. Of a new Arabia.
With Feisal as king. Is that not politics? Or is that just a lie?'
He could no longer keep the fury he felt in check. He strode
over to Noel, who felt a tremor of fear at the wild-eyed man
now before him. 'Are my promises just dead paper?'

'Sit down,' Noel said quietly. 'Please.' He waited until
Lawrence was back in his place before he spoke. He kept his
voice low, knowing he was spilling more state secrets. 'It is
called the Sykes-Picot Agreement.' Lawrence knew Sir Mark
Sykes, who advised the War Cabinet on Middle East Affairs.
He thought him capable but high-handed, with a patrician
view of the Arabs. Picot was, no doubt, his French counterpart. 'It was signed over a year ago, before you started all this.
As you guessed, it is a declaration of intent regarding the
division of post-war Arabia. It gives Syria to the French—'

Lawrence let out a groan of frustration.

'Most of Mesopotamia and Persia to the British. Palestine
to be under international control. The Arabs to rule some
kingdoms, of course—'

'But as British and French puppets.'

Noel felt inexplicably ashamed. 'With His Majesty's backing
and approval, yes.'

Lawrence's fist came down into the scriptor next to him. He muttered something in Arabic, grabbed an envelope and a pencil and on the paper sketched, in a few deft strokes, a map of the Middle East. He passed it to Noel. The hasty draughtsmanship was superb, the new jigsaw of countries unfamiliar and radical.

Lawrence pointed at the rendering with the pencil. 'That is what we should aim for. Nations based on tribes and religions, not colonial borders. An autonomous region for the Kurds and Armenians, a Transjordan covering Syria and Arabia under Feisal. Irak ruled by Abdullah, Feisal's brother. An internationally administered Palestine. Perhaps a home for the Jews. Maybe even a coastal strip for the damned French. That way, there might be a chance of harmony.'

'It's a fascinating idea,' said Noel non-committally. He didn't add that he feared it would remain just that. He held up the map. 'Can I keep it?'

'Show it wherever you think it might do some good.' Lawrence stood and replaced his headdress. 'Thank you, Major, for being so honest about this . . . betrayal. Nobody will know where I heard of it. I must go and consult the Emir.'

'But Allenby wants to see you.' Noel offered the next information like a juicy apple. 'I think he wants you to blow the viaducts on the Yarmuk valley.'

Lawrence had already identified the crossings as the most vulnerable on the railway. The line out of Deraa crossed and re-crossed the river on a series of high bridges. Taking those out would cripple the upper section for at least two weeks, perhaps more. But it would be a long ride north and would need many men and much explosive.

'I must see Feisal. If he hears of this and believes it, then the revolt is finished and the Bull can whistle for his bridges. That is why the Turks are letting the rumours fly about Sykes and Picot and secret agreements.'

'Still, Allenby is your commanding officer.'

Lawrence looked puzzled. 'And Feisal is my king.'

Noel did not know how to answer that. 'What then? After you have seen Feisal?'

'If I can convince him that this is all Turkish propaganda, then we might just save the revolt. It will be a lie, but I am used to those. I can fight the peace and these ridiculous proposals later.' Lawrence spent a long time adjusting his clothes and red and white *keffiyeh*. 'If I succeed in placating Emir Feisal, with words or camels or gold, then I will go and see Allenby.'

'Be careful. I am not certain how much, or anything, even Allenby knows about the agreement.'

'No matter. And I will say nothing of our talk.' He thought for a moment. 'They don't expect us to get as far as Damascus, do they? The Sykeses and Picots of this world?'

Noel hesitated. 'I suspect not. The revolt was a wild idea. The disruption of the Hejaz railway a hope fulfilled, the taking of Aqaba a happy fantasy that came to pass. But an Arab army riding into Damascus . . . they consider it a pipe-dream.'

A mischievous grin came over Lawrence's face and those fiercely blue eyes sparkled. An idea of a different war had come to him, of the kind Wassmuss had waged with his doctored photos of the Kaiser, his bogus radio to Berlin and his propaganda leaflets with the beguiling promises, all helping to convert the Tangistani to his jihad. A war fought with images and information, and instead of bullets, there were lies and half-truths, innuendo and blatant opportunism, but all for a greater good. Lawrence could learn a trick or two from that. But in his case, it wouldn't be the desert warriors he would be recruiting, but the British people to the Arabs nationalists' cause.

'If you hear from that American journalist before I do,' Lawrence said, 'then tell him by all means to come and find me. I have a story for him. A daring tale of the fight for Arab freedom. Of what they are owed for their endeavours. The public should know of their sacrifices, of my sacrifices. Together, maybe we can kick Sykes and Picot up the backside.'

They shook hands. 'You take care of yourself, Lawrence. I am heading off to Cairo. I'm not sure I know when I'll see you again.'

'Oh, I am,' Lawrence said firmly. He smiled once more, a smile of confidence for the future, as if hope had been reborn. He pointed north. 'In Damascus.'

IV

On 1 October 1918, T.E. Lawrence entered Damascus in the Rolls-Royce he had dubbed Blue Mist. Exhausted by two years of gruelling desert warfare, he returned to England shortly afterwards, asking only one thing of a grateful General Allenby before he left. It was that he be promoted to colonel so that he might, after living cheek-by-jowl with his Arabs for so long, enjoy a private berth on the way home. For Colonel Lawrence, the war was over. Thanks to his meetings with the journalist Lowell Thomas and cameraman Harry Chase, the legend of Lawrence of Arabia was only just beginning.

Author's Note

Empire of Sand is a work of fiction, as is my depiction of the character called T. E. Lawrence. The real man remains as elusive and as enigmatic as ever, with even contemporary accounts offering conflicting opinions. I have also played around with the chronology (for example, Lawrence probably knew about the Sykes-Picot Agreement quite early on in his campaign), but the majority of the events in the Prologue and Epilogue happened to Lawrence – his destruction of trains, his alliance with Auda, the mercy killing of his servant and the climbing down the well – albeit in somewhat altered circumstances. I avoided the infamous events at Deraa, where Lawrence claimed to have been whipped and sexually assaulted by the Bey and/or his guards. Academic opinion is shifting towards this being a politically motivated post-war fabrication (see the recently published *Setting the Desert on Fire* by James Barr and *Lawrence of Arabia: Mirage of a Desert War* by Adrian Greaves).

Despite the occasional doubts about his veracity (G. B. Shaw once called Lawrence 'an infernal liar', and Harold Nicholson said that 'his habit of telling fibs was almost pathological'), there is no doubt that Lawrence was, as even his nemesis Mark Sykes admitted, 'a great man'. Relighting the smouldering Arab revolt and dealing with personalities such as Abdullah, Feisal and Auda required a very special person indeed. Perhaps only an Englishman (although both the Welsh and Irish have some claim on him) who felt he was already outside normal 'society' could have done that.

The tactics Lawrence outlined in his remarkable reports (see *T. E. Lawrence in War and Peace*, edited by Malcolm Brown), and later in *The Seven Pillars of Wisdom*, still form the basic rulebook for guerilla and unconventional warfare. And Lawrence did take his Arab forces into Damascus, although an ANZAC unit had passed through a day before, technically liberating it, which Lawrence understandably glossed over in his writings. However, at the end of the war, few knew of his actions outside of a small circle; he was subsequently made famous and christened Lawrence of Arabia by the American journalist and showman Lowell Thomas in his talks and presentations at venues such as the Royal Albert Hall.

The celebrity he courted to help the Arabs, however, backfired and Lawrence had a turbulent time in the 1920s, fleeing his unwanted fame by enlisting under assumed names in the ranks of the RAF and the army. He eventually found some kind of happiness working on the development of the fast rescue boats for the RAF that saved many aircrews' lives in WW2.

He was killed in a motorcycle accident near his beloved Clouds Hill cottage in Dorset in 1935, trying to avoid two messenger boys on bicycles. He was forty-six.

Many questions surround his death, not least a mysterious black car on the same road, seen speeding away by a Corporal Catchpole, out walking his dog, the suspiciously rapid appearance of Special Branch on the scene and the later suicide of the soldier-witness who disputed official events. Conspiracies centre on the fact that Lawrence was due to have lunch the next day with Henry Williamson (*Tarka the Otter*), who was a well-known fascist sympathiser. The thought of Lawrence following Charles Lindberg and becoming an apologist for Hitler, would, the theory goes, be too much for the security services. Personally, I feel this is giving far too much credence to the prescience of the MI6 and MI5 of the day (who were so poor, Churchill helped set up the Z Organisation, an unofficial intelligence-gathering unit, to do their job). Sometimes an accident is just an accident.

Wilhelm Wassmuss was born in the same year as T.E.L., had blue eyes and fair hair, was quite short, and liked Arab dress, military history and Greek philosophers. They were almost twins. My interest in Lawrence's alter ego and the Kaiser's Persian campaign began with the purchase of a book called *Wassmuss: The German Lawrence*, by Christopher Sykes (son of Sir Mark), published in 1935. It is the only biography of the man, although Peter Hopkirk's excellent *Like Hidden Fire* gives the same background from a more modern perspective, and also outlines the remarkable career of Captain Edward Noel, another enigmatic figure. Noel died in 1974 without ever writing his memoirs and his FO reports are still sealed; needless to say I have fabricated certain aspects of his career, but not his involvement with Wassmuss.

The majority of the Wassmuss incidents related here – including the lost luggage, the three Italian books O'Connor requested (Wassmuss didn't actually know it was a ruse: he couldn't speak the language), and the lost codes – are true. Wassmuss survived many attempts by the British to bring him down and returned to Bushire after the war and tried farming, but he died in poverty, a forgotten hero, in Germany in 1931, four years before Lawrence.

Although his story is basically factual, I have introduced one fiction, with the code. It was, in fact, a standard German diplomatic cipher book, but it was broken by Room 40, the British Naval Intelligence cypher unit, and used to decipher a telegram sent to Mexico in 1917 (the so-called Zimmermann Telegram) in which Germany offered Mexico support for an invasion to regain their old provinces, should the US declare war on Germany. This leaked message caused uproar in America and ironically did help faciliate the USA's entry into World War One, thus shortening the conflict. (Wisely, Mexico declined the invitation to invade America.)

Meanwhile, in Cairo, despite the protests in his letters that he was doing very little, Lawrence was more than a mere cartographer. As investigations by *The Sunday Times* first established, he ran a network of spies across the Levant and also debriefed Turkish and Arab prisoners. He would certainly have known about Wassmuss. He was the author of incisive reports on the Arab situation, channelled through D. G. Hogarth, of the Ashmolean Museum in Oxford, who later became head of the Arab Bureau in Cairo.

Lawrence did leave Cairo twice before the Arab Revolt for two periods of 'Special Duty', one in August 1915, travelling to Athens on a little known mission 'to improve liaison' (which is when I have imagined him going after Wassmuss) and the other in March–May 1916 to Kut, above Basra, in present day Iraq. Lawrence is vague on the real reason for that assignment, although the true facts have since emerged. He travelled with a million pounds to bribe the commander of the Turkish army to let surrounded British troops go free. He failed; the British surrendered. Most of the captured troops died on a hideous forced march. Lawrence was scathing in his reports about the British Army in Mesopotamia; his forthrightness earned him many enemies.

Lawrence never did get his Arab kingdom, despite fighting for it at the Paris Peace Conference in 1919 and two years later in Cairo. With some revisions, the Sykes-Picot Agreement held, and Feisal, who was briefly King of Syria, was deposed and driven from the country. He was eventually given the throne of Iraq by the British, taking the country to independence in 1932.

Meanwhile, control of Mecca and the Hejaz and Nejd fell to Ibn Saud and his line. This became the Kingdom of Saudi Arabia in 1932; oil was discovered there in 1938, changing everything for ever.

Lawrence's 'map' of the Middle East respecting tribal and ethnic borders – including a partitioned Iraq – was never adopted. We are still living with the consequences of that.

For Lawrence's background, I have drawn on the work of Jeremy Wilson, Malcolm Brown, Richard Aldington, John E. Mack, Phillip Knightley, Colin Simpson, Adrian Greaves, James Barr and David Garnett among many others. Of course, none of these excellent writers are responsible for my own conjectures. The prologue is loosely based on the memoirs of S. C. Rolls, who became Lawrence's driver. See his book *Steel Chariots in the Desert*.

The letters in the text are versions of Lawrence's actual writings, with the exception of the censored letter to Miss Bell. Copyright on his letters lapsed on 1 January, 2006. For details of the originals and his other writing see the fine and comprehensive www. telawrence.net, edited by Jeremy Wilson.

Gertrude Bell's fascinating career is outlined in two hefty biographies: *Desert Queen* by Janet Wallach and, most recently, the incisive *Daughter of the Desert* by Georgina Howell. Miss Bell provided essential intelligence that made Lawrence's travels possible and was also instrumental in the shape of post-war Arabia.

For Cairo, I used my memory, photographs and notes about the city from visits in the early 1980s and also *Lifting the Veil* and *The Pharoah's Shadow*, both wonderfully evocative books by Anthony Sattin, a man who knows Egypt like the back of several people's hands. Although it deals with a later conflict, Artemis Cooper's *Cairo in the War* was also very useful, as was Andrew Beattie's book on Cairo in the Cities of the Imagination series.

Finally, thanks to Dylan Jones and Bill Prince of *GQ*; David Miller, Christine Walker and Susan d'Arcy, as always, for their guidance and encouragement; the whole team at Headline for their continuing support and especially to Martin Fletcher, for his essential and committed contribution to shaping this particular version of Lawrence of Arabia.

Robert Ryan,
London

Those who dream by night in the dusty recesses of their minds wake in the day to find that all was vanity; but the dreamers of the day are dangerous men, for they may act their dream with open eyes, and make it possible.

T. E. Lawrence, *The Seven Pillars of Wisdom*

Now you can buy any of these other bestselling
Headline books from your bookshop
or *direct from the publisher*.

FREE P&P AND UK DELIVERY
(Overseas and Ireland £3.50 per book)

The Paradise Trail	Duncan Campbell	£7.99
In A Far Country	Linda Holeman	£6.99
Private Eyes	Jonathan Kellerman	£7.99
Murder's Immortal Mask	Paul Doherty	£6.99
A Small Part of History	Peggy Elliott	£7.99
A Carrion Death	Michael Stanley	£7.99
The Guns of El Kebir	John Wilcox	£6.99
The Last Gospel	David Gibbins	£6.99

TO ORDER SIMPLY CALL THIS NUMBER

01235 400 414

or visit our website: www.headline.co.uk

Prices and availability subject to change without notice.

OXFORD

8A

Maths links

Alf Ledsham

Contents

1 Number
Integers 1

2 Geometry
Measures 7

3 Statistics
Probability 13

4 Number
Fractions, decimals and
percentages 17

5 Algebra
Expressions and formulae 24

6 Geometry
Angles and shapes 30

7 Algebra
Equations and graphs 36

8 Number
Calculations 41

9 Geometry
Transformations 50

10 Algebra
Sequences 56

11 Statistics
Collecting and representing
data 60

12 Number
Ratio and proportion 66

13 Algebra
Algebra 72

14 Geometry
Construction and 3-D shapes 80

15 Statistics
Analysing and interpreting
data 88

16 Number
Calculation plus 94

Glossary 99

Homework Book

OXFORD
UNIVERSITY PRESS

Great Clarendon Street, Oxford OX2 6DP

Oxford University Press is a department of the University of Oxford.
It furthers the University's objective of excellence in research, scholarship,
and education by publishing worldwide in

Oxford   New York

Auckland   Cape Town   Dar es Salaam   Hong Kong   Karachi
Kuala Lumpur   Madrid   Melbourne   Mexico City   Nairobi
New Delhi   Shanghai   Taipei   Toronto

With offices in

Argentina   Austria   Brazil   Chile   Czech Republic   France   Greece
Guatemala   Hungary   Italy   Japan   Poland   Portugal   Singapore
South Korea   Switzerland   Thailand   Turkey   Ukraine   Vietnam

© Oxford University Press 2009

The moral rights of the authors have been asserted

Database right Oxford University Press (maker)

First published 2009

British Library Cataloguing in Publication Data

Data available

ISBN 978-0-19-915297-1
10 9 8 7 6 5 4 3 2 1

Printed in Great Britain by Ashford Colour Press Ltd.

Paper used in the production of this book is a natural, recyclable product
made from wood grown in sustainable forests. The manufacturing process
conforms to the environmental regulations to the country of origin.

example

Use a number line to answer these.
a 3 − 5   **b** -2 + 4   **c** -8 + 3

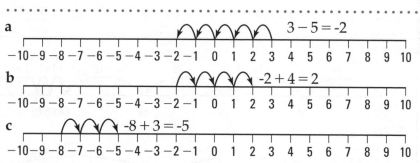

1 Use a number line to answer these.

  a 5 − 8   **b** -4 + 5   **c** 5 − 9   **d** -6 + 10
  e -7 + 9   **f** 3 − 10   **g** -6 + 6   **h** 0 + -4

2 Write these numbers in order. Start with the smallest.

  a 9, -6, 3, -2   **b** 0, -4, 10, 5   **c** -3, 9, -9, 10
  d 2, -4, 8, -7   **e** 0, -3, 8, -10   **f** -5, 0, -12, 7

3 A gardener records the outside temperature over one night.
Here is a record of the temperature for every hour.

10 p.m.	11 p.m.	12 a.m.	1 a.m.	2 a.m.	3 a.m.	4 a.m.	5 a.m.	6 a.m.	7 a.m.
6 °C	5 °C	2 °C	0 °C	-2 °C	-4 °C	-4 °C	-1 °C	0 °C	2 °C

Write out the temperature change between: (the first one is done
for you)

  a 11 p.m. and 12 p.m. — The temperature goes **down** by **3** °C
  b 1 a.m. and 3 a.m.   **c** 3 a.m. and 4 a.m.
  d 2 a.m. and 5 a.m.   **e** 3 a.m. and 6 a.m.   **f** 4 a.m. and 7 a.m.

4 Some garden plants will die if the temperature goes below
freezing (0 °C). How long is the temperature below freezing?

example

Use a number line to answer these problems.

a $24 + 45$ **b** $68 - 23$ **c** $263 + 187$ **d** $476 - 234$

. . . .

a $24 + 45 =$

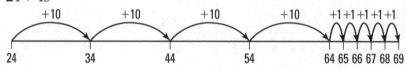

b $68 - 23 =$

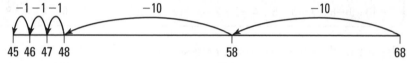

c $263 + 187 =$

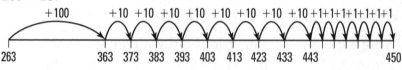

d $476 - 234 =$

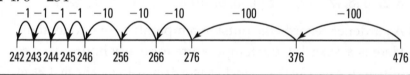

1 Use a number line to answer these addition problems.

a $45 + 23$	**b** $67 + 31$	**c** $34 + 26$	**d** $56 + 38$
e $84 + 34$	**f** $27 + 92$	**g** $145 + 26$	**h** $93 + 139$

2 Use a number line to answer these subtraction problems.

a $55 - 33$	**b** $79 - 34$	**c** $45 - 25$	**d** $62 - 28$
e $74 - 45$	**f** $97 - 39$	**g** $158 - 46$	**h** $143 - 89$

3 Use a number line to answer these addition problems.

a $475 + 112$	**b** $256 + 124$	**c** $475 + 223$	**d** $362 + 328$
e $241 + 54$	**f** $427 + 244$	**g** $288 + 146$	**h** $453 + 379$

Use your times tables to find if these are multiples.
a Is 60 a multiple of 5?
b Is 48 a multiple of 6?
c Is 57 a multiple of 7?

. . . .

a 5 times tables is 5, 10, 15, 20, 25, 30, 25, 40, 45, 50, 55, **60**
 Yes, 60 is a multiple of 5.
b 6 times tables is 6, 12, 18, 24, 30, 36, 42, **48**
 Yes, 48 is a multiple of 6.
c 7 times table is 7, 14, 21, 28, 35, 42, 49, **56**, 63
 No, 57 is not a multiple of 7.

1 Write down any divisibility tests that you know (ask other people in your house as well!)

2 Use divisibility tests or times tables to find if these are multiples.

a Is 28 a multiple of 7?	**b** Is 42 a multiple of 7?
c Is 84 a multiple of 5?	**d** Is 21 a multiple of 3?
e Is 54 a multiple of 9?	**f** Is 43 a multiple of 4?

3 Copy the diagrams, and list all the factors of each number.

a
1
18
18

b
1
24
24

c
1
16
16

d
1
36
36

4 What type of numbers are the following?
a 1, 4, 9, 16, 25, 49, 64, 81, 100
b 2, 3, 5, 7, 11, 13, 17, 19

> *example*
>
> Find the common factors for these numbers.
> **a** 9 and 12   **b** 15 and 8   **c** 6 and 18
> ....
> **a** Factors of 9   Factors of 12   1 and 3 are common
>   **1, 3,** 9   **1, 2, 3,** 4, 6, 12   factors of 9 and 12.
> **b** Factors of 15   Factors of 8   1 is the only common
>   **1,** 3, 5, 15   **1,** 2, 4, 8   factor of 15 and 8.
> **c** Factors of 6   Factors of 18   1, 2, 3 and 6 are common
>   **1, 2, 3, 6**   **1, 2, 3, 6,** 9, 18   factors of 6 and 18.

1 Find all the factors for these numbers. (Use times tables or divisibility tests to find them.)

   a 20   **b** 21   **c** 36   **d** 48   **e** 60

2 Find the common factors for these pairs of numbers.

   a 6 and 10   **b** 8 and 18
   c 12 and 20   **d** 16 and 24
   e 36 and 21   **f** 28 and 60

3 Which common factors do each of these groups of numbers share?

   a 6, 12 and 21   **b** 12, 18 and 24
   c 10, 30 and 110   **d** 24, 36 and 48

4 Find the common factors for these numbers.

   a 7 and 12   **b** 13 and 21
   c 18 and 23   **d** 51 and 20

5 Prime numbers only have two factors; one and the number itself. Give examples of all the prime numbers less than 10.

List all the prime numbers between 10 and 20.

. . . .

11, 13, 17, 19 are all prime numbers because they only have two factors; one and the number itself, for example
$11 = 1 \times 11, 13 = 1 \times 13$
$17 = 1 \times 17, 19 = 1 \times 19$

1 What is the definition of a prime number?

2 Find all the prime numbers in the circle below.

| 3 | 8 | 19 | 9 |

17

11   13   15   45

51   1   2   42

27 7   39

3 Find the factors of these numbers and state how many factors each one has.

a 25   **b** 81   **c** 9   **d** 16   **e** 36

What do you notice about the numbers and the number of factors they have?

The first three square numbers are:

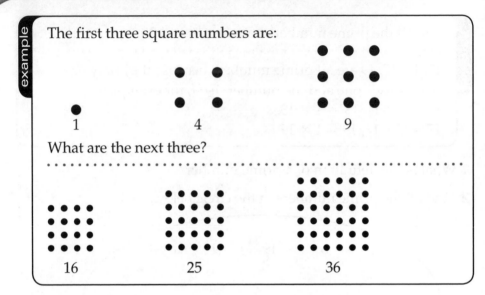

1   4   9

What are the next three?

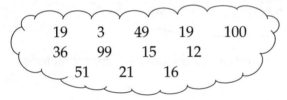

16   25   36

1 List all of the square numbers less than 100.

2 Which of the following numbers are square numbers?

> 19   3   49   19   100
> 36   99   15   12
> 51   21   16

3 Use a calculator to work out the square numbers between 100 and 200.

4 Which of the following numbers are square numbers?

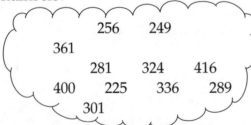

> 256   249
> 361
> 281   324   416
> 400   225   336   289
> 301

example

> **a** Steve has a block of wood that is 25 cm long. He cuts 35 mm from the block. How much is left?
>
> **b** Brian cycles to school. The distance is 12 km. He has cycled 8300 metres. How far is left?
>
> **c** Jasbinder buys 2 litres of orange juice. After breakfast there is 125 ml left. How much has been drunk?
>
> ·
>
> **a** 25 cm = 250 mm. So 250 − 35 = 215 mm.
>
> **b** 12 km = 12000 m. So 12000 − 8300 = 3700 m.
>
> **c** 2 litres = 2000 ml. So 2000 − 125 = 1875 ml.

1 Match up the objects with their correct measurement.

  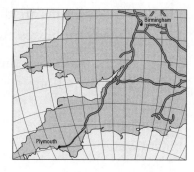

| 250 ml | 200 miles | 80 kg |

2 Copy and complete these conversions.

   a 200 cm = ... m   **b** 3 kg = ... g

   c 2 tonnes = ... kg   **d** 4 km = ... m

   e 3.5 cm = ... mm   **f** 2500 ml = ... litres

3 Tony is running in a 10 km race. He has run 9300 m. How far has he got left to run?

4 Vicki has a 1.5 litre bottle of champagne at her party. She has ten 125 ml glasses. When she has filled these glasses, how much champagne will be left over?

example

Convert these imperial measurements into their approximate metric equivalents.
a 10 pints   **b** 6 feet   **c** 200 yards
d 10 miles   **e** 5 pounds

. . . .

a 1 pint $\approx$ 0.5 litres. So 10 pints $\approx$ 10 × 0.5 = 5 litres.
b 1 foot $\approx$ 30 cm. So 6 feet $\approx$ 6 × 30 = 180 cm.
c 1 yard $\approx$ 1 m. So 200 yards $\approx$ 200 m.
d 1 mile $\approx$ 1.5 km. So 10 miles $\approx$ 10 × 1.5 = 15 km.
e 1 pound $\approx$ 0.5 kg. So 5 pounds $\approx$ 5 × 0.5 = 2.5 kg.

1 a How many seconds are there in 3 minutes?
  b How many grams are there in 1.5 kg?
  c How many millilitres are there in 2.5 litres?

2 Here are the main ingredients for four scones.
  100 g wholemeal flour
  125 g plain flour
  100 ml milk
  50 ml water
  1 egg
  a How much flour is used to make 8 scones (plain and wholemeal together)?
  b How much liquid is used? (excluding eggs?)

3 Convert these imperial measurements into their approximate metric equivalents.
  a 8 pints   **b** 10 feet   **c** 350 yards
  d 50 miles   **e** 12 pounds   **f** 1.5 feet

4 Convert these metric measurements into their approximate imperial equivalents.
  a 90 cm   **b** 3 km   **c** 2.5 kg
  d 3 m   **e** 1.5 litres   **f** 50 kg

example

What measurement is the arrow pointing to ?

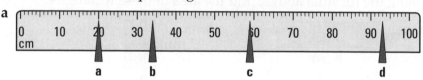

The arrow is pointing to 25 mm.
When reading scales remember these steps.
a What are the units of measure?
b How are the intervals numbered?
c What is each small division worth?
d Approximately, what reading does the scale show?

1 What are the arrows pointing to on each scale?

a

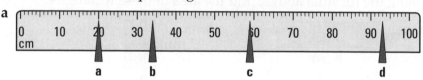

b

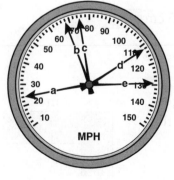

c

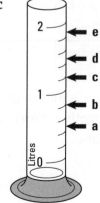

2d Area of a rectangle

Using the formula $A = l \times w$ find the area of these rectangles.

4 cm
11 cm

12 m
5 m

. . . .

a $A = 4 \times 11 = 44\,\text{cm}^2$ **b** $A = 12 \times 5 = 60\,\text{m}^2$
(remember the units for area are square units mm², cm², m² ...)

1 Using the formula above, find the area of these rectangles.

a 2 cm
8 cm

b 3 mm
2 mm

c 12 m
3 m

d 1 cm
11 cm

e 5 mm
7 mm

f 10 cm
2.5 cm

2 Raj's patio is made up of two rectangles joined together. Work out the area of the whole patio.

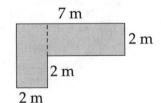

7 m
2 m
2 m
2 m

2d² Shapes made from rectangles

Find the area of this shape.

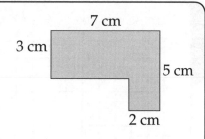

7 cm

3 cm

5 cm

2 cm

. . . .

Step 1 Divide into two rectangles
Step 2 Rectangle B already has
both measurements so find
the area
   Area of B = 2 × 5 = 10 cm²
Step 3 Find the length of rectangle A
   7 cm − 2 cm = 5 cm
Step 4 Find the area of rectangle A = length × width
   A = 5 × 3 = 15 cm²
Step 5 Add the two areas together
   Total area = 10 cm² + 15 cm² = 25 cm²

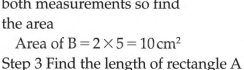

7 cm

3 cm   A

B 5 cm

x cm

2 cm

1 Make a sketch of each shape.
Calculate the area of each shape in either cm² or m².

a

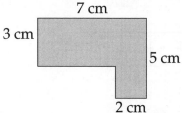

7 cm

3 cm

5 cm

2 cm

b

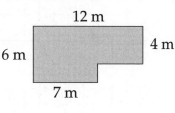

12 m

6 m

4 m

7 m

c

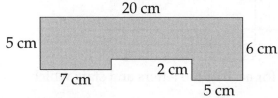

20 cm

5 cm

6 cm

2 cm

7 cm

5 cm

example

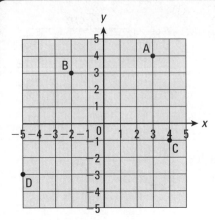

A has coordinates (3,4) and is in the 1st quadrant.
B has coordinates (-2,3) and is in the 2nd quadrant.
C has coordinates (4,-1) and is in the 4th quadrant.
D has coordinates (-5,-3) and is in the 3rd quadrant.

Give the coordinates for each letter and state which quadrant they are in.

1

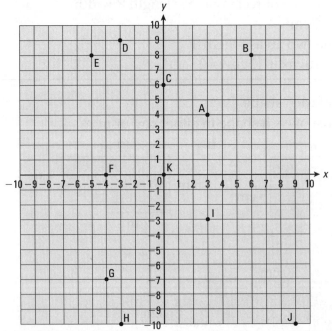

Give the coordinates for each of the letters and state which quadrant they are in.

example

Use these probability words to describe these events
Certain, likely, an even chance, unlikely, impossible
a Rain in November.
b Your teacher will win the lottery.
c You will get a six when you roll a dice.
d You will get an odd number if you roll a dice.

· ·

a It is likely that it will rain in November.
b It is unlikely your teacher will win the lottery and impossible they will win if they don't play!
c It is unlikely you will get a six when you roll a dice.
d There is an even chance you will get an odd number when you roll a dice.

1 Rhiannon puts tickets numbered 1–50 into a bag and picks one out at random. Use the probability words in the example above to describe each of these events.
a Rhiannon picks an even number.
b The number on the ticket is a multiple of 5.
c The number on the ticket is less than 51.
d The number on the ticket is more than 10.
e The number on the ticket is 0.

2 Here are some possible events that could happen when you roll an ordinary dice. Write the list out in order, from least likely to most likely. Explain your answers.
a The score is a 4.   b The score is multiple of 3.
c The score is an even number. d The score is greater than 1.
e The score is greater than 7.

3 If I roll a dice and get a six, am I more or less likely to get a six next time? Explain your answer.

example

Draw a probability scale and label these events.
a You will become famous.
b Your teacher will go abroad this year.
c You will get a head when you toss a coin.
d You will live forever.

· ·

Answers to **a** and **b** may differ

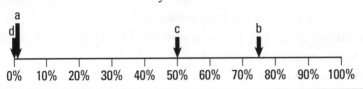

1 Draw a probability scale and add labels to show the probabilities of these events.

  a Meeting someone who is famous.
  b Getting homework tomorrow.
  c It raining this week.
  d An earthquake happening in England this year.

2 Decide where these events belong on this probability scale.

  a Getting a tail when you toss a coin.
  b Getting a one when you roll a die.
  c Picking a number that is greater than 40 from the numbers 1–100.
  d Getting two heads when you toss two coins (hint: think about all of the possible ways two different coins could land).
  e For the fractions that are left on the probability scale add your own events.

3 (Optional) If I play the lottery am I more or less likely to win with the numbers 1, 2, 3, 4, 5, 6 compared to numbers 4, 10, 15, 21, 40, 45? Explain your answer.

example

In Wilson's fish pond there 3 orange and 5 grey fish. What is the probability that he catches an orange fish?

$$\text{Formula} = \frac{\text{Number of outcomes I want}}{\text{Total number of possible outcomes}} = \frac{\text{Number of orange fish}}{\text{Total number of fish}} = \frac{3}{8}$$

1 In a class there are 12 boys and 15 girls. The teacher needs to pick one student to help her. What is the probability that the student chosen will be a boy?

2 Mohammed puts 4 red counters and 3 black counters into a bag. What is the probability that he picks out
a a red counter **b** not a red counter?

3 Gabriel rolls an ordinary six-sided dice. Using the formula in the example calculate the probability that Gabriel's score is
a exactly 4 **b** more than 2
c an even number **d** a multiple of 3
e less than 7.

4 In a raffle there are 50 tickets numbered 1–50. What is the probability that the ticket chosen will be
a less than 10 **b** more than 35
c a multiple of 4 **d** a multiple of 4 and 8
e a prime number?

3d Experimental probability

A football club has 36 players available. Eight of the players are left-footed. What is the probability that a footballer from this club is left-footed?

$$\text{Probability of being left-footed} = \frac{\text{Number of left-footed players}}{\text{Total number of players}}$$

The probability is $\frac{8}{36} = \frac{2}{9}$

1 A nursery asks each child's parents whether or not the child has had the MMR vaccination. The table shows the results.
Use the results to estimate the probability that the next child will have had the MMR vaccination.

Yes	No
43	7

2 Jason has a bag of red and blue balls. He selects a ball at random, records its colour and replaces the ball in the bag. The table shows his results.
Use the results to estimate the probability that the next ball he draws will be red.

Red	Blue
12	28

3 A spinner is spun 250 times. The table shows the results.

Colour	Black	White	Grey
Frequency	120	70	60

a Estimate the probability that the next spin will show
  i Black   **ii** White   **iii** Grey
  Give your answers as percentages.
b Which of these pictures is most likely to be this spinner?
  Explain your answer.

②   ①

example

Which of the two decimal numbers is the larger?
a 0.45, 0.52   **b** 0.32, 0.40   **c** 0.09, 0.30

When numbers have two decimal places it can be easier to
think of them as money.
a £0.45 and £0.52 so 0.52 is the largest.
b £0.32 and £0.40 so 0.40 is the largest.
c £0.09 and £0.30 so £0.30 is the largest.

1 Write these amounts as decimals of one pound (£).
  a 43p   **b** 83p   **c** 93p   **d** 8p   **e** 1p

2 Copy these pairs of numbers and circle the larger
  amount.
  a £0.89, £0.91   **b** £0.34, £0.60   **c** £0.73, £0.29
  d £0.07, £0.21   **e** £0.52, £0.09   **f** £0.20, £0.05

3 Which of these two decimal numbers is the larger?
  a 0.22, 0.19   **b** 0.23, 0.19   **c** 0.06, 0.10
  d 1.02, 0.99   **e** 0.04, 1.00   **f** 0.11, 1.01

4 Put these numbers in order of size starting with the
  smallest.
  a 0.89, 1.01, 0.45, 0.09   **b** 0.16, 1.57, 0.02, 2.01
  c 0.35, 0.10, 0.80, 0.29   **d** 2.01, 0.12, 0.21, 1.20
  e 0.33, 0.30, 3.00, 3.03   **f** 0.99, 0.90, 1.09, 0.09

example

Find the missing number in each set of equivalent fractions.

a $\frac{1}{4} = \frac{\Box}{12}$ **b** $\frac{3}{10} = \frac{9}{\Box}$ **c** $\frac{5}{20} = \frac{1}{\Box}$

. . . .

      $\times 3$ $\times 3$ $\div 5$

a $\frac{1}{4} = \frac{3}{12}$ **b** $\frac{3}{10} = \frac{9}{30}$ **c** $\frac{5}{20} = \frac{1}{4}$

      $\times 3$ $\times 3$ $\div 5$

1 Write these amounts as fractions.

   a 4 out of 7   **b** 8 out of 10   **c** 6 out of 12

2 Make new equivalent fractions by multiplying or dividing the numerator and denominator by the amount shown.

    $\times 2$ $\times 5$ $\times 4$

a $\frac{3}{7} = \frac{\Box}{14}$ **b** $\frac{4}{9} = \frac{20}{\Box}$ **c** $\frac{3}{20} = \frac{\Box}{80}$

    $\times 6$ $\times 3$ $\times 9$

d $\frac{5}{6} = \frac{30}{\Box}$ **e** $\frac{6}{7} = \frac{\Box}{21}$ **f** $\frac{2}{9} = \frac{18}{\Box}$

    $\div 3$ $\div 4$ $\div 7$

g $\frac{9}{30} = \frac{3}{\Box}$ **h** $\frac{12}{20} = \frac{\Box}{5}$ **i** $\frac{21}{35} = \frac{\Box}{5}$

    $\div 7$ $\div 9$ $\div 8$

j $\frac{14}{35} = \frac{\Box}{5}$ **k** $\frac{81}{99} = \frac{9}{\Box}$ **l** $\frac{48}{64} = \frac{\Box}{8}$

3 Simplify these fractions by dividing. Show your arrows and the division(s) you have used. (You can divide the fraction more than once!)

   a $\frac{5}{10}$ **b** $\frac{12}{20}$ **c** $\frac{6}{18}$ **d** $\frac{16}{24}$ **e** $\frac{10}{35}$ **f** $\frac{9}{36}$

example

Use a 100 square to decide which of these symbols $<, >$ or $=$ can be put between $\frac{12}{100}$ and 0.2.

· ·

$0.2 = \frac{2}{10} = \frac{20}{100}$

$\frac{12}{100}$ is less than 0.2

so $\frac{12}{100} < 0.2$

$<$ means less than
$>$ means greater than
$=$ means equal to.

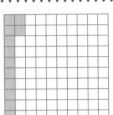 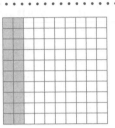

1 Use a 100 square grid to decide which of these fractions is largest.

a $\frac{4}{100}$ or $\frac{3}{10}$ **b** $\frac{31}{100}$ or $\frac{5}{10}$

c $\frac{6}{10}$ or $\frac{45}{100}$ **d** $\frac{8}{10}$ or $\frac{79}{100}$

e $\frac{14}{100}$ or $\frac{4}{10}$ **f** $\frac{7}{10}$ or $\frac{71}{100}$

g $\frac{3}{10}$ or $\frac{33}{100}$ **h** $\frac{5}{100}$ or $\frac{5}{10}$

2 In each pair of numbers below, which of these symbols $<, >$ or $=$ can be put between them?

a $0.4 \,\square\, \frac{4}{100}$ **b** $0.34 \,\square\, \frac{43}{100}$

c $\frac{2}{100} \,\square\, 0.1$ **d** $0.9 \,\square\, \frac{90}{100}$

e $\frac{3}{10} \,\square\, 0.03$ **f** $0.75 \,\square\, 0.08$

g $0.5 \,\square\, \frac{1}{2}$ **h** $0.99 \,\square\, \frac{100}{100}$

3 Are these statements true or false?

a A half is the same as 10 out 20.

b A quarter is bigger than a half.

c If I eat $\frac{6}{10}$ of a pizza, I have $\frac{2}{5}$ left.

d A third is smaller than a quarter.

4d Adding and subtracting fractions

example

Use a drawing to help add

a $\frac{5}{12}$ and $\frac{3}{12}$ **b** $\frac{1}{12}$ and $\frac{9}{12}$

Simplify your answer where possible.

....

a $\frac{5}{12} + \frac{3}{12} = \frac{8}{12} = \frac{2}{3}$
$\div 4$ (applied to numerator and denominator)

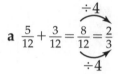

b $\frac{1}{12} + \frac{9}{12} = \frac{10}{12} = \frac{5}{6}$
$\div 2$ (applied to numerator and denominator)

1 Use a drawing to add these fractions. Simplify where possible.

a $\frac{5}{8} + \frac{2}{8}$ **b** $\frac{3}{10} + \frac{3}{10}$ **c** $\frac{1}{4} + \frac{2}{4}$ **d** $\frac{4}{12} + \frac{3}{12}$

e $\frac{3}{7} + \frac{2}{7}$ **f** $\frac{2}{9} + \frac{1}{9}$ **g** $\frac{1}{7} + \frac{2}{7} + \frac{3}{7}$ **h** $\frac{1}{12} + \frac{5}{12} + \frac{2}{12}$

2 Use a drawing to subtract these fractions. Simplify where possible.

a $\frac{6}{8} - \frac{2}{8}$ **b** $\frac{7}{10} - \frac{2}{10}$ **c** $\frac{7}{12} - \frac{2}{12}$ **d** $\frac{4}{8} - \frac{1}{8}$

e $\frac{8}{9} - \frac{2}{9}$ **f** $\frac{5}{6} - \frac{1}{6}$ **g** $\frac{9}{10} - \frac{1}{10}$ **h** $\frac{2}{7} - \frac{1}{7}$

3 Write 5 addition and 5 subtraction questions that would all give an answer of $\frac{1}{2}$. Here is an example to get you started.

$\frac{5}{12} + \frac{1}{12} = \frac{6}{12} = \frac{1}{2}$

example

Calculate $\frac{7}{12}$ of 60 cm.

First find $\frac{1}{12}$. 　　　　　$\frac{1}{12}$ of 60 cm = 60 cm ÷ 12

　　　　　　　　　　　　　　 = 5 cm

Then multiply by 7. 　　　$\frac{7}{12}$ of 60 cm = 5 cm × 7

　　　　　　　　　　　　　　 = 35 cm

1 Calculate

   a $\frac{1}{3}$ of £90　**b** $\frac{1}{5}$ of 80 cm　**c** $\frac{1}{8}$ of 96 kg　**d** $\frac{1}{7}$ of 84 m

2 Use your answers to question **1** to calculate these.

   a $\frac{2}{3}$ of £90　**b** $\frac{3}{5}$ of 80 cm　**c** $\frac{5}{8}$ of 96 kg　**d** $\frac{6}{7}$ of 84 m

3 Calculate

   a $\frac{3}{8}$ of £24　　　　　　　**b** $\frac{4}{9}$ of 18 kg

   c $\frac{5}{6}$ of 30 litres　　　　　**d** $\frac{3}{7}$ of $28

   e $\frac{3}{5}$ of €60　　　　　　　**f** $\frac{7}{10}$ of 50 m

   g $\frac{11}{12}$ of 96 cm　　　　　**h** $\frac{5}{16}$ of 128 MB

4 Calculate

   a $5 \times \frac{1}{7}$　　**b** $4 \times \frac{2}{9}$　　**c** $2 \times \frac{3}{4}$　　**d** $5 \times \frac{2}{3}$

5 Peter is 150 cm tall and his sister Jane is $\frac{5}{6}$ as tall.
How tall is Jane?

6 Harry receives £30 for his birthday. He spends $\frac{2}{5}$ of his money on a
DVD and $\frac{4}{15}$ on a book. Harry puts the rest in his piggy bank.
   a Calculate the price of the DVD.
   b Calculate the amount that Harry saves in his piggy bank.

example

Calculate the following percentages
a 10% of 200 kg   **b** 30% of 200 kg
c 5% of 200 kg   **d** 15% of 200 kg.

. . . .

a $10\% = \frac{10}{100} = \frac{1}{10}$ so to find a tenth divide by 10
so 10% of 200 kg = 200 ÷ 10 = 20 kg.
b 30% = 3 × 10%
so 30% of 200 kg = 3 × 10% of 200 kg = 3 × 20 kg = 60 kg.
c 5% = half of 10%
so 5% of 200 kg = $\frac{1}{2}$ × 10% of 200 kg = $\frac{1}{2}$ × 20 kg = 10 kg.
d 15% = 10% + 5%
so 15% of 200 kg = 10% of 200 kg + 5% of
200 kg = 20 kg + 10 kg = 30 kg.

1 Calculate these percentages.
a 10% of 500 kg	**b** 5% of 500 kg	**c** 15% of 500 kg
d 30% of 500 kg	**e** 35% of 500 kg	**f** 50% of 500 kg
g 25% of 500 kg	**h** 75% of 500 kg	**i** 90% of 500 kg

2 Calculate these percentages.
a 10% of 80 kg	**b** 5% of 80 kg	**c** 15% of 80 kg
d 40% of 80 kg	**e** 45% of 80 kg	**f** 50% of 80 kg
g 55% of 80 kg	**h** 75% of 80 kg	**i** 85% of 80 kg

3 Use a calculator to work out these percentages.
The first one is done for you.
a 45% of £24 Answer: 45 ÷ 100 × 24 = 10.8 so the answer is £10.80
b 15% of £65   **c** 55% of £38
d 35% of £36   **e** 12% of £55

example

Use the signs $<$, $>$ or $=$ between these pairs.

a $\frac{4}{100} \square 5\%$ **b** $\frac{6}{10} \square 60\%$ **c** $0.99 \square 90\%$

. . . .

a $\frac{4}{100} = 4\%$ so $\frac{4}{100} < 5\%$ $<$ means less than

b $\frac{6}{10} = \frac{60}{100} = 60\%$ so $\frac{6}{10} = 60\%$

c $0.99 = \frac{99}{100} = 99\%$ so $0.99 > 90\%$ $>$ means greater than

1 Write these decimals as fractions.

a 0.06	**b** 0.08	**c** 0.85
d 0.70	**e** 0.75	**f** 0.24
g 0.65	**h** 0.95	**i** 0.25

2 Express each of these fractions as percentages.

a $\frac{30}{100} = \square \%$ **b** $\frac{25}{100} = \square \%$ **c** $\frac{15}{100} = \square \%$

d $\frac{4}{10} = \square \%$ **e** $\frac{7}{10} = \square \%$ **f** $\frac{9}{10} = \square \%$

g $\frac{85}{100} = \square \%$ **h** $\frac{1}{4} = \square \%$ **i** $\frac{3}{4} = \square \%$

3 Use the signs $<$, $>$ or $=$ between these pairs.

a $\frac{6}{100} \square 10\%$ **b** $\frac{45}{100} \square 50\%$

c $0.09 \square 90\%$ **d** $75\% \square \frac{3}{4}$

e $85\% \square 0.9$ **f** $\frac{7}{10} \square 75\%$

g $0.11 \square \frac{11}{100}$ **h** $\frac{100}{100} \square 100\%$

4 Put these in order starting with the smallest.

a $0.20, \frac{1}{4}, 0.3$ **b** $35\%, 0.4, \frac{15}{100}$

c $0.9, 85\%, \frac{9}{100}$ **d** $75\%, \frac{1}{4}, 0.08$

example

Draw a picture to represent the expression $3n + 4$.

A packet of crisps contains n crisps so this picture represents $3n + 4$

1 Write an expression for the total number of crisps in each picture below. The number of crisps in each packet is n.

a

b

c

d

e

2 If a packet of crisps contains n crisps draw a picture to represent these expressions.

  a $2n + 1$ **b** $3n + 2$ **c** $4n + 5$

  d $n + 4$ **e** $\frac{1}{2}n$ **f** $\frac{1}{2}n + 1$

3 How would you describe, using packets of crisps, the expression $3n - 2$?

example

Calculate the value of these expressions, if $a = 2$ and $b = 5$.

a $3a$ **b** $\frac{15}{b}$ **c** $a + b$ **d** $10a$

. . . .

a $3a = 3 \times a = 3 \times 2 = 6$
b $\frac{15}{b} = 15 \div b = 15 \div 5 = 3$
c $a + b = 2 + 5 = 7$
d $10a = 10 \times a = 10 \times 2 = 20$

1 Calculate the value of these expressions, if $a = 6$ and $b = 10$.

a $3a$ **b** $4b$ **c** $5a$

d $5b$ **e** $\frac{60}{a}$ **f** $\frac{25}{b}$

g $a + b$ **h** $a \times b$ **i** $a \times a$
j $a - b$ **k** $b - a$ **l** $b \times b$

2 Calculate the value of these expressions, if $x = 8$ and $y = 3$.

a $x \div 2$ **b** $9 \div y$ **c** $24 \div x$

d $4y$ **e** $\frac{21}{y}$ **f** $\frac{18}{y}$

g $\frac{x}{4}$ **h** y **i** $\frac{x}{2}$

3 Calculate the value of these expressions when $a = 2$, $b = 5$, $c = 12$ and $d = 5$.

a $a + b + c + d$ **b** $a + c + d$

c $b \times a$ **d** $\frac{c}{a}$

e $c - a$ **f** $b \times d$

example

Simplify these expressions by adding or subtracting like terms.

a $b + b + b + b + b$ **b** $6c - 3c$ **c** $5d + 2e - 3d + e$

. . . .

a $b + b + b + b + b = 5b$ **b** $6c - 3c = 3c$

c $5d + 2e - 3d + e = 2d + 3e$

1 Simplify these expressions by adding or subtracting like terms.

a $x + x + x$ **b** $3y + y + 2y$

c $2a + 4a + 3a + a$ **d** $3b + 2b + 10b$

e $7p - 5p$ **f** $9r - 4r - 3r$

g $10g - 6g - 3g$ **h** $15h - 10h - 3h$

i $21j - 20j$ **j** $45k - 45k$

k $12a + a - 5a$ **l** $99p - 90p$

2 Simplify these expressions by adding or subtracting like terms.

a $7x + 4x + 2y + y$ **b** $6x + 3y + 2x + y$

c $5a + 6b - 2a + b$ **d** $10h + 3e + 3h - 2e$

e $7j - 2j + 4r - 2r$ **f** $10p - 3p + q$

g $4t + 5r - 3t + t$ **h** $4z + 3w - 3z + 5w + z$

i $6y + y + 6b - b$ **j** $3m - n + m$

k $3q - 3q + 4r - 5t$ **l** $6t + 2w - 2t - w - 4t - w$

3 Write five of your own questions that would give you an answer of $3a + 3b$. Here is one that is done for you.

$a + a + a + b + b + b = 3a + 3b$

example

Expand these brackets.
a $4 \times (a + 2)$ **b** $2 \times (f - 4)$ **c** $6 \times (h - j)$

a $4 \times (a + 2) = 4 \times a + 4 \times 2 = 4a + 8$
b $2 \times (f - 4) = 2 \times f - 2 \times 4 = 2f - 8$
c $6 \times (h - j) = 6h - 6j$

1 Use brackets to write an expression for the
perimeter of these rectangles.

a
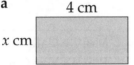
4 cm

x cm

b

2 cm

y cm

c
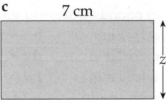
7 cm

z

2 Expand these brackets. Calculate their value.
a $3 \times (5 + 2)$ **b** $4 \times (7 + 2)$
c $(4 - 1) \times 2$ **d** $10 \times (12 - 5)$
e $5 \times (11 + 1)$ **f** $(14 - 3) \times 4$

3 Expand these expressions by removing the brackets.
a $3 \times (b + 2)$ **b** $4 \times (t + 4)$
c $(m + 3) \times 4$ **d** $(z - 3) \times 2$
e $10 \times (a + b)$ **f** $2 \times (m - n)$
g $(e + f) \times 4$ **h** $(p - q) \times 3$
i $4 \times (3 - p)$ **j** $(j - p) \times 4$

4 (Optional) How many questions can you write with
brackets that have an answer of $12a - 16b$?
Here is one that is done for you.
$2 \times (6a - 8b) = 12a - 16b$ ✓

Calculate the value of $A = (p \times 3) + 20$ for different values of p.

a $p = 2$ **b** $p = 4$ **c** $p = 10$

. . . .

a $A = (2 \times 3) + 20$ **b** $A = (4 \times 3) + 20$ **c** $A = (10 \times 3) + 20$
$\quad\ = 6 + 20$ $= 12 + 20$ $= 30 + 20$
$\quad\ = 26$ $= 32$ $= 50$

1 Use the 'Pay as You Go' formula, $C = 12 \times t$ to calculate the cost of these calls. Write your answers in pounds whenever you can.

    a $t = 5\,\text{min}$ **b** $t = 10\,\text{min}$
    c $t = 2\,\text{min}$ **d** $t = 4\,\text{min}$
    e $t = 1\,\text{min}$ **f** $t = 9\,\text{min}$
    g $t = 15\,\text{min}$ **h** $t = 20\,\text{min}$

> Mobile Calls
> Pay As You Call
> 12p per minute

2 Calculate the value of the formula, $A = (q \times 2) + 15$ for different values of q.

    a $q = 2$ **b** $q = 4$
    c $q = 6$ **d** $q = 10$
    e $q = 3$ **f** $q = 20$
    g $q = 7$ **h** $q = 1$

3 This formula is used to calculate speed, $S = \frac{D}{T}$. Substitute the values of D and T into this formula to calculate the value of S (speed).

    a $D = 120, T = 20$ **b** $D = 160, T = 40$
    c $D = 100, T = 25$ **d** $D = 200, T = 20$
    e $D = 240, T = 12$

5f Making formulae

Stephen is 2 years older than Claire.
Write two different formulae to connect Stephen's age and Claire's age.
Use s to stand for Stephen's age and c to stand for Claire's age.

. . . .

$s = c + 2$ and $c = s - 2$

1 James is 8 years older than Lawson.
  a Copy and complete the mapping to show the link between their ages.
  b Write two different formulas to connect Lawson's age and James' age.

Lawson's age		James' age
1	⟶	☐
3	⟶	☐
10	⟶	☐
25	⟶	☐

2 There are 52 playing cards in a pack.
  a How many cards are there in
    i 2 packs
    ii 10 packs
    iii quarter of a pack?
  b Write a formula for the number of cards in any number of packs.
  Use n for the number of packs and T to stand for the total number of cards
  $T = \ldots$

3 This mapping shows how much Nusrat earns compared to Karen.
  a Copy and complete the mapping.
  b Describe in words the relationship between Karen's and Nusrat's wage.
  Start: Karen's wage is ......
  c Write a formula to connect the two wages.
  Use a for Karen's wage and b for Nusrat's wage.

Karen's wage		Nusrat's wage
100	⟶	25
50	⟶	☐
48	⟶	☐
400	⟶	100
16	⟶	☐

example

Calculate the missing angle in each of these.

a

b

c

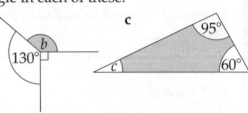

$a + 75° = 180°$ $b + 130° + 90° = 360°$ $c + 95° + 60° = 180°$

$105° + 75° = 180°$ $b + 210° = 360°$ $c + 155° = 180°$

So $a = 105°$ $150° + 210° = 360°$ $25° + 155° = 180°$

So $b = 150°$ So $c = 25°$

1 Calculate the missing angle in each of these.

a

b

c

d

e

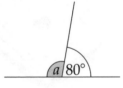

f

g

h

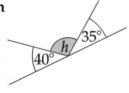

i

2 How many degrees are each of these angles?

  a AB̂C

  b BÂC

  c AĈB

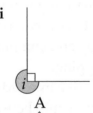

example

Find the missing angles.

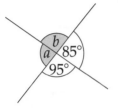

$a = 100°$ angle a is vertically opposite the angle 100°.
$b = 80°$ angle b is vertically opposite the angle 80°.

1 Find the missing angles.

a

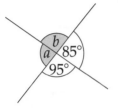

b

c

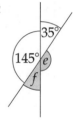

d

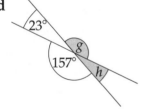

e

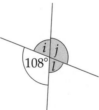

f

2 Find the missing angles.

example

What do you know about
these triangles?
. . . .

a   b

a All three sides are the same length.
All three angles are the same size.
It is called an equilateral triangle.
b Two sides are the same length.
Two angles are the same size.
It is called an isosceles triangle.

1 Sort these triangles in to groups. Give a reason or
reasons and a name for each group.

a   b   c   d

e   f   g   h

i   j   k   l

2 Answer these questions about this triangle.
   a How long is side AB?
   b How many degrees is angle AĈB?

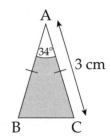

example

Calculate the size of the missing angle.

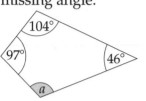
104°
97°
46°
a

Angles in a quadrilateral add up to 360°.

$104° + 97° + 46° + a = 360°$
$247° + a = 360°$
$247° + 113° = 360°$
So $a = 113°$

1 Find the missings angles in each quadrilateral.

a
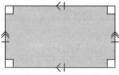

b
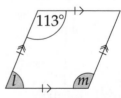
115°
65°
y
z

c
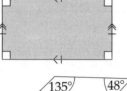
135°
48°
97°
r

d

72°
72°
s
t

e
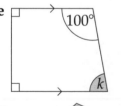
100°
k

f
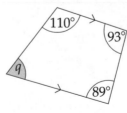
113°
l
m

g
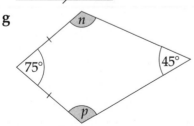
n
75°
45°
p

h
110°
93°
q
89°

Match these names to their correct shape in the previous question.
Some names will be used for more than one shape.
Kite, trapezium, rhombus, parallelogram, rectangle, irregular quadrilateral.

example

Calculate the missing angle.

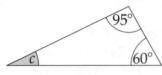

$c + 95° + 60° = 180°$

$c + 155° = 180°$

$25° + 155° = 180°$

So $c = 25°$

1 Calculate the missing angle in each of these.

a

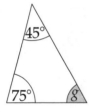

b

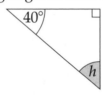

c

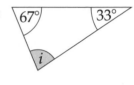

2 Find the missing angles in this diagram.

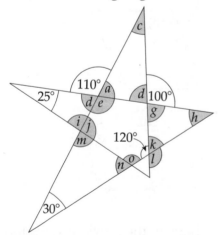

3 What do the angles inside the pentagon (i.e. the centre of the star) add up to?

Draw a cube $3 \times 3 \times 3$ onto isometric paper.

a

Start by drawing
the corner

b

Next add the other
vertical sides

c

Finally add
the top

1 Use isometric paper to draw these shapes.

a 　　**b** 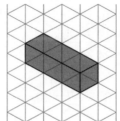　　**c**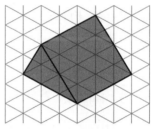

2 Draw these shapes 'free-hand' onto plain paper.

a 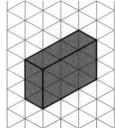　　**b**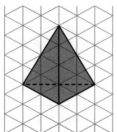

3 Name all of the shapes that you have drawn.

4 Draw 'free-hand' a hexagonal prism.

example

Use the inverse to solve these equations.

a $x + 5 = 8$ **b** $y - 12 = 20$ **c** $r \div 4$

· ·

a $x + 5 = 8$
(subtract is
the inverse)
$x = 8 - 5$
$x = 3$

b $y - 12 = 20$
(add is the
inverse)
$y = 20 + 12$
$y = 32$

c $r \div 4 = 12$
(times is the
inverse)
$r = 4 \times 12$
$r = 48$

1 Calculate the missing number in these equations.

a $30 = 12 + \square$ **b** $10 = 7 + \square$

c $50 = 5 \times \square$ **d** $19 + \square = 25$

e $45 = 60 - \square$ **f** $24 \div \square = 6$

g $\square - 5 = 20$ **h** $6 = 6 \times \square$

i $15 + \square = 15$ **j** $20 \div \square = 20$

2 Solve these equations using inverse operations.
Calculate the missing value of the letter.

a $x + 5 = 12$ **b** $y + 20 = 30$

c $h - 8 = 12$ **d** $p \div 3 = 12$

e $s \times 5 = 30$ **f** $t + 2 = 9$

g $y - 3 = 13$ **h** $40 - q = 40$

i $d \times 4 = 16$ **j** $20 \div a = 5$

3 Make up five equations (and show the worked
solutions) where the value of the letter is 4.
The first one is done for you.

$a + 5 = 9$ (subtraction is the inverse)
$\quad a = 9 - 5$
$\quad a = 4$

Solve the equation to find the value of r.
$2r + 4 = 16$

. . . .

$2r + 4 = 16$ (subtract 4 from the left and right)
  $\quad 2r = 12$ (divide the left and right by 2)
  $\quad\quad r = 6$
  $\quad\quad r = 6$

1 Calculate the weight of the parcels in the cartoons.

a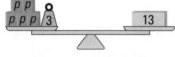

$5p + 3 \quad = \quad 13$

b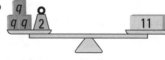

$3q + 2 \quad = \quad 11$

c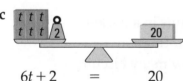

$6t + 2 \quad = \quad 20$

d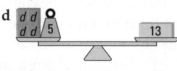

$4d + 5 \quad = \quad 13$

2 Solve these equations to the values of the letters.

a $2p + 3 = 13$	**b** $4r + 3 = 19$	**c** $5z + 4 = 14$
d $11p + 1 = 23$	**e** $7t + 4 = 53$	**f** $4h + 6 = 18$
g $8j + 5 = 21$	**h** $3g + 9 = 30$	**i** $7y + 3 = 31$
j $9t + 5 = 50$	**k** $7y + 3 = 17$	**l** $4k + 6 = 10$

3 John has £50. He buys 4 tickets and has £18 left.

a Write an equation from this information.

b Solve the equation to find out how much each ticket cost.

4 Write five equations (with worked solutions) where the
value of the letter is 7.
Here is one that has been done for you.
$4q + 5 = 33$ (subtract 5 from the left and right)
  $\quad 4q = 28$ (divide the left and right by 4)
  $\quad\quad q = 7$

---

example

There are 3 full boxes of matches and 4 loose matches.
Altogether there are 124 matches.
a Using n for the number of matches in a box, write an
equation for the above information.
b Solve the equation to find the number of matches in a box.
· ·
a $3n + 4 = 124$
b $3n + 4 = 124$ (subtract 4 from the left and right)
  $3n = 120$ (divide the left and right by 3)
  $n = 40$
Each box has 40 matches.

---

1 There are 5 packets of biscuits and 4 loose biscuits.
Altogether there are 64 biscuits.
a Let n stand for the number of biscuits in a packet.
Write an equation for the above information.
b Solve the equation to work out how many biscuits
there are in a packet.

2 Fiona pours 12 full buckets of water plus another
4 litres in her paddling pool. The capacity of her
paddling pool is 100 litres.
a Let m stand for the number of litres of water in a
bucket. Write an equation for the above information.
b Solve the equation to work out the capacity of one
bucket of water.

3 Imran takes part in a competition. The first four judges
gave him the same score, the last judge gave him a
score of 8. His total score for the competition is 36.
a Write an equation for the above information.
b Solve the equation to find the score the first four
judges gave him.

Complete the mapping diagram and function machine.

x	y	:	x	y
5	1	:	5	1
25	5	:	25	5
35	7	:	35	7
50	☐	:	50	10

$x \longrightarrow \boxed{\square} \Longrightarrow y$: $x \longrightarrow \boxed{\div 5} \Longrightarrow y$

1 Use the function machines to complete each mapping.

a $\boxed{+7}$

x	y
2	☐
4	☐
5	☐
10	☐

b $\boxed{\times 4}$

x	y
5	☐
6	☐
10	☐
20	☐

c $\boxed{\div 6}$

x	y
6	☐
18	☐
24	☐
36	☐

2 The cost, c, of phone calls on a certain mobile phone is 12 pence per minute.

a Copy and complete the mapping diagram for different number of minutes, m.

b Plot your values for m and c onto a grid like this.

c Use your plotted values to work out the cost of 25 minutes of phone calls.

m	c
3	☐
5	☐
15	☐
30	☐

3 Plot points for the mappings in question **1** onto suitably sized grids. From each mapping diagram work out the values for y when x is 42.

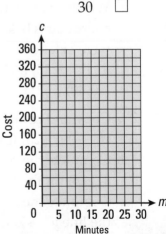

Algebra Mappings and functions

example

a Plot the points (0,0) (1,6) (2,12) (3, 18) onto a grid.
b Which of these points would lie on the line if it was extended?
   (5,32) (6,36) (7,42) (8,50) (9,54)
c Write the name of the line.

· ·

a

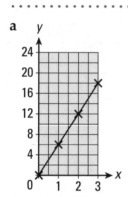

b (6,36) (7,42) (9,54) because all of
   these fit the rule which is ×6.
c $y = 6 \times x$ (or $y = 6x$)

1 a Plot these three sets of coordinates
onto a copy of this grid.
Line a: (1,2) (2,4) (3,6) (4,8)
Line b: (0,0) (1,5) (2,10) (3,15)
Line c: (0,0) (1,3) (2,6) (3,9)

b Write the name for each line.

c Which of the three lines would these
coordinates belong to, if the lines
were extended?
(6,12) (5,25) (8,16) (5,15) (10,50)
(20,40) (7,21)

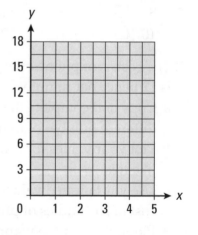

2 a Copy and complete the coordinates (4,□) (□,9)
(10,□) (□,25) for the line $y = 3 + x$.

b Complete the coordinates (6,□) (□,8) (11,□)
(□,15) for the line $y = 20 - x$.

c Complete the coordinates (5,□) (□,16) (□,24) for
the line $y = 4 \times x$.

Round these to the nearest whole number.

a 13.7   **b** 23.2   **c** 20.5

. . . .

a 13.7 will 'round up' to 14.

b 23.2 will 'round down' to 23.

c 20.5 is half-way but will 'round up' to 21.

1 Round these numbers to the nearest whole number.

a 15.3	**b** 45.2	**c** 42.1
d 52.6	**e** 16.5	**f** 24.8
g 81.6	**h** 9.5	**i** 10.4
j 19.9	**k** 0.9	**l** 99.5

2 Round these numbers to the nearest 10.

a 14	**b** 57	**c** 23
d 55	**e** 81	**f** 3
g 123	**h** 168	**i** 96
j 291	**k** 235	**l** 299

3 Round these numbers to the nearest 100.

a 234	**b** 87	**c** 258
d 50	**e** 595	**f** 145
g 45	**h** 467	**i** 295
j 1321	**k** 1695	**l** 1299

4 Round these numbers to the nearest 1000.

a 1264	**b** 8374	**c** 4268
d 5001	**e** 6595	**f** 7155
g 1500	**h** 6750	**i** 2499
j 500	**k** 9499	**l** 9500

example

Copy these questions.
Insert brackets to make each problem correct.

a $4 \times 3 + 2 = 20$ **b** $20 \div 4 + 1 = 4$

. . . .

a $4 \times (3 + 2)$ **b** $20 \div (4 + 1)$
    $= 4 \times 5 = 20$ $= 20 \div 5 = 4$

1 Copy and complete these problems.

a $4 \times (5 - 1) =$ **b** $(4 + 5) \times 3 =$ **c** $2 \times (9 - 2) =$
d $15 \div (5 - 2) =$ **e** $5 \times 2 + 3 =$ **f** $20 \div 2 - 2 =$
g $15 \div 5 - 2 =$ **h** $5 \times (2 + 3) =$ **i** $20 \div (2 - 1) =$

2 Copy these problems.
Insert brackets, if they are needed, to make each
problem correct.

a $4 \times 2 + 1 = 12$ **b** $3 \times 2 - 1 = 5$ **c** $20 \div 5 - 1 = 5$
d $20 - 2 \times 3 = 14$ **e** $12 - 2 \times 3 = 30$ **f** $14 \div 3 + 4 = 2$
g $4 + 3 \times 4 = 16$ **h** $5 \times 2 + 2 = 20$ **i** $12 + 2 \div 2 = 13$

3 Copy and complete these problems.

a $5 \times (3 + 3) + 2 =$ **b** $20 - 6 \div 2 + 5 =$
c $(20 - 6) \div 2 + 5 =$ **d** $(20 - 6) \div (2 + 5) =$
e $(12 \times 2) \div (3 + 1) =$ **f** $30 - 3 \times 4 + 3 =$

4 Write five problems containing brackets that give an
answer of 10.
Here is one that has been done for you.

$(7 - 2) \times 2 = 10$

example

Do these additions and subtractions in your head.

a $41 + 23$ **b** $68 - 44$

a First estimate; about $40 + 20 = 60$

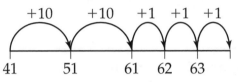

so $41 + 23 = 64$

b First estimate; $70 - 40 = 30$

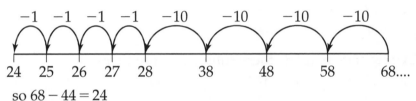

so $68 - 44 = 24$

1 Using jumps of 10, add these numbers.

  a $34 + 30$ **b** $23 + 20$ **c** $45 + 30$

  d $34 + 50$ **e** $39 + 40$ **f** $35 + 60$

  g $24 + 50$ **h** $39 + 60$ **i** $53 + 60$

2 Using jumps of 10 backwards, subtract these numbers.

  a $35 - 20$ **b** $46 - 20$ **c** $43 - 30$

  d $56 - 30$ **e** $69 - 40$ **f** $34 - 30$

  g $98 - 40$ **h** $101 - 40$ **i** $119 - 50$

3 Do these problems in your head.

  a $24 + 53$ **b** $31 + 56$ **c** $47 + 32$

  d $64 + 23$ **e** $46 + 43$ **f** $55 + 36$

  g $44 - 32$ **h** $66 - 24$ **i** $55 - 24$

example

Lay these problems out in columns and complete them.

a $24.5 + 17.3$ **b** $272.5 - 69.3$

. . . .

a 24.5
    $+17.3$
     $\overline{41.8}$

b 272.5
   -69.3
   $\overline{203.2}$

1 Copy and complete these addition problems.

a 23 **b** 46 **c** 63
   $+34$ $+32$ $+34$

d 65 **e** 75 **f** 38
   $+26$ $+26$ $+57$

2 Copy and complete these subtraction problems.

a 45 **b** 57 **c** 83
   -24 -45 -51

d 75 **e** 83 **f** 92
   -36 -16 -77

3 Copy and complete these addition problems.

a 14.6 **b** 44.4 **c** 46.3
   $+51.3$ $+52.3$ $+34.8$

4 Copy and complete these subtraction problems.

a 25.5 **b** 35.4 **c** 89.4
   -14.3 -26.8 -51.9

5 Lay these problems out in columns and complete them.

a $145.9 + 23.5$ **b** $213.8 - 45.6$ **c** $145.6 + 98.3$

d $294.4 - 149.6$ **e** $309.4 - 153.9$ **f** $435.6 + 32.7$

example

Use jottings to help you answer these multiplication problems.

a 16×5 **b** $104 \div 8$

....

a $16 \times 5 = (10 \times 5) + (6 \times 5)$ **b**
$16 \times 5 = 50 + 30$
$16 \times 5 = \mathbf{80}$

$$
\begin{array}{rl}
104 & \leftarrow\ 8 \times \mathbf{10} \\
\underline{80} & \\
24 & \leftarrow\ 8 \times \mathbf{3} \\
\underline{24} & \underline{}\mathbf{13} \\
0 &
\end{array}
$$

$104 \div 8 = 13$

1 If $7 \times 6 = 42$ **a** what is $42 \div 6$?   **b** what is $42 \div 7$?
If $8 \times 9 = 72$ **c** what is $72 \div 9$?   **d** what is $72 \div 8$?
If $12 \times 13 = 156$ **e** what is $156 \div 12$?   **f** what is $156 \div 13$?
If $15 \times 16 = 240$ **g** what is $240 \div 15$?   **h** what is $240 \div 16$?

2 Multiply each of these numbers by 10.
   a 3.4   **b** 128   **c** 34.9
   d 140   **e** 13.9   **f** 99.0

3 Divide each of these numbers by 10.
   a 560   **b** 130   **c** 45
   d 135   **e** 1440   **f** 56

4 Use jottings to help you answer these multiplication problems.
   a 23×5 **b** 35×6 **c** 19×7
   d 45×3 **e** 63×8 **f** 78×6

5 Use jottings to help you answer these division problems.
   a $64 \div 4$ **b** $108 \div 6$ **c** $85 \div 5$
   d $112 \div 8$ **e** $57 \div 3$ **f** $117 \div 9$

example

Complete the multiplication 14×17 using a grid.

Estimate/approximate; $10 \times 20 = 200$

	10	7
10	100	70
4	40	28

170 (add first row)
68 (add second row)
238

So $14 \times 17 = 238$

1 All of these numbers end in zeros. Multiply them mentally, make jottings if necessary.

a 40×30 b 80×20 c 50×60
d 130×20 e 300×30 f 200×120
g 140×30 h 260×40 i 280×50

2 Copy and complete these multiplications involving whole numbers using a grid. Remember to estimate your answer first.

a 15×18 b 18×14 c 16×17
d 19×16 e 23×18 f 32×44
g 24×35 h 56×42 i 46×82

3 Copy and complete these decimal multiplications using a grid.

a 14×3.5 b 15×2.3 c 13×6.3
d 19×1.7 e 21×1.9 f 14×3.5

4 Copy and complete these multiplications using bigger grids.

a 234×43 b 274×89 c 23.5×13

example

Complete this division problem $35.7 \div 2.1$

Multiply both numbers by 10 to change the question to $357 \div 21$ (there are the same number of 21s in 357 as 2.1s in 35.7).

$$21\overline{)357}$$
$$\underline{210} \quad 21 \times 10$$
$$147$$
$$\underline{105} \quad 21 \times 5$$
$$42$$
$$\underline{42} \quad 21 \times 2$$
$$0 \quad \overline{17}$$

So $357 \div 21 = 17$ and $25.7 \div 2.1 = 17$ as well.

1 Copy and complete these division problems.
There are no remainders.

a $96 \div 6$	**b** $105 \div 7$	**c** $152 \div 8$
d $180 \div 15$	**e** $252 \div 14$	**f** $234 \div 13$
g $272 \div 16$	**h** $306 \div 18$	**i** $368 \div 16$

2 Copy and complete these division problems.
There are remainders.

a $145 \div 8$	**b** $146 \div 6$	**c** $198 \div 7$
d $194 \div 12$	**e** $321 \div 11$	**f** $362 \div 14$
g $362 \div 15$	**h** $476 \div 16$	**i** $458 \div 21$

3 Copy and complete these division problems.
There are no remainders.

a $273 \div 2.1$	**b** $462 \div 6.6$	**c** $747 \div 8.3$
d $315 \div 6.3$	**e** $392 \div 9.8$	**f** $1196 \div 9.2$

example

Use your calculator to solve this problem $(3 \times 5) - (20 \div 4) =$
Write down the buttons you used.

. . . .

Either

| (| 3 | × | 5 |) | − | (| 20 | ÷ | 4 |) | = |

Or
Students may use the memory function instead.
The answer is 10.

1 Copy and complete these questions using your
calculator.
Write down the buttons that you pressed.

a $(4 \times 10) \div (5 - 3)$ **b** $30 - (2.2 \times 6.6) \div 3$

c $5.9 \div (4.5 + 7.2) \times 3.4$ **d** $13.3 - (2.4 \times 5.2) \div 2$

2 Copy and complete these calculations using a
calculator. Some of the working have been set
out for you to complete.

a Ahmar has three £5 notes in his wallet, and
£3.24 in change in his pocket.
How much money does he have?
$(\square \times \square) + \square =$

b Zoya buys 4 pens at 89p each and 1 pencil case for
£2.99. How much change does she get from £10?
$\square - (\square \times \square) - \square =$

c Teresa gets paid (after tax) £4.89 an hour. She works
for 8 hours. Whilst at work she pays £2.95 for her
lunch. How much money does she make that day?

d Make up a 'story' for this calculation.
$25 - (3 \times 2.99) + 4.24$

example

Use your calculator to work out

a £3.30 + £0.60　　　**b** 1.46 m + 1.24 m.

....

a The answer is £3.90, the calculator says
Remember when giving an answer with
money you may need to add an extra zero.

3.9

b The answer is 2.7 m, the calculator says
If the answer is needed in metres and centimetres then
remember '0.7' stands for 70 cm so the answer is 2 m 70 cm

2.7

1 Here are some answers Philip got on his calculator.
'Tidy up' these answers by rounding them to
2 decimal places (2 dp).

a 4.564　　　　**b** 12.344　　　　**c** 8.4633

d 12.456　　　　**e** 20.547　　　　**f** 14.566

2 Use a calculator to work out these division problems.
Make an estimate first. Give your answers to 2 dp.

a 48 ÷ 17　　　　**b** 86 ÷ 15　　　　**c** 91 ÷ 19

d 123 ÷ 18　　　　**e** 453 ÷ 46　　　　**f** 563 ÷ 53

3 Use your calculator to copy and complete these money
problems.

a £4.50 + £3.30 =　　**b** £8.80 + £1.20 =　　**c** £3.90 + £12.10 =

4 Use your calculator to complete these measurement problems.
Give your answers in metres and centimetres.

a 2.45 m + 1.15 m =　**b** 4.67 m + 2.03 m =　**c** 6.92 m + 2.48 m =

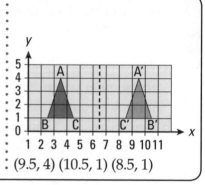

example

Reflect the shape in the mirror line.
Give the coordinates of the image.

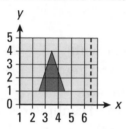

(9.5, 4) (10.5, 1) (8.5, 1)

1 Copy these shapes and draw their reflections in the
mirror line.

a   b   c

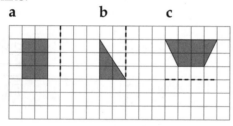

2 a Copy the grid and draw and label the
    parallelogram.
  b Reflect the parallelogram in the mirror line.
  c Label the image A′, B′, C′, D′.
  d Give the coordinates of A′, B′, C′and D′.

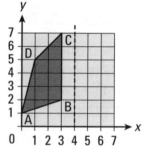

3 a Copy the grid and draw and label
    the trapezium.
  b Reflect the trapezium in
    the mirror line.
  c Label the image
    A′, B′, C′, D′.
  d Give the coordinates of
    A′, B′, C′ and D′.
  e What do you notice?

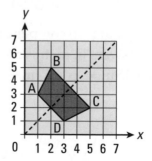

example

Copy these shapes onto square paper.
Draw one line of symmetry onto each shape.

You can use a mirror or, trace
the shapes, cut them out
and then fold them to help
find the line of symmetry.

1 Copy these shapes onto square paper.
Draw one line of symmetry onto each shape.

a   b   c   d

e Draw your own shape that has only one line of symmetry.
Draw the line of symmetry on your shape.

2 These shapes have more than one line of symmetry.
Copy these shapes onto square paper, and draw the
lines of symmetry.

a   b   c   d

e Draw your own shape that has more than one line of symmetry.
Draw the lines of symmetry on your shape.

3 (Optional) Write down as many capital letters as you can think of
that have
a only one line of symmetry
b more than one line of symmetry.

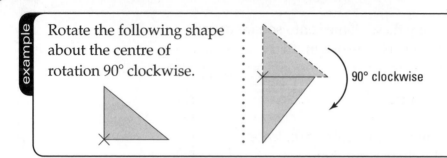

example

Rotate the following shape about the centre of rotation 90° clockwise.

90° clockwise

1 Copy each shape onto squared paper. Follow the instructions and rotate the shapes through the centre of rotation.

a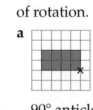

90° anticlockwise

b

180° clockwise

c

270° clockwise

d

90° clockwise

e

180° anticlockwise

f

270° anticlockwise

2 Copy each shape onto squared paper. Follow the instructions and rotate the shapes about the centre of rotation.

a

180° clockwise

b

90° anticlockwise

c

270° clockwise

3 Write down another instruction that is the same as
   a rotate 90° clockwise
   b rotate 270° clockwise
   c rotate 180° anticlockwise.

9d Rotational symmetry

Copy this shape and state the order of rotational symmetry.

Instructions

1 Trace shape and mark one corner.
2 Put your pencil in the centre of the shape.
3 Turn the tracing paper until the shape on the tracing paper is in the same position as the shape in the book.
4 Count how many times this happens until you get back to the beginning (count this move as well).

The order of rotational symmetry for the shape above is 4.

1 Copy each shape and state the order of rotational symmetry.

a

b

c

d

e

f

g

h

i

2 (Optional) Draw a shape that has
  a 2 lines of symmetry and rotational symmetry of order 2
  b 3 lines of symmetry and rotational symmetry of order 3
  c 1 line of symmetry and no rotational symmetry.

example

The coordinates of a trapezium are A(2,2) B(3,4) C(5,4) D(6,2). The trapezium is translated 3 squares to the right and 4 squares up. What are the new coordinates?

Draw trapezium ABCD on a coordinate grid.
Slide the trapezium 3 squares to the right and then 4 squares up.
Read off the new coordinates.
A' (5, 6) B' (6, 8) C' (8, 8) D' (9, 6)

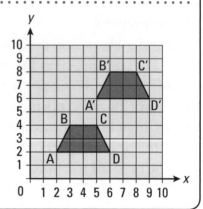

1 Copy the grid and trapezium ABCD from the example. Move the trapezium using these translations and give the new coordinates.

a $\begin{pmatrix} \text{left 2} \\ \text{up 6} \end{pmatrix}$

b $\begin{pmatrix} \text{right 1} \\ \text{up 6} \end{pmatrix}$

c $\begin{pmatrix} \text{right 3} \\ \text{up 5} \end{pmatrix}$

d $\begin{pmatrix} \text{left 1} \\ \text{up 6} \end{pmatrix}$

e $\begin{pmatrix} \text{right 4} \\ \text{down 1} \end{pmatrix}$

f $\begin{pmatrix} \text{right 5} \\ \text{up 0} \end{pmatrix}$

2 Give the translation if the trapezium ABCD ended up in these positions.

a A'(4,3) B'(5,5) C'(7,5) D'(8,4)
b A'(6,1) B'(7,3) C'(9,3) D'(10,1)
c A'(9,0) B'(10,2) C'(12,2) D'(13,0)
d A'(0,0) B'(1,2) C'(3,2) D'(4,0)
e A'(-2,4) B'(-1,6) C'(1,6) D'(2,4)
f A'(-3,-3) B'(-2,-1) C'(0,-1) D'(1,-3)
Explain how you got your answers.

example

Tessellate this shape 10 times.

Remember you can turn shapes upside down, on their side etc to help fit them together.

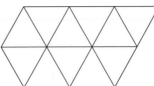

1 Copy each of these shapes onto square paper and tessellate them 10 times.

a

b

c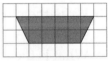

d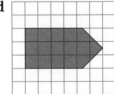

e

f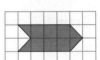

g

h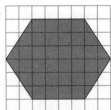

i

2 (Optional) Do you think these shapes would tessellate? You do not need to draw them.

a

b

c

10a Describing sequences

example

a Write the term-to-term rule for each of these sequences.
i 4, 9, 14, 19, 24, ...   **ii** 160, 80, 40, 20, ...
b Write the next two terms in each sequence.

· ·

a i Add five   **b i** 29, 34
  ii Divide by 2   **ii** 10, 5

1 a Copy the drawing and add two more patterns.

  b Write the number of squares in the pattern as a number sequence. Write the first five terms.
  c What is the term-to-term rule for the number sequence?

2 a Copy the drawing and add two more patterns.

  b Write the number of squares in the pattern as a number sequence. Write the first five terms.
  c What is the term-to-term rule for the number sequence?

3 a Write the term-to-term rule for each of these sequences.
  b Write the next two terms in each sequence
    i   8, 14, 20, 26, ...   **ii**   40, 20, 10, 5, ...
    iii 3, 6, 9, 12, ...   **iv**   0, 0.5, 1, 1.5, 2 ...
    v   29, 26, 23, 20, ...   **vi**   810, 270, 90, 30, ...
    vii 10, 5, 0, -5, ...   **viii** 12500, 2500, 500, 100, ...

10b Generating sequences

example

Use this position-to-term rule to generate the first five terms in the sequence. **Position** → $\times 2$ → $+3$ → **Term**

· ·

Position				Term
1st	$\times 2$	2	$+3$	5
2nd		4		7
3rd		6		9
4th		8		11
5th		10		13

So the sequence is 5, 7, 9, 11, 13

1 a Copy the pattern and draw the next shape.

b Write out the first five terms of the sequence.

c Show that this position-to-term rule works for the sequence.

Position → $\times 4$ → $+1$ → **Term**

2 a Copy the pattern and draw the next shape.
b Write out the first five terms of the sequence.
c Show that this position-to-term rule works for the sequence.

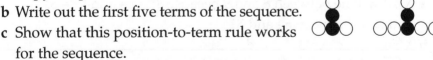

Position → $\times 3$ → $+2$ → **Term**

3 Use these position-to-term rules to generate the first five terms in each sequence.

a Position → $\times 3$ → $+2$ → **Term**

b Position → $\times 5$ → -1 → **Term**

c Position → $\times 6$ → $+5$ → **Term**

Algebra Generating sequences

example

Use your calculator to find these amounts.

a 30^2 **b** $\sqrt{324}$

· ·

Press the following buttons

a [3] [0] [x^2] [=] 900   **b** [$\sqrt{}$] [3] [2] [4] [=] 18

1 Copy and complete these calculations.

   a $6^2 = \square \times \square = 36$ **b** $9^2 = 9 \times \square = \square$

   c $12^2 = \square \times \square = \square$

2 Use your calculator to find these amounts.

   a 40^2 **b** $\sqrt{361}$ **c** 25^2

   d $\sqrt{225}$ **e** 4.5^2 **f** $\sqrt{72.25}$

   g 200^2 **h** $\sqrt{2025}$ **i** 0.5^2

3 Write down all of the square numbers between 0 and 100.

4 Without using a calculator, work out between which two whole numbers the following square root will be.

Give a reason for your answer.

The first one is done for you.

   a $\sqrt{70}$ will lie between 8 and 9 because $8^2 = 64$ and $9^2 = 81$ and 70 is between 64 and 81

   b $\sqrt{50}$ **c** $\sqrt{33}$ **d** $\sqrt{21}$

   e $\sqrt{89}$ **f** $\sqrt{10}$ **g** 105

5 Check your answers to question 4 with a calculator.

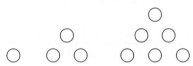

Use dots to draw the first three triangular numbers.

example

1, 3, 6 are the first three triangular numbers.

1 Use dots to draw the first five triangular numbers.

2 Describe how you work out a triangular number.

3 Write down all of the triangular numbers less than 100.

4 Which number between 0 and 100 is both a triangular number and a square number?

5 Square numbers can be made up of two triangular numbers, as shown in the example below.

 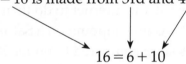

$4^2 = 16$ is made from 3rd and 4th triangular number

$$16 = 6 + 10$$

a Which two triangular numbers would make $7^2 = 49$? Draw it, as in the example above.

b Draw diagrams to show how these square numbers can be made from two triangular numbers.

i 6^2

ii 8^2

iii 9^2

iv 10^2

v 11^2

example

Jonaid wants to carry out a survey to see how healthy people are. Suggest some questions that could be used.

· ·

How many pieces of fruit do you usually eat each in a day?
How much exercise do you do usually do in a week?
How much time do you spend watching TV each evening?

1 Explain whether each of these is primary data or secondary data.

  a Data from the internet.

  b Results from a survey in a magazine.

  c The results from an experiment you did at school.

  d Results you collected from a survey.

2 Alika wants to find out how much time people spend shopping and whether it is different for certain age groups. Alika wants to ask these questions.
How many households use the internet to do their shopping?
How many Year 8 students go shopping on a Saturday?
How much do over 40s shop compared to under 20s?
Suggest some sources of information that Alika could use to answer these questions.

3 Dionne wants to carry out a survey to see how healthy people are. She writes a plan for her project.
"I am going to find out how much fruit and vegetables people eat each day and how much exercise they take. I will go to the local swimming pool and ask as many people as I can."

  a Explain why this is not a good plan.

  b Suggest a better way for Dionne to find out how healthy people are.

4 Suggest a topic that you could investigate and some questions that could be asked.

example

Jonaid wants to carry out a survey to see how healthy people are. Suggest how these questions that could be improved.

How many pieces of fruit do you usually eat?

| 0–1 | 2–3 | 4–5 | 6+ |

How much exercise do you do usually do in a week?

| None | A bit | A lot | 5 hours |

The first question doesn't say over how much time.
A better question is:
How many pieces of fruit do you eat in a day, a week, a month etc.
The second question is too vague. 'A bit' and 'a lot' could mean different things to different people.

1 Elvy designed a questionnaire for a school project. She wants to find out how people spend their time and whether there is a difference between age groups, gender etc.

a How old are you?

b What is your gender?

c How much money do you earn?
   None   OK amount   Quite a lot   Loads

d What do you do in your spare time?
   Watch TV   Play sport/exercise   Shopping   Chilling

Explain how each of these questions could be improved and then rewrite/improve each question.
Add one of your own questions.

2 Sonia is trying to find out how many people use public transport. She decides to ask all of her friends at school.

a Explain why this is the wrong approach.

b Suggest a better way to collect this data.

example

John collected the shoe sizes of
20 people in his class.
The results were
4, 5, 4, 6, 5, 7, 6, 6, 7, 5, 6,
6, 3, 5, 4, 7, 5, 8, 4, 5
Tally the information and
complete a frequency table
to show the data.

Shoe size	Tally	Frequency
3	I	1
4	IIII	4
5	JHI I	6
6	JHI	5
7	III	3
8	I	1

1 The total number of goals scored in 20 football matches were
1, 2, 1, 0, 3, 4, 2, 1, 3, 2, 2, 1, 0, 0, 4, 5, 3, 2, 2, 5.
Create and complete a tally chart and frequency table
to show this information.

2 Frances made a note of the number of cars that drove
past her house every 5 min for 100 min. Her results were
8, 6, 6, 8, 7, 9, 10, 6, 7, 5, 7, 8, 4, 5, 8, 6, 7, 6, 8, 8.
Create and complete a tally chart and frequency table
to show this information.

3 The ages of 20 people in Claire's hockey club were
25, 30, 26, 22, 24, 31, 19, 24, 27, 32, 29, 36, 18, 16, 21, 26,
32, 26, 30, 32.
Create and complete a tally chart and frequency table
to show this information.

4 Collect some data to display in a frequency table.
Here are some suggestions.
 – Shoe size of 20 people in your class.
 – Colour of cars that pass your house/school over
   a 20 min period.
 – Number of pets that people have.

example

This frequency table shows the shoe sizes for 20 people in Jonaid's class. Display this information in a bar chart.

Shoe size	Tally	Frequency
3	I	1
4	IIII	4
5	ЖI	6
6	Ж	5
7	III	3
8	I	1

Bar chart to show the shoe sizes of Jonaid's class.

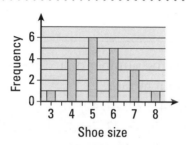

1 This table shows the scores when a die is rolled 30 times.
Draw a bar-line chart for this data.

No. on die	1	2	3	4	5	6
Frequency	4	5	6	6	4	5

2 This table shows the colour of 35 cars that drive past the school.

Car colour	Red	Silver	Black	Blue	Other
Frequency	4	5	6	6	4

Draw a horizontal bar chart for this set of data.

3 The data below shows the number of goals scored in 36 premiership games last year.

3	3	4	1	0	4	1	1	0
3	6	2	1	1	0	1	2	2
1	0	1	1	4	1	0	1	1
3	2	4	1	2	1	2	1	0

a Construct and complete a frequency table for this data.
b Use your frequency table to draw a bar chart.

example

These are the ages of 20 people in Ravi's football club.
22, 32, 34, 15, 26, 29, 38, 27, 21, 20, 27, 33, 25, 39, 18, 30, 22, 28, 24, 29
Organise the data into groups.

Age (years)	Frequency
15–19	2
20–24	5
25–29	7
30–34	4
35–39	2
40+	0

1 Michelle records the number of text messages she gets each day for a month.
24, 20, 16, 34, 12, 45, 20, 24, 40, 31, 12, 32, 33, 35, 25, 38, 29, 15, 16, 16, 35, 37, 22, 26, 32, 41, 26, 29, 26, 30
a Organise the data into groups.
b Use the grouped data to draw a bar chart.

2 Justin asks 30 people to time, in minutes, how long it takes to get to work on one Monday morning.
34, 23, 8, 35, 23, 12, 39, 40, 23, 41, 31, 19, 37, 35, 12, 15, 16, 21, 23, 33, 12, 14, 11, 8, 6, 14, 46, 24, 25, 30
a Organise the data into groups.
b Use the grouped data to draw a bar chart.

3 A traffic survey measured the number of cars that passed a hospital every hour during one full day.
12, 13, 9, 8, 5, 16, 30, 45, 70, 65, 34, 20, 45, 65, 58, 54, 58, 61, 47, 55, 59, 24, 45, 21
a Organise the data into groups.
b Use the grouped data to draw a bar chart.

This frequency table shows the favourite colour for 18 people. Draw a pie chart to represent this information.

· ·

One person is represented by an angle of $360 \div 18 = 20°$

Colour	Frequency	Angle
Red	5	$5 \times 20° = 100°$
Blue	3	$3 \times 20° = 60°$
Green	4	$4 \times 20° = 80°$
Purple	3	$3 \times 20° = 60°$
Yellow	1	$1 \times 20° = 20°$
Other	2	$2 \times 20° = 40°$

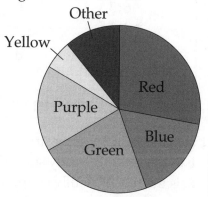

1 Maude carried out a survey about favourite hobbies.

Hobby	Sport/ exercise	Reading	Listening to music	Watching TV/Films	Shopping	Playing games
Frequency	6	4	7	5	6	8

Draw a pie chart to represent this information.

2 Kalpesh surveyed people's favourite fruits.

Fruit	Apples	Banana	Orange	Berries	Pear	Other
Frequency	4	5	3	4	1	1

Draw a pie chart to represent this information.

3 Brian carried out a survey to find out which of the following foods students liked to eat in the school canteen.

Food	Salad	Pasta	Chips	Curry	Baked potatoes	Sandwiches
Frequency	12	16	9	7	14	2

Draw a pie chart to represent this information.

example

Which of these ratios are equivalent to $3:1$?

a $6:3$ **b** $9:3$ **c** $12:4$ **d** $18:3$

....

To simplify ratios, divide both amounts by the same number,

a $\div 3 \left(\dfrac{6:3}{2:1}\right) \div 3$ **b** $\div 3 \left(\dfrac{9:3}{3:1}\right) \div 3$

c $\div 4 \left(\dfrac{12:4}{3:1}\right) \div 4$ **d** $\div 3 \left(\dfrac{18:3}{6:1}\right) \div 3$

So $9:3$ and $12:4$ are equivalent to $3:1$.

1 a Is the ratio $3:1$ fully simplified? Explain your answer.

  b Is the ratio $12:4$ fully simplified? Explain your answer.

  c Is the ratio $5:4$ fully simplified? Explain your answer.

2 Simplify these ratios.

a $10:5$	**b** $12:4$	**c** $9:15$	**d** $8:2$
e $16:4$	**f** $18:9$	**g** $24:12$	**h** $36:9$
i $12:32$	**j** $14:35$	**k** $26:13$	**l** $48:30$
m $65:30$	**n** $56:32$	**o** $75:125$	

3 Which of these ratios are equivalent to $4:5$?

  a $12:15$ **b** $32:36$ **c** $8:12$ **d** $20:25$

4 To make pink paint you mix white and red paint.
Different ratios give you different shades.

Dark pink	Mid pink	Light pink
white:red	white:red	white:red
$1:4$	$2:5$	$3:1$

Using the same mixture ratios, what shade is each of
these mixtures?

a $4:10$	**b** $12:4$	**c** $2:8$	**d** $30:10$
e $10:25$	**f** $4:16$	**g** $8:32$	**h** $18:6$
i $5:12.5$	**j** $0.5:2$	**k** $4.5:1.5$	**l** $3.5:14$

example

Nancy and Todd divide £20 in the ratio 4:1.
How much will they receive?

. . . .

By sharing
Nancy : Todd
    4:1 ⟶ 5
    4:1 ⟶ 5
    4:1 ⟶ 5
    4:1 ⟶ 5
£16 : £4 ⟶ £20

By dividing
Nancy : Todd
    4:1 ⟶ 5 (£20 ÷ 5 = £4)
4 × £4 : 1 × £4
So, Nancy will have £16 and Todd £4
Check £16 + £4 = £20

1 Krystal has 12 sweets and shares them with her
friend in the ratio 2:1.

Divide the sweets to show how many sweets each of
them get.

2 Glody and Aleem are paid £25. Glody works
harder than Aleem so they share the money
in the ratio 3:2.
How much does each one get?

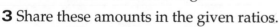

3 Share these amounts in the given ratios.
  a £14 in the ratio 5:2   **b** £15 in the ratio 2:3
  c £24 in the ratio 3:5   **d** £30 in the ratio 5:1
  e £44 in the ratio 3:1

4 Purple paint is red and blue paint mixed.
The ratio is red : blue
              3:1
How much red and blue paint is needed to mix
12 litres of purple paint?

example

There are 10 boys in a class. Six of them have brown hair.
a What proportion of the boys have brown hair?
b What percentage of the boys do not have brown hair?

· ·

a 6 out of 10 is $\frac{6}{10}$ as a fraction.
b 4 out of 10 is 40% as a percentage.

1 a Match up the fractions to their equivalent percentages.

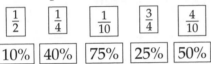

$\boxed{\dfrac{1}{2}}$ $\boxed{\dfrac{1}{4}}$ $\boxed{\dfrac{1}{10}}$ $\boxed{\dfrac{3}{4}}$ $\boxed{\dfrac{4}{10}}$

$\boxed{10\%}$ $\boxed{40\%}$ $\boxed{75\%}$ $\boxed{25\%}$ $\boxed{50\%}$

b Add a few more pairs of your own.

2 James and Sonia share a pizza. It has been cut into four
equal pieces. James eats three pieces and Sonia one piece.
a What proportion of the pizza did James eat?
b What percentage did Sonia eat?

3 Write these statements replacing the fraction with a
percentage.
a $\frac{8}{10}$ people prefer the summer to winter.

b $\frac{2}{10}$ cats are black cats.   **c** $\frac{6}{10}$ cars made are silver.

4 Write these statements replacing the percentage with a
fraction.
a 75% of students live within 1 mile of their school.
b 50% of teachers live within 5 miles of their school.
c 20% of schools are in cities.

5 There are 20 students in a class. Four of them are
absent on one particular day.
a What proportion, as a fraction, of the class are absent?
b What proportion, as a percentage, of the class are
present?

example

David pays £60 for 4 bottles of champagne.
How much will 16 bottles of champagne cost?

. . . .

David buys 4 times more champagne so he pays 4 times more
money. The scale factor is **4**.

Cost   Number of bottles

$\times 4 \left(\begin{array}{c} £60 \\ £240 \end{array} \right.$ $\left. \begin{array}{c} 4 \\ 16 \end{array} \right) \times 4$

David will pay £240.

1 Harriet bought 2 kg of potatoes for £1.50. How much
would it cost for 1 kg?

2 Teresa is paid £30 for 4 hours work.
How much will she be paid for 28 hours work?

3 Abu buys 5 bananas for £1.50.
How much will it cost for 15 bananas?

4 Helena can deliver 13 newspapers in 2 hours.
How many newspapers can she deliver in 6 hours?

5 Claire can run 7 miles in 60 minutes.
How long would it take to run 21 miles?

6 Abdi can type 35 words a minute.
How long would it take him to type 280 words?

7 Maros can do 5 press ups in 10 seconds.
How many could he do in one minute (if he didn't
get tired)?

example

Concrete is mixed from cement and aggregate.
The ratio is cement : aggregate 1 : 5
How many kilograms of cement are needed to mix with 20 kg of aggregate?

$\times 4 \left(\begin{matrix} 1:5 \\ 4:20 \end{matrix} \right) \times 4$ You would need 4 kg of cement.

1 Using the information in the example about making concrete, answer these questions.

  a How much aggregate do you need to mix with 3 kg of cement?

  b How much cement do you need to mix with 15 kg of aggregate?

  c How much aggregate do you need to mix with 0.5 kg of cement?

  d How much cement do you need to mix with 7.5 kg of aggregate?

2 Stephen and Paul share some money in the ratio 3 : 2. Stephen gets the bigger share. How much does Paul get if Stephen gets £15?

3 To make pink paint you mix white and red paint in these ratios.

Dark pink	Mid pink	Light pink
white : red	white : red	white : red
1 : 4	2 : 5	3 : 1

  a How much white paint do you need to mix with 12 litres of red paint to make dark pink?

  b How much red paint do you need to mix with 4 litres of white paint to make mid-pink paint?

  c How much white paint do you to mix with 0.5 litres of red paint to make light pink?

Which of these offers is the best deal?

a $\frac{1}{3}$ of 90 kg or $\frac{1}{2}$ of 80 kg

b 20% of £30 or 40% of £20

· ·

a $\frac{1}{3}$ of 90 kg = 90 kg ÷ 3 = 30 kg

$\frac{1}{2}$ of 80 kg = 80 kg ÷ 2 = 40 kg $\frac{1}{2}$ of 80 kg is the better deal.

b 20% of £30 = (£30 ÷ 10) × 2 = £6

40% of £20 = (£20 ÷ 10) × 4 = £8   40% of £20 is the better deal.

1 Calculate these percentage proportions.

  a 10% of 60   **b** 10% of 40   **c** 10% of 120

  d 30% of 60   **e** 40% of 40   **f** 60% of 120

  g 60% of 60   **h** 70% of 40   **i** 90% of 120

2 Which of these proportions is the better deal?

  a $\frac{1}{10}$ of 20 or $\frac{1}{4}$ of 12   **b** $\frac{1}{3}$ of 18 or $\frac{1}{2}$ of 14

  c $\frac{1}{5}$ of 30 or $\frac{1}{3}$ of 24   **d** $\frac{1}{8}$ of 24 or $\frac{1}{3}$ of 15

  e $\frac{1}{7}$ of 35 or $\frac{1}{4}$ of 24   **f** $\frac{1}{10}$ of 40 or $\frac{1}{5}$ of 25

3 Which of these proportions is the better deal?

  a 10% of £50 or 30% of £20   **b** 40% of 120 or 50% of £100

  c 30% of £30 or 70% of £10   **d** 60% of £80 or 30% of £60

  e 90% of £90 or 60% of £140   **f** 70% of £150 or 30% of £310

4 Which of these is the larger amount?

  a $\frac{4}{5}$ of £35 or $\frac{2}{3}$ of £30   **b** $\frac{3}{7}$ of £42 or $\frac{2}{3}$ of £33

5 Which of these is the better deal?

Sale: $\frac{1}{3}$ off
Original
price £33

Sale: 30% off
Original
price £30

example

Simplify these expressions.

a $5m \times 3$ **b** $5g + 3h - 3g + 2h$

c $4f \times 3g \times 2h$ **d** $\frac{12a}{6b}$

. . . .

a $5m \times 3 = 15m$ **b** $5g + 3h - 3g + 2h = 2g + 5h$

c $4f \times 3g \times 2h = 24fgh$ **d** $\frac{12a}{6b} = \frac{2a}{b}$

1 Simplify these expressions by collecting like terms.

  a $b + b + b + b$ **b** $m + m + m + m + m$

  c $3g + 4g$ **d** $h + 3h + 2h - h$

  e $5k + 3k - k + 2k$ **f** $2w - w + 4w + 3w$

2 Simplify these expressions by collecting like terms.

  a $3e + 2e + 4d$ **b** $2a + b + 3a + 5b - a$

  c $6y + x + 2y - x + y$ **d** $10f + 3g - 7f + g$

  e $15d - d + 3p + 2d - 2p$ **f** $2e + f + 7e + 5f - e$

3 Simplify these expressions.

  a $5m \times 3$ **b** $5t \times 2$ **c** $8h \times 3$ **d** $6k \times 5$

  e $3e \times 2f$ **f** $5t \times 7y$ **g** $6s \times 8g$ **h** $2t \times 9p$

  i $3r \times 8w$ **j** $12d \times 3c$ **k** $m \times 3d$ **l** $s \times t$

4 Simplify these expressions by division.

  a $3a \div 3$ **b** $12b \div 4$ **c** $25t \div 5$ **d** $100h \div 10$

  e $\frac{16h}{4}$ **f** $\frac{24p}{4}$ **g** $\frac{45j}{9}$ **h** $\frac{36h}{6}$

  i $\frac{10y}{2x}$ **j** $\frac{32e}{8p}$ **k** $\frac{27m}{9n}$ **l** $\frac{40r}{10s}$

5 (Optional) Write down five expressions that would simplify to $24h$. Here is one that has been done for you.

  $13h + 4g + 7h - 4g + 4h = 6 \times 4h = 24h$

example

The cost of calls on a mobile phone is recorded in this table.

Minutes	5	10	15	20	25
Cost in pence	70	140	210	280	350

a Use the table to write a formula to describe the relationship between the number of minutes and the cost of the calls.

b Use your formula to work out the cost of a 35 minute phonecall.

. . . .

a Cost = Number of minutes $\times$ 14 or $C = m \times 14$ or $C = 14m$.

b $C = 14 \times 35 = 490$ pence = £4.90

---

1 This table shows the cost of a taxi journey over different distances.

Miles	5	10	15	20	25
Cost in pounds	£10	£20	£30	£40	£50

a Use the table to write a formula to describe the relationship between the number of miles travelled in the taxi and the cost.

b Check the formula works using a pair of values from the table.

c Use your formula to work out the cost of a 45 mile journey.

2 This table shows the cost of hiring a bike by the hour.

Hours	1	2	3	4	5
Cost in pounds	£8	£16			

a Copy and complete the rest of the values in the table.

b Write a formula for the cost of hiring a bike against the number of hours.

c Check the formula works using values from the table.

d Find the cost of hiring a bike for 9 hours.

example

Find the value of these symbols by balancing these equations.
a $x + x + x + 3 = x + x + 5$
b $y + y + y + y + 5 = y + y + 8$

. . . .

a

b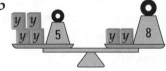

$$3x + 3 = 2x + 5$$
So $x + 3 = 5$
$$x = 5 - 3$$
$$x = 2$$

$$4y + 5 = 2y + 8$$
So $2y + 5 = 8$
$$2y = 8 - 5$$
$$2y = 3$$
$$y = 1.5$$

1 Find the value of these symbols by balancing these equations.

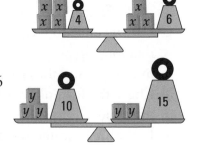

a $x + x + x + x + 4 = x + x + x + 6$
b $y + y + y + 10 = y + y + 15$
c $r + r + r + r + r + 12 = r + r + r + r + 16$
d $s + s + 10 = s + s + s + 7$
e $t + t + t + 20 = t + t + t + t + 16$
f $q + q + 12 = q + q + q + q + 6$
g $n + n + n + n + n + 20 = n + n + n + 30$
h $m + m + m + m + 3 = m + 15$

2 Find the value of these symbols by balancing equations.
(Remember $3a$ means $a + a + a$)
  a $4s + 2 = 3s + 7$ **b** $5r + 4 = 4r + 6$
  c $6t + 1 = 5t + 4$ **d** $4h + 2 = 5h + 1$
  e $4f + 3 = 2f + 15$ **f** $7h + 3 = 5h + 11$

3 Make up a question of your own. Make sure it works by showing the solution.

13c² Making equations

There are 3 bags of sweets and 5 loose sweets. There are 32 sweets altogether. How many sweets are in each bag?

. . . .

Let x stand for the number of sweets in each bag.

$$x + x + x + 5 = 32$$
$$\text{So} \quad 3x + 5 = 32$$
$$3x = 32 - 5$$
$$\text{So } 3x = 27$$
$$\boldsymbol{x = 9}$$

1 The perimeter of all three shapes is 50 cm.

a   20 cm

8 cm ⟋‾‾‾‾‾‾⟍ 8 cm

r cm

b   15 cm

s cm ▭

15 cm

c   8 cm ⟍ 8 cm

t cm ⟍_____⟋ t cm

10 cm

i Write an equation for the perimeter of each of these shapes.

ii Solve the equations to find the length of sides r, s and t.

2 There are 4 bags of sweets and 3 loose sweets. There are 47 sweets altogether.

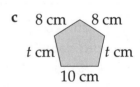

a Write an equation for the total number of sweets.

b How many sweets are in each bag?

3 Laura and Jade have the same number of sweets.
James has 3 bags of sweets and 15 loose ones.
Sonia has 4 bags of sweets and 5 loose ones.

a Write an equation to show that the number of sweets that both Sonia and James have are equal.

b Solve this equation to find the number of sweets in a bag.

example

a Use the rule to copy and complete a table of values for the *x*- and *y*-coordinates.
b Plot the *x*- and *y*-coordinates onto axes.

$x \rightarrow \boxed{\times 2} \rightarrow y \rightarrow \boxed{+3} \rightarrow$

a

x-coordinate	0	1	2	3	4
×2	0	2	4	6	8
+3	+3	+3	+3	+3	+3
y-coordinate	3	5	7	9	11

b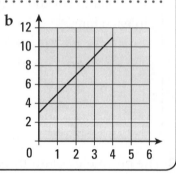

1 Copy and complete these mappings to calculate the *y*-coordinates.

a $x \boxed{\times 3} y$
0 ⟶ ☐
1 ⟶ ☐
2 ⟶ ☐
3 ⟶ ☐
4 ⟶ ☐

b $x \boxed{+5} y$
0 ⟶ ☐
1 ⟶ ☐
2 ⟶ ☐
3 ⟶ ☐
4 ⟶ ☐

c $x \boxed{\times 6} y$
0 ⟶ ☐
1 ⟶ ☐
2 ⟶ ☐
3 ⟶ ☐
4 ⟶ ☐

d $x \boxed{+11} y$
0 ⟶ ☐
1 ⟶ ☐
2 ⟶ ☐
3 ⟶ ☐
4 ⟶ ☐

2 a Use the rule to copy and complete the table of values for the *x*- and *y*-coordinates.

$x \rightarrow \boxed{\times 3} \rightarrow \boxed{+4} \rightarrow y$

x-coordinate	0	1	2	3	4
×3	0				
+4	+4	+4	+4	+4	+4
y-coordinate					

b Plot the *x*- and *y*-coordinates onto axes.

13e Straight line equations

> **a** List four coordinates shown on the line.
> **b** Use the coordinates to work out the two operations and complete the sentence below. 'To work out the y-coordinate you multiply the x-coordinate by ..... and add ...'
> **c** Write the equation of the line: $y = ...x + ...$
>
> ....
>
> **a** Coordinates are $(0,1)$, $(1,3)$, $(2,5)$, $(3,7)$.
> **b** To work out the y-coordinate you multiply the x-coordinate by 2 and add 1.
> **c** $y = 2x + 1$

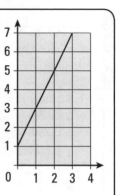

1 Match each rule with the set of coordinates which belong to it (copy the grid and draw the line for each one). One has been done for you.

$y = x + 3$	$(0,-2)\ (1,-1)\ (2,0)\ (3,1)$
$y = 2x + 3$	$(0,0)\ (1,4)\ (2,8)\ (3,12)$
$y = 3x - 1$	$(0,3)\ (1,5)\ (2,7)\ (3,9)$
$y = x - 2$	$(0,3)\ (1,4)\ (2,5)\ (3,6)$
$y = 4x$	$(0,-1)\ (1,2)\ (2,5)\ (3,8)$

2 a List four coordinates shown on the line.

b Use the coordinates to work out the two operations and copy and complete the sentence below. 'To work out the y-coordinate you multiply the x-coordinate by ..... and add ...'

c Write the equation of the line $y = ...x + ...$

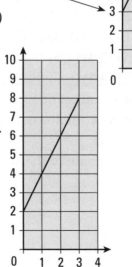

example

On the grid is a parallelogram.
a Write the equations of the four sides.

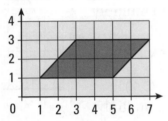

b Where do these lines intersect?

a $y = x$
$y = x - 4$
$y = 1$ $y = 3$

b The lines intersect at $(1,1)$ $(5,1)$ $(7,3)$ $(3,3)$.

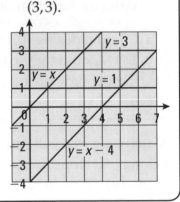

1 a Draw axes like these.
b Plot these sets of coordinates. Join each set to make straight lines.
Set 1 $(3,0)$ $(3,1)$ $(3,5)$ $(3,6)$
Set 2 $(7,0)$ $(7,1)$ $(7,4)$ $(7,6)$
Set 3 $(2,1)$ $(2,4)$ $(2,5)$ $(2,8)$
Set 4 $(2,7)$ $(5,4)$ $(6,3)$ $(8,1)$
c Write the equation of each line.
d Write the coordinates where the lines intersect.
e What is the name of the shape the four lines make?

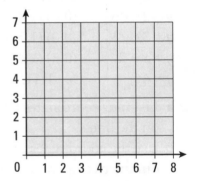

On a particular day, the exchange rate for Pounds (£) to US Dollars($) is $1.90 to £1.

a Draw a conversion graph to help convert dollars($) into pounds (£).

b Use the graph to estimate how many dollars there are to £70.

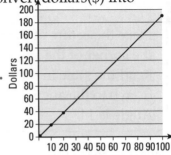

· ·

a First make a table.

Pounds (£)	1	10	20	100
Dollars ($)	1.9	19	38	190

Then plot the graph.

b Reading off the graph at £70 gives approximately £130.

1 Say whether the following values in the table would make a linear graph.

x	0	1	2	3	4
y	0	2	6	12	20

2 Shabana is visiting Jamaica. She exchanges currency in UK pounds to Jamaican dollars. The exchange rate is 131 dollars to the pound.

a Copy and complete this table of values.

Pounds (£)	1	10	20	100
Dollars ($)	131			

b Use your values to plot a conversion graph. Use your graph to make these conversions.

  i £30 into Jamaican dollars.   **ii** £70 into Jamaican dollars.

  iii £85 into Jamaican dollars.   **iv** 1000 Jamaican dollars into pounds

  v 800 Jamaican dollars into pounds.

c Whilst on holiday Shabana spends 1250 Jamaican Dollars. She has 680 Jamaican dollars left which she exchanges back into pounds. How much money will she get in pounds?

3 (Optional) Research other exchange rates and draw a conversion graph for one of them.

example

Measure this angle.

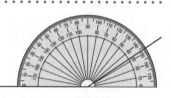

Place the centre of the protractor on the corner of the angle.
Read the scale in the correct direction from 0 to the angle.
Angle is 147°.

1 Measure these lines accurately.

a ├──────────────────────┤

b ├──────────────────────────────────────┤

c ├────────────────────────────────┤

d ├────────────────────────────┤ e ├──────────────┤

f ├──┤

2 Draw these lines accurately.

  a 3.4 cm   **b** 10.2 cm   **c** 12.6 cm   **d** 5.3 cm   **e** 8.9 cm

3 Measure these angles accurately.

a

b

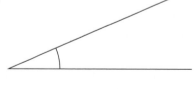

c

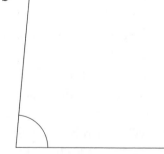

4 Draw these angles accurately.

  a 34°   **b** 123°   **c** 19°   **d** 173°   **e** 95°

Remember when constructing a triangle you will need.
- A sharp pencil
- A protractor or angle measurer
- Ruler
. . . .
Accuracy is important so don't rush it!

1 Construct these triangles accurately.

a
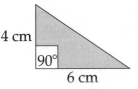
4 cm
90°
6 cm

b
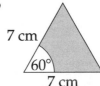
7 cm
60°
7 cm

c
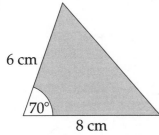
6 cm
70°
8 cm

d

75° 75°
4 cm

e Match the triangles above with these names-
isosceles, scalene, right angle or equilateral.

2 Use your ruler and protractor
accurately draw this triangle.

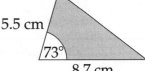
5.5 cm
73°
8.7 cm

3 Decide whether it is possible to construct
these triangles.
Explain your answers.
a Sides = 2 cm, 4 cm, 7 cm   **b** Sides = 4 cm, 5 cm, 6 cm
c Angles = 25°, 65°, 90°   **d** Angles = 55°, 85°, 50°

1 Construct these triangles accurately.

a

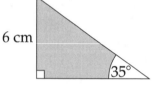

6 cm

35°

b

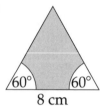

60°   60°

8 cm

2 Copy and complete these triangles.

a

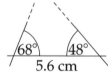

68°   48°

5.6 cm

b

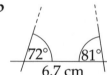

72°   81°

6.7 cm

c

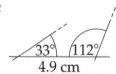

33° 112°

4.9 cm

d

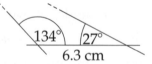

134° 27°

6.3 cm

3 Construct triangle ABC from this information.

A

B   C

Base BC is 8.5 cm long.

Angle AB̂C is 58°.

Angle AĈB is 43°.

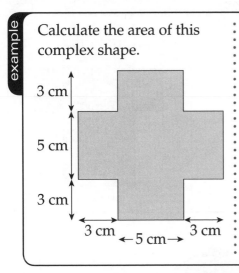

example

Calculate the area of this complex shape.

3 cm
5 cm
3 cm
3 cm ←5 cm→ 3 cm

Step 1 Divide the shape into rectangles.
Step 2 Calculate the area of each rectangle.
  Area A = 3 cm × 5 cm = 15 cm².
  Area B = 5 cm × 11 cm = 55 cm².
  Area C = 3 cm × 5 cm = 15 cm².
Step 3 Add the areas together;
  Total area = 15 cm² + 55 cm² + 15 cm² = 85 cm².

A
B
C

1 Calculate the area of each rectangle. Give your answers in the correct units (mm², cm², m²).

a
3 cm
12 cm

b
3 mm
2 mm

c
10 m
8.5 m

2 Calculate the area of each complex shape. Give your answers in the correct units.

a
7 cm
3 cm
5 cm
2 cm

b 2 mm
7 mm
2 mm
3 mm ←15 mm→ 3 mm

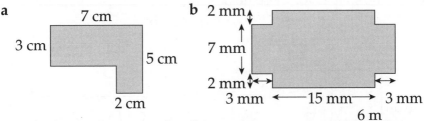

3 Mr Patel is laying a wooden floor in his kitchen. Here is a plan of his kitchen floor. What is the area of the kitchen?

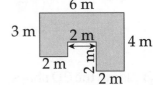

6 m
3 m
2 m
4 m
2 m
2 m
2 m

example

Draw the net of this cuboid.

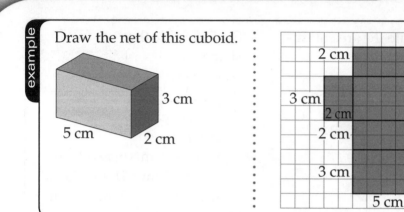

3 cm

5 cm   2 cm

2 cm

3 cm

2 cm

2 cm

3 cm

5 cm

1 Draw the nets for these shapes.

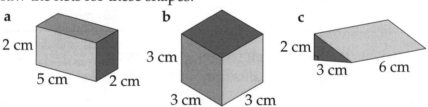

a
2 cm
5 cm   2 cm

b
3 cm
3 cm   3 cm

c
2 cm
3 cm   6 cm

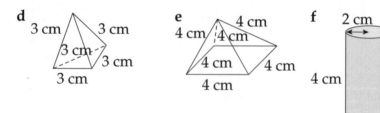

d
3 cm   3 cm
3 cm
3 cm
3 cm

e
4 cm
4 cm 4 cm
4 cm   4 cm
4 cm

f
2 cm
4 cm

2 Draw the shapes for these nets.

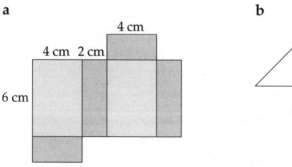

a
4 cm
4 cm   2 cm
6 cm

b
5 cm
4 cm

3 Name the 3D shapes above.

example

What is the surface area of the cuboid?

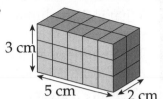

3 cm

5 cm   2 cm

Find the area of each face of the cuboid
Area A = 2 cm × 5 cm = 10 cm²
Area B = 3 cm × 5 cm = 15 cm²
Area C = 2 cm × 5 cm = 10 cm²
Area D = 3 cm × 5 cm = 15 cm²
Area E = 2 cm × 3 cm = 6 cm²
Area F = 2 cm × 3 cm = 6 cm²
   Total area = 62 cm²

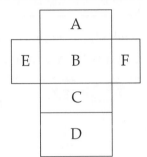

1 What is the surface area of each cuboid?

a
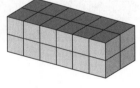

b
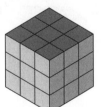

c

2 What is the surface area of each cuboid?

a
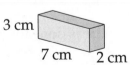
3 cm
7 cm   2 cm

b
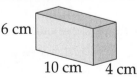
6 cm
10 cm   4 cm

c
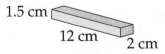
1.5 cm
12 cm   2 cm

3 a Draw your own cube and workout its surface area.
  b Draw your own cuboid and workout its surface area.

14·f² Volume of a cuboid

What is the volume of the cuboid?

. . . .

The volume of each layer is $5 \times 2 = 10$ cubes (each cube is $1 \, cm^3$).
There are 3 layers.
The volume of the whole cuboid $= 5 \times 2 \times 3 = 30 \, cm^3$.

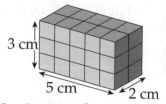

3 cm

5 cm   2 cm

1 Each shape is made from $1 \, cm^3$ cubes stuck together.
What is the volume of each shape? Remember to give the units.

a   **b** 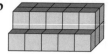   **c**

d Sketch a shape that has a volume of $12 \, cm^3$.

2 What is the volume of these cuboids?

a 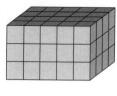   **b** 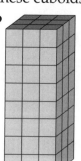   **c**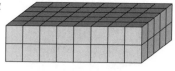

3 What is the volume of these cuboids? The first one is done for you.

a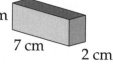
3 cm
7 cm
2 cm

b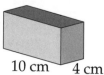
6 cm
10 cm   4 cm

c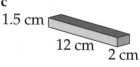
1.5 cm
12 cm   2 cm

Volume $= 7 \, cm \times 2 \, cm \times 3 \, cm$
$= 42 \, cm^3$

4 Draw as many cuboids as you can that have a volume of $24 \, cm^3$.

Rio is drawing a plan with a scale of 1 : 100. His shed is 2.5 m long and 1.5 m wide. What will the measurements be on his plan?

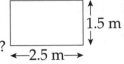

1.5 m

←2.5 m→

The scale of the plan is 1 : 100 this means 1 cm : 100 cm or 1 cm : 1 m.

So the plan will be 2.5 cm × 1.5 cm or 25 mm × 15 mm

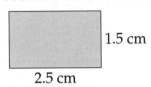

1.5 cm

2.5 cm

Tip: When drawing a plan you don't need to worry about how tall things are.

1 David measures his living room. He makes a sketch of the dimensions. Redraw the sketch as a plan.
Use a scale of 1 cm : 1 m (1 : 100)

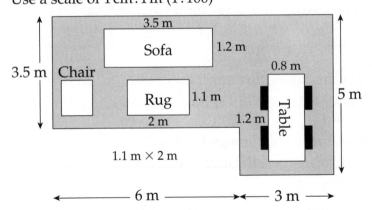

2 Draw a plan of your garden or a room in your house.

example

Find the mode, median and range for these numbers.
6, 5, 3, 6, 6, 3, 7, 4, 2, 3, 2, 4, 6

· ·

First rewrite the data in order 2, 2, 3, 3, 3, 4, 4, 5, 6, 6, 6, 6, 7
  Mode = 6   (most popular)
  Median = 4   2, 2, 3, 3, 3, 4, **4**, 5, 6, 6, 6, 6, 7 (middle number)
  Range = 7 − 2 = 5   (biggest − smallest)

1 Find the mode, median and range for these numbers.
 a 3, 4, 5, 5, 6, 6, 7
 b 5, 5, 6, 6, 6, 7, 7, 8, 8

2 Find the mode, median and range for these numbers.
 a 3, 3, 4, 4, 5, 5, 6, 7
 b 4, 7, 7, 7, 8, 9, 9, 10

3 Find the mode, median and range for these numbers.
 a 12, 4, 1, 0, 3, 5, 6, 5, 3, 7, 5, 2, 5, 5, 6
 b 1, 6, 7, 4, 4, 7, 9, 11, 4, 7, 8

4 Eight people were asked how much they earn.
  £10 000   £21 000   £12 000   £15 000
  £12 000   £38 000   £10 000   £10 000
 Find the mode, median and range for this data.
 Which of these averages is the most representative?
 Explain your answer.

5 Manpreet takes part in a long jump event. She has
 five jumps. The distance she jumps each time is given
 below: 2.45 m, 2.15 m, 1.98 m, 2.45 m, 0.97 m
 a Find the mode, median and range.
 b Which is the most representative? Explain your answer.

Find the mean of these numbers.

4, 5, 6, 4, 6, 7, 5, 8, 6, 7, 5, 10

$$\text{Mean} = \frac{\text{Total of all of the numbers}}{\text{Number of values}}$$

$$= \frac{4+5+6+4+6+7+5+8+6+7+5+10}{12}$$

$$= \frac{73}{12}$$

$$= 6.08 \text{ (to 2 dp)}$$

1 Find the mean of each of these sets of numbers (without a calculator).

   a 5, 3, 4, 8   **b** 7, 5, 6, 5, 7   **c** 15, 12, 10, 12, 11

2 Find the mean of these sets of numbers (with a calculator).

   a 8, 5, 6, 7, 4, 8, 10, 4   **b** 10, 8, 5, 7, 5, 6, 9, 7, 11

   c 4, 11, 15, 9, 6, 7, 6, 7, 10, 9, 3

3 Eight people were asked how much they earn.

£10 000	£21 000	£12 000	£15 000
£12 000	£38 000	£10 000	£10 000

   Find the mean wage.

4 In a dance competition the judges gave Aimee these scores

   5.9, 5.8, 5.5, 6.0, 5.9, 5.8, 5.7, 6.0

   Find the mean score.

5 In a class test five of the students' scores were

   45%, 87%, 67%, 70%, 69%.

   a Find the mean score.

      The students wanted to improve their mark so they were allowed to take a retest. This time their scores were 55%, 88%, 80%, 78%, 66%.

   b How much did the mean score go up by?

example

The frequency table shows the number of brothers and sisters a class of 30 students have.

Number of brothers and sisters	0	1	2	3	4	5
Frequency	4	12	8	3	2	1

a Find the modal number of brothers and sisters.
b Find the median number of brothers and sisters.
c Find the mean number of brothers and sisters.
· ·
a The modal number of brothers and sisters is **1**.
b The 15th and 16th people, both have one brother or sister.
   Therefore the median is **1** brother or sister.
c Mean $= \dfrac{(0 \times 4) + (1 \times 12) + (2 \times 8) + (3 \times 3) + (4 \times 2) + (5 \times 1)}{30}$

   $= \dfrac{50}{30} = 1.66666\ldots = \mathbf{1.7}$ (1 dp)

1 The frequency table shows the scores in a mental arithmetic test where there were five questions.

Score	0	1	2	3	4	5
Frequency	1	4	5	10	9	1

a Find the modal score.   **b** Find the median score.
c Find the mean score.

2 The frequency table shows the number of points awarded in a competition.

Score	3	4	5	6	7	8	9	10
Frequency	1	0	0	8	15	20	9	2

a Find the modal score.   **b** Find the median score.
c Find the mean score.

3 (Optional) Ask 20 people their shoe size. Record the data in a suitable table.
Calculate the mean, median and mode shoe size.

1 The bar chart shows how students travel to school.

 a How many students are included in the survey?

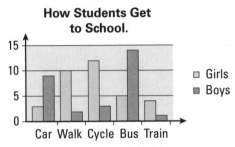

How Students Get to School.

Which is the most popular way to travel to school for

i girls **ii** boys?

 b Describe the differences between how boys and girls get to school.

Tennis Club Members **Football Club Members**

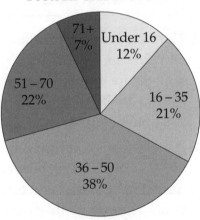

2 These pie charts show the proportion of members by age at a tennis club and a football club.

 a Which is the most popular age group at the

  i tennis club   **ii** football club?

 b Which age group is least popular in both clubs?

 c Describe the main features of the two clubs.

 d Is it correct to say that the tennis club has more under 16 members than the football club? Explain your answer.

example

The test scores for Classes 7A and 7B are recorded. Which class did best in the test? Explain your answer.

Score	0	1	2	3	4	5
7A	1	4	5	10	9	1
7B	0	2	4	8	15	1

The mean score for each class are

7A $\dfrac{(0 \times 1) + (1 \times 4) + (2 \times 5) + (3 \times 10) + (4 \times 9) + (5 \times 1)}{30} = \dfrac{85}{30} = 2.83.$

$= 1.7 (1\ dp)$

7B $\dfrac{(0 \times 0) + (1 \times 2) + (2 \times 4) + (3 \times 8) + (4 \times 15) + (5 \times 1)}{30} = \dfrac{99}{30} = 3.3$

Using the mean it can be concluded that Class 7B did better than 7A.

The mean is a good measure as there are no extreme values which could skew the mean.

1 The scores for a competition for boys and girls are recorded.

  a Compare the boys' and girls' results.

Score	0	1	2	3	4	5
Boys	0	6	2	0	10	2
Girls	4	1	0	12	2	1

  b Who did better in the competition? Explain your answer.

2 A survey was conducted to see if memory gets worse with age. Ten items were shown for people to memorise. They were then removed and the volunteers had to recall the items. How many they remembered is recorded in the table.

Number of items	4	5	6	7	8	9	10
25 and under	3	1	2	5	5	9	1
Over 25	0	0	1	5	3	5	4

Compare these two sets of data using

  a mode **b** median **c** mean.

What is your conclusion?

3 (Optional) Conduct the above experiment yourself!

example

At the beginning of a statistical enquiry you need to decide exactly what question you are going to investigate, and how i.e.

"In my investigation I will collect data to see if girls are better at spelling compared with boys. I am going to ask 20 boys and 20 girls to spell 10 words. I will record how many each person gets correct in a frequency table, then draw a comparative bar chart to compare the results. I will also calculate the mean, median and mode."

After the experiment you will then need to write a conclusion.

1 Carry out an investigation of your own. Use one of these suggestions or make one up yourself.
Here are some ideas.

- Younger people have a better memory than older people (ask people to memorise 10 items then take them away to see how many thay can recall).
- Girls are better at spelling (see example).
- Boys have bigger feet than girls.
- Children are better at mental arithmetic than adults.
- Boys are better at shooting baskets compared to girls (ask people to shoot 10 and record the number that go in).

Whatever you decide to investigate the data you collect must be a number. If it's not a number you will not be able to calculate the mean, median or range.

In your investigation
- Decide on the question you are going to investigate.
- Write a plan to show what you are going to do.
- Draw a suitable statistical diagram to show your results (pie chart, bar chart, etc.).
- Calculate mean, median, mode and/or range.
- Write a conclusion.

example

Javid buys some equipment for school in a sale. He buys a memory stick, a calculator and pencil case. He pays with a £50 note.

a How much did he spend?

b How much change should he be given?

c How much did he save?

> BACK TO SCHOOL SALE
> Memory stick WAS £19.99 NOW £16
> Pencil case WAS £4.99 NOW £3
> Calculator WAS £7.99 NOW £5

. . . .

a Spent £16 + £3 + £5 = £24

b Change £50 − £24 = £26

c Save   Full price £19.99 + £4.99 + £7.99

$= £20 + £5 + £8 − 3p = £33 − 3p = £32.97$

Savings = £32.97 − £24 = £8.97

1 Behzad buys a memory stick and a calculator. He pays with a £20 note and a £10 note.

a How much does he spend?

b How much change should he get?

c How much does he save?

2 Four students at Fowey school run a 100 m race. These are their times.

Jacob   16 seconds

Paul   15 seconds

Adil   17 seconds

Tristan   22 seconds

a How much longer did the slowest person take compared to the fastest person?

b If they ran a 400 m relay (one after the other) how long would it take?

example

Lloyd weighs his suitcase and hand luggage. Their total weight is 24.7 kg and his suitcase weighs 19.8 kg.
How much does his hand luggage weigh?
....
24.7 − 19.8 = 4.9 kg

1 The Singh family are going on holiday. They have a total luggage allowance of 80 kg. Here are the weights of their suitcases and hand luggage.

Rupinder's luggage   25.3 kg
Parmjit's luggage   18.4 kg
Jasbinder's luggage   22.5 kg
Jitender's luggage   17.5 kg

a What is the total weight of their luggage?

b How much are they over or under their weight allowance?

2 Laura, Jade and Sonia run the 1000 m race at Sports Day. Here are their times.

Laura's time   326.5 seconds
Jade's time   332.9 seconds
Sonia's time   319.9 seconds

a Who won the race?

b By how many seconds did the winner beat the other two runners?

c The school record for the 1000 m is 298.9 seconds. How many seconds was the winner away from breaking the record this Sports Day?

example

Here are some Back to School items.
Manjit wants to buy her children
some equipment.
She buys 3 calculators, 4 pencil
cases and 2 memory sticks.
How much change does she get
from £100?

> BACK TO SCHOOL
> Memory stick WAS £19.99
> Pencil case WAS £4.99
> Calculator WAS £7.99

Total cost
$2 \times 19.99 + 4 \times 4.99 + 3 \times 7.99 = (2 \times £20) + (4 \times £5) + (3 \times £8) - 9p$
$$= £40 + £20 + £24 - 9p$$
$$= £84 - 8p = £83.91$$
Change $= £100 - £83.91 = £100 - £84 + 9p = £16.09$

1 Jordan buys some equipment to sell in the school
stationary shop. He buys 12 memory sticks, 20
pencil cases and 10 calculators.

  a How much does he spend?

  b He sells the memory sticks for £22, the pencil
cases for £6 and the calculators for £8.50. How
much profit could he make?

  c He has an extra £100. Does he have enough
money for 2 memory sticks, 5 calculators and
7 pencil cases? If so how much change would
he have?

  d Jordan's teacher wants to buy a class set of
calculators. How many could she buy for £150
at £7.99 each?

2 Charlie wants to buy 2 adult tickets and
3 child tickets. He only has £30.
Does he have enough money to pay for
the tickets?

Cinema Tickets	
Adults	£7.90
Children	£5.80

> Claire runs a mile in 8 minutes and cycles a mile in 5 minutes.
> How long will it take her to run 6 miles and cycle 12 miles?
> ....
> $(6 \times 8) + (5 \times 12) = 48 + 60 = 108$ minutes $= 1$ hour 48 minutes

1 Nico runs a mile in 6 minutes and cycles a mile in 4 minutes.

   a How long will it take him to run 6 miles and cycle 12 miles?

   b How much quicker will he do it compared with Claire?

2 Miss Hook takes 68 students and 8 adults to a football match. Each minibus can hold 15 students and 2 adults. Miss Hook orders 6 minibuses.
Has she ordered the correct number? Explain your answer.

3 Shannara is saving to go on holiday. She saves £9 a week from her paper round and £4 a week from her pocket money. She saves for 12 weeks.

   a How much money does she have for her holiday?

   b She is on holiday for a week. How much money can she spend each day?

4 Ruth is travelling to Scotland. The journey is 420 miles. She travels at an average speed of 60 miles per hour.

   a How long does it take her to travel to Scotland?

   b She needs to be there for 3 p.m.. She wants to stop for lunch for half an hour and also add an extra hour for any delays. What time should she leave home?

example

Claire wants to run a marathon (26 miles) in less than 4 hours. How fast must she run each mile?

. . . .

4 hours = 4 × 60 minutes = 240 minutes
240 ÷ 26 = 9.2307... minutes
0.2307... needs to be changed to seconds:
0.2307... × 60 = 13.8 seconds
She must run each mile in less than 9 minutes 13 seconds to get under 4 hours.

1 Sanjay wants to drive from Cornwall to Coventry in less than 4.5 hours. The distance is 290 miles. How many miles must he do each hour?

2 Sid is working out the cost of his motoring each month.
Diesel costs £1.32 a litre.
His car travels 7 miles for each litre of diesel.
Each month he travels 680 miles.
Tax and insurance cost £70 a month.
  a How much money does Sid spend on motoring
    i each month   **ii** each year?
  b The car repayments also cost Sid £340 a month.
    Including these car repayments what is his weekly motoring cost?

3 Mrs Furze is taking students to Drayton Manor theme park for the day. There are 395 students and 20 adults.
A coach seats 54 passengers and a mini bus 15.
Mrs Furze orders 7 coaches and 3 mini buses.
Has Mrs Furze ordered the correct amount?

Glossary

add, addition

Addition is the sum of two or more numbers or quantities.

adjacent (side)

Adjacent sides are next to each other and are joined by a common vertex.

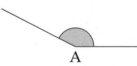

AB and BC are adjacent sides.

algebra

Algebra is the branch of mathematics where symbols or letters are used to represent numbers.

amount

Amount means total.

angle: acute, obtuse, right, reflex

An angle is formed when two straight lines cross or meet each other at a point. The size of an angle is measured by the amount one line has been turned in relation to the other.

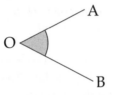

An acute angle is less than 90°.

An obtuse angle is more than 90° but less than 180°.

A right angle is a quarter of a turn, or 90°.

A reflex angle is more than 180° but less than 360°.

angles at a point

Angles at a point add up to 360°.

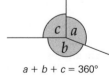

$a + b + c = 360°$

angles on a straight line

Angles on a straight line add up to 180°.

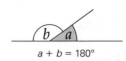

$a + b = 180°$

Glossary

answer   An answer is the solution to a calculation or question.

approximate, approximately   An approximate value is a value that is close to the actual value of a number.

approximately equal to (≈)   Approximately equal means almost the same size.

area: square millimetre, square centimetre, square metre, square kilometre   The area of a surface is a measure of its size.

average   An average is a representative value of a set of data.

axis, axes   An axis is one of the lines used to locate a point in a coordinate system.

axis of symmetry   An axis of symmetry of a shape is a line about which the shape can be folded so that one half fits exactly on top of the other half.

bar chart   A bar chart is a diagram that uses rectangles of equal width to display data. The frequency is given by the height of the rectangle.

bar-line graph   A bar-line graph or chart is a diagram that uses lines to display data. The lengths of the lines are proportional to the frequencies.

base (of a plane shape or solid)   The lower horizontal edge of a plane shape is usually called the base. Similarly, the base of a solid is its lower face.

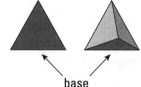
base

base angles   The angles measured from the base of a shape are called the base angles.

bearing

brackets   Operations within brackets should be carried out first.

calculator: clear, display, enter, key, memory	You can use a calculator to perform calculations.
cancel, cancellation	A fraction is cancelled down by dividing the numerator and denominator by a common factor.

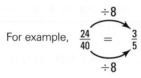

For example,

capacity: millimetre, centilitre, litre, pint, gallon	Capacity is a measure of the amount of liquid a 3-D shape will hold. 1 litre = 1000 ml = 100 cl 1 pint ≈ litre (568 ml) 1 litre ≈ 1.75 pints 8 pints = 1 gallon
centre	Centre means middle point. The centre of a circle is an equal distance from any point of the edge.
centre of rotation	The centre of rotation is the fixed point about which a rotation takes place.

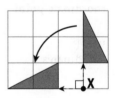

certain, uncertain	An event that is certain will definitely happen.
chance	Chance is the probability of something happening.
class interval	A class interval is a group that you put data into to make it easier to handle.
common factor	A common factor is a factor of two or more numbers. For example, 2 is a common factor of 4 and 10.
compare	Compare means to assess the similarity of.
conclusion	A conclusion is a statement that summarises your findings.

Glossary

congruent   Congruent shapes are exactly the same shape and size.

consecutive   Consecutive means following on in order.
For example 2, 3 and 4 are consecutive integers.

construct   To construct means to draw a line, angle or shape accurately.

continuous   Continuous data can take any value.

conversion graph   A graph that converts between units is a conversion graph.

convert   Convert means to change.

coordinate pair   A coordinate pair is a pair of numbers that give the position of a point on a coordinate grid.
For example, (3, 2) means 3 units across and 2 units up.

coordinate point   A coordinate point is the point described by a coordinate pair.

coordinates   Coordinates are the numbers that make up a coordinate pair.

currency   Currency is the particular type of money in use in any country.

data, grouped data   Data are pieces of information. Grouped data is information that is collected about a group or class.

database   A database is a collection of data, especially in a form that can be used by a computer.

data collection sheet A data collection sheet is a sheet used to collect data. It is sometimes a list of questions with tick boxes for collecting answers.

decimals, decimal fraction A decimal fraction shows part of a whole represented as tenths, hundredths, thousandths and so on.
For example, 0.65 and 0.3 are decimal fractions.

decimal place (d.p.)   Each column after the decimal point is called a decimal place.
For example, 0.65 has two decimal places (2 d.p.).

degree (°)   A degree is a measure of turn. There are 360° in a full turn.

denominator   The denominator is the bottom number in a fraction. It shows how many parts there are in total.

depth   Depth is a measure of distance from top downwards or from a surface inwards.

diagonal   A diagonal of a polygon is a line joining any two vertices but not forming a side.

This is a diagonal.

diagram   A diagram is a line drawing to illustrate a situation.

dice   A dice is a cube with the six sides marked one to six, used for games of chance.

difference   You find the difference between two amounts by subtracting one from the other.

digit   A digit is any of the numbers 0, 1, 2, 3, 4, 5, 6, 7, 8, 9.

direction   The direction is the orientation of a line in space.

discount   A discount is an amount deducted from a cost. Items in a sale are sold at discounted prices.

discrete   Discrete data can only be whole numbers, and take a certain value.

distance   The distance between two points is the length of the line that joins them.

divide, division   Divide ($\div$) means share equally.

Glossary

divisible, divisibility
A whole number is divisible by another if there is no remainder left.

divisor
The divisor is the number that does the dividing.
For example, in 14 ÷ 2 = 7 the divisor is 2.

double, halve
Double means multiply by two. Halve means divide by two.

edge (of solid)
An edge is a line along which two faces of a solid meet.

edge

enlarged
If a shape is enlarged, it is made bigger.

equal (sides, angles)
Equal sides are the same length. Equal angles are the same size.

equally likely
Events are equally likely if they have the same probability.

equals (=)
Equals means having exactly the same value or size.

equation
An equation is a statement linking two expressions that have the same value.

equidistant
Points that are equidistant from a line are exactly the same distance away from the line.

equivalent, equivalence
Equivalent fractions are fractions with the same value.

estimate
An estimate is an approximate answer.

evaluate
Evaluate means find the value of an expression.

even chance
An even chance means no event is more likely to happen than an other.

event
An event is a trial occuring.

exact, exactly
Exact means completely accurate.
For example, three divides into six exactly.

experiment   An experiment is a test or investigation to gather evidence for or against a theory.

experimental probability   Experimental probability is found by dividing the number of times the required outcome occurs by the total number of trials done.

explain   To explain an answer means to give your reasons.

expression   An expression is a collection of numbers and symbols linked by operations but not including an equals sign.

face   A face is a flat surface of a solid.

face

factor   A factor is a number that divides exactly into another number.
For example, 3 and 7 are factors of 21.

factorise   A number is factorised by finding all the numbers which divide into it exactly.

fair   In a fair experiment there is no bias towards any particular outcome.

favourable   When finding a probability of something happening, a favourable outcome is the one you want, that is, the one for which you are calculating the probability.

finite, infinite   A finite sequence has a definite beginning and end. An infinite sequence goes on for ever.

formula   A formula links two or more variables together in an equation.
For example, the formula for the area of a rectangle is
$A = l \times w$.

fraction   A fraction is a way of describing a part of a whole. For example $\frac{2}{5}$ of the shape shown is red.

Glossary

frequency	Frequency is the number of times something occurs.
frequency diagram	A frequency diagram uses bars to display grouped data. The height of each bar gives the frequency of the group, and there is no space between the bars.
frequency table	Data is grouped into classes in a frequency table so that a frequency diagram may be drawn. This can be called a frequency chart.
function	A function is a rule. For example, +2, −3, ×4 and ÷5 are all functions.
function machine	A function machine links an input value to an output value by performing a function.
general term	The general term is the rule that describes how a sequence is made up.
generate	Generate means produce.
graph	A graph is a diagram that shows a relationship between variables.
greater than (>)	Greater than means more than. For example 4 > 3.
grid	A grid is a repeated geometrical pattern used as a background to plot coordinate points. It is usually squared.
height, high	Height is a vertical measurement, between the top and bottom of a shape.
highest common factor	The highest common factor of two numbers is the largest whole number that divides exactly into both.
horizontal	Horizontal means flat and level with the ground.
hundredth	A hundredth is 1 out of 100. For example 0.05 has 5 hundredths.

hypothesis	A hypothesis is a statement of an idea which you can test using an experiment or survey.
identical	Identical means exactly the same. Identical triangles have matching angles and sides of exactly the same size.
image	When a shape is reflected, translated or rotated, the new shape is called the image.

object   image

imperial	Imperial measures are no longer used in the UK. The most common ones are mile, inch, stone, pound, ounce, pint.
impossible	An event is impossible if it definitely cannot happen.
improper fraction	An improper fraction is a fraction where the numerator is greater than the denominator. For example, $\frac{8}{5}$ is an improper fraction.
increase, decrease	Increase means make greater. Decrease means make less.
index, indices	Index is another word for power. In 3^2, the number 2 is called the index.
input, output	Input is data fed into a machine or process. Output is the data produced by a machine or process.
integer	An integer is a positive or negative whole number (including zero). The integers are: ..., -3, -2, -1, 0, 1, 2, 3, ...
interpret	You interpret data whenever you make sense of it.
intersect, intersection	Two lines intersect at the point, or points, that they cross.

intersection

Glossary

interval

An interval is the size of a class or group in a frequency table.

inverse

An inverse function is one which has the opposite effect to its related function. It carries out the opposite operations in the opposite order.
For example, for a function $(+3 \times 2)$ the inverse function is $(\div 2 -3)$.

investigate

To investigate a problem you solve it in a series of steps.

length: millimetre, centimetre, metre, kilometre; mile, foot, inch

Length is a measure of distance. It is often used to describe one dimension of a shape.

less than (<)

Less than means smaller than.
For example, 3 is less than 4, or $3 < 4$.

like terms

Terms that use the same letter are called like terms
For example, $2x$ and $5x$ are like terms.

likelihood

Likelihood is the probability of an event happening.

likely

An event is likely if it will happen more often than not.

line of symmetry

A line of symmetry is a line about which a 2-D shape can be folded so that one half of the shape fits exactly on the other half.

line segment

A line segment is a straight line of fixed length.

line symmetry

A figure has line symmetry if it can be divided by a straight line so that when the figure is folded along the line the two halves fit exactly on each other.

lowest common multiple

The lowest common multiple of two numbers is the smallest number that is a multiple of them both.

mapping	A mapping diagram plots inputs and outputs via a function.
mass: gram, kilogram, ounce, pound, tonne	The mass of an object is how heavy it is.
maximum, minimum	The maximun value is the greatest possible value. The minimum value is the least possible value
mean	The mean is an average value found by adding all the data values and dividing by the number of pieces of data.
measure	When you measure something you find the size of it.
median	The median is an average which is the middle value when the data is arranged in size order.
metric	Metric measures are used in the UK and abroad. The mose common are metre, litre, kg.
mirror line	A mirror line is a line or axis of symmetry.

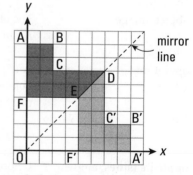

mixed number	A mixed number has a whole number part and a fraction part. For example, $3\frac{1}{2}$ is a mixed number.
modal class	The modal class or group is the most commonly occurring class when the data is grouped. It is the class with the highest frequency.
mode	The mode is an average which is the data value that occurs most often.

Glossary

multiple A multiple of an integer is the product of that integer and any other.
For example, these are multiples of 6: 6 × 4 = 24 and 6 × 12 = 72.

multiply, multiplication Multiplication is the operation of combining two numbers or quantities to form a product.

nearest Nearest means the closest value.

negative A negative number is a number less than zero.

net A net is a 2-D arrangement that can be folded to form a solid shape.

nth term The nth term of a sequence is the expression that describes the general term in algebra.

numerator The numerator is the top number in a fraction. It shows how many parts you are dealing with.

object, image The object is the original shape before a transformation. An image is the same shape after a transformation.

operation An operation is a rule for processing numbers or objects. The basic operations are addition, subtraction, multiplication and division.

opposite (sides, angles) Opposite means across from.

The red side is opposite the red angle.

order To order means to arrange according to size or importance.

order of operations The conventional order of operations is: brackets first, then powers or indices then division and multiplication, then addition and subtraction.

order of rotation symmetry	The order of rotation symmetry is the number of times that a shape will fit on to itself during a full turn.
origin	The origin is the point in a coordinate grid where the x-axis and the y-axis meet. It is the point $(0, 0)$.
outcome	An outcome is the result of a trial or experiment.
parallel	Two lines that always stay the same distance apart are parallel. Parallel lines never cross or meet. 
partition; part	To partition means to split a number into smaller amounts, or parts. For example, 57 could be split into 50 + 7, or 40 + 17.
path	The path of an object is the shape its movement describes.
pattern	Number patterns can be expressed as sequences. For example, the pattern of triangular numbers form the sequence 1, 3, 6, 10 ...
percentage (%)	A percentage is a fraction expressed as the number of parts per hundred.
perimeter	The perimeter of a shape is the distance around it. It is the total length of the edges.
perpendicular	Two lines are perpendicular to each other if they meet at a right angle.
pie chart	A pie chart uses a circle to display data. The angle at the centre of a sector is proportional to the frequency.
place value	The place value is the value of a digit in a decimal number. For example, in 3.65 the digit 6 has a value of 6 tenths.

Glossary

plane
A plane is a smooth level surface such as one side of a cube.

plus, minus
Plus (+) is the symbol for addition and minus (−) is the symbol for subtraction.

point
A point is a fixed place on a grid or on a shape.

polygon: pentagon, hexagon, octagon
A polygon is a closed shape with three or more straight edges.

A pentagon has five sides. A hexagon has six sides. An octagon has eight sides.

positive
A positive number is greater than zero.

possible
A possible situation is one which may or may not occur.

powers
In the number 3^4, 4 is the power. It tells the number of times the 3 must be multiplied by itself.
So $3^4 = 3 \times 3 \times 3 \times 3 = 81$.

predict
To predict is to estimate or guess what will happen in a future situation.

primary data
Primary data is data you collect yourself.

prime
A prime number is a number that has exactly two different factors.

prime factor
A prime factor is any factor of a number which is a prime number.

probability
Probability is a measure of how likely an event is.

probability scale
A probability scale is a line numbered 0 to 1 or 0% to 100% on which you place an event based on its probability.

probable	Something that is probable is likely to happen.
problem	A problem is a question to be answered by investigation, calculation or proof.
product	A product is the result of a multiplication. In $5 \times 3 = 15$, the product is 15.
proper fraction	A proper function is one in which the numerator (top number) is less than the denominator (bottom number).
proportion	Proportion compares the size of a part to the size of a whole. You can express a proportion as a fraction, decimal or percentage.
protractor (angle measurer)	A protractor is an instrument for measuring angles in degrees.
quadrant	A coordinate grid is divided into four quadrants by the x- and y-axes.
quadrilateral: arrowhead, delta, kite, parallelogram, rectangle, rhombus, square, trapezium	A quadrilateral is a polygon with four sides.

ractangle

All angles are right angles. Opposite sides equal.

parallelogram

Two pairs of parallel sides.

kite

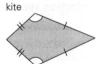

Two pairs of adjacent sides equal. No interior angle greater than 180°.

rhombus

All sides the same length. Opposite angles equal.

square

All sides and angles equal and all angles are right angles.

trapezium

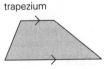

One pair of parallel sides.

Glossary

questionnaire

A questionnaire is a list of questions used to gather information in a survey.

quotient

A quotient is the result of a division.
For example, the quotient of $12 \div 5$ is $2\frac{2}{5}$, or 2.4.

random

A selection is random if each object or number is equally likely to be chosen.

range

The range is the difference between the largest and smallest values in a set of data.

ratio

Ratio compares the size of one part with the size of another part.

reduced

If something is reduced, it is made smaller.

reflect, reflection

A reflection is a transformation in which corresponding points in the object and the image are the same distance from the mirror line.

reflection symmetry

A shape has reflection symmetry if it has a line of symmetry.

regular

A regular polygon has equal sides and equal angles.

relationship

A relationship is a link between objects or numbers.

remainder

A remainder is the amount left over when one quantity is divided by another.
For example, $9 \div 4 = 2$ remainder 1.

results

The results of an experiment are the data you get.

rotate, rotation

A rotation is a transformation in which every point in the object turns through the same angle relative to a fixed point.

rotation symmetry	A shape has rotation symmetry if when turned it fits onto itself more than once during a full turn.
rough	A rough calculation is an approximation.
round	You round a number by expressing it to a given degree of accuracy. For example, 639 is 600 to the nearest 100 and 640 to the nearest 10. To round to one decimal place means to round to the nearest tenth. For example 12.47 is 12.5 to 1 d.p.
row, column	In a table the horizontal lines of data are rows and the vertical lines of data are columns.
rule	A rule describes the link between objects or numbers. For example, the rule linking 2 and 6 may be +4 or ×3.
ruler	A ruler is an instrument for measuring lengths.
sale price	A sale price is a discounted price, that is, less than the normal price.
scale	A scale is a numbered line or dial. The numbers usually increase in sequence.
sector	A sector is a section of a circle.
sequence	A sequence is a set of numbers or objects that follow a rule.
side (of 2-D shape)	A side is a line segment joining vertices.
simplest form	A fraction (or ratio) is in its simplest form when the numerator and denominator (or parts of the ratio) have no common factors. For example, $\frac{3}{5}$ is expressed in its simplest form.
simplify	To simplify an expression you gather all like terms together into a single term.

Glossary

simulation

A simulation is the imitation of a situation by using alternative methods.

sketch

A sketch is a rough diagram to show the main points of a problem before attempting to solve it.

secondary data

Secondary data is data that has already been collected.

solid (3-D) shape: cube, cuboid, cylinder, hemisphere, prism, pyramid, square-based pyramid, sphere, tetrahedron

A solid is a shape formed in three-dimensional space.

cube

six square faces

cuboid

six rectangular faces

prism

the end faces are constant

solve (an equation)

To solve an equation you need to find the value of the variable that will make the equation true.

spin, spinner

A spinner is an instrument for creating random outcomes, usually in probability experiments.

square number, squared

If you multiply a number by itself the result is a square number.
For example 25 is a square number because
$5^2 = 5 \times 5 = 25$.

square root

A square root is a number that when multiplied by itself gives a square number.
For example, 5 is the square root of 25 because
$5 \times 5 = 25$:

statistic, statistics

Statistics is the collection, display and analysis of information.

straight line	A straight line is the shortest distance between two points.

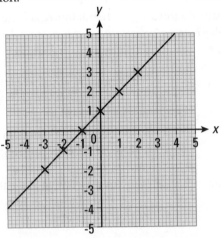

straight-line graph	When coordinate points lie in a straight line they form a straight-line graph. It is the graph of a linear equation.

substitute	When you substitute you replace part of an expression with a value.
subtract, subtraction	Subtraction is the operation that finds the difference in size between two numbers.
sum	The sum is the total and is the result of an addition.
surface, surface area	The surface area of a solid is the total area of its faces.
survey	A survey is an investigation to find information.
symmetrical	A shape is symmetrical if it can be divided into two identical mirror image shapes by a straight line.
systematic	To work systematically means to break a problem down into simple steps, which you can solve individually.

Glossary

table	A table is an arrangement of information, numbers or letters usually in rows and columns.
tally	You use a tally mark to represent an object when you collect data. Tally marks are usually made in groups of five to make it easier to count them.
temperature: degrees Celsius, degrees Fahrenheit	Temperature is a measure of how hot something is.
tenth	A tenth is 1 out of 10 or $\frac{1}{10}$. For example 0.5 has 5 tenths.
term	A term is a number or object in a sequence. It is also part of an expression.
tessellation	A tessellation is a pattern made by identical shapes that fit together to cover a whole surface with no gaps or overlaps.
theoretical probability	Theoretical probability is calculated by dividing the number of favourable outcomes by the total number of possible outcomes.
three-dimensional (3-D)	Any solid shape is three-dimensional.
time	Time is a measure of duration. There are: • 60 seconds in a minute • 60 minutes in an hour • 7 days in a week • 28–31 days in a month • 365 days in most years • 10 years in a decade • 100 years in a century • 1000 years in a millennium
title	All graphs should have a title, that is, a short name to show what they represent.
tonne	A tonne is a measurement of mass equal to 1000 kg.

to one decimal place	A number rounded to the nearest tenth is rounded to one decimal place. For example, 5.78 is 5.8 to one decimal place.
total	The total is the result of an addition.
transformation	A transformation moves a shape from one place to another.
translate, translation	A translation is a transformation in which every point in an object moves the same distance and direction. It is a sliding movement.
trial	A trial is your experiment to determine an outcome.
triangle: equilateral, isosceles, scalene, right-angled	A triangle is a polygon with three sides.

equliateral

isosceles

three equal side

two equal sides

scalene

right-angled

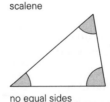

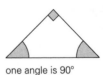

no equal sides

one angle is 90°

triangular number	A triangular number is the number of dots in a triangular pattern: The numbers form the sequence 1, 3, 6, 10, 15, 21, 28 ...

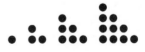

two-dimensional (2-D)	A flat shape has two dimensions, length and width or base and height.
unfair	In an unfair experiment all possible outcomes are not equally likely.

Glossary

unknown   An unknown is a variable. You can often find its value by solving an equation.

unlikely   An event is unlikely if it will probably not happen.

value   The value is the amount an expression or variable is worth.

variable   A variable is a symbol that can take a range of values.

verify   To verify a solution you put your answers back into the original question to check that they work.

vertex, vertices   A vertex of a shape is a point at which two or more edges meet.

vertical   Vertical means straight up and down.

vertically opposite angles When two straight lines cross they form two pairs of equal angles called vertically opposite angles.

$$a = c \quad b = d$$

width   Width is a dimension of an object describing how wide it is.

x-axis, y-axis   On a coordinate grid, the x-axis is usually the horizontal axis and the y-axis is usually the vertical axis.

x-coordinate, y-coordinate The x-coordinate is the distance along the x-axis. The y-coordinate is the distance along the y-axis. For example, (-2, -3) is -2 along the x-axis and -3 along the y-axis.

zero place holder   In a number such as 15.07 where there are no tenths but there are hundredths, the zero is called a zero place holder.

maths